STAR TREK®
THE NEXT GENERATION

STAR TREK: THE NEXT GENERATION NOVELS

STAR TREK: THE NEXT GENERATION GIANT NOVELS

STAR TREK®
THE NEXT GENERATION
METAMORPHOSIS
THE FIRST GIANT NOVEL

JEAN LORRAH

TITAN BOOKS
LONDON

STAR TREK THE NEXT GENERATION GIANT 1:
METAMORPHOSIS
ISBN 1 85286 288 2

Published by
Titan Books Ltd
42–44 Dolben Street
London SE1 0UP

First Titan Edition March 1990
10 9 8 7 6

British Library Cataloguing-in-Publication Data. A catalogue
record for this book is available from the British Library.

Printed and bound in Great Britain by Cox and Wyman Ltd, Reading,
Berkshire.

Foreword

I would like to thank Gene Roddenberry, the creator of *Star Trek,* which has been such an important influence in my life; Hans Christian Andersen, Melinda Snodgrass, and Jacqueline Lichtenberg, all of whom provided a measure of inspiration for this novel; and Dave Stern, editor at Pocket Books, who supported my efforts to finish this novel during a very difficult time in my life.

I have been a *Star Trek* fan since 1966, when Classic Trek first appeared. I learned to write through fanzines, and have made many wonderful friends through Trekfandom. By this time I doubt anyone can dispute that *Star Trek: the Next Generation* carries on the dream that Classic Trek first brought to life.

Readers may be familiar with my Classic Trek novels, *The Vulcan Academy Murders* and *The IDIC Epidemic.* To the many who have asked, yes, I do hope to write more Classic Trek novels in the future. However, I do not see any discrepancy between Classic Trek and *Next Generation;* they are both part of the same vision. The spirit of Trek continues—I hope you can feel it in this novel and in my previous *Next Generation* novel, *Survivors.*

If you have not read *Survivors,* don't worry. These books are written like *Star Trek* episodes: If you have missed some you can still enjoy others. When you catch earlier episodes in reruns, though, you may discover new depths in the ones you have seen before. So after you have read *Metamorphosis,* if you are curious about the story of Tasha Yar and Darryl Adin, referred to here, you may decide to seek out *Survivors,* available wherever *Star Trek* books are sold.

If you have been a *Star Trek* fan for years, you may already know about fandom. If you have just joined us via the new series, welcome! Paramount sponsors a fan club with a bimonthly newsletter to tell you all the latest news about the movies, the TV series, the actors, and the creators:

The Official *Star Trek* Fan Club
P. O. Box 111000
Aurora, CO 80011

But Trekfandom is not limited to the fan club. If you write or draw or make music or costumes or want to interact with other fans, you want the original fandom: friends and letters and crafts and fanzines and trivia and costumes and artwork and filksongs [sic] and posters and buttons and games and conventions—something for everybody.

The way to that fandom is not through me, or any other author of *Star Trek* novels. You want that wonderful organization, *The Star Trek Welcommittee.* Be *sure* to include a *stamped* self-addressed envelope, as this is a volunteer organization of people who love *Star Trek* and are willing to answer your questions and

put you in touch with other fans. Their current
address:

The *Star Trek* Welcommittee
P. O. Drawer 12
Saranac, MI 48881

In both Trekwriting and my other professional
science fiction, I have a strong belief in the interaction
between authors and fans. Authors want your con-
structive comments. They cannot collaborate with
you, write the stories you want to tell (you'll have to
do that yourself), or critique your novels (they're too
busy writing their own). Neither can they write you
long, involved letters about how to write books; you
can find that information at your local library. You
can't learn to write that way anyway; you must learn
by doing. Get involved in fanzines and develop your
skills as so many of us did. Writing workshops can be
a great help, too—the authors conducting them have
set that time aside specifically for that purpose, and
will welcome you.

All authors are happy to receive comments about
their books, and most will answer questions—within
reason. Authors have lives, families, jobs, just like
you, and book deadlines on top of all that.

Almost everyone who writes Trek novels also writes
other science fiction; if Trek novels by a particular
author appeal to you, you might very well enjoy that
author's other work. Chances are, the themes he or she
chooses to develop in Trek are the same ones he or she
treats in other books. Ask at your booksellers for other
books by your favorite *Star Trek* authors.

If you would like to comment on this or any of my
other books, you may write to me in care of my

publishers, or at P. O. Box 625, Murray, KY 42071-0625. If your letter requires an answer, please enclose a stamped, self-addressed envelope.

Keep on Trekkin'!

Jean Lorrah
Murray, Kentucky

Historian's Note

Metamorphosis takes place in the second season of *Star Trek: the Next Generation,* beginning immediately after "The Measure of a Man." Data had to fight for his very existence in that episode; the experience has lingering aftereffects.

"No, sir . . . I never wanted to compound one . . . illusion . . . with another. It might be real to Q, perhaps even to you, sir. But it would never be so to me. Was it not one of the captain's favorite authors who wrote, 'This above all: to thine own self be true'? Sorry, Commander. I must decline."

> —Lieutenant Commander Data,
> to Commander Riker's offer of
> humanity, "Hide and Q"

"You may find that having is not so pleasing a thing, after all, as wanting. It is not logical, but it is often true."

> —Commander Spock,
> "Amok Time"

"Legends . . . are the spice of the universe, Mr. Data, because they have a way of sometimes coming true."

> —Captain Jean-Luc Picard,
> "Haven"

Chapter One

THE U.S.S. *ENTERPRISE* swung in orbit about Starbase 173, with only a skeleton crew on duty. On the holodeck, a party marked the homecoming of Lt. Commander Data—a celebration as intense and cheerful as if it had been months or years that he had been separated from their ranks, instead of less than seventy-two hours.

The holodeck was set to duplicate parkland on an Earthlike planet; one entered by crossing stepping stones over a stream, leading to a path through a patch of woods. Beyond that there were open lawns with blue sky, green grass, and a fresh breeze stirring the trees dotted here and there in the landscape. From a distance, as if a band were playing somewhere just out of sight, music drifted pleasantly, not loud enough to interfere with conversation.

Of the participants, however, the one least cheered by the music and laughter was the guest of honor. Data smiled, and tried to keep up conversation with his friends, but there were some who knew him too well to miss noticing that at least a part of his good cheer was artificial.

As artificial as I am, he thought as he deliberately turned to answer a question from Wesley Crusher, just to avoid addressing the concern radiating from Geordi La Forge.

"How does this work?" Wesley asked excitedly, peering into the startube that Data had just presented to him. From their acting ensign, the question did not mean "How do I start it?" or even "How do I change the display?" but "What is the principle behind its operation?"

"I suggest you examine it at leisure and when you have figured it out, explain it to me," Data replied, never forgetting his responsibility for Wesley's education.

The boy grinned. "I'll figure it out. Did you build this, Data?"

"No, I used the matter transformer."

"But did you design it? I've never seen anything like it," Wesley added, holding the tube to his eye and twisting its rings to bring various starfields into focus. "It's as if it knows the direction I turn it, and actually shows me stars too far away to be seen with our instruments!"

Dr. Kate Pulaski came up to them as Wesley spoke. She gave a puzzled frown. "Surely it's a trick—a hand-held instrument that could read distant stars would be invaluable."

"It is up to Wesley to determine how—or whether —it does what it appears to do," Data replied.

"Ah—another lesson," the doctor said.

"Data's lessons are fun," Wesley said, grinning.

"Technological, you mean," Pulaski said. "I'm not certain you're getting the well-rounded education you ought to have, Wesley."

"I take history and music and literature classes," the boy protested. "I just like science better, that's all."

Data took the opportunity to offer Dr. Pulaski the gift he had chosen for her, carefully wrapped in soft paper. When he had recently resigned his post, in an attempt to thwart Commander Bruce Maddox's plan to take him apart, his friends had given him a "going-away party," complete with a present from each of them. When he had returned so soon, he had pondered what to do about those presents. It seemed inappropriate to keep them, since he had not gone away, and yet impolite to return them. So he had settled on giving each of his friends a present in return. They were displayed at one end of a picnic table with a bright checkered cloth, while food and drinks were laid out at the other end.

Of the crew, he had known Dr. Pulaski for the shortest time. She was also the person he understood least, and he knew that the feeling was mutual. Therefore, unable to choose a gift with personal significance, he had opted for something he knew to be universally admired: a bellflower from Artemis Three, or as close as he could come to reproducing one. The live plants did not thrive outside their natural environment, and so were never exported. For the past two centuries—since the discovery of the delicate and precious blooms whose soft chiming was said to relieve stress—artists, artisans, and horticulturists had striven to copy the bellflowers. Some came

3

very close, and their work commanded great respect and huge prices.

The *Enterprise* computer contained the DNA pattern of the bellflowers, but Data did not want a cut flower that would die in a few hours. He had quickly abandoned any idea of mutating a living plant, opting instead for as near-perfect an artificial replication as possible. A product of the holodeck, the artificial bellflower would seem as real and solid and beautiful as a naturally grown plant with one exception—it would last forever. And unlike an actual holograph, there was no need to turn the "plant" on or off. It was a perfect permanent fake. Data had wrapped the asymmetrical shape in the softest of tissue.

Other crew members gathered around as Dr. Pulaski removed the wrapping. Loosed from the muffling material, the bellflowers began to chime, drawing "ooohs" from the audience, and the attention of an uninvited guest.

Mystery, a Siamese cat who considered the entire ship her domain, had been wandering about, garnering stroking or bits of food here and there. There were many pets on the ship, but they were supposed to remain in the living quarters. Mystery, though, might show up anywhere at any time, despite concerted efforts to confine her to areas appropriate to animals. No one knew how she got through or around doors, detectors, or forcefields; hence her name.

Now the cat jumped up on the table to examine the source of the new sound. Pulaski ignored her, looking from the flowers to Data. "They're absolutely beautiful!" she exclaimed in genuine amazement.

"I hoped they would please you."

"But, they *can't* be real," she said, gently fingering one of the leaves. "Oh, Data—you wouldn't reproduce something so lovely that would only wither and die?"

"It's a replication, Doctor," Geordi explained, "created through transporter matter conversion."

"Really?" Wesley asked, tapping one of the blooms. "It even *smells* organic."

Mystery put up a hesitant paw, and set the flowers chiming again.

"If I have succeeded in my attempt," Data said, "the flowers should seem real to all human senses."

Dr. Pulaski gave Data a smile with a touch of sadness in it. "But you can tell the difference, can't you, Data?"

"Only if I access other means of analysis than the normal range of human senses."

"To which," the doctor said flatly, "you usually confine yourself. I don't understand why you should want to limit your abilities that way."

"I do," said Geordi, laying a hand on Data's shoulder.

"So do I," put in Commander Will Riker. After being forced to argue the case against Data's right to make his own life choices, the *Enterprise* First Officer had not intended to come to the celebration. Data had gone to get him, understanding his uneasiness, but the usually ebullient Riker had been uncharacteristically quiet thus far, as if he hoped to escape notice.

Geordi tensed. Data knew his friend resented Riker's claim to understanding. But Data knew Will Riker better than Geordi did, had seen him take in

5

stride new life-forms, customs, and laws, no matter how bizarre. Unlike most humans, Riker did not have to understand before he accepted; he had accepted Data from the moment they first met.

Irony was one human emotion Data understood; it was ironic that the first person to whom the android had confided his desire to be human was the very person forced to argue that he was mere equipment, Starfleet property. Riker had lost the case but won the resentment of Data's friends.

Even those he had not considered close friends, for Kate Pulaski told Riker, "You claim to understand Data, yet you called none of us to testify at the hearing."

"Did you think I wanted to win, Doctor?" Riker replied.

The woman's green eyes flashed. "Do you think I would have wanted you to? Commander, the disagreements I have with Mr. Data have nothing to do with his autonomy. He is unique in all history—and no experiment should ever be permitted to threaten that uniqueness."

"Then you think no more Datas should be built?" Geordi asked, picking up Mystery just as she was about to pounce on the bellflowers. He stroked the cat, and she started to purr.

"I have no objection to other *androids* being built," Pulaski replied. "As briefly as I've known Data, I know that his particular set of positronic circuits and heuristic algorithms have a distinct and individual personality. So, I assume, would another android, even if built in his image. Each would be a different person, as unique as any human. No, my differences with our friend have to do solely with his desire to be something else, instead of exploring the possibilities of what he is."

Mystery wriggled out of Geordi's arms and back onto the tabletop. To distract the cat from the flowers, Riker offered his hand. She rubbed against it, purring loudly as she wove her way from his hand to Pulaski's, and then to Data's.

"There—you see?" Pulaski said.

"See what?" asked Riker, Wesley, and Geordi, almost in chorus.

Data knew; it happened every time he touched the cat, and he could not explain it.

Mystery was perfectly content to rub against Data, to accept petting from him as she would from anyone else, to take food from his hand . . . but when he touched her, she did not purr. Up to now, no one else had noticed.

"Animals know," Pulaski affirmed. "Mystery knows Data is a machine."

"What do you mean?" Geordi asked.

"Geordi, I've heard you complain about finding her on consoles in the Engine Room," Pulaski said with a slightly smug smile.

"Cat hair is not beneficial to delicate components," he replied.

"Nor do I like it in my medical instruments, yet not a week goes by that I don't find that creature curled up on one of my diagnostic units. Nothing I've tried will keep her out of sickbay."

"Mom gave up on it," Wesley said, "after she discovered that Mystery never enters a quarantined area. She says cats have senses we'll never understand."

"She may be right," Pulaski said. "Cats like nice,

warm machines, but they don't purr for them. Mystery likes Data, but she knows perfectly well what he is."

Silence fell as everybody listened intently. Mystery was still winding back and forth between Data's hands, more rubbing him than being petted. He had discovered this kept the animal with him longer than attempting to impose his own ideas on her. Just now, though, he wished she would go on to someone else, for Dr. Pulaski was correct—the cat moved without a sound.

Riker broke the silence. "The fact that Data is a machine was never the issue. He's alive and sentient, and that's what makes him a person."

"My point exactly!" Pulaski exclaimed. She turned to the android. "Data, it disturbs me to see anyone trying to be something else, instead of exploring his own potential."

"I understand, Doctor," Data said. "Still, it would be pleasant to be accepted without question."

"Nobody has that luxury, Data," Riker pointed out. "Everyone faces challenges."

"Of course," Data said with a nod, "challenges to one's ideas, one's skills, one's authority—things one can prove or disprove. Were I a flesh-and-blood being, my consciousness would never be questioned."

"At least it's settled now," Geordi declared. "No one can dispute it after the trial."

"You are wrong, Geordi," Data said. "Legal rulings are appealed every day, and frequently overturned. I do not think Commander Maddox will appeal, but there may easily come a time when someone else with the authority to do so may have what he considers a good reason."

8

"Data, that was a landmark decision," Riker reminded him. "It's not going to be overturned."

"Perhaps not overturned, but given the estimates of my life span the probability approaches 100 percent that it will be challenged. What *I am* has been debated three times in only twenty-seven years: when I was first activated, at my application to Starfleet Academy, and again when Commander Maddox sought to disassemble me. I did not question the necessity the first two times. Now I realize that there will always be those who are not satisfied. Judge Louvois put it very aptly when she said that the question is whether I have a soul. Even she admits that that is something that cannot be proven."

"No more for us than for you, Data," Geordi said.

"The difference," Data explained, "is that if souls exist, you are automatically assumed to have one, and I am not."

"So you must keep proving yourself," put in Worf, who had listened in silence to the previous conversation. "Among Klingons, an unchallenged life is not worth living."

Data smiled at their security chief. "But I am no more Klingon than I am human."

"Maybe you're more than human, Data," Geordi suggested. "You're the only person I know with a halo. Only saints have halos."

What Geordi called his "halo" was nothing more than the aura of electromagnetic energy generated by his nonorganic components. Only the engineer could perceive it, with the VISOR that gave him vision far beyond the spectrum available to human, or even android, senses.

Geordi had teased Data about it before—but Dr.

Pulaski evidently didn't recognize the attempt at levity. "All innocents are saints," she said.

Almost without volition, Data accessed his memory concerning metaphysics and theology, and realized, "If I am innocent in that sense—incapable of sin— then I do not have free will, and the verdict of today's hearing was wrong."

There was a moment of stunned silence. Then Riker said, "If you didn't have free will, there would have been no hearing. You would have accepted the transfer without question."

As his friends seemed relieved to accept that rationalization, Data didn't pursue the question further. He stored it for future consideration, though. Was he capable of wrongdoing? Not mistakes; having to make decisions with insufficient information provided frequent opportunity for those. Not disobeying orders; there were times when any officer did so, in the firm belief that some other factor overrode the force of the order.

But deliberate wrongdoing, referred to in a religious context as sin. Had he ever in his life placed his own desire before duty? Was he capable of doing so? He had never been tempted, he realized. *I am simply untested in that area of life,* he told himself firmly. Still—

Just then Counselor Deanna Troi appeared on the path leading from the woods to the picnic area. She stopped in her tracks, her huge dark eyes even wider with surprise. "What has happened? This was supposed to be a happy celebration."

"We just found out that Data's not a Klingon," Geordi said, still trying to lighten the mood.

"But Worf is right," Data said. "I must accept that the challenge to my sentience is one I can never say I have won permanently." *And what shall I do if I discover that Maddox was right? No, I do not believe he was. Let it go for now.* "However, I did win this round, so I have cause for celebration. Counselor, I have a present for you."

The mood lightened, the rest of the presents were opened, and the party settled down into comfortable conversations among people who knew and liked one another. Data deliberately stayed with Troi and Riker for a time, having observed that humans often understood actions better than words. He knew that some would think he had forgiven Riker, and wondered if there were any way to show them there was nothing to forgive. They were all Starfleet officers, after all; every one of them must at some time have had to perform a duty against his will.

Wesley teased Mystery with the ribbon from one of the presents until the cat grew tired of the game and disappeared as enigmatically as she had come. Pulaski, Worf, and Geordi got into a heated debate over the book Data had given Worf: a copy of *Moby Dick* complete with nineteenth-century woodcut illustrations. Data knew the adventure/revenge format would appeal to the Klingon, and looked forward to discussing its literary merits with him.

Right now, though, Worf had other things on his mind. Never one to forget his duty, the Security Officer broke off his conversation with Geordi and Pulaski to remind Wesley, "We leave orbit at 0600 hours. You'll need a full night's sleep if we are to trust you to navigate."

"Come on, Worf—it's a *party,*" Wesley protested, thus proving to everyone there that he must be tired indeed.

Worf rose to his feet.

Wesley was weary enough to complain, "Most of the crew are taking shore leave on the Starbase—lots of them won't come back till the last minute. I could've gone—"

Worf stalked toward the boy, a low growl sounding in his throat.

Wesley scrambled to his feet, picking up the startube. "Okay, okay—I'm going. Portal! Good night, everyone. Thanks, Data!" and he darted out the nearest holodeck door.

Worf paused a moment, staring after him, then turned to the others. "Perhaps this night I ought literally to tuck him in. You have provided our charge with a most fascinating toy, Data." He, too, made his farewells, and one by one the others left until only Kate Pulaski remained, carefully picking up the bellflower.

"It cannot break," Data assured her. "Shall I carry it to your quarters for you?"

"Thank you," she replied. "It's incredible how you can put together something as complex as this, and that gadget for Wesley, in a few hours. The people in Ship's Supplies can't turn the designs for my new medical equipment into reality when they've had them for nearly a month now!"

"Do you wish me to see if I can help them, Doctor?" Data offered.

"No. That was a gripe, not a hint. It's not your job, and the people in Supplies need to learn to do it." Then, as they walked through the nearly-deserted corridors, she turned back to an earlier topic of conversation. "Did you really think I didn't consider you a person, Data?"

"I did not think about it."

"Don't give me that. I've seen you react to some of the things I say. I'm a blunt woman; I generally speak my mind without thinking much about it first." She sighed uncharacteristically. "You fascinate me, Data. You are so much more than the sum total of circuits, sensors, organic fluids, and heuristic algorithms. I want to understand you as *you,* not some imitation humanoid."

"I *am* an imitation humanoid."

"Nonsense!" she flashed. "The humanoid shape is one of the most versatile; otherwise, so many species would not have evolved along the same pattern. You were obviously intended to be as versatile as possible, hence your form."

They stopped before Pulaski's door, and she took the bellflower from him. "Data," she said, "I wish I could wave a magic wand and turn you human for a few days. You need to find out that there's nothing so special about *us,* so you can get on with being *you.*" With that, she stepped into her quarters, leaving Data standing by himself in the corridor.

Data did not sleep. The extra free time it gave him allowed him to assuage his voracious curiosity with the computer or on the holodeck. There was never "nothing to do" for Data.

Yet this night he found himself feeling alone.

Chapter Two

THE NEXT DAY, the U.S.S. *Enterprise* left Starbase 173 with new orders: update sector maps of an area of Federation space Starfleet Command now planned to open to civilian traffic. It was far off the usual routes, but led to some of the oldest starbases still functioning —those responsible for monitoring the Romulan Neutral Zone.

In his seat at the bridge Ops console, Data diverted his attention from the primary systems monitor to run a brief check on recent Starfleet reports of the area they planned to survey. He noted recurring mentions of border disputes with the Waykani, a nonaligned, technologically advanced race—something the Romulans would undoubtedly take an interest in, as the Waykani controlled territory close to both Federation and Romulan space.

Geordi was using the long journey to run stress tests on the engines, pushing the ship to warp nine for extended periods of time. At those speeds the *Enterprise* devoured parsecs at a rate faster than Wesley, manning Conn at the station next to Data, could follow the tumbling numbers on his monitor. The young ensign let out a sigh of frustration.

"Change the display to give you reports at one-second intervals," Data suggested.

"You haven't changed it on your board," Wesley pointed out.

"I can follow it, as can the ship's computer. There are some things machines can do better than humans, Wesley. Let them."

Wesley gave him a curious glance, but adjusted his display without further comment.

Data's own board continued to show the *Enterprise* on course for Starbase 32, all systems normal. All was quiet on the bridge as well; without turning, Data sensed Lieutenant Worf manning the security station at the top of the bridge horseshoe, while directly behind the android, Commander Riker and Captain Picard silently watched the warp-dilated starfield fly past them on the main viewscreen.

The captain had put in only a brief appearance on the bridge yesterday, and today, though he had resumed his normal schedule, he seemed a little more relaxed than usual. Shipboard gossip in the Ten-Forward lounge had it that Phillipa Louvois was responsible for the change in his demeanor.

Data knew only the bare facts of the captain's relationship with Captain Louvois: She had been the prosecuting attorney at Picard's court-martial after he lost the *Stargazer,* and he had not trusted her judgment thereafter . . . until her decision as judge in Data's case. It seemed their friendship, and perhaps something more, had now been revived. Data was glad of it; he did not know how to deal with antagonisms among humans, particularly those he considered his friends.

He listened now as Captain Picard took advantage of the lull in activity to bring his log up to date.

"Captain's Log, Stardate 42528.6. Federation survey ships charted the star clusters through which we are now traveling more than a century ago, reporting no inhabited planets and few with life-form readings. The single exception is a planet called Elysia, charted 107 Federation Standard Years ago by the U.S.S. Clarion. *Their survey team reported intelligent and friendly humanoid life. Yet after they had been there only three days, they were abruptly asked to leave.*

"The sociologist's report suggests that the crew unknowingly trespassed on sacred ground. He theorizes that only an act which to the Elysians was sacrilege could account for the sudden demand that they depart, which the Elysians claimed was issued by their gods. In accordance with the Prime Directive, the Clarion *crew left the planet at once. As Elysia was at that time far from major space lanes, the Federation never attempted to follow up on that first contact.*

"There has been no official exploration in this sector since. Today, however, with modern warp drive systems and expanding trade, the geodesic which skirts the Elysian solar system may become a corridor between the Federation and the farthest extent of the Romulan Neutral Zone, particularly Starbase 32, which lies precariously far from Federation neighbors. Whether the non-Federation worlds near the starbase would provide aid in an emergency is an unknown factor. Recent territorial disputes must be carefully monitored lest the Federation be drawn into conflict.

"With the recent re-emergence of the Romulans into galactic politics, the Federation have decided to survey some of the uninhabited worlds in this quadrant to determine whether any are suitable for colonization. The Federation Council believe such colonies are a peaceful means of establishing a Federation presence in a sector of space which is currently unoccupied, at the same time alleviating population pressures on some of the inner worlds.

"Therefore the Enterprise *is proceeding—"*

There was a flicker on Data's board, the tumbling numbers halting so briefly before resuming that even the ship's computer did not note it. Data said, "Captain, instruments show a variation in warp speed."

"What?" Picard sprang forward to look over the android's shoulder as Data replayed the readings. The captain punched the communications button. "Engineering! Why did we have a drop in power?"

"No drop in power, sir," came Geordi La Forge's voice, sounding somewhat puzzled. *"Engines are running at optimum."*

"Continuing at normal speed, Captain," Data reported, punching up current reports from all systems. "The fluctuation in velocity did not originate within the ship. There was a temporary change in the gravitational field of this area of space."

"How?" Geordi asked. *"What's going on up there, Data? Giant meteor go by or something?"*

"Nothing so obvious," Data replied, too concerned that his instruments gave no answers to remind Geordi that it would have been the *Enterprise* going by a body in space, not the reverse. Something powerful enough to affect the speed of a Galaxy-class starship, even for a nanosecond, ought to be instantly obvious. Instead, scans showed this sector of space normal, as charted.

"Well, Mr. Data?" Picard demanded.

Data shook his head. He was thoroughly familiar with the feeling of frustration; it usually came when he exercised his primary function as the perfect data-retrieval instrument, and the captain cut him off in midreport. Now, though, he experienced the reverse: he was unable to provide information the captain wanted.

"Instruments show all systems normal," Data said as he studied the replay of the fluctuation. "Sensors indicate only that there was a brief surge of—"

"Shh!" the captain interrupted, laying his hand on Data's shoulder.

This time the shift was stronger: a faint, momentary difference in the subliminal hum of warp travel. It was gone in an instant, but Data's perfect memory automatically recorded it. Whatever it was, it was real.

Now Will Riker stepped forward to stand behind the captain.

"Whatever that was," he said, "it made the hairs on the back of my neck stand on end."

"What're you guys doing up there?" Geordi's voice demanded. *"Slaloming around star systems?"*

"Engineer, transfer to the bridge. Captain out." Picard turned back to Data. "That was a gravitational anomaly."

"Agreed, sir. However, saying so is merely to label it, not to define it."

"Then *define* it, Commander!"

"I am trying, sir." Data set the ship's sensors to scan at the broadest range, attempting to determine the source of the surges.

Two minutes passed before another occurred, but this time Data pinpointed its origin. "Powerful electromagnetic and gravitational fluxes are being generated in the vicinity of the planet Elysia."

"Elysia?" Riker asked. "A century ago they had a simple agricultural society. The survey report indicated nothing to suggest the birth of industry, let alone a technology that could produce that kind of power."

"It may not be artificially induced," Data said as he refocused the sensors. "Possibly the planet is undergoing natural gravitational stresses. If so, the populace may need our help."

"If their . . . *gods* do not object," muttered Picard. "What can you find out, Data?"

"I have focused all sensors on Elysia. We ought to be able to determine the epicenter of—"

"Captain!" Worf interrupted. "We are intercepting a radio transmission. Subspace, but not Starfleet frequency."

"From Elysia?" Riker asked.

"Open all frequencies," the captain instructed.

"It is from the direction of Elysia," Worf confirmed, changing the configuration of his board so that the *Enterprise* could receive any broadcast, not merely Starfleet transmissions.

"Dare! I can't hold course!" came a voice over the bridge speaker.

"We're caught, too. Hang on, Poet! Maintain—"

"I know those people," Captain Picard said in a tone Data recognized as meaning that he could not place the circumstances under which he knew them. This time, he was able to provide the information his captain sought.

"Yes, sir, Darryl Adin and his associates." He checked his sensors. "It appears one of their ships is caught in Elysia's gravitational flux."

It had been several months since Data first met Darryl Adin and his band of mercenaries, who at that time had been operating outside the Federation. Only Adin, however, had ever been a fugitive from justice: a former Starfleet security officer falsely convicted of treason and murder.

Darryl Adin was also the man who had rescued the *Enterprise*'s late security chief, Tasha Yar, from the hellhole of a planet where she had been born, abandoned, and victimized. Dare and Tasha had fallen in love—only to have their plans destroyed when Dare was accused and convicted of treason and murder.

The evidence was false, but Tasha didn't know that when, years later, she and Data met up with Dare on a mission to the planet Treva. Tasha was forced to arrest her former love. But when Data uncovered computer tampering used to frame Adin, Starfleet had cleared him of all charges. Tasha and her former mentor made plans for the time when Tasha's tour aboard the *Enterprise* would be completed . . . plans that died with Tasha on Vagra II.

"What in God's name are they doing out here? Mr. Worf, open hailing frequencies," Picard directed, but even as Worf reached for the controls they heard calamity unfolding.

"Don't try to grab us, Dare—you'll only go down with us," Poet's voice, oddly calm, came again. *"I'll try bouncing off the atmosphere and into orbit. We who are about to—"*

"You are not about to die!" Adin's—Dare's—voice

20

ordered. *"You just make that orbit. Aurora and I will merge our tractor beams to pull you—"*

The second voice was drowned in a burst of static. Another gravitational flux vibrated through the *Enterprise* just as Geordi La Forge burst out of the turbolift. "What's going on up here?"

"That's what we called you to find out," Riker told him.

"We have discovered massive electromagnetic and gravitational fluxes emanating from the planet Elysia," Data offered.

"Elysia?" Geordi asked, transferring control of Engineering to his bridge station. "Where the hell is that?"

"Where we're headed, Mr. La Forge—where you'll have ample opportunity to find a reason for those surges," Picard replied.

"Hailing frequencies open, sir," Worf announced.

Picard toggled open a communications frequency. "U.S.S. *Enterprise* to Darryl Adin. Maintain your position. We are within—"

"Seven minutes," Data supplied softly.

"—seven minutes of your location. We have the power to pull your companion's ship to safety. Do not risk your vessels."

Darryl Adin and his people had fine warp-capacity vessels, the epitome of private spacecraft technology, but their engines could not produce enough power to break free of the gravitational surges that barely affected a Galaxy-class starship.

"We hear you, Enterprise," Adin replied. *"Thank God—we thought we were alone out here. Poet, did you get that?"*

"We heard. Dare, my instruments are out. I'll have to make orbit by eye."

"Be careful, Poet," a third voice—a woman's—interrupted. *"Dare, we can track him on our screens, maybe help—"*

"And if there's another surge?" Adin asked in frustration. *"Damn—we've got to risk it. Aurora, swing out 120 degrees in front of Poet, and I'll take a position 120 degrees behind him. With the cross-reckoning, we won't lose track of him."*

By this time Data had Elysia on the main screen. Three ships, too small to be visible, were indicated by blinking lights. The orbit of one was decaying rapidly. It changed course, diving toward the atmosphere in a maneuver not particularly dangerous for an experienced pilot under ordinary circumstances.

But these were not ordinary circumstances.

If the planet emitted another gravitational surge while Poet attempted the maneuver, not only his ship would be affected; the other two could be pulled out of orbit as well.

"Data," Picard said, "I want you on the transporter. The instant we're close enough, get a fix on the people—if we have to, we'll pull them clear and let the ships go. Adin, how many in your company?"

"Eight—four in my ship, two each in Poet's and Aurora's."

As Data moved toward the turbolift, Picard instructed, "Mr. La Forge, ready tractor beams. Mr. Crusher!"

"Yes, Captain?"

"We'll need that tractor beam enhancement of yours on-line if we're going to be dividing power in three directions."

"Aye, Captain," the youngest bridge crew member said as the turbolift doors closed the bridge off from Data's hearing. In the corridor outside the transporter room, another gravitational surge shifted the floor beneath his feet.

Transporters were normally off-line during warp travel, but Transporter Chief O'Brien had orders to start operation the moment they made contact with vessels in distress. While the systems checks were being finished, Data took over the primary console, all the while listening to the intercom from the bridge.

"—out of control!" came Poet's voice. "Rory— don't forget me."

"Enterprise, do you read?" came Adin's voice. "That surge blanked our instruments. We can't operate tractor beams!"

"Slow to impulse!" Picard ordered. "Ensign Crusher—"

"Enhancement on-line, sir!" The boy's voice cracked with tension.

"Mr. La Forge, focus the tractor beams. Data, do you have a fix on the people?"

"Negative, Captain—the distance is too great."

"One of the ships is behind the planet," Picard said. "Change course to two one five mark naught—"

Data turned his primary attention from the bridge conversation and concentrated on the transporter controls. He cross-circuited, seeking to locate life-forms in what the sensors insisted was empty space. Then there was the slightest flicker—

"We're breaking up! Enterprise, your tractor beam's too powerful!"

"Survival suits," said a woman's voice Data also recognized: Pris Shenkley's. "Hurry—"

But by this time Data had a fix on two life-forms. Engaging the transporter, he watched apprehensively as two striped columns of light appeared on the transporter platform, remained fragmented for almost ten seconds, then, as his hands nursed the controls, coalesced into two figures.

He had caught them unprepared. One of them, an oddly nondescript man, was seated on nothing, his hands poised over a nonexistent control board. The other, a tall, slender blond woman, had one survival suit slung over her arm and a second in her hands, ready to drop into the man's lap. As they integrated, the man fell backward onto the transporter platform. But he was up in a flash. He spun and caught sight of Data at the console.

"Did you get the others?" he demanded.

At the same moment, Picard's voice came over the intercom. *"Data—we lost one ship! Did you get those people aboard?"*

"Two aboard safe," he replied.

"Thank God," the captain replied. *"We've got the other ships in tow—they'll be in the shuttle bay in another few minutes."*

The man and woman grinned at one another, and then the woman came around the console to hug Data. "Once more to the rescue. This is starting to become a habit."

"Welcome aboard, Pris Shenkley. I am pleased that the *Enterprise* was available," Data replied. "I shall maintain transporter readiness until the other ships are safely aboard. Then I will take both you and Poet"—he nodded a greeting to the man—"to the shuttle bay."

Data was pleased to see Pris again. They had first met on the planet Treva, but at that time he had been so enmeshed in his mission—concerned about Tasha Yar's attraction to Darryl Adin—that he had hardly responded to Pris's overtures of friendship.

Now, perhaps, he would have the chance to get to know her better.

The other two shuttles were brought aboard without incident. Shortly thereafter, Data led Pris and Poet to a reunion with the other members of Darryl Adin's band in the shuttle bay.

He had a reunion of his own there as well.

"Mr. Data," Darryl Adin said, striding over to meet him. "Thank you. That is twice I owe you . . . or is it three times?"

Data saw a shadow appear in the man's dark eyes on the last words. "Only twice," he replied. "The last time was my choice. You owe me no debt."

Adin was referring to the last time he had seen Data—several months ago, after Data had delivered to Adin the personal farewell message prepared by Tasha Yar for the man she loved. After Adin had viewed the message, sharing memories of Tasha, he had talked quietly for hours, never questioning Data's understanding. The android had felt that his responses were inadequate, and yet Adin seemed somehow comforted—as much so as a man could be who had been so often betrayed by fate.

Data, like his human colleagues, was unable to reconcile Tasha's senseless death with any kind of justice in the universe. Slowly, in his search to comprehend human nature, he was coming to accept that a primary characteristic of being human was paradox: *not* understanding certain things gave him more in common with man than understanding them did.

The dark clothing, and Adin's human-average brown-hair/brown-eyes coloring, might have caused another man to blend inconspicuously into the background. But not Adin; even in the middle of a crowded shuttle bay, he was the center of attention.

Their conversation was interrupted by the arrival of Captain Picard.

"Mr. Adin, I'm glad to see you in one piece."

"I'm glad to see you as well, Captain—though I must admit, these aren't the circumstances I'd have chosen for our meeting."

Picard nodded. "What are you doing here? This isn't a recommended civilian space lane."

"Starfleet opened it three months ago," Adin replied. "It may not be recommended, but there's nothing warning private craft away."

"He is correct, Captain," Data added. "This is the fastest route for any craft capable of Warp Four or above to the quadrant of explored space along the neutral zone. Small craft are warned only that there are no inhabited planets or space stations, hence no refueling or repair depots. It might be foolhardy to take this route in a single ship, but there is nothing to indicate that it is not safe for three ships in convoy."

Adin smiled. "I'm sure we can repair our ships, Captain Picard—if you will permit us to work here in your shuttle bay . . ."

"Of course," Picard replied. "The engineering staff are currently on alert, because of those power surges from Elysia. Once we are back to normal status I shall assign some of our crew to help you."

"There's no need—"

"We *owe* you," Picard interrupted firmly.

Adin seemed surprised; Data didn't understand why, as Starfleet policy was to offer aid in repairing any ship in distress. It was also Starfleet policy to make good on its mistakes, such as the one that had resulted in Dare's unjust conviction.

"Now, I want all of your crew examined in sickbay, then assigned to guest quarters," Captain Picard continued. "Feel free to work on your ships. And don't hesitate to ask for assistance or equipment. In the meantime—" Picard tapped his communicator. "Bridge—anything new to report, Number One?"

"It's stopped—as if those surges never existed." Riker's voice hesitated. *"Data, could your friends have done something to provoke the Elysians?"*

"Nothing," Adin asserted. "We were merely cutting through this sector on the way to Brancherion. We had no intention of coming near Elysia—the first surge pulled us off course. The planet's listed on the charts as pre-industrial and not desiring contact. We were skirting the outer edge of the star system when it just reached out and grabbed us."

"I find it unsettling," Picard added, "that something powerful enough to affect a starship can turn on and off like that."

"Perhaps it is artificial," Data suggested. "But we did not show even radio transmissions from Elysia."

"Captain—can we risk going closer?" Riker asked.

"And if the surges begin again?" Picard asked.

"The *Enterprise* withstood them before and pulled three other ships free," Data replied. "I believe we can establish standard orbit and still maintain the ship's safety. The question is whether we should risk an away team."

"We'll survey the planet from standard orbit then, Number One," Picard instructed. "And make our decision afterward." He closed the channel to the bridge. "Data, see what you can salvage from Mr. Adin's onboard computers. With your permission, of course," he added to Adin.

The mercenary replied with a sardonic smile, "Pass up the help of the best computer expert I know?" He shook his head sadly. "There's nothing to hide in those computers; the question is whether there's anything left in them at all."

For the next few hours, the *Enterprise* orbited Elysia, circling the planet repeatedly with a slight change of angle on each pass, as if winding an invisible ball of yarn, thereby gaining a complete picture of the planet below.

Meanwhile, Data joined Darryl Adin's crew in the shuttle bay. While the others tore apart the instrument panels and demagnetized or replaced the scrambled equipment, he and Sdan, Dare's science expert, connected the shuttle's memory storage to the *Enterprise* system. They spent hours locating every byte of unscrambled data, managing to recover most of the ships' logs. Pieces of the ships' programs were recoverable, but they would be far easier to replace than to debug.

By this time, most of Adin's gang were growing weary. Sdan, who appeared superficially Vulcan (but did not act it because he was actually a mix of Vulcan, Romulan, human, Orion, and possibly other ancestry), also had Vulcanoid stamina. He and Data spent the time until Data's next duty shift restoring the navigational programs and began the adaptation of the shuttlecraft operations program, which would take many more hours of work.

Data reported to the bridge, to find that while he was occupied the survey orbit of Elysia had almost been completed. Calling up the information on his console at the fastest rate his positronic brain could absorb it, he transferred the data to his own memory within minutes, and was already sifting through it for significant information when the captain entered the bridge.

"Mr. Data, Number One, Counselor Troi, my ready room," said Picard. "And you, too, Lieutenant," he added as Worf stepped out of the turbolift.

Data saw Wesley Crusher's eyes follow the captain eagerly, but their young acting ensign was certainly not going to be invited on an away team to a potentially dangerous planet. At the door, though, Picard turned.

"Mr. Crusher—"

With a quick "Yes, sir!" Wesley was halfway out of his chair before the captain finished his instructions.

"—ask Mr. La Forge and Dr. Pulaski to come to my ready room, please. And Mr. Thralen from Sociology."

The boy's disappointment showed, but all he said was "Aye, Captain," as he slid back into position and keyed the intercom to Engineering.

As they waited for Geordi and the ship's CMO, Data gave his assessment of the planetary survey. "There can be little doubt that this planet is artificially maintained. Humanoid life could not have evolved naturally on Elysia, for the atmosphere is made up of

29

gases poisonous to carbon-nitrogen-oxygen based life-forms. Except for small areas of extreme cold near the poles, Elysia is a planetwide noxious swamp."

"But there are settlements of intelligent humanoid beings," Riker argued. "We have tricorder records from the original survey team, who met and spoke with them, and our own survey verifies their existence today."

"That is correct," Data said with a nod. "There are nine inhabited areas, where the land is arable, the atmosphere appropriate to a class-M planet. Such a configuration is not possible under natural conditions. Something must keep the poisonous atmosphere from overwhelming the settlements. Something must prevent the cloud cover which holds temperature and moisture at intolerable levels over the swamplands from blocking sunlight to and heat radiation from the inhabited areas."

Before Data could continue with his list of impossible things "something" was doing on Elysia, Picard interrupted to suggest, "Forcefields?"

"None that our sensors can detect," Data replied.

"Physical barriers, then?"

"None, sir."

The doors opened to admit Kate Pulaski, Geordi La Forge, and the Theskian sociologist Thralen, just as the captain challenged, "Magic?"

"Magic?" Pulaski repeated skeptically.

"By the definition," Data suggested, "that any technology sufficiently advanced as to be beyond our comprehension may be defined as magic, then it appears that yes, we may be dealing with magic on Elysia."

Seating herself across from Data, Pulaski snorted

derisively. "We need to *understand* what is happening on Elysia, not pin some obscure definition on it."

"I do not claim that the definition explains what we have observed on Elysia, Doctor," Data protested. "I merely agree with the captain that without more information we cannot solve the puzzle."

"That's always your answer, isn't it? Gather more data." She pronounced the first syllable of the last word with a short vowel.

"In this case Mr. Data is right, Doctor," Picard observed. "I assume you've all seen the recordings of the original survey team's encounters with the Elysians, a century ago. What we've observed from orbit indicates that nothing's changed. The society is still agricultural, with no evidence of industry. The gravitational shifts have stopped, but as we've not been able to trace their source—"

"Captain," Data said, "we do not know their *cause;* their *source* is in all probability the single anomalous mountain in Elysia's terrain."

"How could it be?" Riker asked. "There are undefined energy emanations from that region, but the readings from the mountain hardly impact on the sensors. It's probably just low-grade volcanic activity."

"Yeah," Geordi added, "there's nothing regular about it. If it's natural, then it couldn't be connected with the gravitational shifts or it would show aftereffects. But if it's artificial, then it ought to show the kind of regularity that you don't get in nature, Data."

"But it does," said the android.

"Explain," Picard directed.

Data turned the captain's computer terminal so he could call up a holographic image of Elysia. "First, the fact that the planet has only one mountain is unique to my knowledge."

"That's what I'd call unique!" Geordi put in.

"Otherwise," Data continued, "the topography of the planet appears normal enough. There is the expected gravitational bulge at the equator and flattening at the poles. There are various hills and valleys, even though all but the gently rolling lands in the protected habitats are within the swamp. The valleys there are filled with water, the hilltops emerging as hummocks or small islands. The locations of the unexplained inhabitable areas appear haphazard . . . until we change the view from topographical to topological."

"I see!" gasped Geordi, the only one in the group with the engineering background to make it instantly obvious.

So the others could also see, Data adjusted the display, flattening out the irregularities of Elysia until the planet's surface was a perfect sphere, with the exception of the single mountain. With the unevenness smoothed out, the pattern became apparent to everyone seated around the table: each one of the nine habitats covered the same area of ground, and all were equidistant from the mysterious mountain. "I think this is sufficient evidence that the mountain is central to whatever force maintains the habitats," said Data. "The design is patently artificial."

Captain Picard nodded and began soliciting suggestions on how to proceed with the study of Elysia.

"Obviously, somebody has to go down there," Geordi said. "I volunteer."

"As do I," Data added.

"I don't recommend it," Riker warned. "Your abilities would be extremely helpful, but neither of you could pass for Elysian. We don't know whether the natives will order strangers away, as they did the people who offended them a century ago."

"Mr. Thralen?" Captain Picard prompted.

The sociologist nodded. "I have studied the records of the original survey team very carefully. As long as they remained within the inhabited areas, the Elysians made them welcome. However, although none of the great power surges we have witnessed were recorded by the *Clarion,* they did note those energy anomalies, and beamed several crew members down onto the mysterious island. They attempted to climb the mountain, and suddenly, wherever Starfleet personnel were on the planet, Elysians came and informed them that they were no longer welcome."

"So we steer clear of the mountain," Riker said, "and try to keep the natives from equating us with the *Clarion* crew. It's probably best to avoid contact with the Elysians, but it may be impossible to prevent it. I suggest that everyone who beams down be capable of passing as Elysians. If we are questioned we can claim to be from a different habitat."

"Mr. La Forge, I'm afraid Commander Riker is right," said Picard. "You've seen the records: Elysians look much like humans, and certainly do not have the technology to comprehend an android, or even your VISOR. There is no response to our attempts to communicate with them from here. If it weren't for the danger these gravitational anomalies pose to travel through this quadrant, we wouldn't go near the native settlements at all."

"Captain," Worf said, "I believe there is an easier way to prevent the Elysians from equating our away team with the *Clarion* crew."

"What do you suggest?" the captain asked.

"Send Data, Geordi, Thralen, and me."

Pulaski broke into a moment's laughter, but controlled herself at Picard's stern glance. "You have to agree, Captain," she said, "Lieutenant Worf is absolutely right."

"Thank you, Doctor," the Klingon replied.

"It's perfect!" Geordi exclaimed. "My vision, Data's ability to accumulate information, Lieutenant Thralen's knowledge of sociology to help us with local customs, and Worf for security."

Picard shook his head. "I'll consider you four as a secondary team. However, I believe Commander Riker's plan to avoid contact with the Elysians is preferable. If you four were seen, even from a distance, the natives would certainly investigate. Mr. Thralen, do we have any indication as to whether the Elysians intended to send away all strangers, all humans, all Starfleet personnel, the crew of the *Clarion* in particular . . . ?" He stopped, a raised eyebrow asking the Theskian to choose an option or provide one of his own.

"No, sir," Thralen replied calmly, in the clear, sibilant tones characteristic of his race. The Theskians were related to the Andorians, with similar slender physique and high-strung nervous energy, but culturally they were far more gregarious. The deepening of blue coloration in his face and the slight quivering of the curved antennae which thrust up through his furlike yellow hair indicated Thralen's frustration. "It is not even clear whether the Elysians grasped the fact that the *Clarion* crew came from off the planet. The proscription could apply to any strangers. On the other hand, it may no longer be in effect—the present-day inhabitants may know nothing about it."

The captain rubbed his chin, then nodded. "We'll proceed with our original plan, and go to Mr. Worf's, in a different habitat, if the away team encounters hostility."

"Although I agree that we should not seek contact with the Elysians," added Counselor Troi, "their habitats are quite small. Encounters with the natives may be unavoidable. Therefore I volunteer for the away team to act as liaison."

Picard nodded. Argyle from Engineering and Johnson from Security were chosen to fill out the team.

"One final note," the captain added. "If we discover that the Elysians or whoever keeps them here in such an obviously artificial environment has control over those gravitational anomalies, we still must not violate the Prime Directive."

"What will we do in that case, Captain?" Pulaski asked.

"Nothing," Picard answered. "Absolutely nothing except to record every bit of information, close this space lane to all traffic, and refer the problem to the Federation Council."

"And if the surges turn out to be a natural phenomenon?" the doctor asked.

"I can't answer that until we know, one way or the other," Picard replied. "So far as we can tell, the surges don't affect life on the planet's surface. If the populace appear to be in danger, then we'll deal with further philosophical questions. For now, let's get the away team down to the surface and replace speculation with facts."

Once again, Picard asked Data to operate the transporter. The away team, dressed in simple homespun garments such as the Elysians wore, beamed down less than an hour later to a habitat that was not one of the three visited by the *Clarion* crew. Dawn was just breaking there, allowing them hours of daylight to complete their study. No anomalies disturbed the beaming; indeed, there were no traces whatsoever of the huge fluctuations of power that had taken place only a few hours before.

Once the away team reported that they had landed unobserved on the perimeter of one of the protected areas, Data returned to the bridge. The reports came in on schedule as the hours passed—they had located the dividing line between swamp and farmland and avoided the attention of the natives; however, their instruments could not identify what held the poisonous gases of the swamp away or kept clean, fresh air within the invisible boundaries.

"Magic," Data commented when the final report scheduled for his duty shift came in.

When Data's replacement was due, the android turned to the captain. "Shall I stay at my post, sir?"

"No, Data," Picard replied. "Ensign Gibson can take 'no new information' reports as well as you can. If anything does happen, you'll be called. Go help your friends with their ships; at least you're accomplishing something there."

But Darryl Adin and his gang were not in the shuttle bay. The ensign on duty told Data, "They quit a while ago. Said they needed rest and recreation. I recommended the Ten-Forward lounge, sir."

Indeed, Data found his friends in that favorite leisure spot. Sdan was at the bar, talking to Guinan, the hostess who everyone aboard assumed had as colorful a past as the Vulcanoid, although no one, not even Data, could find out much about it.

Over near the ports, through which Elysia could be seen filling half the view, several tables were pushed together so that some of the *Enterprise* crew could talk with the famous "Silver Paladin." Kate Pulaski was there, as was Pris Shenkley; Sandra Murchison, one of the secondary-level history teachers; Worf and three other off-duty security personnel; and Wesley Crusher with two of his young friends from the advanced science seminar Data conducted for the best and brightest students among the families on board.

Adin's reputation as mercenary and adventurer attracted most of the crew, Data supposed, but those who had been close friends with Tasha Yar were undoubtedly curious about this man who had loved her and lost her, twice over.

Tragic love, Data knew from cold statistics, held great appeal for the human psyche. Why, he could not comprehend. The pain of losing a close friend was bad enough—he had experienced that and did not doubt he understood it as much, or as little, as any human. As he did not comprehend love, however, he made no claims to understand what Adin had suffered at Tasha's death, even though he had observed the man at the time. And although he could recite word for word such classics as *Romeo and Juliet,* Data could not fathom the appeal of vicarious suffering, unless it was the sense of community which sometimes resulted from sharing such emotions.

As the android approached, Adin broke off his conversation. "Data—come and join us," he invited, gesturing to a chair near his own. "What's happening on Elysia? Or is it classified?"

As it was not, Data told the group around the table the frustrating findings, or lack thereof, of the away team. "They will return to the ship soon," he added, and frowned. "I cannot help thinking that they are missing something. It is not possible that no barrier separates swamp from habitat. Geordi might be able to see something the tricorders do not, but he cannot do so without his VISOR, which would identify him as non-Elysian were he observed. I do not understand why I cannot go, however."

Not unexpectedly, that comment drew a snort of laughter from Dr. Pulaski. "You don't think an android would be a dead giveaway that we're not Elysians?"

"I had hoped," Data replied, "that you would be willing to help disguise me, Doctor. I would not be alone; if an encounter with Elysian natives became unavoidable, I could remain in the background and say nothing. Surely my skin could be temporarily colored like that of a human."

Pris Shenkley smiled at him from across the table. "I could help you do that—but I'm afraid there's no way to change your golden eyes, Data."

"My eyes are kept clean and lubricated by a fluid which serves the same function as human tears," he explained. "Therefore I could wear contact lenses."

"I've never prescribed them except as a temporary protection while an eye injury heals," Pulaski said.

"But they were once used for both corrective and cosmetic purposes. Your medical laboratory could easily manufacture a set that would make my eyes appear brown or blue."

"Data's got you, Doctor," Adin said with a grin. "I see no reason he couldn't pass for human in a brief encounter, and that's all an away team would allow."

Pulaski shook her head. "He'd give himself away with every act, every movement. No one would believe for a moment he was a living humanoid."

Adin scowled at the doctor. He was a man used to authority, but in this case Data sensed that something other than having his opinion challenged disturbed him. He looked from Data to Pulaski, and then asked her, "How long have you known Data, Dr. Pulaski? You weren't aboard when I was last on the *Enterprise.*"

"I've been aboard for several months," she said.

Adin shook his head. "Well, you've hardly gotten to know Data in that time, or you'd never question that, at the very least, he is a 'living humanoid.' Data, you have an open invitation to come and work with me if Starfleet fails to appreciate you."

"There are times when we could certainly use you, Data," Pris Shenkley added, staring at Pulaski with a glare that rivaled Dare at his most glacial.

The doctor, however, was intent on explaining her position further. "I should have said 'organic' humanoid; Data has been designated a life-form. That he is a sentient being, a person, has been established by law, and rightly so." She turned her gaze to Data. "But you're not a human being—and I'm afraid I'll never understand your desire to become one."

The table fell silent for a moment. Data saw no cause for offense at Dr. Pulaski's words—after all, his desire to be human (impossible as he knew it to be) was no secret—but he could sense that Dare and Pris were upset.

Pulaski obviously sensed it, too, for she continued, "You can all"—she spread her hands to indicate the table at large—"anthropomorphize Mr. Data as much as you wish, but he acts and thinks like a machine. Elysians might not understand what he is, but they would certainly recognize that he is not one of them."

"Would you care to make a wager on that?" Adin asked, baring his teeth with a faint smile.

Pulaski rose to the challenge: "What do you want to bet?"

"My money's on Data," Pris put in. "I know how charming he can be when he sets his mind to it."

"And I have never observed him to misstep in a fight," added Worf. "What is the wager?"

Pulaski smiled sweetly at Worf. "What do you suggest?"

Data was astonished at the trust his friends placed in an ability he was not certain he had—but the point was moot, anyway. "I cannot join the away team in an attempt to win a bet, and even if the captain sent me for other reasons I could certainly not attempt contact with the Elysians merely to test your faith in my acting ability."

Pulaski laughed. "We should have wagered—I'd have won by default."

"Oh, no," Adin said. "You don't get off that easily, Madame. Or you either, Data. Elysia may not provide the opportunity, but if we reach a starbase or a Federation planet—"

"You're on!" Pulaski said with that sweet smile Data knew concealed supreme confidence. "Like taking candy from a baby."

Adin responded with an almost identical expression. "Then we must agree upon terms."

Data considered warning Dr. Pulaski that Adin was an experienced gambler who rarely lost, but decided against it, remembering the doctor's skill at poker. Besides, he wished to attempt the challenge. Appearing human might allow him to understand human behavior just that much better.

"It's too bad you won't be going to Elysia, Data," Dr. Pulaski said. "Perhaps the forces you call 'magic' would be able to grant that desire of yours."

"Unlikely," Data told her. "Whatever forces govern Elysia, they cannot grant the impossible."

"Now isn't that funny?" the doctor replied. "You recognize that you want the impossible. That's about as good a definition of being human as I've ever heard."

"Doctor, we are in grave danger of being in agreement," Dare said. "Data, your very desire for the impossible makes you one of us."

"Which is not what we were proposing to bet on," the doctor reminded him. "The question is whether Data can make strangers, not friends, accept him as the human he is modeled on."

"Done," Dare agreed, "the challenge to be implemented at the first opportunity that does not interfere with a mission."

"Done," said Dr. Pulaski, reaching across the table to shake Dare's hand. "Now—what shall we bet?"

The conversation was interrupted by the chirp of combadges.

"Mr. Worf, Mr. Data," Captain Picard's voice instructed. "Report to Briefing Room Three for away team assignment to Elysia."

Chapter Three

DATA FOUND GEORDI LA FORGE already with Captain Picard in Briefing Room Three. The two were watching Commander Riker's away team giving their report, which was being transmitted openly from the outskirts of a small city the natives knew as "Quinaria." Elysians stood all about them, looking curiously at the tricorders but exhibiting no hostility.

"I sense open welcome from these people, Captain," Counselor Deanna Troi was saying. "If they pose a threat to us, they are not aware of it." The counselor's long hair was drawn back from her face and fastened with a thong at the nape of her neck in the same style Data could see worn by native women in the picture.

"Mr. Riker, please explain this situation." Picard demanded. "Under no circumstances were these people to be approached—"

"We didn't approach *them*, sir," Riker's voice interrupted. *"They* came to *us*."

The picture jolted for a moment, then steadied as

their first officer apparently handed his tricorder to someone else in the party and stepped into view. He had combed his hair down into bangs such as the native males wore; with the beard he had recently grown he looked rustic enough to pass, as long as the hood of his tunic hid the fact that his hair was much shorter in the back than the Elysians'.

Riker spoke again. "We meant to pass on by them, exchange greetings as per our orders, and then go back to our studies when they were out of sight."

"But it turned out," Troi took up the story, "that they had been sent in search of us—they had been told to expect a visit from 'strangers from a far land.' But let Drahanna, their Speaker, explain."

Troi beckoned an Elysian woman into the picture. She was tall, middle aged, with iron-gray hair and hazel eyes that looked with steady curiosity into the lens. "If I speak to this object, your leader will hear me?"

"I will hear you, Drahanna," Picard replied.

The only sign of surprise the woman gave was a slight widening of her eyes. "The gods told me of your magical implements, and that you are on a Quest far greater than any of our people have achieved. We have been instructed to make you welcome, and told that among you are some who are very different from ourselves. We are preparing a feast in your honor, oh blessed of the gods. Please join us, and allow us to aid you on your journey."

"We are honored," Picard replied. "Thank you for making welcome those we sent ahead. Now I must speak to my people."

Drahanna moved away. After a moment, Riker

said, "We're out of range, Captain. Whatever it is the Elysians call gods seem to know a great deal about us. We haven't detected *them*, though. The natives apparently think we've come across the swamp from another land, in some kind of boat. They certainly have no concept of the size of our ship or crew."

"No," Troi confirmed. "They were amazed at four of us 'questing' together, as they see it. I've gathered that quests are usually undertaken by one person, or occasionally two. I am quite certain they would be shocked to learn that there are more than, oh, perhaps ten of us at most. Captain, I get no sense of these 'gods' at all, but from what they have told these people, through Drahanna, it almost appears that they are sending *us* instructions about the role we are to play."

"And they'll throw us off the planet again if we don't go along with it," Riker added peevishly.

"We'll take what we can get," Picard said. "These 'gods' may be assessing our strength just as we are attempting to assess theirs."

"I sure haven't found any trace of them using our instruments up here," Geordi added. "Or of those power surges."

"What if they're at the mercy of those power surges as well, Captain?" Riker suggested.

Picard nodded thoughtfully. "It could be that they don't know whether they dare trust us enough to ask for help. Very well, Number One. We'll play along for now. They've set the stage for me to send Data and Geordi down, and I know Lieutenant Worf won't be satisfied with security unless he's down there supervising it."

"I suggest that you make no attempt to disguise them," said Counselor Troi. "The natives are prepared for people quite different from themselves."

Within the hour, Data beamed down, along with Geordi, Worf, and the sociologist Thralen, in uniform and undisguised. There was no one at the beamdown point, which was close to where the undetectable barrier kept the swamp from encroaching on the habitat, but there was a road nearby that took them to the village in less than half an hour's walk. There, they joined the first landing party, as well as most of the village natives.

The Elysians were friendly, but ferociously curious. They surrounded Thralen first, for the Theskian's blue skin, furlike yellow hair, and antennae were furthest in appearance from the Elysian norm. But soon they tackled Worf and Geordi as well, bombarding each with questions.

Data was intrigued to be the last one noticed—and only for the color of his skin and eyes. "I think Darryl Adin will win his bet," he told Worf.

"Agreed," the Klingon said, but they had no time to discuss it further, with the Elysians plucking at their uniforms, demanding to know how they made such cloth, so different from any weave they knew.

Eventually, though, the away team was granted some privacy. Drahanna led them all to one of the houses in the village, which had been cleared for their use. It was built of mud and wattle on a stone foundation, the floor strewn with clean straw. The construction was simple but sound, the roof made of wooden shingles that showed no light except for the central smoke-hole.

The Elysians had not yet invented the chimney. How could they be in control of forces that could shake a starship?

"Thralen," said Riker, "what do you think?"

"Either the Elysians do not know of our predecessors at all, or they have not connected us with them. This is a very preliminary report—I was too busy trying to think of neutral answers to their questions to ask many of my own. As the novelty of our appearance wears off, I hope to learn more."

"What *did* you learn?"

"'Afar' is the only word they seem to have for 'not within this habitat.' The great difficulty of traversing the swamp apparently makes contact between the habitats close to impossible, so they have little idea what other lands are like. They find it much harder to comprehend how we have come here than that we are so different from them. For all they know, the other side of the planet could be peopled with Klingons and Theskians."

"Here there be dragons," Riker commented.

Data's automatic memory search showed him maps of Earth from many centuries before, unexplored regions marked with that phrase. "Yes," he said, "but not 'Here there be androids.' The Elysians are incapable of recognizing me as a machine because they have no machines more complex than a plow or a pulley. They have not even invented clockwork."

"Why should they?" Geordi asked. "These gods of theirs give them a protected environment in which they don't have to do more than hunt, herd, plow, plant, and harvest to live comfortably. There's no challenge to them to create a technology."

"If they did," Thralen added, "and thereby increased their life spans, they could easily overpopulate these small habitats. I need to go out among them more, Commander," he said to Riker, "let them get used to me so I can ask questions to determine whether their population is stable, or whether the habitats expand to accommodate an increase."

They all tried to steer the conversations at the feast prepared for them in such directions, but the Elysians countered every question with a question of their own. The away team would have been completely frustrated had not their instruments given them some answers: Their tricorders and Geordi's VISOR showed that the village had been expanded over a period of centuries, even though the style and method of building remained the same.

"No ingenuity," Geordi muttered to Data. "Very little variety. Look at the food—about as plain as it ever comes."

Data nibbled at the food, always interested in trying new flavors, but found nothing of special interest. There was fresh fruit, a grain that had been boiled in water to the consistency of cooked rice, meat roasted over an open fire, and small crystals of a sweet substance produced by a local insect in the same way bees produced honey. But there were no sauces, no spices, not even the concept of blending ingredients into bread or cakes. Plain fare, nutritionally adequate, but uninteresting.

So Data did not take more than a taste of each dish except for the meat, which he did not try. He might not feel the revulsion some of his colleagues did at the thought of eating meat produced by killing animals, but he shared the same ethical considerations. Their hosts were not offended, for Worf and Riker showed no such reluctance.

After the meal, things became much more interesting. It seemed that on those rare occasions when there were guests "from afar," tradition required a ritual ceremony.

Drahanna stepped forward and began: "We welcome you, oh beloved of the gods. Feast with us in praise of the gods who have suffered you to brave the perils of the swamp, an honor few Elysians are granted. Tell us, blessed ones, of your journey to the sacred mountain."

Riker frowned, clearly trying to decide how best to respond. Troi spoke up for him. "We have not reached the sacred mountain, Drahanna. We have not come near to it."

"The gods must have further tests for you then," said the Speaker. "May you prove worthy, and some among you be allowed the challenge when you have completed your arduous journey across the Great Swamp."

If Drahanna was to be believed, Thralen had guessed right: The gods of Elysia wanted no one attempting to climb their sacred mountain without permission. Unfortunately, it appeared they would find out very little about the gods and their relationship to the mysterious and dangerous power surges by visiting only the Elysian habitats. The "gods" seemed determined to remain hidden.

The away team had already determined to stay the night, as if they were truly weary travelers grateful for rest from an arduous journey. After the conclusion of the ceremony, most of them were led back to their hut, but Data and Thralen (who was too eager to gain more information about this enigmatic culture to be interested in sleeping) stayed behind, and spent the night talking with Drahanna.

By morning they had gleaned a few more facts about Elysia's gods: each village had a Speaker, who was attuned to the gods; he or she received the messages the gods wanted delivered, which were usually such things as when to begin planting, or to stop hunting a particular animal until it had a chance to repopulate.

When Thralen asked how she received the messages, Drahanna explained that the gods spoke to her, but refused to explain further. After a time she must have decided their questions indicated they were nervous about their journey to the sacred mountain. "It is true," she told them, "that some reach the sacred isle only to be turned back, for the final test comes there. But be not afraid: The gods have chosen you to undertake the journey. That in itself shows their favor. Only one or two of your group will be permitted the final quest to the top of the mountain. I cannot tell you which ones—the gods do not speak to me of you, any more than they foretold your destiny to your own Speaker at home." She smiled. "Your future shifts with each thought; except for certain foreordained truths, nothing is certain until it happens."

At sunrise the team left the hut, walked back to the beamdown point, and transported up to the *Enterprise*. Drahanna had conveniently instructed the villagers not to accompany them to the edge of the swamp; whatever the gods were, they obviously did not want their subjects to see people vanish into thin air.

Aboard ship, there was a briefing to decide whether to try exploring another habitat.

"I do not think we shall find further information about the Elysian gods or the power surges among the natives," Data said. "Mr. Thralen and I did learn that the reason the landing party from the *Clarion* were driven away was that they attempted to climb the Elysians' sacred mountain without passing a test of the gods."

Thralen added, "I've played back and carefully studied Drahanna's words. It appears we would be in no violation of Elysian law if we set an away team down on the island, at the foot of the mountain. As long as we did not attempt to climb it, we might be able to take readings that would tell us something about the power surges."

"I might be able to see something," Geordi put in. "Captain, those same undetectable barriers that keep the swamp gases from poisoning the habitats also keep a habitable environment on that island, yet we transport through it as if it weren't there. As we haven't been able to detect the barrier, we don't know how much it screens. Assuming the island is its source, we may be able to find out something there about these mysterious gods."

Picard rubbed his chin. "I would prefer more direct communication from these 'gods' about what they consider acceptable, but we've hailed them on every frequency we can transmit. If they don't want to be found, the very act of attempting to locate them may be deemed aggressive."

"If so," said Riker, "how are we any worse off?

There's no reason to think they'll do more than order us off the planet, like the *Clarion* crew. We can give up, file a report, and close this convenient geodesic to Federation traffic because of those damned power surges. Or we can make one more attempt to find the gods—that might even be the test Drahanna spoke of. If we can locate them, maybe they'll talk to us. If they either control the power surges or can predict their occurrence, they may be willing to send out warnings beforehand, so ships can avoid the area."

Picard nodded. "We need this space lane open if we are to offer protection to our colonies near the Neutral Zone. Very well, Number One. Take Data and Geordi, beam down to that island, and see what you can find out."

"Request permission to accompany them, sir," Worf said. "I also recommend that we take phasers. We should not meet any Elysians there, but we do not know what else we may encounter."

The captain seemed about to protest, but finally nodded reluctantly.

Unlike the habitats, the sacred island was barren and gloomy—or at least the side on which they landed was. The mountain was so large that it seemed as if they weren't on an island at all; rocky beach stretched in either direction as far as they could see.

Between the swamp and the foot of the mountain there was perhaps a hundred meters of more or less flat beach, but even that was difficult to traverse. It was made up of rocks ranging from fist size up to giant boulders, tumbled haphazardly, their sharp edges unweathered in the still air.

The stillness—that's what made the place so

strange. They were outdoors, yet the air didn't move. It was as if they were in a holodeck rather than on the surface of a planet.

Data noticed his human companions hunching and shivering slightly. The temperature was nine degrees Celsius, warm enough for humans to come to no harm, but cool enough to be uncomfortable if they did not keep moving. Data, of course, was unaffected, and if Worf felt the chill he refused to show it. The Klingon did, however, move out quickly, scouting the territory as if he expected enemies behind every rock.

Riker walked toward the swamp, where they could see the gray mist of poisonous vapors swirling against the invisible barrier. Sounds came through, though: the lapping of water moved by some breeze that stirred the vapors, but stopped dead at the barrier. There were other noises, too, but not knowing the fauna of this planet, Data could not identify them. All seemed to resound in a minor key. Such tones, he knew, had an unsettling effect on humans.

At the edge of the water, Riker put out a hand, and was stopped. It looked as if he were holding back the swamp vapors. He pushed, but succeeded only in shoving himself backward. "Just like the barrier around the habitats," he noted.

Data tried all his own instrumentation, as well as every detection device in his tricorder. All said there was nothing between the swamp and the clean air on the island. Yet the two remained sharply separated, and the away team could not penetrate the barrier. Neither could their tricorders detect life-form readings through it, although they could see the swamp teeming with life.

"Yet the ship's instrumentation read the Elysians right through it, from orbit," Data pointed out. "There should not be such a discrepancy."

"It's not natural," Geordi agreed. "I guess it's our job to find out if it's supernatural."

"Supernatural, Geordi?" Riker asked skeptically.

"Magic, sir," Data answered. "Technology so far above ours it seems—"

Riker held up his hand to stop Data. "I get the picture." He motioned them forward. "Come on."

Both Data and Geordi could penetrate the mist with infrared vision, and see farther into the swamp. It was not an appealing place. Dark, dank hummocks of rotting wood mingled with the roots of live trees. Reptilian beasts slithered through the water, which in some areas was several meters deep but in others just a shallow layer over mud so saturated that it would act as quicksand.

Flying creatures sailed from one gray tree to another on batlike wings. Data saw one dive into the water, emerging with something snakelike held between rows of sharp teeth. Its victim put up a valiant fight as it twisted, coiling about the flying creature until it bound its wings, and the two, still entwined and struggling, fell into the water and sank.

No wonder the Elysians, with no technology to build protected, motorized craft, honored anyone who managed to travel alive through such a place.

Geordi, meanwhile, had turned to study the mountain. "Commander!" he said suddenly, and both Riker and Data turned. "Riker, what do you see up there—about ten meters up, just to the right of center?"

"Nothing, Geordi, just a sheer rock wall."

54

"Data?"

"The same—and the tricorder indicates solid rock."

"Tune it to my Visual Acuity Transmitter," Geordi instructed, switching on the addition to his VISOR which, for brief periods, would allow their instruments to pick up exactly what he was seeing.

Data adjusted his tricorder to the frequency of Geordi's transmitter. In the middle of the solid rock wall, there appeared an uneven . . . opening? None of the frequencies Data could access with his own eyes showed it, but Geordi's VISOR did.

By this time Riker and Worf were on either side of Data, looking over his shoulders at the tricorder screen. "I wonder," Riker mused, "whether this is the test. Are we supposed to go *into* the mountain rather than climb it?"

"Shall we attempt to enter, Commander?" asked Worf.

"Hold on a minute," Riker said, tapping his combadge. "Captain, we've found what appears to be an opening in the mountainside. I would like to explore it."

"Not so fast, Number One," came Picard's voice. "Get every piece of information you can *without* approaching the mountain first, and report your findings. Then we will decide whether to attempt to explore the cave."

"Roger." Riker closed the channel; at his command, the four away team members spread out around the mountain.

Five hours later, they met back at the same spot. None of them reported anything new. They prepared to beam up along with rock samples and readings, and recommend to the captain that they see if the cave was merely that, or an opening into the realm of Elysia's elusive gods.

"Wait," Data said as they moved into position for beamup. "There is a life-form reading—but it is faint. No . . ." He frowned at the faint flicker on the tricorder screen, and turned up the gain. "Commander, I cannot get an accurate directional reading, and on open range your readings interfere."

Riker nodded. "We'll get out of your way, then." He tapped his combadge. "Three to beam up, Mr. O'Brien. Mr. Data to follow at his command."

Data stepped away from the other three. They dissolved in the transporter beam, and he turned up the gain on his tricorder again. Nothing. He turned full circle, annoyed; he could not have been fooled by that flicker—

He was about to signal for beamup when he heard a sudden splashing noise.

Looking toward the swamp, he saw nothing until he used infrared vision to penetrate the fog. There was someone coming!

It was a flat-bottomed boat, poled by a single person whose slow efforts, head down, bespoke desperate tiredness—yet over and over the weary traveler retrieved the pole, placed it, and shoved again.

They had wondered how anyone could traverse the swamp with its poisonous atmosphere. Now Data saw that the boat was surrounded by a bubble of fresh, clear air, obviously generated by the same mysterious means as the atmosphere of the habitats. That was what Drahanna had meant when she said the gods "allowed" some Elysians to cross the swamp: they provided such protection only to those they deemed worthy of the quest to the sacred island.

Fascinated, Data watched the boat with its lone occupant approach the shore. Suddenly she looked up, and he saw for the first time that it was a woman, tired and bedraggled from her arduous journey. And he also realized that she was now close enough to glimpse him through the swamp fog.

He backed off, reaching for his combadge, intending to let her think weariness had made her see visions in the fog—

Too late. The woman's eyes widened, her face was suffused with wonder—and the pole she was using to steer the boat with slid out of her grasp. Eyes still on Data, she bent to recover it—and set the boat rocking from side to side.

The bubble of clear air around it quivered and burst. Swamp gases poured in around her, and she began to choke and cough, rocking the boat even more wildly—attracting the attention of something that lived in the water. Ropy arms reached into the boat to grab at the hapless woman.

Data dropped his hand to his phaser, whipped it out and fired—or tried to. The weapon was dead!

That woman would be, too, if the thing pulled her under, or just held her in the noxious gases long enough to suffocate.

Data ran to help her, jumping from one sharp rock to another and then into the water. He sank ankle-deep into swamp ooze with every step, but the boat was less than ten meters from shore. If he could only get her away from that thing and to the protection of the island—

He reached the boat, and grasped the woman about the waist with one arm while he tried with the other hand to pry loose the arms of the thing pulling her overboard. As fast as he tore one tentacle loose, another refastened on its victim—and some were now fastening about Data as well.

There was no use attacking the arms, he realized—but did the thing even *have* a head?

Time was running out; the woman was unconscious, her lips turning an unhealthy blue.

Data lifted woman and beast together, and struggled back toward shore. The swamp creature wrapped some of its arms about tree roots, but android strength prevailed. Refusing to give up its victim, it was dragged, still clinging, onto the rocky shore, along with the boat to which it also clung.

Data laid his burden down on a flat rock, and began drawing in air again himself, for his system had automatically turned off its oxygen-gathering mechanism when he plunged into a potentially corrosive atmosphere.

But it was the woman he was concerned about—had she breathed in enough poison to damage her lungs?

The swamp creature loosed its hold on the woman, and allowed Data to pull its twining arms off her without further resistance. It was shriveling in an atmosphere that was poisonous to *it,* even as he flung it back toward the swamp . . . and saw it bounce off the barrier and onto the rocks.

One part of Data's mind realized that he had just gone through that barrier and back again himself—but he had no time to contemplate the impossible when he had a life to save. The woman had stopped breathing, but his android hearing told him her heart still beat. Quickly, he pressed the poisonous gases from her lungs, being careful not to lean hard enough to do her harm. Then he began the process of breathing air into her lungs.

Maintaining the rhythm, he tapped his combadge.

There was no sound from it, not even the normal chitter of opening the frequency. He remembered that his phaser would not work, and after the next breath picked up his tricorder to analyze the woman's condition. That instrument, too, was inoperative.

Data's own instrumentation seemed to be operating as well as ever—or was there some distortion that caused him to see the woman take a breath on her own, then another, and normal coloration returning to her complexion far too rapidly for what she had been through?

Then she opened her eyes.

"Oh, that I am so blessed as to look upon one of the gods themselves! Have I offended thee? Forgive, please forgive, for the sake of my people," she pleaded, trying to sit up.

"Do not try to move," Data told her. "I am not one of your gods. I am—" he fell back on the away team cover story, "—a traveler like yourself, seeking the gods here on the sacred island." It was the truth, after all.

The woman broke into a smile. "Then it is as was foretold! You are the One from Afar who will join me in my Quest. I did not understand at first. You are very different from my people."

She sat up, and tried to stand, despite Data's

protests. As she seemed fully recovered, as well as determined, he helped lift her to her feet.

Standing, she took in his appearance from head to toe. His uniform was still wet—and only now did it occur to him how much danger he had placed himself in to rescue her. He could not swim, and while he could walk under water that went over his head, he could do so only if the bottom were solid ground. If Data stepped into a patch of quicksand, he would sink as fast as a human.

But, as he had not been harmed, there was no use being concerned about it now. It was simply fortunate that he had been available to rescue the young woman. His current problem, with his combadge out of order, was how to contact the *Enterprise*. They might beam him up at any moment, once they realized he was out of contact . . . unless, of course, the Elysian gods prevented it. Considering the way they played with that undetectable forcefield, they were undoubtedly the reason his equipment would not function. Perhaps, then, the *Enterprise* would be unable to detect him at all, much less beam him up.

Meanwhile, the woman was saying, "You are the One from Afar the gods promised would await me here. All is fulfilled, then—we will quest together."

Data remembered the way Drahanna's words had guided the away team to what the Elysian "gods" expected of them before. Perhaps because they had followed those instructions in good faith there had been no protest then, or when they beamed down to this sacred island. Were these more instructions? Did the gods want Data to undergo their testing? He was certain they were responsible for cutting him off from contact with the *Enterprise*. He remembered a human

60

saying which applied to such situations: "The only way out is through."

So he looked at the woman he had rescued and nodded. "Yes," he agreed, "it does appear that the gods have decided we shall undergo their Quest . . . together."

Chapter Four

THE WOMAN PUSHED a strand of dark hair out of her eyes. "My name is Thelia. I come from Atridia."

"I am called Data," he replied.

"Data," she repeated, trying the sound. "Your name is as different as you are. What is your land called?"

Stay as close to the truth as possible, he remembered, and replied, "Starfleet."

"Starfleet," Thelia said. "What a beautiful name. Do the stars truly move more swiftly there?"

"They do, in fact, appear to do so," Data replied, bemused.

"It must be a magical land," Thelia said, dreamily.

It would seem so to you, Data realized, but he did not say so aloud. Despite his reticence, Thelia asked, "Are you under a spell? Is that why you are questing?"

"A spell? No."

"Then is everyone in your land like you?" the young woman wanted to know.

"No, not like me," he explained, "but many in

Starfleet are very different from you." He assumed that would not offend Elysia's gods, who had allowed a similar explanation in the habitat the away team had visited. "You have obviously had a long and difficult journey," Data continued. "You should rest before—"

"The Quest begins now."

Data spun around, but there was no one else to be seen, no one else he could hear, even with his augmented senses. Was this what Drahanna had meant— that the "gods" literally spoke out loud to those they had chosen to hear?

Thelia's face again took on a look of joy and wonder. "I am permitted? Ah, blessed gods, let me pass through with the help of this One from Afar, and reach your sanctuary."

"This sanctuary," said Data. "There we will meet the gods themselves?"

"So it is spoken."

He nodded. "That is what I came seeking." He tapped his combadge again, but it was still dead, as was his tricorder. By this time the *Enterprise* crew would have used every means at their disposal to locate and recover him. Elysia's gods must have blocked their efforts—their technology was clearly far beyond that of the Federation. They must have assessed the away team members, decided they desired contact, and determined that the android was best equipped to record such a meeting.

But he would not get that far if he did not succeed in this Quest. The Elysian gods obviously insisted that even visitors from other worlds play by their regulations, something the *Enterprise* crew had encountered on enough other planets to consider it the rule rather than the exception. So Data said, "I am honored to undertake the Quest. I hope we both succeed."

"May it be so," Thelia replied formally. "We should begin the climb now, I think. Where are your supplies?"

"I have nothing else," he said, putting phaser and tricorder into their holsters. They might be useless now, but he was sure that once he had done whatever the Elysian gods required they would function normally again.

"You have not brought food?" Thelia asked. "Or did you use it up on your journey? I will share mine with you if need be."

Data decided to postpone further explanations until they were better acquainted. Elysians were not accustomed to machines at all, let alone sentient ones. So, as she turned to the boat she had come in and lifted out a pack designed to be worn on the back, he said, "I will carry that for you, as I am sure the way will not be easy."

"Thank you," she replied, and reached for a pouch of animal skin—a water bag, he realized. Of course; she could not have drunk the water of the swamp. But the container was nearly empty. "I was four days in the swamp," she said, pulling the cork and offering the bag to Data. He shook his head, and she drank— carefully, he noticed, not spilling a drop despite the awkward vessel, taking only two measured swallows although he suspected that after her exertions she was thirsty enough to empty it.

"There is a spring not far away," Data said, remembering a flow of clear water they had seen while circling the mountain. "We can refill that."

"Yes," she agreed, and as they set off over the rocks, she asked, "You've been here long enough to explore, then? Did your Speaker tell you to expect my arrival?"

"No," he replied honestly, as he wondered how, more than four days ago, the gods could have told the Speaker in Thelia's land that a stranger would be on the island when she arrived. But then, if they were capable of detecting subspace radio messages they could have known that the *Enterprise* was in the vicinity. Had they deliberately lured it here with the power surges? Was the rescue of Darryl Adin and his gang one of the gods' tests? If Data concentrated on whatever these gods required of him, he might earn the opportunity to question them directly. He could only hope he would also earn some answers.

As Thelia struggled over the sharp boulders, she could not help but notice the ease with which Data jumped from one to another. "You are very quick and agile," she said as he offered a hand to help her across a wide gap.

"It is my nature," he replied. "I will explain, but it might be better to wait until we have easier going."

Thelia did not let go of his hand immediately. Instead she spread his fingers, looked from his hand down to his feet and then up his body to his face. She was only a little shorter than he was; most of the Elysian males the away team had met were taller than Data, and broad shouldered from the hard work of pre-industrial survival.

"You are far stronger than you appear," Thelia noted. "Have you already a gift from the gods? Perhaps from one of your ancestors, as I have?"

"Not in exactly that way," he replied, "but yes, I am physically stronger than the people I live among. I promise, Thelia, I will explain. I just do not wish you to become frightened of me."

"You are the One from Afar of the Speaker's prophecy. You have already saved my life." She smiled. "Do you think me a child, to fear your golden eyes? Data, you have already proved yourself to the gods, or you would not be here."

Her confidence in her gods would make it easier, he realized. But it was too early to tell her the whole truth—and perhaps he was not intended to. Should he try to pass for an organic being? Under the close scrutiny of a genuine organic life-form he doubted he could do so for long—but then, if Elysia's gods did not want Thelia to know what he was, they might help him avoid the issue.

At the spring Thelia drank eagerly, and then refilled the water pouch. Data was not thirsty, of course; his cooling system did not operate by evaporation as many organic beings' did, so he required no replenishment of liquids after exercise. He did wash the swamp mud off his uniform—and saw Thelia's surprise at the way it rinsed right off.

"What excellent cloth," she said. "I wish you were not from such a distant land. My people would be pleased to trade for such material."

"Do you trade with the people of other lands?" he asked, for they had heard nothing of that in Quinaria.

"Only with the people of Tosus, the land closest to our own, and even that is very difficult. That is the purpose of my Quest, Data—if I succeed, I will ask the gods to unite our two lands, for without each other's help our lands are dying."

Progress! And the idea came from the Elysians themselves, no taint of outside interference. "I shall do everything I can," he told Thelia, "to help you succeed in your Quest."

When Data started to lead the way back, Thelia asked, "Do you know of an easier slope to climb?"

He stopped. "Do your legends say we are to climb the outside of the mountain?"

"What other way is there?" she replied.

"There is an opening into the mountain, near where you came ashore," he told her. "Let me at least look into it—if it is a dead end, we will climb the outside."

But when they reached the spot from which Geordi had seen the opening, Data was sure that they were meant to go in. His infrared vision showed a definite cold spot at the cave mouth, while around it the rock wall reflected the warmth of Elysia's sun.

Thelia stared. "There is no opening."

"It is there," Data insisted, searching for handholds on the steep rockface. Once he was on the ledge, though, the opening was invisible once more to the spectrum he could command.

Undaunted, Data walked straight through what appeared to be solid rock—only to be called back by Thelia's startled shout of his name. She stared at him, wide-eyed. "You walked through stone. You *are* one of the gods!"

"No, I am not," he told her. "Thelia, it only *looks* like solid rock. Where I come from, we would call it a holographic projection. Come up and I will show you." He did not tell her he could detect any ordinary hologram, and that this was technology beyond anything in his experience. Making contact with these Elysian "gods," no matter how many questions were left unanswered, was worth overcoming whatever obstacles they placed in his way.

The rock face Data had climbed was too high for him to lift Thelia from below, or to reach down and pull her from above. He had to let her find her own hand- and foot-holds until she was within his reach; then he lay down on the ledge and held out his hand.

She looked up, panting. "I'll pull you over."

"No—I am well centered here," he replied, for he had stretched the length of his body away from the edge to counterbalance her weight.

Thelia, though, still sought her own way up. Only when she could find no handholds suited to her organic strength did she take his hand. Even then she scrambled up much on her own, far underestimating Data's strength and mass.

Data was reminded of Tasha Yar. Although Thelia had dark hair and eyes, and features more gamine than Tasha's classic beauty, she seemed to be about the same small size under her loose clothing. It was the spirit and determination that Data recognized, the ability to call up emotional strength beyond physical ability.

He recognized also the movements of an athlete— like Tasha, this woman had honed her native abilities to their keenest edge in preparation for her Quest.

When she stood beside him, she frowned at the apparently solid rock face, put out a hand—and swallowed hard as it went right through. "The gods thus show their presence." Squaring her shoulders, she stepped forward. Data followed, and they found themselves in a cave dimly lit by spots of fluorescent lichen, the first life, other than themselves and the swamp creatures, that Data had seen on the island.

"You were right," Thelia said. "This must be the way we are to go. It is different for each one who comes here, they say." She shook her head. "I could not have found the opening alone."

"The gods must be observing us, and matching their tests to our abilities. When you were attacked, they opened the barrier so that I could reach you. They disguised the cave opening, but in such a way that I could still find it. It appears that they wish you to trust me."

"We must trust each other," she said. "We'd best go on now, I think," and she started farther into the cave.

Data adjusted his vision to the dim light. A steep trail led upward, easy for him, tiring for Thelia. They climbed for over half an hour without incident.

Thelia sat down on a rock formation, took a drink, and again offered the water bag to Data. "I do not need water at this time," he explained. "My body does not excrete fluids to cool itself, as yours does."

"No, you're not perspiring," Thelia agreed. "Your strength, and lack of need for food and water—are these gifts of the gods, Data?"

He saw that she would keep asking until he gave her an answer. How much of the truth would the Elysian gods allow her to know? For that matter, did *they* know exactly what Data was?

Again he tried an abridged version of the facts. "I have no gifts from these gods, Thelia. I simply use energy resources efficiently. Eventually I will need nutrients, but—"

With hardly a warning rumble, the roof caved in!

Data shoved Thelia under a shallow overhang, shielding her with his own body.

It lasted only moments, and Data was not hit by any rocks large enough to do him serious injury.

When the deluge ended, Data and Thelia scrambled

up the steep trail to where they could look back on the rockfall. It had been aimed specifically at them— the fallen stones covered no more than ten square meters.

As they moved on, though, Data turned his attention to a message from his diagnostics. He looked down to see a glitter of circuits where the skin on the back of his right hand had been scraped aside. He was leaking chemical nutrients from a ruptured conduit to that extremity. His automatics had shut off the valve at his elbow, but what fluid had been present continued to drip.

Data covered his damaged right hand with his left as Thelia came up beside him. "I am unhurt," she said, "but you are bleeding!" for fluid leaked between his fingers. She reached for his hand, and he instinctively pulled it away. "Let me see," she insisted.

"Thelia," Data said, "I think the gods have decided you must know what I am," and he lifted his hand away.

A small gasp escaped her as she saw the metal skeletal structure, the sensor mesh, neural net, and control circuitry. She backed off, and for the first time he saw fear in her eyes. "What *are* you?"

"I am an android. A machine."

"No! Plows and wagons and windwheels are machines! They do not move on their own. They do not speak. You look like a man, speak like a man."

Holding his damaged right hand up, pinching off the leaking conduit with his left, Data searched for an explanation she might understand. He recalled the way Will Riker often referred to him. "Are you familiar with puppets, marionettes?"

"Toys? Dolls with jointed limbs?" Thelia's eyes

70

widened. "You . . . you are such a creature brought to life?"

Sudden terror lit the woman's dark eyes. Her gaze darted fearfully back to where the rockfall blocked her escape downward. Then she turned and tried to run the other way, slipping in her panic, for the upward trail was far steeper now than a few moments ago.

Data made no attempt to follow her, for the gods were clearly determined that she not escape confronting his nature. There was moisture on the smooth rock that had not been there before; Thelia struggled and scrabbled for purchase, only to slide and tumble back to Data's side, gasping and panting.

She flung herself away from him, her back against the rock wall, terror replaced by resignation. "I was taken in," she said. "Kill me, then, and be done with it."

Data was astonished. "Thelia—I have no reason to kill you! Why are you so frightened? What do you think I am?"

"A golem. A homunculus."

Data accessed his memory banks: the legends were ancient and inconsistent, but basically they dealt with man-created beings, either soulless or animated with evil spirits, which turned upon their creators to destroy them—usually after murdering a number of innocents. The Elysians, it seemed, had similar legends.

"I do not know how to show you that I mean you no harm," Data said sadly. "Can you determine why your gods would choose to test you in such an unusual fashion?"

"They couldn't think I would trust you!" she snapped.

"Thelia, I did not lie to you," said Data, "but I did not know whether your gods wanted you to know my true nature. Obviously they do, but terrifying you cannot help you succeed in your Quest. I am sorry that you are frightened." He tried a different approach. "Do you not trust your gods to protect you from harm?"

The fear in her eyes was replaced by wariness. "Which is the test? How am I to know? Are you an evil spirit, in the form of the dolls I so loved in childhood? Or are you truly the One from Afar that I was promised?"

"Perhaps if you told me about your dolls—?" Data suggested.

"I had many as a child. I loved them and made up stories about them, until my mother heard me say one day I wished my favorite could come to life. Then she told me the tales of others who had made such wishes, and the evil they brought upon themselves and others. I put my dolls away then, and grew up."

She looked him up and down again, no longer panicked, trying to make a reasoned decision. "Are you temptation, in the form of my childish fantasies? Or are the gods telling me it is time to set aside old fears?"

"I do not know how to resolve your dilemma," Data admitted. "All I can offer is to leave you to continue your Quest alone, and return to where we entered."

"You cannot get past the rockfall."

"I can; I have the strength to lift rocks you could not budge."

"If I asked, you would go, and not return somewhere along the way to oppose my progress?"

72

"To interfere with your Quest would violate one of the laws of my people," Data replied.

"You would abandon your own Quest?"

Data considered, and spoke truthfully. "Not unless I am told to do so by the gods. I am very eager to meet them. I will continue as far as they will allow me, but I will not interfere with you."

"And if I demand that you abandon your Quest?"

"You do not have that right," he replied. "The gods have permitted me this Quest, and only they can revoke that permission."

Thelia let go a tensely held breath. "You are not a toy to do my bidding. An evil spirit would not so trust in the gods, nor would one unworthy of the Quest. Yet . . . I fear to continue in your company. Your solution seems best for both of us."

So Thelia started up the trail once more—it was again difficult, but no longer impossible to climb. Apparently the gods approved of their decision.

As he turned back Data twisted a wire around the leaking conduit to prevent the loss of further fluid, but without the organic component his right hand lost a good deal of sensory capacity. That, however, was not his major problem.

When he reached the rockfall, he found that he was trapped.

The blockage had originally been composed of stones from pebbles to boulders, none too large for Data to shift. Now it was all gigantic boulders, packed so tightly into the passageway that his android strength could not budge the first one.

How had the Elysian "gods" done it? They had to be using technology similar to that of the holodeck, although Data's sensors insisted the rocks were exactly what they appeared to be. But then, if he cared to take the time, it would be possible to adjust the *Enterprise* holodeck to compensate for android senses. This was simply more evidence that the Elysian gods had analyzed him very thoroughly.

This whole Quest idea . . . it seemed similar to games the holodeck provided: the players entered an unknown environment armed with general knowledge of such games, but had to discover the rules specific to the current game as they went along. It was too bad, Data thought, that he had had to part company with someone who must know the general conventions for the Elysian Quest.

He stopped wasting effort on the pile of rocks, verified that he could not climb out over the top, and considered quietly following Thelia until there was a branch in the path, where he would take the one she did not choose.

A scream—Thelia's scream—sounded in the distance.

Data raced back to where they had parted, then up the steep trail and through a narrow passage. Dashing down the smooth tunnel that led from it, he found the trail empty until he came to the water pouch lying against the wall. He accessed every frequency of his vision and hearing. There were scuff marks on the rocky floor, and in the distance he heard the faint sound of something—or someone—being dragged. He bolted forward—and came around an outcropping just in time to see Thelia sink her knife into an apelike creature trying to drag her along the tunnel. The thing roared, and backhanded the woman.

Thelia struck the wall, but did not go down. Data leaped between her and the creature. It roared again, baring vicious fangs, but it was distracted by the knife in its flesh.

Its hands had only four fingers, Data noticed as he crouched in front of Thelia, ready to throw the ape-being should it attack. One of those hands closed on the knife and withdrew it, but instead of trying to wield it just threw it aside. Gouts of purplish blood spurted from the wound.

The creature yowled, looming over Data. He was ready—but before the beast could lunge, something hit it in the side of the head. It looked beyond Data, and he turned as it lunged past him, threatening Thelia again. Data leaped on the creature's back with the impact of his full weight at an acceleration no human could achieve.

The creature rolled, dislodging Data, and both jumped to their feet at the same time. Now Thelia was in Data's range of vision, swinging something. She released it. Another rock hit her attacker solidly on the head.

This time the creature's cry was more of fear or pain than threat. Weakened from loss of blood, it put both hands to its head. Then it turned and ran away down the trail.

Retaining his audio input at its highest range, lest the thing return with reinforcements, Data turned to Thelia. She was readying another rock in her sling. "Are you injured?" he asked.

For a moment he thought she would fling the stone at him. Then she let her arm relax. "Just scratched and bruised. I am not succeeding well. The gring should not have been able to sneak up on me."

"Gring? You are familiar with this animal, then?"

"There are packs of them in the highlands, usually

no problem except to solitary travelers. They do not like people encroaching on their territory, and they are afraid of fire. It never occurred to me to bring torches, though."

"There cannot be many such animals on the island," said Data, "as there does not appear to be anything for them to live on. I think we can assume that the gods placed that one in your way." He picked up the bloody knife, giving it to her handle-first. "You will need this, I fear."

"I am sure of it," Thelia replied, taking it from him warily and cleaning it with a cloth she took from her pocket. Then she looked up at Data. "You did not leave."

"My way was blocked—just as the gods made the trail too steep and slippery for you to get away from me before. I was considering what to do when I heard you scream."

"You saved my life . . . again." She spoke flatly, as if she did not know what feeling she ought to have.

"You might have defeated it. You are very good with that sling."

"No," Thelia said firmly. "I never would have—" She squared her shoulders. "It must be the will of the gods. Please forgive me, Data, and continue the Quest with me."

"There is nothing to forgive," Data said, attempting a brief smile.

"I see that even though you are not flesh and bone, you can be injured," Thelia said suddenly. Data followed her glance to his hand, and saw that it was leaking again, his temporary repair inadequate to his exertion. Thelia offered, "I have cloth in my pack to make a bandage."

76

"That will not be necessary. I can stop the leakage. If I wipe away the fluid, the skin will bond well enough to protect my circuitry until I can repair it properly."

Thelia found her pack, took out a cloth, and insisted on cleaning away the organic fluid. The conduit was not ruptured, but detached. Tying it off was not an adequate solution.

Data said, "I do not have the proper tools—and I would ordinarily ask Geordi to help when I cannot use both hands. But perhaps I can reattach the tube. I lose some function in that hand without the organic component."

"Geordi," Thelia said. "The one who . . . built you?" He could hear in her voice that she was still disturbed by his mechanical nature.

"No—but he is a friend," Data explained. "Perhaps you can help me. The principle is simple enough: remove the retaining ring, stretch the tubing back into place, and tighten the ring over it again."

"Yes, I see. We can use my knife," Thelia said. "Perhaps I can pry the ring loose—but how will you tighten it again?"

"I cannot if you pry it loose. There is a tiny slot for a tool to go into. If your knife tip will fit into it, we may be able to loosen and then retighten it."

It would have taken less than five minutes with proper tools. With only a knife, it took them nearly half an hour in the dim light, complete with losing the retaining ring twice—once down inside Data's arm, and a second time onto the cave floor. Finally they were able to tighten it about the tubing so that Data could release the organic fluids into his forearm again.

With that restoration came the unpleasant sensation that served, as pain did for organic beings, to warn him that something was wrong. He reran the diagnostics, cleared some unnoticed fluid out of his sensory mesh, and slid the skin back into place. It appeared whole but scarred. When he used the right instrument on it back on the ship, it would meld together as if it had never been torn.

Thelia was shivering. "I am sorry," said Data. "It still disturbs you to know what I am."

"No!" she said, shuddering even more strongly. "I'm cold!" She began rummaging in her pack as she added, "The gods are listening to us, Data. I wanted to know what you are, so they showed me—and then showed me that I need your help." She shook out a cloak of some material much like wool, and wrapped it about herself. "Be careful what you ask, here in the gods' sacred place. Often, they give it, but never without exacting a price."

"I will," he replied. "I think, though, that if there are other things I should know about the Quest, you had better tell me before we go on."

"There are only two others. A wrong choice brings a penalty, and we must watch for guideposts."

"Guideposts?"

"Objects, or even living creatures which are clues when there is a choice to be made. A white animal must always be followed. But most guideposts are more subtle, and if you miss one you will certainly be delayed, and may even fail the Quest."

"Let us hope that will not happen," Data said. The temperature had dropped while they were working on Data's hand. It made no difference to him, but Thelia needed her cloak.

"Can you go on for a while before you must rest?"

Data asked her. "We may be able to find a warmer spot, or some means to build a fire."

"I am ready," she agreed, and they resumed their climb.

Their way continued to be lit by dim fluorescence. Data watched for anything they might use for a fire, but there was no organic matter except the lichen. Thelia could not go on indefinitely without rest, but the temperature was by now low enough that she would be miserably uncomfortable, even wrapped in her cloak. Sleep would benefit her little under those conditions.

The trail turned between high rock walls, twisting so as to hide from their sight anything more than a few paccs ahead, winding and backtracking incessantly. Although they took many steps, they made little progress. There seemed no purpose in such a passage except to tire Thelia even further.

She stopped at last, wiping sweat from her brow, but shivering from a combination of the cold and fatigue. "This has to be the right path," she said uncertainly. "We have been offered no other choice."

"Are you capable of going on?" Data asked.

"We must go on," Thelia insisted. "It is the only way to succeed in the Quest."

Thelia began to explain the lore of the Quest as they walked along—but after less than fifty meters of twists and turns their way was blocked by a wall with two doors.

"We must choose one," Thelia said.

"Why not both?" asked Data, grasping a knob in either hand. Both doors were locked. For the moment, he did not try to break the locks. The gods were aware of his android strength, so probably this was a test of something else. "Do you know anything about a key?" he asked Thelia.

"If there is one, we must have it with us," she replied. "I do not have one."

"Nor I. Where I come from, doors open to one's voice or palmprint, or just one's presence."

"Really?" she asked. "Perhaps these are also magical doors." She stepped up beside him. "Doors, I am Thelia of Atridia. Will either of you open to me?"

The door on the left swung open, revealing a meadow, some cultivated fields, a patch of woodland, and in the distance a fair-size town dominated by a castle that seemed to come straight out of a fairy tale. "It's home!" Thelia exclaimed. But when Data started to step through she put her hand on his arm. "No—look there." She pointed to a pile of objects only a few paces inside the door. It took Data a moment to realize that they were primitive torches, stacked next to a pile of firewood.

"Ah," he said, "you are cold. Shall we not retrieve materials to build a fire?"

"No," she replied, shivering. "It is a temptation, Data. We must make do with what we brought or what we find along the way. The Quest would be finished for me if I stepped through the portal. I would be at home, failed, all my journeying gone for nought."

Data nodded. She was the expert on Elysian Quest lore, after all. "Very well. Then let me try the other door." He spoke to it as if he addressed the holodeck portal. "I am Lieutenant Commander Data of Starfleet. Will you open to me?"

Sure enough, this door slid aside, just like the doors on the *Enterprise*. It did not lead to the ship that he called home, however. There was nothing but a whirling dark mist that not even his android vision could penetrate. As they watched, a vortex formed—and within it distorted forms and faces. The stars. The computer station in his cabin. Captain Picard. Wesley Crusher. Tasha Yar. Darryl Adin. And Geordi, VISORless, his sightless eyes open and staring at nothing.

Out of the mist, the figure of Geordi gained substance and held out its hands. "Data. My friend. When you have need to see beyond sight, use this." His VISOR appeared in his hands. Automatically, Data put out his hands—the object dropped into them.

But it was not Geordi's VISOR that Data held as the door before them slid shut again with a clang. It was . . . a metal cylinder, apparently empty. Data peered through it, but saw nothing except Thelia looking back at him.

"What is it?" she asked.

"I do not know," he replied honestly. "Perhaps we will discover a use for it later."

"The one who gave it—do you trust him?" Thelia asked warily.

"With my life," Data replied.

She nodded. "Then keep it. You will certainly need it before your Quest is through."

Data slid the cylinder into the holster beside his tricorder—and when he looked up, wall and doors were gone. The trail continued upward. "I think we are intended to go on now."

So they continued on the ever-steeper trail.

It narrowed and the roof lowered until they had to crawl single-file through a tunnel, coming out into a small cavern of crystal formations of exquisite beauty. To one side was a smooth slab of rock perfectly sized to make a camp for two people—if there were only a way to warm it. To add to the chilling effect, the formations looked only too much like ice and snow.

When Thelia dragged herself into the cavern, she did not climb to her feet but sat with her knees drawn up, huddled into her cloak. She was shaking with cold and weariness. "We must stop," Data told her. "You need sleep, Thelia."

"It's t-too cold," she protested. "The gods m-must intend that we go on to a warmer area."

"It may be that they are testing our ingenuity. My body continues to generate heat. If we wrap up in your cloak together, I can keep you warm enough that you can sleep."

"You are not tired," she said flatly.

"No. I do not tire as you do, nor do I sleep. I shall keep watch."

"Then I am delaying your Quest."

"Thelia, it is obvious that the gods want us to quest together. I thought you overcame your fear of touching me when you helped to repair my arm. What do you fear now?"

She frowned. "It is strange . . . it is as if my mother disapproves. Ah, I remember: when I wished for the seja doll I slept with to come to life, she took it from me, and told me all the terrible legends of dolls brought to life. Do you have seja in your land, Data?"

"No."

"They are animals with soft wool, and often children's toys are made in their image. Mine was dressed like a prince, and he was the one I made up the most stories about. To me he was a handsome prince from a far land who rescued me from great perils and then quested for permission to marry me and join our lands." She smiled sadly. "Joining Atridia with the land of Tosus was the great concern of both my father and my mother, and everyone in our land, from the time I can remember. As a child, I dreamed that someone would come and solve our problems."

"And now you have grown up, and are solving them yourself," Data pointed out, wondering why this slight young woman had been chosen to Quest for all her people. For once, he curbed his curiosity: Thelia needed to sleep, not tell stories. "I am not the doll your mother took from you," he pointed out. "I am not covered with wool, nor am I a prince."

As he had hoped, Thelia laughed, though wearily. Then she removed her cloak and draped it over his shoulders.

"I remember another ancient fable, but it was not one my mother told me. It was about a woodcarver who made a doll so lovely he wanted to marry her, and quested that the gods might bring her to life." Thelia took Data's hand. "But you are not carved out of wood. You are living flesh over the strange machinery inside."

"My skin is designed to feel like flesh," he told her, "but it is not. Thelia, if the doll actually came to life in the story you know, then, in some ways, I am like her."

"Ah, I hope not," said Thelia, "for her story is very sad. It's odd: when I was very young, I did not realize how sad it was that she got everything she desired, and yet never found happiness."

As she talked, Data sat against the wall and took

Thelia on his lap, wrapping the cloak about them both. She took food from her pack, dried fruit and seeds and tough meat. Data drank some water to replenish the fluid he had lost. If this Quest lasted more than a day or two he would need sustenance, but that did not mean depriving Thelia of the food her organic system needed so much more.

There might be trace elements he could take directly from mineral formations, but with his tricorder nonfunctional he would be safer with organic nutrients. He had no need to taste the glowing lichen in order to analyze its constituents; he already knew that the energy his system would use in filtering out fluorescent elements would outweigh any benefits he might gain from consuming such vegetation. There was also the danger of some element his sensors could not detect, like the drug Lore had once used to render him unconscious, but that risk was minimal. He wondered if the Elysian gods could tell from their study of him what few elements were a threat to his existence.

After a time, Thelia got up and went out of the cavern, back the way they had come. Data had lived too many years among organic beings to embarrass her by asking where she was going or what for; besides, her desire for privacy indicated that she regarded Data as a person rather than, as she perceived it, a toy.

The gods also respected Thelia's privacy; nothing happened except that she returned a few minutes later and came into Data's arms, shivering with renewed cold. For once wishing he were not built quite so compactly, he tried to keep as much of himself as possible between her and the cold stone, for even a layer of warm woolen cloak was little protection against the warmth-leeching rock.

As she settled herself, Thelia asked, "Am I too heavy on you?"

"No," he replied. "My design even precludes your putting one of my limbs to sleep, as it were. Rest, Thelia. There is no way you can harm me."

She turned her head to look sidewise at him, and with an odd smile said, "No, I don't suppose there is."

He expected her to fall off to sleep at once, but apparently she was too keyed up from the day's events. Her breathing remained uneven. She sighed and shifted her weight. After a time, apparently realizing that sleep was going to elude her for the moment, she asked, "Data, what are you questing for?"

"To meet the gods," he replied.

"Yes—but what gift will you ask of them if your Quest is successful?"

"Knowledge of great importance to me and the people I live among," he replied. "What will you ask?" he continued, before she could ask him what that knowledge was.

"I have inherited the gift of my ancestor who quested before me—but it does my people no good unless the gods allow the lands of Atridia and Tosus to be joined," she replied.

"As you said your people have long talked of. Why?"

"Because the people of my land are in dire need, while we have things the people of Tosus need equally. When our population was small, we had enough of the proper foods to give everyone a healthy diet. But much of Atridia is rocky highlands. We graze seja

85

there, use their wool, their milk, their meat, and have plenty we could trade with other lands for the grains and fruits our land will not grow in the quantities our people need. If the gods would but allow it," she concluded sadly.

"Why do the gods not allow it?" Data asked.

"You don't know?" she asked in surprise.

"No, I do not."

"Do you mean that that story also has been lost in your land? Or that you have never been told it?"

"I have never been told it," Data replied, avoiding admitting that he did not come from one of Elysia's lands.

"It is the oldest of stories," she said. "When the gods first placed our people on Elysia, all were in one great land. With the aid of the gods, the Elysians grew and thrived—until they began to quarrel with one another over the best land, food, property, even marriages. The quarrels grew into a great conflict, and the Elysians began to kill one another.

"The gods saw that our people were still as children, to fight over what should be decided according to the common good. Therefore they divided the people into many separate lands, with the great swamp all in between, so that none might do battle with another land. It is said that the people were so enamored of war that they tried to defy the gods, raising armies that died attempting to cross the swamp for no reason other than to kill people they thought were their enemies."

Thelia shook her head at such inexplicable foolishness. "After a time, the attempts were abandoned. Each group of Elysians learned to survive in their own land. Peace brought prosperity, and the gods smiled upon them once again. Eventually a few were allowed to cross the swamp and undergo the Quest, but only those who proved themselves worthy. And so it is to this day."

Thelia's voice grew softer, and a yawn interrupted. But she continued, "In Atridia, we understand how foolish it is to fight over what may be properly divided by peaceful means. We hope the gods will understand . . . that we . . . have grown up." Her words trailed off. Thelia snuggled sleepily against Data, growing relaxed and heavy as she settled into slumber.

He held her, pondering the story she had told, wondering if the gods would allow what she was asking, considering that they had separated the Elysians in the first place. The legend corroborated what *Enterprise* sensors had discovered: the planet could not have evolved its population, and the habitats could not exist naturally.

Could these "gods" possibly be a surviving colony of the legendary Preservers, who had once gathered endangered intelligent races from around the galaxy and "seeded" them on uninhabited planets? What a discovery that would be! Starfleet had been searching for further information on the Preservers for over two hundred years.

There was little enough in Data's memory banks about the Preservers. He accessed records on similar guarded colonies, of which there were few. As usual when one accessed Starfleet exploratory records, he came quickly to the name *Enterprise,* this time their own vessel, but Data did not have to call up Starfleet reports on the planet of the Edos; he had been there.

Annoyingly, the being or beings those people called God had taken a great deal of information from him, but given little in return. They had not demonstrated as much power as these Elysian gods—but then, they had not had occasion to, for the *Enterprise* had backed off at their mere approach. Data added another question to the long list he would ask the Elysian "gods" if this Quest finally did bring him face to face with them.

Thelia slept on, secure in Data's arms. Nothing disturbed them as the hours passed, although Data had set his sensors to bring a full scan of their surroundings to his central consciousness every ten minutes while his attention was occupied elsewhere. Finally, though, he had followed every lead he could think of, and had no more information to access.

Although there was nothing more for him to do than wait for Thelia to waken, Data was not frustrated at his forced inaction. He recalled how Tasha had found the inability to take action the most frustrating of all situations . . . and then realized that that was not the reason Tasha Yar had come into his mind.

It was the feel of a woman asleep in his arms that reminded Data of Tasha once again. She was the last to have rested there. It had felt good to have her trust, her friendship, to know he had given her pleasure— and it had taken many months after her unexpected denial for them to become close friends again. He was unutterably glad that they had done so before her death, and that when they were assigned together on the mission to Treva they had overcome the last lingering obstacles and resumed, even deepened, their friendship.

If that mission had not reunited Tasha with Darryl Adin, her first love, it might have led to—

Data broke away from such thoughts. There were times when he was glad to be a machine, with heuristic algorithms he could control instead of a subconscious he could not.

Fond memories, on the other hand, were something he shared gratefully with his human friends. Not just factual memory, which for him was far more accurate than for any organic being—no, it was what he had come to describe as the "flavor" of the moment that he had learned to savor. The metaphor he chose to describe it came from a conversation he had once had with Tasha, when she had described how associating certain foods with pleasant occasions made her appreciate them more when she encountered them again. That was when Data discovered that, without being consciously aware of it, he did the same thing with all sensory experiences: they were neutral to him until associated with specific company or occasions, whereupon they were forever after pleasant or unpleasant.

So, although he had not known Thelia long enough to do more than admire her spirit and determination, and her courage in overcoming superstitious fears, he felt pleasure in holding her because of his memories and associations. As the hours passed, though, and Data reviewed what had happened thus far on his unplanned Quest, he recalled that the Elysian "gods" had provided images not only of his crewmates, which they could easily take from the *Enterprise* in orbit, but of Tasha. He had not spoken of her to Thelia; could they have accessed his memory banks without his knowledge? To Data, that was a most alarming thought.

On the other hand, the *Enterprise* logs contained gigabytes of information on all present and former crew, including a transcript of Data's recent trial at Starbase 173. The holographic image of Tasha was back in his quarters. The "gods" could have gotten the information for their series of images without invading Data's memory banks. He assumed that either they could not invade his mental privacy, or that they conformed to an ethical system that would forbid it.

Wherever the truth lay, he realized that for the moment there was nothing he could do but proceed with the Quest, and hope that in the end he would receive answers to his questions.

When Thelia stirred awake, she smiled shyly at Data. "Thank you," she said. "I would have been most uncomfortable without your help. As it is, I rested well, and am ready to go on."

The trail continued steep and difficult for more than two hours, but at the end of that time the temperature finally began to rise. Thelia repacked her cloak. As the temperature continued to climb, her quilted vest joined it in her pack, and she stopped often to drink from the water bag.

"It must be a further test of your endurance," Data said. "We have been winding around the outer edge of the mountain; if the heat were geothermal, it would be higher at the core."

"I do not care where it comes from," Thelia said, wiping the sweat from her brow, "so long as it does not stop us."

"An increase of many more degrees will not harm me," said Data, "but the temperature is now close to upper tolerances for organic beings."

"How hot must it be to harm you? Would the fire not burn you?" Thelia asked.

"Not unless I were foolish enough to leave my hand in it for several minutes."

"The heat of the smith's forge?" she asked. "It melts iron and steel."

"Oh, that heat could damage me," Data agreed. Recalling that the Elysian gods appeared to tailor their tests according to what they overheard from the questors, though, he did not elaborate. Actually, a forge such as Thelia's people could build would not do more than external damage; that could be temporarily incapacitating if it destroyed his sensors or motor functions, but such damage was repairable. It would take the heat of an atomic firestorm to endanger his most vital and well shielded components.

They had stopped again. Thelia took another measured drink, then shook her head. "I cannot help but envy your strength and endurance."

Data smiled sadly. "I envy your spirit, your creativity, your belief in a purpose to your existence. I would gladly give up all my mechanical strength and sensory acuity to be human."

"You are not happy as you are?" she asked him.

"I . . . do not truly comprehend happiness," he admitted. "I find satisfaction in performing my functions. I understand friendship and loyalty. But there are things that will be forever beyond me, experiences I observe in those I live among, but can never comprehend."

To his consternation, he found her smiling at him. "Do you not realize that that is true of everyone, Data? No one is ever truly satisfied."

Data recalled Dr. Pulaski's remark that lack of satisfaction was a good definition of being human. Unfortunately, he was not satisfied with the definition.

Thelia was still panting, but she continued, "We must go on now. The gods wish to test us, not destroy us."

Data opened his mouth, then closed it again. She was right: there was no reason for the gods, as she had described them, to use "test to destruct" on their people. That they would not, judging from Thelia's confidence, was apparently part of her knowledge of Quest lore.

The path narrowed to another tunnel, which opened into a rectangular chamber, obviously artificial. To the left was an archway through which they could see caverns glittering with ice; Thelia gravitated toward the cool breeze wafting from it. To the right the trail led upward, but blasts of heat poured from that narrow entrance.

"Burn or freeze," Thelia said. She moved deliberately away from the coolness and toward the entrance from which came the hot air. She could not even reach the archway, but threw her arms over her face and retreated. "It is too hot, Data. I cannot go in there."

"Then it must be the other way," he replied. "I can keep you warm if necessary." He strode forward into the ice cavern.

Here the formations were real ice. Thelia put her vest and cloak back on. The trail was level and easy, compared to the climbing they had done for the past few hours. Thelia said, "Let's run. That will keep me warm."

Data jogged easily beside her, noting that she knew how to pace herself. They continued this way for perhaps twenty minutes—until Data realized, "Thelia, we are going in circles."

"What do you mean? I see nothing we have passed before."

"The formations change, but we remain on the same level. We are making no progress. The scenery changes, while we waste time and energy running the same path repeatedly."

She stopped, and turned to him, breathing heavily. "You are certain?"

"I am certain."

"Then we must go back," she said. "I don't know how I can stand that heat, but I must."

When they turned back, though, the scenery changed again. The smooth path became uneven, and suddenly there were rock formations in their way that had not been there before.

"A penalty," Data said, "for making a wrong choice. I am sorry."

"How could you know?" Thelia gasped, slipping down the side of an icy rock to land beside him. She rubbed her chapped hands together.

Data took Thelia's hands between his. "You should have brought gloves."

"Whats?"

"Coverings for your hands." He filed away another piece of information as to the level of culture of the Elysians: they had not yet even invented gloves. Little wonder they believed in magic.

They continued doggedly backtracking. While they remained on one level despite clambering over obstacles, at least they were not descending. The caverns closed in on them again—and there was the archway, up ahead.

"Thank the gods!" Thelia exclaimed, and hurried

toward it. Data kept pace with her, and they moved through together—but not into the chamber where they had made the choice. There was no other archway, only the trail straight ahead of them, leading upward.

"This is not—" Data began.

The rest of his sentence was drowned by the slam of a metal door falling behind them, centimeters from their heels. There would be no backtracking from *this* choice.

"We have but one way to go now," Thelia said. She started forward—and the ground opened under her feet!

Only the speed of Data's reflexes enabled him to pull her back as a chasm yawned.

The earth shook with the throbbing crack of tearing rock. They backed against the door, with less than a meter of rock to stand on, the gap growing—

Data could jump it, but if it kept growing it would soon be beyond even his ability. "We must get across at once," he said as he swung Thelia into his arms, crouched—

A wall of flame roared up out of the chasm, yellow, then blue—then white!

A firestorm of unbearable heat poured over them. Data's back was to a solidly shut door, he was walled off from turning right or left, and before him white-hot flames threw off such heat that Thelia turned from it with a whimper, shielding her face against his shoulder as the odor of her singed hair set off his warning sensors: fire, smoke—death to humans, and heat of such intensity that in seconds it would do irreparable damage to Data himself!

Chapter Five

Speed was their only chance. Data said, "Hold your breath!" not breathing himself lest superheated air affect delicate internal components. He wrapped Thelia's cloak over her head, and leaped through the firestorm.

Every microsecond of the passage through the flame registered on Data's consciousness, warnings first of danger, then damage—

He landed running, sensors in discordant uproar. Ignoring them, he sprinted away from the blast-furnace heat until finally the trail turned and he could no longer hear the roaring flames.

The massive temperature differentials turned the caverns into a wind tunnel; sand and small rocks scoured Data as he fell to his knees, still shielding Thelia.

He could not tell the temperature: after blasting his circuitry with messages of destruction, his surface sensors had gone dead. But when he drew in a cautious breath, internal sensors told him the air was tolerable. His automatics set about preserving his systems as the heat his skin had absorbed penetrated into his body.

When the wind died, Data sat up and opened his eyes.

Leaving his automatics to restore his own systems, he pulled the scorched cloak away from Thelia. She was unconscious, but alive.

When Data tried to adjust his vision to examine her, he found that it was limited to the human range he had accessed when the light increased. That indicated damage to the sensors that served him as eyes—but at least he could see well enough to tell that Thelia was alive and breathing.

Her face, which had been pressed against his chest, was unharmed, just as the front of Data's body was undamaged where she had shielded him. The backs of her hands were reddened and blistered, for where she had clung to him they had been protected only by the single layer of her cloak. The sleeves of her heavy shirt, though, had put another layer between her arms and the terrible heat; they seemed to have suffered little damage. Her legs and feet were covered by trousers and sturdy boots, and her hair had protected the back of her neck. If her lungs were not scorched, she would recover.

Data reached for his tricorder, wondering if the gods would allow it to work for purposes of medical diagnostics—but pulled his hand away with a lightning-quick reflex. The tricorder, fully exposed to the firestorm, was red-hot.

The sensors on Data's palms and fingers, protected by his hold on Thelia, had come through unharmed, and his systems were slowly adjusting to compensate for lost function.

Thelia stirred, coughed, and opened her eyes. She sat up, wincing as she put one hand over the back of the other. Data recalled that the pain of burns was the most severe that humanoid beings could suffer.

But although she frowned as she flexed her hands, she quickly said, "I'll be all right." Her voice was husky, and she coughed again. Then she looked at Data and her eyes widened in concern. "Oh—you are badly hurt!"

"All my damage can be repaired." It was not just a reassuring lie; replacements for his surface sensors were readily available aboard the *Enterprise*, and after he and Geordi were satisfied that everything was once again functioning properly, Dr. Pulaski would replace his full synthoskin if necessary. A few hours of work, and there would be no evidence that he had ever been damaged.

Thelia coughed again, but Data recognized throat irritation, not the lung damage he had feared. He found the water bag—dripping the last dregs of their supply.

Thelia stared. "How could that be damaged? It is not burnt."

Data examined it. "The extreme heat turned the water to steam and burst the bag. So we are without a way to carry water. We had best assess the rest of the damage," he added, handing her her pack.

Data had wrapped the cloak about Thelia, not giving a thought to the pack or water bag. The pack had protected a section of his left hip and back, but it was thoroughly scorched, and so were its contents.

Thelia's food supply was a blackened mess, as were what had apparently been spare garments.

Only the leather sling did not crumble when Thelia picked it out of the ashes. She brushed it as clean as she could, looped it over her belt beside her knife, then looked up at Data and said, "The gods will supply our needs. Let me see how badly you are hurt, Data. Perhaps there is something I can . . . repair."

"We have no tools or replacement parts," he said. "Please do not be concerned, Thelia. The damage is superficial and will be quickly repaired when I get . . . home."

But Thelia insisted on examining him. She confirmed what his sensors—or lack thereof in some areas—told him. On much of his back, the sides of his legs, and the backs of his arms, the synthetic material of his uniform and skin had melted and fused together. His hair had melted, too, but had done its job of protecting the delicate sensory components housed in his head.

Subdermal sensors were out in the fused areas, but other than the damaged circuit that restricted his vision, his other sensory apparatus seemed to work now that it had cooled to its range of function. He could not see his face, but could feel that the skin of his forehead had bubbled. It probably looked like that on the back of his left hand: like organic skin horribly scarred. The rest of his face had been pressed against Thelia's cloak for the leap across the chasm; it had suffered little or no damage. The previously damaged skin of the back of his right hand had burned away entirely, though, leaving the skeletal structure and neural net exposed.

After much argument, he was able to persuade

Thelia that he could go on, and they continued their climb onward. "The gods temper the wind to the shorn seja," observed Thelia, and Data realized that the temperature was within a normal range for humanoid comfort for the first time since the rockfall.

He almost began to answer her quote by telling her that his people said the same thing about shorn lambs, but remembered the unspoken agreement with Elysia's gods not to inform their people of other worlds. Then he began to wonder whether his strangeness was being repeatedly demonstrated to Thelia to determine whether her people were ready to be introduced to that very concept.

The trail continued upward, until Data judged that they were more than two-thirds of the way up the mountain. Thelia lagged, though, licking her lips in thirst. She must also be hungry; the sensors that informed him of the state of his organic components were prodding Data with reminders that they should be replenished. Stress of this magnitude to his electronic components affected his organic parts, creating excessive electron resistance across the neural filaments at the mechanical-organic interface. Without that interface, his positronic brain could not function.

It was impossible for an android to "starve to death." However, if Data could not replenish certain organic nutrients soon, his safeties would shut him down. He would remain in stasis until found by someone who knew how to reanimate him. Inside Elysia's sacred mountain, that could mean forever.

He wondered if Elysia's gods knew that. After all, his design was unique. Even if they had encountered other androids, they might not know his personal specifications.

So he said to Thelia, "We are in need of nutrients and water."

"There is no choice but to go on until we find some. It is a test of endurance."

"Humans are capable of going on beyond their endurance," Data said.

"What do you mean?" she asked.

"If you refuse to give up, you cannot be stopped short of death. There are situations, though, in which my will has no effect: I am designed with safeguards which will stop my function so as to retain my systems in a state from which I can later be revived."

"Do you mean you cannot die?" she asked.

"Oh, no, I can certainly die. In fact, my friends remind me often that I am not indestructible. If I had fallen into that flaming chasm I would have been as dead as you. However, I cannot die from attrition. If my power source is damaged, or when in the future it simply wears out, if it cannot be immediately replaced my systems will shut down to preserve my memory banks for revival when power can be restored. The same is true of my organic components."

"You have not eaten since our Quest began," said Thelia, "and you have been injured. If you do not find food you will—?"

"Cease to function," he supplied. "To you it would appear that I was asleep or unconscious."

"Is this about to happen?"

"The nutrients in my system have reached the critical level, giving me a thirty-minute warning. If I do not restore the balance in that time my systems will shut down."

Thelia nodded. "Continuing to climb hastens the use of . . . nutrients?"

"Yes." There was no use trying to explain that what he needed were trace elements. They might be readily available in the rocks surrounding them, but the gods had apparently made certain Data would not be able to ascertain that without his tricorder.

"You must stay here and rest while I seek ahead for food," Thelia told him.

"There may be dangers—"

"Not dangers beyond my capabilities, if I am alert," she replied. "The gods do not require that which we are not capable of, only that which tests us to our limits."

Data remembered how she had driven off the gring. Yet she was a small woman, frail flesh and blood, and had needed his aid to pass every obstacle.

But then, that might be the test. If he were human, it would be a test of pride. Or perhaps it was of trust, that the Elysian gods could indeed provide what an android required. 'Go, then," he told her, sitting down with his back against one of the ubiquitous rock formations. "I trust that the gods will not ask what you cannot provide."

Thelia stood, checking the knife and sling at her waist, and started purposefully up the path. She disappeared around a twist in the trail, but Data turned up his hearing to keep track of her footsteps. They did not fade out, but paused. He heard softer noises—apparently she had to crawl through another tunnel.

Suddenly Thelia's laughter drifted back to him. "Data!" she called, her voice echoing hollowly, "come and join me."

Wondering if it were a trap, he went somewhat cautiously around the bend in the trail and stooped to crawl through the tunnel that appeared before him. There was bright light at the other end.

He emerged into daylight.

No—it was the kind of "daylight" projected on a holodeck when no specific planet had been selected and so the program did not place a sun in the sky. It was a generic pastoral scene: a lake, a few trees, and strategically placed woods and hills so that one could not see off into the nonexistent distance.

Thelia knelt beside the lake, drinking from her cupped hands. She looked up when he joined her, saying, "The gods provide. Look."

There were plants growing in the water, some of them bearing blossoms, others fruits ranging from green through red to purple. Thelia plucked two purple ones, handing one to Data. "Do you have pears in your land?" she asked.

"Not exactly like these," he hedged, accepting the fruit and taking a small bite. His sensors analyzed it as containing some of the components he needed, in small quantities, so he ate it as she did, leaving the core.

Thelia tossed the core of hers, with its seeds, back into the water. "More will grow," she said.

Or would if this were a real place, Data thought, but did not contradict her. He tossed the core of his own fruit into the lake, then drank some of the water.

Thelia plucked another water pear, and ate it as she walked over to a nearby tree. "Look," she said, "gring nuts. But people like them just as well." She started to climb the tree, but Data came over and picked her up so that she could reach the clusters in the branches overhead. When she had both hands full, he set her down and she looked around. "Nothing but rocks until we need some," she commented.

"Rocks?" Data asked, puzzled.

"To crack the nuts open," Thelia explained.

"Ah," said Data, taking one from her and squeezing it between his fingers until the shell cracked. Then he separated it neatly into two halves and handed it to her.

Thelia laughed again. "I forget how very strong you are. Eat now, and restore yourself."

But Data needed only a few nutmeats along with the fruit he had already consumed. Interestingly, they provided exactly the electrolytes the pears were missing. Despite the drain of maintaining the organic interface with mechanical components operating at low efficiency, he would not need to replenish his organic nutrients for some time now.

When Thelia had eaten her fill, she pocketed the rest of the nuts and said, "I need to sleep again, Data. What about you? Do you not sleep even to heal after injury?"

"No. I shall keep watch again, although I suspect that you are right: The gods have provided us a place of refuge to restore ourselves before we go on."

She stared at him. "I did not say that, although I was thinking it." She took his right hand, studying the exposed mechanical components. "You say that you were made, like a doll, and magically brought to life. Yet you think and act like a person." She raised her dark eyes to his. "There is only one thing you can be questing for, is there not?"

"I have told you, I wish to meet the gods."

"Yes—for only the gods can give you a soul."

"That is not possible," he said.

"Anything is possible for the gods," Thelia insisted.

"But," Data asked, "is not the soul, if it exists at all, a consciousness capable of existing beyond the limits of the physical body?"

"That is not the wording taught in my land, but the idea is the same."

"Then a soul is not something that can be manufactured and installed. It must exist from the time a person becomes self-aware. Actually," he added, "I have official permission to attempt to discover whether or not I have one. Perhaps I should add that to the list of questions I shall ask the gods."

Data's Starfleet colleagues would probably have considered that statement facetious, but Thelia's eyes widened. "You do not know whether you have a soul?"

"I have consciousness. I share in common with humans the question of whether that consciousness will continue after my body ceases to function."

"Oh, I hope yours is not a sad story, like that of Calatina."

"Is that the doll you mentioned earlier, whom the gods brought to life?" Data asked. "Please tell me. I do not know that story."

"A woodcarver made a doll so beautiful that he fell in love with her, and even gave her a name, Calatina. So great was his devotion that the gods permitted him to Quest, that Calatina be brought to life. When he returned home again, lo, there she was, walking and talking, but . . . like you, Data, she was not living flesh. She was still made of wood, but even more beautiful now that she could move and speak and dance. But the story says she had no soul. The woodcarver loved her, but she could not love him in return."

Data was familiar with that lack. He understood friendship and caring, but he often felt set apart from that elusive emotion humans call love. "I know how she felt," he replied. "Did she then Quest for a soul?"

Thelia smiled. "You said you did not know the story."

"If she were sentient, having been taught that that was the reason for her lack, she would undoubtedly attempt it."

"Yes, Calatina did attempt it—and she succeeded. When she faced the gods in their sanctuary, she asked that she be made capable of loving, that she might marry a living man and make him happy.

"The gods agreed—and she found herself back in her homeland, in the body of a flesh and blood woman."

"Intriguing," Data said. "She quested for a soul, but instead was given a body. It appears that like so many others, your people believe that only those of flesh and blood have souls."

Thelia frowned. "I never thought of it that way. All of the stories about inanimate beings brought to life are unhappy ones. In most, the creature is a monster who turns on the one who brought him life. Calatina is the only one depicted as a nice person, but even she is foolish."

"It is no wonder you were afraid of me," said Data. "Your culture says I should not exist. In my . . . home, although there are indeed stories in which such creations turn on those who made them, there is a story similar to yours in which a woodcarver makes not a woman, but a little boy, Pinocchio."

Data told Thelia the story, adding, "A friend introduced me to that story, and has reminded me of it since. Pinocchio first came to life because of an old man's love, but became a flesh and blood person—gained a soul, as I suppose you would put it—only after he had undergone many trials and adventures. But his story has a happy ending, Thelia: he was reunited with those who were family to him, able to be the son his human father wanted."

Thelia smiled. "What a beautiful story. I wonder why it is not known in Atridia? I shall tell it when I get home."

Oh, no, Data thought, *what have I done?* But could introducing a story so similar to those that the Elysians already knew break the Prime Directive any more than letting them know of the existence of androids? The Elysian gods, not Data, had forced Thelia to face that. Nor had they interrupted his telling of the story. So he said, "Tell me the rest of the tale of Calatina."

"It is different from your Pinocchio story. Both the woodcarver and the woman he created went on selfish quests, and each was granted precisely what he asked for. Calatina came to life, but could not love him. Her quest made her capable of loving—but it was not the woodcarver she came to love. On her way home she met a handsome young man, and fell in love with him. However, he did not desire her."

"A triangle," Data observed.

"A tragic one. The man Calatina fell in love with did not love her. The woodcarver loved her, but she did not love him in return. She pined after the other man, while the woodcarver pined for her. Calatina could not accept that the man she loved did not want

106

her, until he married another. On his wedding day she finally became free of his spell and returned to the woodcarver. But by that time he had grown so ill from unrequited yearning that he lay on his deathbed.

"Calatina came to him in tears—the first tears she had ever shed—vowing her love. He whispered his to her as he died. With one last sigh, her heart burst, and she fell dead upon him—but the story says they are together now, for in that one moment of love's unity, their souls were at last joined."

Data shook his head. "That is a sad story."

"What it's really about is the reason for questing," said Thelia. "Neither the woodcarver nor Calatina asked for what they really wanted, because they did not understand what that was. He asked for her to come to life, when what he wanted was for her to love him. She asked to be made capable of love, when what she wanted was to love the woodcarver." She smiled. "I suppose that means she did not have to be flesh and blood to love."

"Yes," Data mused, "that fits a story my gr—a teacher of the man who made me once told me. It was about a man made of tin, who yearned to have a heart. He, too, went on a quest, only to discover in the end that he had had a heart all along."

"He was not transformed?" Thelia asked.

"No, but he was satisfied," said Data, who had looked up the entire story.

"Yet you wish to be transformed."

"Yes, Thelia, my fondest wish is to know what it would be like to be human, but what happens in legends and fairy tales is one thing. What can happen in actuality is quite another."

"Data, do you wish to offend the gods? They give such gifts as the Voice of Power or the Kiss of Bonding—surely nothing is beyond their power."

"More folktales?" he suggested.

"No. I have personal knowledge of these gifts. No one can disobey the one with the Voice of Power, while the Kiss of Bonding binds the one kissed in total and selfless love. These are rare and dangerous gifts, and seldom bestowed, for they may cause mischief, even disaster, if misused."

"Those gifts are easy enough to understand," Data replied, knowing the power of suggestion on unsophisticated people like the Elysians. "They operate because people believe they do."

"They also affect those who do not know of their existence," Thelia said. "If I—" She halted, curbing the first signs of anger Data had seen in her. Obviously he had offended her with his skeptical attitude toward her sacred beliefs. "Data," she went on, "if you do not believe in the powers of the gods, how can you quest?"

"I know they have great powers," he assured her. "That is why I wish to speak with them, to try to understand how they do what they do. But I will not ask for the impossible."

"Nothing is impossible for the gods," she asserted.

"Even gods cannot break the laws of nature, Thelia."

Thelia looked into Data's eyes with concern. "Be very careful what you wish for, Data. If you deny your true desire, you will find the gods' gift no boon at all."

Thelia seemed confident now that they would both make it to the sanctuary. Data was aware of the dangers of overconfidence, but as Thelia sleepily made a nest of her abused cloak and prepared to rest, he realized that he was coming to agree with her. She knew the powers of these gods after all. What might happen if he *did* ask for his true desire?

As he had told her, even severe damage did not cause him to require sleep. Were two organic beings on this Quest, he was sure there would be a test of alertness at this point, when both would be exhausted. Weariness, however, was another human experience Data could only observe without understanding. He could malfunction from damage, but not from being overtired.

Data left Thelia to sleep, and explored the small habitat they had been provided, to determine which way to go when they left it. On the other side of the lake he could see a trail that seemed the most likely exit.

It was a small lake; Data should be able to walk around to the other side in less than fifteen minutes. When he attempted to round the end, however, he ran into the wall of the illusion.

With his sight restricted to human range, he could not see even a holodeck wall at the moment—but the Elysian gods produced illusions he could not detect even with all sensors fully functioning.

He turned in the opposite direction, but encountered a similar wall at the other end of the lake. They were not to be allowed to walk around it.

They must either build some kind of boat, or go through the water. Swimming such a short distance would be no problem for Thelia, Data was sure, but he hesitated to go into the water with one gaping hole in his protective synthoskin and the molecular structure of other areas weakened. With so many of his sensors inoperative, Data could not detect flaws in areas of synthoskin he could not see, or tell whether some interior insulation might have melted or charred away entirely. Exposed circuits could short out in contact with water.

Once Data had discovered the perimeter of their little habitat by bumping his nose on it, he saw that the trees they might have built a raft from were all beyond their reach, part of the illusion of background scenery. Only the gring-nut tree was "real," but the widest point of its trunk was hardly as thick as his neck. Even if Data had had the tools to cut it into lengths to build a raft, he doubted it would provide enough buoyancy to counteract his density.

However, the gods had certainly scanned him thoroughly by now; they might not know all his capabilities, but he was sure they had discovered every detail of his physical structure. Possibly that tree would yield a raft just barely able to float Data across the lake. If so, what would he fasten the logs together with? The closest thing to ropes he could see were the tangled stems of the water pears. When he tested them, however, they broke at the slightest tug.

Another test, it seemed. Data could attempt to cut up the tree, but the only tool available was Thelia's knife. His strength might allow him to complete the task with such an inadequate tool, but not without dulling it beyond function. Before he risked that, he had to know if there was any use in the exercise.

Data chose a tree limb slightly bigger around than his arm, and twisted until it splintered away from the trunk. He stripped away leaves and twigs, and dropped the limb into the lake.

It sank.

That wasn't possible.

His sensors could not be so garbled that he would not have felt it to be excessively heavy. And organic material almost always floated.

Is this an answer to my assertion that even gods cannot break the laws of nature?

But then, if Elysia's gods wanted to have trees too dense to float, they could do so here, in their own domain. It was nothing more than a holodeck program could achieve. But their powers surely could not affect anything beyond Elysia, any more than a holodeck figure could walk out into the corridors of the *Enterprise*.

Apparently the gods were determined that Data go through that water. He would send Thelia across first, he decided. She must not be in the water at the same time, in case his circuits shorted out. He would not allow her to risk electrocution. Once Thelia was safely on the opposite shore, Data would walk across on the bottom of the lake. If it was not too deep, perhaps he could keep his right hand, with its gap in the synthoskin, out of the water entirely.

He wondered how deep the lake was at its center. With his normal range of vision, he could have seen it. Geordi would certainly have known with a glance—

Geordi.

Suddenly Data remembered the cylinder the Elysian gods' version of Geordi had given him. *"When you have need to see beyond sight, use this."*

Data had put the cylinder into the holster with his tricorder. It was still there, undamaged. It hadn't shown him anything before, but perhaps it would only work at the time it was intended for.

Data peered through the cylinder at the lake. Yes . . . he could see beyond surface reflections now, beyond the water pears' tangled stems and the murk beneath. The vision grew clearer. The bottom sloped gently downward for perhaps ten meters, then dropped off sharply.

Data waded out until the water was nearly up to his knees. From there he could see into the depths . . . bottomless depths.

The chasm beneath the lake went down beyond the measurement capability of the instrument he held. Its sides were sheer verticals, as smooth as glass. Not even Data could climb such a wall.

The chasm was a good fifteen meters across, a leap that would test Data's ability on dry ground. With the drag of water against him, it was far beyond his tolerance. The chasm extended the entire width of the lake; there was no skirting around it in the shallows.

So, Data was stopped here. If the trail on the other side of the lake was the way the Elysian gods intended them to go, he had failed the Quest.

That did not seem likely, however. Thelia said that the gods did not expect more than questors were capable of. They would have to leave the way they had come in—and chances were, the gods would have a new trail, with new challenges, waiting for them.

Data waded out of the lake. Nothing in his legs had shorted out, but his undamaged anterior warning sensors informed him that water had leaked into his legs and feet. Where the synthoskin on the backs of his legs had melted and fused with the material of his uniform, he discovered cracks. Now the water was seeping out again.

Data pressed gently, meaning to temporarily widen a crack on his left ankle just above the top of his boot, to let the water out more quickly. Instead, the entire section of fused synthetics came loose in his hand, the water pouring out with a soft "sploosh." Another section of his internal workings was exposed.

He did not tamper with the back of his right leg, but made his way toward the tunnel through which they had entered this temporary shelter. When he squatted down to try to see the tunnel, though, the skin of his right calf could no longer stretch to accommodate the movement. It, too, peeled away.

He now knew the effects of cold water on the areas of synthoskin melted by the firestorm. So must Elysia's gods. They would have to provide him with alternatives to going into the lake.

He quickly discovered that the alternatives did not include going back the way they had come. The mysterious cylindrical instrument located the back wall of this holographic illusion, but nowhere did it reveal tunnel, doorway, or any other exit.

And when Data turned around, the scenery had changed.

The lake was still there, its contours unchanged. Gone, however, were the water pears, the grass, the gring-nut tree. The scene was desolate wasteland, rocks and sand with a few scrubby bushes clustered around the lake. There was an orange sun in the sky now, causing the rocks and hills to cast maroon shadows.

Thelia still slept, unaware of the change, and Data went to sit beside her, reassuring himself that she was safe. In the short time he had known her she had proved courageous, capable, flexible, and loyal. What did the gods expect of her now? Or of Data? They had effectively trapped him here, it seemed. He accessed everything in his memory banks on the archetype of the Quest, and found that while the questor often had companions for much of his journey, there always came a point at which he or she must face a final test alone.

Perhaps Thelia must go on without him. If that were so, he could only wish her well, and hope that when the gods released him from this trap, they would allow him to continue alone until he had earned answers to at least some of his many questions.

Dismissing his own concerns, Data considered how to send Thelia onward with the best chance of success. The change in the scene obviously had meaning. Would there be a threat to Thelia now? If his vision was not functioning fully, his hearing was; he set it again to highest level and 360-degree scan, alert for poisonous reptiles or insects such as might inhabit a desert wasteland.

No such menaces threatened, but off in the distance Data heard faint, harsh cries. Far on the other side of the lake two creatures circled in the air—birds or flying reptiles his curtailed vision could not discern.

When he looked through the cylinder again, it acted as a telescope. They were birds, raptors with curved beaks and vicious claws. They seemed not to have noticed Data and his sleeping companion, but given their purpose here he doubted that lack of notice would continue.

Data kept an eye on the birds while he maintained a close watch, expecting something to happen nearby if he allowed his attention to be fixed on the other side of the lake. As an android, Data did not exhibit tension through sweating or nervous gestures or stomach pains, but he shared with humans the frustration of sensing that something unpleasant was inevitably going to happen.

Thelia slept on, and after a time Data decided nothing would happen until the gods were sure she had had enough rest to maintain health, if not a sense of well-being. Having thoroughly explored the habitat, Data remained at Thelia's side until she woke.

When she stared at the changed scenery, he explained what had happened, and led her to feel the walls that would not allow them to walk around the lake. She ate the handful of leftover gring-nuts while she verified what Data had discovered.

"We must swim the lake," she said at last.

"Thelia, I cannot swim, nor can I walk through the lake because of the chasm. The tunnel has closed behind us. It appears that this is where you and I must part company."

"Data—no!" Thelia exclaimed.

He smiled at her as reassuringly as he could manage. "It is your Quest, Thelia. I was on the island, so the gods let me help you for a time. You have overcome your fear of me, although they have shown you all my strangeness. Now they have placed a barrier which you can cross easily, but which is impossible for me. Perhaps," he added, "to show you that every being, no matter its strengths, also has its weaknesses. I have considered every possibility and probability, Thelia. There is no choice for you but to leave me here."

"But what of *your* Quest, Data?"

"Perhaps mine is an impossible request. Or perhaps the gods have other plans once you have gone ahead. One thing the gods have certainly made clear: unless they plan to carry me miraculously across that lake, I cannot go with you to the other side."

"Oh, Data," said Thelia, tears in her eyes, "I shall miss you. I am sure the gods will allow you to complete your Quest. I just wish we could go on together."

"So do I. But you must go now."

She nodded. "Yes. I have come to depend on you, as I dreamed as a child of having a protector. My mother made me leave such foolish dreams behind and learn to depend on myself. Now it is time to do so again. I shall miss you, Data—far more than I missed the seja doll that was only a prince in my imagination. You are real—and I hope that the gods will grant that which you most desire."

"I wish the same for you, Thelia," he told her solemnly.

"If my Quest is successful," she added, "if two lands are united, and we show that we will not go to war again—then one day the gods may allow travel more easily between distant lands. Perhaps we shall meet again."

"I wish that could be so," Data replied honestly.

Thelia wrapped her boots in her battered cloak, and balanced the package on her head. She walked to the edge of the chasm, then pushed off and swam easily across. She was a strong swimmer; she walked out the other side, turned as she wrung out her clothes, and waved to Data—

Who suddenly saw movement behind her!

"Thelia! Look out!" he shouted.

Out of nowhere, it seemed, the two raptors dived from the other side of the lake.

Thelia turned, and ducked quickly as they sailed right by her.

The birds were gigantic!

Unable to judge distance with his handicapped visual sensors, Data had thought the birds perhaps the size of eagles. Now he realized that they had been much farther off than he had thought—and that they were as big as horses!

Nothing that big could fly on wings that size.

But here inside their sacred mountain the gods of Elysia broke the laws of nature as they pleased—why not the inverse-square law?

Data's fear was for Thelia; it never occurred to him that the predators might see *him* as dinner until one of them dived directly at him. He heard Thelia's shout, but her warning was of no more help than his own.

There was no place to hide. He stood and braced himself, striking out at the bird as it reached for him—

The creature grabbed his arm in one claw, and his waist in the other.

To his astonishment, the bird carried him off as if he weighed no more than a rabbit!

He battered at the creature's leg and breast with his free arm, to no avail. The raptor might as well have been built of the same material as the android.

Even as it registered that that was the case, Data had no time for speculation; the other bird was closing on them, screaming avian curses as it delivered a blow to Data's bird's neck with its sharp beak, then grappled in midair, trying to grab the android's dangling legs.

Data kicked and squirmed, seeing a chance to escape—until he looked down. They were over the lake!

He ceased struggling and tried to grab the claw that gripped him, just as the attacking bird dealt another blow to his captor's head. Stunned, the bird loosed its grip and plummeted. Data's only chance was to dive for the shallows.

He let go, twisting out from under the great falling body and trying to use wind resistance to fall at an angle, but his weight was too much for friction to have much effect in the short distance he fell. He landed in the chasm, reaching desperately for the side, kicking with all his strength.

The water closed over his head as exposed circuits shorted out and his sensors exploded in overload.

His hands struck the side of the chasm, mirror-smooth and slippery. Clawing for a nonexistent hold, Data sank.

Chapter Six

WATER FLOWED INTO DATA. His circuits went berserk.

His body twitched helplessly, convulsing, diminishing to occasional spasms as he sank into the chasm beneath the lake.

So this is death.

Claws grabbed him.

One of the birds had dived in after him!

He was dragged helplessly upward, twitching and writhing, water draining from fissures in his synthoskin. As the last sparks spit and sizzled, the bird gripped him more firmly. His damaged skin could take no further abuse; what was left on his back flayed off and fell away as water poured out of him.

Data was vaguely aware that they were no longer over the lake, but his remaining sensors could not give him an accurate reading. He hung helpless in the bird's claws, limp as a puppet with its strings cut.

He heard shouting, could not make it out—then the bird carrying him screamed.

It was a scream of pain, not challenge.

The claws loosed their grip.

Data fell again—this time onto a rocky surface. Unable to break his fall, he landed on his side with a jolt, one leg flung over the other, arms spread wide, eyes and mouth open. Dust from the impact entered his eyes, nose, mouth. Sensors warned of potential damage, but he could not blink or move his jaw.

After far too long a pause, the fluid which cleansed his eyes emerged—too much, dripping over his nose and cheek as he lay helpless. Finally he could blink, although there was a perceptible delay between his autonomic system's issuing the order and its being obeyed.

He struggled to close his mouth . . . and slowly succeeded. There was sand between his teeth.

Footsteps, a shadow. Thelia's voice. "Data! Data, are you alive?"

He was aware of his body vibrating slightly seconds before the feel of her hand on his shoulder registered. Thelia scrambled over him, to peer into his face. His eyes focused on hers. She saw that, and smiled. "You're alive! Oh—I hope that means you can be repaired!"

By whom? he wondered, but could not say it. With a supreme effort, he moved the arm that was pinned beneath him a few centimeters, allowing him to fall over onto his back.

Unfortunately, that movement drove even more sand into his exposed components. Some seconds later, his diagnostics confirmed it. The sand might be bad news, but the fact that some part of his diagnostic system was still operative was good.

He had no strength to use the vocal apparatus which made him sound like an organic being. With an effort, he managed to say, "I . . . must . . . recover." To his ears, the words sounded like mistuned subspace radio through an ion storm. What must they sound like to Thelia?

She understood, though. "As you did after you jumped through the flames?" she asked. "I understand. I'll guard you."

Guard? he wondered, but could not focus on the question because systems which should operate automatically demanded conscious attention. His damaged repair system could not function without his guidance.

Sensors came on-line, one by one—only a small fragment of the hundreds of thousands in his normal operation. But if there were enough for him to get around, assuming he was able to move, he could continue to the point at which the Elysian gods decided he had either passed their tests or should be released to return to the *Enterprise.*

Thelia watched over him, mopping water and eye-cleansing fluid from his face. Lake water was still dribbling out of him. When he was finally able, with great effort, to sit up, his undamaged uniform front, no longer connected to a back, peeled forward off his undamaged chest and the front of his arms.

His movement did not go unnoticed. One of the raptors still circled above them, determined not to be cheated of its prize. Sighthawks, he recalled, were often intrigued by shiny objects. The glitter of his exposed metal attracted it.

His software, Data realized, seemed to have come through unharmed. But his hardware was not cooperating. He tried to say, "Cover me with your cloak" to Thelia, but could not get it out before the bird dived for him.

Thelia was on her feet, sling in hand. She flung a stone, and the bird missed its mark and slanted upward.

Thelia squatted beside Data, saying grimly, "I need something besides a sling, Data. The gring was no real menace, but I cannot fight this creature with just rocks."

"Cov—" he tried again, but Thelia was on her feet, flinging another stone at the oncoming raptor. It struck the bird's breast, but did not stop it. Claws raked across Thelia's shoulders as she ducked barely in time to escape death. The back of her shirt was shredded.

The raptor whirled and dived again, too fast for Thelia to impose herself between it and Data. "No!" she shouted. "No—you won't hurt him again!"

The claws came straight at Data, the cruel beak ready to strike.

The best he could do was fall back; he could not even roll aside.

Not two meters above Data, the raptor gave a sudden shriek, feathers floating behind ichor as the bird rose, shrieking and flying in wobbly circles.

Thelia had managed to hit the creature in the eye.

Fortunately, the giant bird chose safety over revenge, winging off into the distance as Thelia bent over Data once more.

But there had been two of them. "Where . . . is the other . . . bird?" Data managed to whisper.

"You didn't see?" Thelia asked. "When it fell into the lake with you, and the fire came out of you—it seemed to have a fit, and then it sank. It must have drowned."

Electrocuted, Data realized, but there was no use

trying to explain that to Thelia. Had it been organic, then? Probably it had been programmed to react like an organic being. They were apparently safe from the raptors for the moment, but he was not sure what good that would do them if he could not move.

However, some of his function was returning. He sat up again, his arms obeying better than before. Cautiously, he pulled his feet under him, and tried to stand.

"Don't!" Thelia ordered, while instinctively trying to support him.

Data sat back down slowly. "My . . . self-repair units . . . are functioning," he explained. "Rerouting commands through . . . undamaged circuits."

"Then stay still until you are healed," Thelia told him. "There is no time limit to the Quest."

It took almost an hour before his diagnostics informed him that all possible self-repairs had been completed. He was able to stand and walk, but the main connectors to the flexors that served him in lieu of muscles were inoperative. With only the auxiliaries working, he could not exercise android strength for lifting, shoving, or leaping. He hoped there would be no more chasms to jump.

As he tested his limbs, Thelia smiled in relief. Then she chuckled. "You look like a scarecrow." At least that is what his translator circuits made of what she said.

Data was sure whatever birdlike creatures Elysians tried to frighten from their fields were not called crows, but the concept of placing some model of a person amid the newly-planted fields was ubiquitous in agricultural societies.

"I did not frighten that creature who tried to carry

123

me off," he pointed out, grateful that his speech circuits no longer created perceptible pauses.

Nor did he frighten Thelia, although he wondered if he might not frighten himself if he could see the damage. From his eyebrows down, the front of his body had escaped the firestorm, so that skin remained in place. From his eyebrows back over the whole of his skull, though, and down his back to his waist, skin and hair that had been burned and fused had fallen away, leaving his skeletal structure, neural net, sensor mesh, and insulation exposed.

From his waist halfway to his knees, his sides and back had been protected by Thelia's pack and water bag. That skin and uniform remained intact, but the insides of his legs showed from there down to where his feet disappeared into the protection of his boots.

The top part of the front of his uniform still hung 'loose. Data was not sure he could have torn that strong synthetic when he had his full strength; he certainly could not now, so he wrapped what was left of his sleeves around his waist to tie at the back. The fronts of his trouser legs flapped loosely as he and Thelia started out once more on the clearly marked trail.

"We must be more careful what we say," Thelia remarked.

"Why?" Data asked.

"The gods are listening. You said you could not get to this side of the lake unless they sent something to carry you. Next time, ask for a boat. Or a bridge."

"I shall keep that in mind," he replied.

As he labored to climb a hill that would ordinarily have taken no effort, Thelia looked at him with concern again. "Data, do you feel pain?"

124

"Not exactly. To inform me of a malfunction, my sensors create signals which cannot be ignored. The sensations are extremely unpleasant until repairs are set in motion. Once that is done, there is no further need for unpleasant sensations, and so they cease."

"People feel pain all through the healing process. Yet you wish to be human."

"Not in that sense."

"But you said you were willing to give up your strength, your special senses, to be human, Data. The gods were obviously listening to you. Isn't that what they are testing now?"

"So it appears," he was forced to agree. "Thelia, your gods do not seem to be bound by the laws I comprehend. You are correct: I shall tell them of my wish to know what it is to be human. The worst that can happen is that they will be unable or unwilling to grant it."

They hiked over the top of a rise, and saw the trail ahead disappear into the mouth of a cave. "How much farther?" Thelia asked. "What more can they ask of us, Data?"

"I think," he replied, "we must leave that up to the gods."

Inside the cave the climb became steeper yet. Data tried to help Thelia, but had not enough strength. They struggled on, Data hampered by his own weight as he labored up the steep slope.

His sensors might be unreliable, but they had to be very near the top of the mountain now.

At last they reached the top of a rock formation, and faced a level cavern out of which led . . . seven archways.

"Which way?" Data asked.

"I do not know," Thelia replied. "We have never been given so many choices before."

They moved closer. Through the first archway they could see a patch of woods with a small stream running through it, and stepping stones on which to cross the stream. "Water," Thelia remarked.

"No," Data said, putting a hand on her arm. "You were not to enter your home when it appeared before. That is *my* home," for he recognized his own favorite holodeck recreation of a nature park on Earth.

"Your land is lovely," Thelia said. "But you are right; we must not go that way."

Their other choices were less obviously right or wrong: more rocky passageways, desert scenery, frozen caverns, two closed doors . . . and a mirror.

Thelia gasped. "I have never seen such a huge looking-glass!"

Data was more startled to see what a ragamuffin pair they looked. Thelia was scratched, bruised, sunburned, her hair trailing wild wisps from the sensible braid she had started with, her shirt torn, face dirty, eyes huge with wonder, but underlined by dark smudges of exhaustion.

But he, normally imperturbable, impeccable in Starfleet uniform—no wonder Thelia had called him a scarecrow! His face was stuck incongruously on the front of the metal skull protecting the sensors in his head; his chest was a pale triangle streaked with dirt, and his uniform hung in shreds. His arms and legs showed the rods, tubes, and mesh of his internal structure, with the occasional diode flickering weakly.

He was . . . absurd.

Of all beings in the universe, Data should have the least concern over appearances. Yet he felt disturbed at this distortion of his usual neat image.

Distortion? No—this mirror showed what he really was: a physical housing containing a consciousness that had somehow developed the same vanity as humans, even while it sought to understand their nobler virtues. How ridiculous. How—

How funny!

At the spectacle, and at the revelation of his own smug pride . . . Data laughed.

Thelia chuckled. "We *are* a sight, aren't we? But it doesn't matter. We've come this far, and we'll make it the rest of the way."

Data's laughter faded as he realized that Thelia had no idea of his revelation.

Nor could he attempt to explain. So he said, "This is surely the last obstacle. Is there nothing in your Quest lore to help us decide which path to take?"

As if on cue, a woolly white animal suddenly darted out of the passageway from which they had come, and sped past them through one of the arches. Data saw a collar of gleaming jewels about its neck.

"Follow the white seja!" Thelia exclaimed, sprinting after it.

Data followed, but his auxiliary locomotion systems could no longer propel him as quickly as Thelia could run. No matter—she would tire, and he would catch up. He heard her footsteps echoing ahead as they traversed a narrow rocky passage that twisted and turned every few meters.

He came out into a long, straight pass, seeing Thelia perhaps twenty meters ahead of him, still pursuing the animal. But hardly had he glimpsed them when a door slammed down in front of him, so close and so fast that with his impaired reflexes Data ran into it. He bounced off—into a second door that had closed behind him!

He was trapped in a featureless box of stone, the top only centimeters over his head, the width in any direction not enough to stretch his arms out.

When he stood still, he could hear nothing, even with his audio input on its highest setting. A patch of the ubiquitous fluorescent lichen gave him dim light, but there was nothing to see.

Testing the limits of his prison, Data tried the walls in every direction, then the ceiling, to no avail. Even with his normal strength, he doubted he could have broken free. Certainly not if the Elysian gods did not want him to.

What danger was Thelia rushing into now, without his help? A memory surfaced, unwanted: Tasha Yar forever striding bravely into danger, until that time on Vagra II when she had met death before Data's helpless eyes.

These Elysian gods had powers the *Enterprise* crew could not comprehend. Had those powers made them as corrupt as the creature that had killed Tasha? Were they toying with their people's lives? Thelia's life?

"Let me out of here!" Data demanded.

To his amazement, one of the doors slid upward.

It was not, however, the one that led to the path Thelia had taken. "If you want to be literal," he said, "you have picked a worthy opponent. Let me go to Thelia."

That is not permitted. You have completed your Quest. She must be permitted to complete hers. If she

succeeds, you will be allowed to see one another before
you are returned from whence you came."

Shocked at getting an answer, Data did not realize
for a moment . . . "Completed my Quest?"

"The pathway will now lead you to the sanctuary."

Data found himself smiling. He had passed the
tests—now he would be able to ask all those questions
he had been storing!

The path no longer twisted and turned. It was
smooth and easy to walk, but it went on and on,
through caverns, then gardens, and only after almost
an hour of steady walking into a courtyard leading to
a building that seemed built of rainbows.

"Data!"

He turned. "Thelia!"

She had come in at another entrance, as bedraggled
and unkempt as before, but radiant with happiness.
"We have both achieved the Quest," she said. "I was
so afraid for you when I reached the labyrinth and
realized you had not followed."

He recalled that labyrinths were common in the
Quest motif, but said truthfully, "A maze is no
challenge to me. Was that your last obstacle?"

A slight frown crossed her face. "There was something else—the white seja led me to my childhood
prince, but—"

When she hesitated, Data said, "I understand. I,
too, experienced something I cannot explain to you.
But I could not have reached that point without your
help, your knowledge of Elysian Quest lore."

"Nor I without your strength and kindness." Suddenly she took his hand, looking at the exposed
mechanical components. Then she looked up, into his
eyes. "I can never thank you enough, Data. I have

129

nothing to give you but my friendship. You will be forever welcome in the land of Atridia." She threw her arms about him, oblivious to the exposed metal and synthetics her arms embraced. Then she studied his face again, as if to memorize it. "Surely it is safe for me to accord you a token of affection."

And saying that, she leaned forward and kissed him on the cheek.

For an instant, Data felt something. Something like what he'd felt for Tasha, but different. . . .

"Come now," Thelia said, smiling. She took his hand. "Let us go into the sanctuary."

There was no door; they passed through a rainbow into a place of glowing color. The patterns playing over the floor formed a circle of white light at the center.

"Thelia of Atridia."

Letting go of Data's hand, Thelia stepped into the light circle.

"In your Quest, you have come to know your strengths and your weaknesses. You have overcome your fears and demonstrated that you can work with another, no matter how different from you. When he was injured, you protected him at your own risk. When you proceeded alone, you avoided the temptations we placed in your path. Your request is granted: Atridia and Tosus will be joined, and your people will prosper."

The circle of light began to pulse, as if a transporter were in operation. Within the glow, Thelia changed, her injuries healed, her clothing transformed from the rough shirt and trousers to a magnificent gown of gold and white. Her dark hair was arranged in an elegant style, surmounted by a small golden crown.

She was beautiful.

And then, before Data could even say good-bye, she faded away. It *was* a transporter, he realized. By now Thelia was safely at home in her own land.

"Data of Starfleet."

Data stepped into the circle of light.

The voice declared, *"Although a stranger to our planet, you have obeyed our laws and aided one of our people. For this alone we would offer you our gratitude. But beyond that, you, also, have expanded your limitations. That you may understand the nature of what you perceive as limits, we grant your fondest wish."*

The Elysian transporter effect pulsed around Data, and in a moment he was standing, off balance, on one of the tilted rocks littering the beach below the mountain. When the beam let him go he staggered, could not maintain his footing, and fell forward, landing on hands and knees on the pebbled shards.

Data pushed himself quickly to his knees—to an increase of unpleasant sensation in one place, a decrease in another. *Pain,* some analytical portion of his mind informed him, increasing in his knees when he put pressure on them, decreasing in his hands when he relieved the pressure there.

His hands . . . Data stared at the backs of his hands.

And saw not metal rods and mesh showing through gaping holes, but skin. And the sleeves of his uniform, whole and clean, came neatly down to his wrists as usual.

As usual?

He tried to process what was wrong—and could not access his diagnostics.

His hands were the wrong color: a pinkish hue with a few dark hairs showing near the wrists.

Numb with disbelief, he staggered to his feet and stood swaying—his sensory balance was off—as he turned his hands over and saw sharp pebbles embedded in the palms. He brushed them away and looked at his hands again, and a strange pounding rose in his ears.

Through numerous small cuts on the palms of his hands welled bright red blood.

Chapter Seven

DATA STOOD STARING at the blood on his palms, feeling the pain in his hands and knees. Sheer disbelief fought with wonder in his mind. It could not be real! *He* could not be . . . real?

. . . human?

What he felt was different from any previous experience. He was used to feedback circuits bringing the results of diagnostics immediately to his conscious attention. Now there was no indication of the type or extent of his damage, just this extremely unpleasant sensation calling his attention to the four points of his body that had taken the brunt of his fall.

The sensations began to fade. That must mean he was not badly hurt, as he would not expect a human to be from a similar mishap. A human . . . but even if it were true, he had duties. Guilt stabbed him. He had been sent here to study the island, the mountain—not indulge his personal desires!

He was on the rocky beach from which he had first

spotted Thelia, facing the swamp. He turned toward the mountain, looking for the entrance to the caverns, but he could not see it. Not sensor damage: organic eyes simply could not access the frequencies necessary to locate it. He reached for the cylinder Geordi had provided for his Quest—but it no longer hung beside his tricorder in its holster.

Still, he knew where the opening was. Traversing the uneven ground took as much effort as he had needed to walk when confined to auxiliary locomotive power. The farther he went, though, the more effort it took. He grew uncomfortably warm as he worked his way to the sheer rock wall, and almost fell several times as he searched for the hand- and foot-holds that had been so easy for an android. Finally, panting and sweating, he pulled himself onto the ledge and faced the entrance.

Or where the entrance had been.

His hands touched solid rock: pushing on it only made the cuts on his palms burn. It occurred to him to try his tricorder. It now worked, but read exactly what he saw: solid rock.

Data stood back and looked up toward the top of the mountain. "Gods of Elysia!" he shouted.

There was no answer.

Had he really expected one?

They had given him what he had asked for and now they were through with him.

He had passed their tests, and now he was—

A sudden bubble of pain/pleasure rose up inside him, and he felt himself smile. Why was he fighting it?

He was human!

For better or for worse, he truly was what he had longed to be. It terrified and delighted him at the same time.

For long moments Data stood rapt at the very idea of being human, feeling his flesh react as he shivered in the cold air, before the habit of duty prompted him again. If his tricorder was working, then—

He tapped his combadge. "Data to *Enterprise.*"

Worf's voice said, *"Captain—"*

Before the Klingon could continue, Picard's voice exclaimed, *"Data! Are you all right?"*

"Yes, sir, but—"

"Transporter room—get a lock on that signal and beam Commander Data up at once!"

"But the power surge—" protested the transporter chief's voice.

"Get him aboard before there's another one!" Picard ordered.

Data was caught in the familiar sensation, the mountain fading, the *Enterprise* transporter room coalescing before him. Yellow Alert lights were flashing—presumably because of the power surge they had mentioned.

Data suddenly realized what Elysia's power surges were: the "gods" exercising their power for something as seemingly impossible as turning an android into a man. He must proceed directly to the bridge and inform the captain—

Transporter Chief O'Brien frowned at something on his console, looked up, and slapped the alarm. "Intruder alert! Security to Transporter Three!"

Data was too stunned to get a word out before two guards appeared, phasers trained on him. With them flanking him, O'Brien stalked forward. "Who are you?" he demanded. "What have you done with Commander Data?"

"I *am* Data. Chief O'Brien, you know me—I cannot appear *that* different—"

"What kinda game are you playing? How'd you get Data's uniform and equipment? If you've harmed him, there'll be hell to pay, bet on it! Now hand over that phaser—and no tricks!"

As Data gingerly unholstered his phaser and proffered it handle-first to one of the guards, the doors slid open again, this time admitting Picard, Worf, Troi, and Riker. Picard stared, then glared. "Who *are* you?" he repeated O'Brien's first question. "Where is Data?"

"Captain, I *am* Data," he tried again. What had the Elysian gods done—placed his consciousness in a body that looked nothing like his android appearance? His uniform fit, his hands had the same slender fingers that had always belied his android strength . . . but from the reaction of his friends, his face must be that of a stranger.

A stranger they assumed had brought harm to one of their colleagues. He saw anger on every face in that room, except—

Deanna Troi put a hand on Picard's arm. "Captain," she said, "this man absolutely believes what he is saying. He is bewildered at our reactions. He truly believes he is Lieutenant Commander Data."

"Thank you, Counselor," Data said in relief. "Captain, I can explain. The Elysian gods—they might as well be truly supernatural for all we are capable of understanding. They put me through their tests, and because I aided one of their subjects . . . they granted my fondest wish. That was the source of the power surge you experienced just before I contacted you: they must access tremendous power to do what to us appears impossible."

"Good God!" Riker whispered. "Is it true?"

Data grasped at the opening. "Commander—surely you can verify my identity. Ask me something an impostor could not know, something not in the ship's logs."

Riker studied him for a moment, then asked, "Where did we first meet?"

"On the *Enterprise* holodeck."

"What song were you singing?"

"I was not singing; I was trying to whistle 'Pop Goes the Weasel.'"

"You told me about wanting to be human. What did I say?" Riker asked.

Human or android, Data would never forget his feelings when he accessed the reference. "You said, 'Nice to meet you, Pinocchio,' and I knew that I had been right to tell you. You understood then. Please understand now."

Riker stared at him a moment longer. Then he said, "Captain, I can't imagine how it could be done . . . but it appears our Pinocchio has become a real, live boy."

"Or someone," Worf growled, "has accessed all of Data's memory banks."

"No," Troi said. "This is definitely an organic being. It would not be possible to transfer an android's entire memory into an organic brain."

"You prefer to believe," the Klingon said skeptically, "that someone waved a magic wand and turned an android into a man?"

"There was no magic wand involved," Data supplied helpfully.

Picard started. "That's Data. Or at least he reacts like Data." He folded his arms across his chest and stared at Data again. "We're getting nowhere standing here. Take him to sickbay and see if Dr. Pulaski can sort out who he is."

It had not occurred to Data that his friends would not recognize him. Strange feelings coursed through the alien body he now wore. It was breathing hard, and he could feel a pounding in the chest—the heart beating too fast, he realized. His android body had never reacted to his feelings, but he knew that human bodies did. Strange how he had fantasized about a heart skipping with joy, but never thought of it pounding in fear.

What if they could not verify his identity? Would they return him to Elysia, abandon him there? Or, thinking he had done away with the second officer of the *Enterprise,* try him for murder, or at least kidnapping? The truth verifier at a formal trial would reveal that he believed what he said—he could be placed in a hospital where doctors would attempt to cure him of what they would certainly believe was insanity!

None of these difficulties had ever occurred to him. Why should they? He had never dreamed of *really* being human.

By the time they reached sickbay, Data was trembling. Of all people, the pragmatic Dr. Pulaski was the least likely to accept his story.

When the doors opened, the CMO was turned away from them, studying a chart of Data's specifications on the screen behind one of the diagnostic couches. Geordi La Forge was with her, also refreshing his memory.

Hearing the doors swish open, Pulaski said, "It's about time. I don't care who it is, when a crewman is missing for more than 48 hours he is to be checked out in sickbay before . . ." She turned on her last words, eyes widening to find not a single android, but Picard, Riker, Troi, Worf, O'Brien, two security guards, and . . .

Pulaski's eyes traveled up and down Data's frame, then back to his face. She frowned, squinting slightly. "Data?" she said in wonder.

He nodded. "Yes, Doctor."

"What happened? No, I can see *what's* happened, but *how?*"

"Doctor," said Picard, "you recognize him?"

"Don't you?" she asked, as if surprised. "Captain, he looks exactly the way Data would if—"

Geordi, who had been standing immobile all this while, his mouth hanging open, stepped forward to finish the statement. "—if Data had been born human. Data, how—" Geordi clasped Data's shoulders with both hands and stared into his eyes, shaking his head in wonder. "It's you, isn't it? It's really you."

"It is I, Geordi," Data said, the corners of his mouth twitching upward in an involuntary smile. Relief shot through every pore of his body at his friend's acceptance of him.

Geordi smiled back, and gripped him harder around the shoulders. "It's really you."

"You have said that already, Geordi," Data pointed out.

"I still don't see it," Riker said. "Doctor, can we verify his identity?"

"Of course I— Oh. No DNA scan."

"Yes there is," Geordi said, "but it still may not match. Data has—had—organic components."

"Of course," Pulaski responded. "Data, please lie down on the diagnostics couch. Mr. La Forge, it looks as if I won't be needing help from engineering, but if you'd like to stay—"

"You couldn't drag me out of here with a tractor beam." Geordi helped Data onto the diagnostics couch. "Data, what happened to you?"

"It is a long story, Geordi," Data said, feeling his heartbeat slowing now, as the fears passed.

"You've got time to tell it, Data," Dr. Pulaski said, stepping to his side. "These tests will take a while."

"Yes, Lieutenant, tell us," Picard agreed. "Computer, record the statement being given by the person claiming to be Lieutenant Commander Data."

Between pokings and probings, Data told his story. By the time he was finished, Dr. Pulaski had her report.

"My findings agree with what Data has just told us," she said. "His fingerprints are the same. The computer identifies his voice and inflections. His DNA is not a perfect match for that of the nutritive fluid in his android body, because that fluid, although organic, was not human. If, however, someone were attempting to create a human clone of Data, keeping as much of the original DNA pattern as possible, this man's DNA would be one potential outcome."

"Then you're saying these Elysian gods created a clone of our Data, and transferred his consciousness into it?" Picard asked.

"At a guess," the doctor replied. "From what Data has told us, his android body might have been damaged beyond repair."

"No, Doctor," said Data, sitting up on the couch. "There was no damage you and Geordi could not have repaired—so it certainly could not have been beyond the capabilities of the Elysian gods. They *chose* to do this to me. Do you remember how it seemed they were sending our away teams instructions through the Elysian people? It appears that they listen to their own people in the same way. Time after time, the tests that befell us came out of things that Thelia and I had spoken aloud."

"And of course at some point," Riker surmised, "you told her of your wish to be human."

Data nodded. "Yes. I did verbalize my desire to meet with these 'gods,' but they chose to ignore that."

Picard nodded. "Unsurprising. Gods rarely commune with mere mortals. You have had far more communication with them than we have managed to achieve. So far as our sensors can perceive, Elysia's 'gods' might as well be purely mythical. They will not answer our messages on any frequency—and we tried every method short of smoke signals when we lost contact with you."

"I know, sir," Data replied. Then he shook his head. "I hope you believe that I did not intend to place my own desires above my duty. To be honest, I did not believe even the Elysian gods capable of making me . . . literally human." He looked down at his hands again, still hardly believing that it was true.

"You told us they appeared to be able to change the laws of nature," Geordi mentioned, "at least as we know them, Data. Remember, only four centuries ago the best human scientists thought they had absolute mathematical proof that faster-than-light travel would violate the laws of nature. Look how far we've come since then. These Elysian gods might not be any more advanced over us than we are over twentieth-century scientists."

Dr. Pulaski nodded. "They gave you a brand-new, perfect body, Data, perhaps by cloning, perhaps by some technique we haven't yet dreamed of. You have no scars, not even calluses." She shook her head. "I can't imagine doing it. *We* certainly don't have the technology. We could produce a clone, yes—but to transfer consciousness? My God, we're still trying to figure out what consciousness *is!*"

Through all this, Captain Picard had kept his mind on the main issue: the safety of his ship and crew. "You are satisfied, then, that this is Data? He could not be held captive somewhere, and his memories *duplicated* rather than transferred into this body?"

"Captain, I do not think so," Troi said. "Memories alone do not make personality—the personality that Data feared losing if Commander Maddox had been allowed to experiment with him. I think it is obvious to all of us that the person we have been talking with here for several hours is indeed our Data."

"Of *course* he is," Geordi said.

"I agree," Riker added.

"So do I," Worf seconded.

"That's what my instincts tell me as well," Picard added. "Doctor, are there any other tests?"

"We could do a brain scan," she suggested, "although a negative result would be inconclusive."

"Try it," instructed Picard.

So Data was subjected to yet another test—but the captain's instincts were sound. "Look at this!" Pulaski said excitedly.

She had the graphs on two screens, side by side: a scan of Data done when they were using him as a model to activate Lore, and the results of the present scan. At first glance they appeared incompatible, but the doctor explained, "The electromagnetic activity of a positronic brain and an organic brain are completely different, but when we remove everything but the line that represents conscious thought patterns—"

The wildly different red, yellow, pink, purple, and green lines disappeared from both graphs, leaving only jagged blue lines. Although they were not identical, the similarity was obvious.

"You won't get perfect correspondence in thought patterns," Pulaski forestalled the objection, "not even from the same person at different times. No one thinks exactly the same thing in exactly the same way except in a trance or dream state. But the overall pattern, the *way* this person thinks, is not the way a human does. He is still attempting to access and process information like an android. Captain, I don't think there can be any further doubt."

"Well, Mr. Data," said Picard, "you have been through a shock, and I'm sorry we added to it by doubting you."

"I understand, sir," Data said.

"Doctor," the captain asked, "is he fit for duty?"

"He's in perfect physical health," she replied. "Data, I want you to report back here in forty-eight hours for another brain scan. We mustn't miss this opportunity to study the process of your adapting to a human body. And if before then you feel the slightest discomfort, I want you in here on the double."

"Yes, Doctor," he replied. "Captain, shall I report for duty?"

Troi intervened. "Not yet. Captain, Data is human now; he will need some time to adjust."

"I agree, Counselor. Data, take the next twenty-four hours off, and then report for limited duty."

"Yes, sir."

"I would also suggest adding your name to the regular exercise and self-defense sessions," Worf said. "An organic body does not maintain itself without effort. Sir."

"Let's give Data some time to adjust to his new body before you start throwing it around the holodeck, Worf," Dr. Pulaski suggested.

The captain nodded agreement, and everyone then left except Geordi and Pulaski.

"Time to adjust, Data?" Geordi teased. "Time to celebrate—show you some of the things you've been missing. I think we'll start in Ten-Forward—"

Pulaski held up a hand, and turned away. "Count me out of this one. I've got work to do."

Data bent down to put his boots on, wondering if Geordi would think him rude if he, too, asked to be "counted out" of this one—and was suddenly seized with the sensation that the room was moving. He rabbed hold of the couch to steady himself, and Geordi was there at once with an arm about his shoulders, lifting him to his feet. "What's wrong, Data? Doctor!"

Data blinked. He had never felt anything like this

before. "The room appears to be turning. Is this dizziness?"

"My God," Geordi said, "he probably has no immunities, Doctor. Can he have caught something that fast?"

Pulaski came at him with her scanner, concern clear in her eyes as she said, "He showed nothing only hours ago—" Then she looked at the readings and chuckled. "Low blood sugar. Of course—the body scan showed nothing in your digestive system, Data. You've been under stress bordering on shock for several hours, running on adrenaline. All you need is some nutrition."

Geordi guided Data to a chair while Pulaski brought him a cup of fruit juice. "Drink it slowly," she warned. "Have some soup in an hour or so, and something easy to digest, like custard, before you go to bed. If you don't have any problems, go to solid foods tomorrow. Do you want me to give you an appropriate maintenance diet?"

"No, thank you, Doctor. I am familiar with foods appropriate for humans," Data replied, sipping the juice.

Suddenly his awareness focused on an entirely new sensation.

As an android, he had assumed that his senses were more acute than those of humans. He could take a sip of something like this juice and analyze instantly its pH, chemical structure, density, temperature, and viscosity. None of that information was available to him now—but something far more amazing was.

The liquid seemed to explode on his tongue, sending little pleasurable sensations up into his nasal cavity, then down inside his body as he swallowed reflexively. Yes—he remembered that aroma was a major constituent of flavor for humans. That was why he felt it in his nose.

But the "why" no longer mattered. The *experience* was nothing like his former analysis-by-sensor. It was pure delight, untinged by logic or reason. Eagerly, he gulped more of the juice.

"Easy—easy, Data!" Geordi warned him. "If you're that thirsty you'll shock your stomach. Sip it slowly."

Curbing his desire to increase the pleasant sensations, Data lowered the cup and smiled at his friend. "It just—tastes so good!" he explained inadequately.

"You sound surprised," Dr. Pulaski observed.

"I am. I had no idea how . . . how *different* it would be. Because as an android I could analyze more specifically, I always assumed that human senses were less powerful. I never expected to find them so overwhelming!"

"You ain't seen nothin' yet!" Geordi told him with a grin.

"Data," Pulaski said, approaching him with a hypodermic, "I'm giving you the standard broad-spectrum inoculation all human crew members receive." There was a slight stinging sensation as it hissed against his arm. "There should be no occasion for you to leave the ship for the seventy-two hours required to be certain it has taken effect. I will inform the captain of that restriction, and also my recommendation that you not attempt anything beyond the most routine duties until both Counselor Troi and I clear you for

146

full duty status." She put the hypodermic away, asking, "You keep a personal log, don't you?"

"Yes, of course I automatically—" He stopped, realizing, "It is gone."

"Gone?" she asked.

"It was in my memory banks."

"Of course," she said. "Well, use the computer, like everyone else. Your experiences are unique—please don't neglect to record your feelings, your reactions, your descriptions of what has happened to you. I realize that some of it will be too personal to share, but I would ask that you grant access to an edited version—senior officers only, if you prefer."

"Certainly," he replied, feeling some relief. "I always stored such an edited version in the ship's computer before. So all my records are not gone, after all." He frowned. "Why did I not think of that immediately?"

"After what you've been through?" Geordi sympathized. "How can you possibly be thinking straight?"

"Geordi's right," Pulaski agreed. "How do you feel now?"

"Normal?" he asked. "No physical discomfort? I am sorry, Doctor—I do not yet know how I am supposed to feel when in optimum condition."

"Pretty much the way you do now, but without the stress caused by shock," she replied. "I'm releasing you, then, but don't hesitate to come back here, or call for help if anything happens that you don't understand."

So Data rose, and found his legs steady. The spray Dr. Pulaski had used on his cuts had stopped even that slight pain.

"I guess Ten-Forward's out for now," Geordi said ruefully.

"Yes," Data nodded. "I think I will just go to my quarters."

"Do you want me to come with you, Data?" Geordi asked.

"I have *not* forgotten the way," he replied, more harshly than he intended.

Geordi stared at him, hurt etched on his face.

"I did not mean—" Data began, then shook his head. "Forgive me, my friend," he said sadly. "I think I want to be alone for a while. This is all so new—let me find out what it feels like to be human without trying to hold a conversation at the same time. I think, later, we will have much to talk about."

"Sure, Data," Geordi replied softly. "I understand."

It took more effort than Data was accustomed to just for the simple act of walking the corridors of the *Enterprise*. His door did not open at his approach, for when he had left the ship the computer had routinely placed it on privacy lock. When he palmed the keyplate, though, it accepted his identity and the door slid open.

"Computer," he instructed, "discontinue privacy lock." No one on board the *Enterprise* would enter his quarters without invitation. Only Bruce Maddox had ever done so, in the belief that Data was not a person and therefore not entitled to privacy.

If he could see me now. Oh, yes, there was one person who would be sorely disappointed at what had happened to Data—but Data himself was at the beginning of a whole new life, a little frightened, but also eager to see what else besides taste he had been missing for twenty-seven years.

The first thing to do—

With trepidation, Data walked to where he could see himself in the full-length mirror on his cabin wall.

He stared. No wonder his friends didn't know him! Who was this dark stranger?

But that was just a first impression. Actually, he was pale, but no longer android-pale. His skin had the color of human flesh untouched by the sun, a rather sickly light pink hue. It was as Dr. Pulaski had said: he was brand new. But the ship's lighting was designed to provide the spectrum of light required by the various species aboard, without including harmful radiation. Soon his skin would acquire a more natural color without any effort on his part.

The impression of darkness came from hair and eyebrows and a shadowy hint of beard. He felt his mouth twitch at the idea that he would have to shave, and saw his reflection smile back at him. His lips were darker pink than his skin, and therefore appeared fuller. Instead of sketchily molded in pale lines, his eyebrows were heavy and thick, and his hair—!

It wasn't darker, exactly, but more . . . shadowed than it had been. His android hair had been all of one shade; organic hair had depths and highlights. Furthermore, it waved, and despite being cut in the same variation of Starfleet regulation style that he had worn as an android, a strand fell over his forehead in an unkempt fashion. Automatically, he pushed it back— succeeding only in dislodging even more recalcitrant strands.

Abandoning the attempt to control his hair, he

studied his figure. There were no changes that he could detect; his uniform fit precisely as it always had. He stepped up to the mirror for a closer examination of his face.

His eyes, he was startled to discover, were blue.

Why that should surprise him he could not fathom; it was the second most common eye color among humans. Probably, he decided, he would have been equally surprised to find them brown, green, or hazel —any color except the gold that had always looked back at him.

Just then Data felt the vibration of the ship change. They were leaving orbit—and accelerating to high warp speeds. It did not take android senses to feel the increasing stress as the great vehicle was pushed to its limits.

Without thinking, Data turned and left his quarters. Only when the turbolift doors opened to deliver him to the bridge did he recall that he was off-duty.

Captain Picard looked up from his center seat. "Mr. Data, you are not scheduled for this shift."

"Yes, sir. But why are we proceeding at highest warp?"

"Commander," the captain said dangerously, "you do not have bridge clearance at the present time."

Wesley Crusher was at the helm. At that he turned, and stared wide-eyed at Data.

The scene was tense, but the viewscreen showed nothing but passing stars, and the ship was not on alert status. Data backed off. "You are correct, Captain. I shall be in my quarters."

When he had returned there, Data did what he now realized he should have done in the first place: called up the bridge log on his computer.

The *Enterprise* was responding to a priority directive from Starfleet Command: a planet in the Samdian Sector reported attacks from a race of beings called the Konor. Their attempts to engage their attackers in any kind of dialogue had failed. They knew only that their people were being slaughtered.

None of the three planets in the Samdian Sector were members of the Federation, or even allies. They had always been fiercely independent, trading with one another but showing no interest in the Federation or any other culture. However, they were calling for help now from anyone who might be willing to heed their plea. As "anyone" included Orions, Ferengi, and possibly even Romulans, the Federation had a vested interest in responding to their call for help.

The *Enterprise* was the closest Federation ship with personnel qualified to take on the job. Their orders were to contact both sides and find out what the dispute was about, in hopes of finding a peaceful solution. The messages from the Samdians indicated they had no idea why they were being attacked. There *were* no messages from the Konor.

Even at top warp, it would take several days to reach the Samdian Sector. Data was glad; he had lost nothing of his insatiable curiosity, and was determined to be back to full duty status by the time they arrived.

That might be more difficult than he had thought at first. His *faux pas* in going to the bridge just now—some of his automatic programming must have translated as habit. As an android, had he been instructed to remain off duty for a specific period, he would have placed a temporary "cancel" on his "in case of emergency, unless otherwise instructed report to the bridge" response.

But as a human, he had no way to cancel a conditioned response except to keep his mind carefully on his first priority: getting accustomed to his new physiology so that he could return to duty as quickly and efficiently as possible. He instructed the computer to inform him of any new developments, and returned to his personal objectives.

Data had the strangest sense that there were a thousand things he ought to do next, and he could not think of one of them. His new body was throwing sensations at him, but none seemed particularly overpowering. His impressions were mostly visual, it seemed, so he shut his eyes.

His feet hurt.

Not particularly alarming, but both feet had slight, unpleasant burning sensations. He had no calluses, he remembered; climbing over the rocks and then up the cliff wall in his unsuccessful attempt to contact Elysia's gods had given his new body quite a workout.

Now it had a sort of vague overall ache.

Data realized he was experiencing tiredness, and sat down to take off his boots. He rubbed at one annoying ache, and discovered how good *that* felt. Data had given massages in his life as an android, but had never received one. To an android body, it was pointless.

He smiled at the world of simple pleasures opening to him. He pulled his socks off, knowing that if there had been any real damage Dr. Pulaski's instruments would have indicated it, but still needing to see for himself. Like his hands, his feet were the same size and shape as before, but there were red marks across the toes and on each heel.

They also gave off an odor. Humans bathed daily, Data knew. He had only ever needed to do so when he got dirty. Now he must add bathing and shaving to his daily schedule.

He stood and unzipped his uniform—to discover a veritable coat of fur on his chest! What other surprises lay in store? He stripped, and turned in front of the mirror. Yes, it was his own familiar body shape beneath the human coloration and the extra hair. He decided to clean it and cover it up again.

The sonic shower warmed and vibrated his abused muscles as it whisked him clean. Officers' quarters included water showers as well. Data had occasionally used water for cleansing when that was the method provided on a planet, but aboard ship he had always used the more efficient sonics. He was tempted to try the water shower, aware that humans considered water more pleasurable than sonics, but his stomach was sending him a message he recognized from sickbay: he was hungry.

So he completed his shower quickly, tossed his used uniform into the cleaning unit, and put on his spare. But he didn't want to put his boots back on.

He didn't own slippers; android feet did not require changes of footwear. What else did he need? There was nothing in his closet now but his dress uniform; his other everyday uniform would be cleaned and returned automatically.

The carpeting felt good beneath his bare feet, so Data padded to the food dispenser. Soup, Pulaski had said. But what kind?

"Give me a menu of soups suitable for human consumption," he instructed.

"Alphabet, apple, argramine, asparagus, betaresnis, cavistat, cheddar cheese, chicken broth, chicken consommé, chicken noodle, chicken vegetable, cream of asparagus, cream of broccoli—"

"Stop!" Data ordered. Eating was obviously going to be an adventure. He might as well begin at the beginning. "Alphabet soup," he instructed, trying to remember what that was. He wasn't sure if he had ever known.

How much memory loss had he suffered in his transformation? Enough to impair his performance as a Starfleet officer? That was the most frightening thought he had had yet.

The dispenser provided a steaming bowl of soup. Data carried it to his computer console, and punched up the analysis of Elysia's power surges that he had begun before they had received the distress call from Dare's gang.

His fingers flew over the keyboards as naturally as ever. That was a relief. He also understood everything on the screen; his mathematical competence seemed unimpaired.

However, he had to slow the information feed; his human brain could not assimilate data so quickly. While he watched the information scroll, he picked up the bowl of soup. It smelled wonderful, and the combination of heat and melded flavors proved delicious. It was a vegetable broth laden with pasta shaped like letters of the Roman alphabet. Hence, he assumed, the name. But why had anyone thought to form the pasta that way? It added nothing to the flavor.

Suddenly Data realized that while his attention had drifted to the soup, two screens of information had passed by without his assimilating them. When he tried to access that information, as he had formerly been able to do with any data passing within range of his sensory apparatus, there was nothing there.

He scrolled back to pick up the thread of the analysis again, and frowned. Someone else had continued it after he left the ship. He called up the user's I.D.: Wesley Crusher. Of course.

Data smiled at his star pupil's diligence. If he had known he would be gone for days, he would have given Wesley that assignment.

The boy had done well. He had not solved the problem of tracing the source, but he had eliminated several approaches. Data doubted he could have done more in the same time, although he would not have considered some of Wesley's more imaginative attempts.

Satisfied that his basic knowledge and skills were intact, Data called up from ship's stores the list of items available for crew quarters. He chose "Toiletries and Clothing" from the main menu, and the subcategory "Suitable for Humans."

He already had hairbrush, comb, and tooth cleanser. The latter, though, was designed for android use; he ordered a toothbrush and the first dentifrice on the list. Data chose an automatic shaver, then watched with increasing wonder as the list of other possibilities scrolled by. Although with a sonic shower soap and shampoo were unnecessary, the ship stocked more than twenty varieties of each. Data let those pass for the time being.

He also passed by perfumes and colognes, but having discovered how sharp his own sense of smell had become he ordered a deodorant by the same process of designating the first on the list.

He skipped past cosmetics, but paused over nail clippers and files, realizing that his nails would grow now, and it would be up to him to keep them at a utilitarian length. He ordered those implements, beginning to wonder how, with all the care it took to maintain a human body, he would ever find time to do his work.

Brushing that tickling strand of hair off his forehead again, Data backtracked to hair-care products. While he had no interest in changing his hair color, or molding it into some fashionable style, he could use something to keep it in place. This time he did not choose the first thing on the menu, but consulted with the computer as to Commander Riker's preference, and ordered that.

Foot comfort? Sexual enhancements? Skin care? The list was endless. Data decided he would wait and order further items as he identified a need for them.

From the clothing menu he ordered a pair of soft slippers, and hesitated over sleepwear, reminded that he would have to sleep, too. Probably he should do so now, except that he was still too excited to feel the need. He was glad to have lived among humans for long enough to understand that this was a normal state of affairs.

When he did sleep, though, he would need a bed. That was not something the dispenser could provide, so he called ship's stores directly for a cabin refit, then turned back to the dispenser menu.

He knew that human taste in sleepwear ranged from nothing at all to some very exotic and ornate costumes. Best to take a middle course until he found a personal preference: he ordered a set of Starfleet issue pajamas and bathrobe.

That was enough, he decided, and instructed implementation. When he walked over to retrieve the items from the dispenser, he became aware of a heavy sensation low in his abdomen. It wasn't a pain, but he sensed that he ought to do something to alleviate it.

His mind still operated logically: juice and soup meant an accumulation of more liquids than his body needed. He knew all about human anatomy—his degree in exobiology included study of all Federation races. However, he was going to have to learn the feelings from the inside now; things commonplace to a small human child were alien to Data. He hoped he could learn enough in the twenty-four hours Captain Picard had given him that he would not embarrass himself in public.

Having successfully put into practice what he had previously known only from theory, Data considered again what he ought to do next. When *was* he due on the bridge?

For the first time in his life he hadn't the slightest idea what time it was!

The computer, of course, informed him immediately upon his request.

At this time the bridge crew of his duty shift would be on free time. Data could probably find some of his friends in Ten-Forward. Wesley should be studying— perhaps Data should go and discuss the boy's work on the Elysian mystery with him.

Just then the ship's intercom chimed. "Data? Are you in?" came Darryl Adin's voice.

"Yes, Dare, I am here."

"We just heard the most incredible story about

what happened to you on Elysia. Are you up to company, or would you be uncomfortable to have some of us come and gape at you?"

"I suppose I had better get used to it," Data said. "I think I might welcome some company just now. Be warned: what you have heard is true."

Dare, Poet, Sdan, and Pris came to visit, hard on the heels of the crew who set up Data's bed. Data was glad of the sudden crowd: the two ensigns from ship's stores were encouraged to exchange the modular components and leave without satisfying the curiosity betrayed by their surreptitious glances.

Poet shook his head, looking Data up and down. "What a piece of work. Don't know why you wanted a ticket to this ruddy vale of tears, but welcome anyway."

"Don't be so cynical, Poet," Pris said. "Data hasn't had time yet to learn the advantages of being human." She went up to Data, adding, "Let me give you a proper welcome to humanity." She put her arms about him and kissed him.

Data was swamped with sensation: her warmth, her scent, but most of all her *femaleness*. Too startled by the way his body instantly responded, he could hardly do more than bring his arms stiffly around her.

Before Data could muster his thoughts, Pris stepped back. She smiled. "Data, you're blushing. First kiss?"

"No. But the first since . . ."

"How strange!" she said. "I'd have thought all your female colleagues would've welcomed you home by now. But then, I suppose they're bound by some sort of rules."

"Starfleet protocol," said Dare, who had moved in past the others to usurp the comfortable armchair.

That left Data and Pris the small sofa. Poet and Sdan leaned over Data's computer, engrossed. The ship's vast library was at their disposal; of course, it would release to them only information on the security level Data had coded to their voice prints when he began helping them repair their ships.

Meanwhile, Dare was saying, "What are you going to do with yourself now, Data?"

"I do not know," he replied honestly. "I have hardly had time to think about the future. If I am still fit for duty, I shall certainly serve out my current tour in Starfleet. Right now, I cannot think beyond tomorrow."

"That sounds like a sensible approach. I trust you haven't lost your logic."

"I hope not," Data said.

"Then let me admit that I have come here for a selfish reason: I need you to use your persuasive powers on Captain Picard."

"Why? What has happened?"

"While we've been stranded here—no, Data, it was not your doing. We couldn't have had our ships spaceworthy by now anyway, and if it weren't for the *Enterprise* we'd all be dead. But before we got caught by those Elysian power surges, we were due at Brancherion in three days' time. Now we're late, and the Brancherions are calling for an explanation."

"And we have just warped off in a direction almost opposite to that in which Brancherion lies," Data realized. "But Dare, we are under Starfleet priority orders. We cannot divert to deliver you to Brancherion."

"I understand that," Dare replied. He had once been a Starfleet officer himself, so Data knew he truly did comprehend. "But Captain Picard has placed the entire crew on alert status. That means no one is available to help us complete our repairs."

"And so," Data concluded, "the longer your repairs take, the longer it will take you to get from the *Enterprise* to your destination."

"All that's left," said Sdan, "is debugging the navigation computer program. If you're off-duty anyway—"

"I shall help you," Data said. "However, I return to duty tomorrow. I think I could persuade Captain Picard to let me work with you under ordinary circumstances, but given my current status I must be retested for standard Starfleet skills. I shall have to practice to bring some of them up to standard. I am afraid my free time will be very strictly limited."

"Especially if you add time in sickbay, after that Worf character wipes up the holodeck with you," said Dare with his wolfish smile.

Data could not help but agree; although he was sure the Klingon would not actually harm him, he was concerned about his Security testing.

At his grim silence, Dare added, "I'll help you with that if you like, Data. Before you face your Chief of Security, I'll show you a few tricks for handling larger, stronger opponents."

"Thank you, Dare," said Data. "I wish I could do more to help you." He thought a moment. "Alert status does not relieve Wesley Crusher of his studies. I shall assign him the practical application of his navigation skills, helping you with your repairs."

"That child?" asked Pris.

"Believe me," Data said, "Captain Picard would

not trust the helm to our acting ensign if he were not qualified."

"To fly the ship, certainly," said Dare. "Kids his age have great reflexes, so long as there is a cool head to keep them from running straight into trouble. But we don't need a pilot; we need a computer expert."

"Try him," Data suggested. And yawned. Another new experience, this one neither pleasant nor unpleasant. When he realized everyone was staring at him because he was sitting silently analyzing, Data said, "Forgive me. I believe the day's experience is beginning to tell on me. Tomorrow, before my duty shift, I shall help you. At this moment, Wesley can do you more good than I can. This is his study time. Let me call him, and assign—" Another yawn interrupted him.

"We'd better go," Pris said. "You're exhausted, Data. You've been through so much today—it's normal letdown setting in."

"I'll give you a lesson in unarmed combat tomorrow, too," Dare said. "Reserve the holodeck for an hour."

When his guests had left, Data managed to make the holodeck reservation and then call Wesley, who was delighted at the new assignment. Data suspected it had more to do with getting to work with the Silver Paladin's gang than with the rather tedious computer program adaptations.

Weariness was overtaking Data with a vengeance now. It took immense effort to clean his teeth and change into the pajamas he had ordered.

Finally he was able to lie down and pull the cover over himself—a most luxurious feeling of comfort.

"Mrrowrr?"

Something poked the side of the bed.

Data opened leaden eyelids to find two round blue eyes staring at him from a dark brown mask.

"Roorrr?" Mystery queried as she stretched a paw to tap his arm.

"How did you get in here?" Data asked the cat. She had never come visiting his quarters before.

She took that as an invitation to jump up on the bed, where she proceeded to stare Data solemnly in the eyes as she kneaded the bedclothes, purring.

Tentatively, he stroked her. She rubbed herself against his hand, her purr increasing in volume.

Data smiled. So Mystery granted him humanity. Her soft fur felt lovely under his hand, but she did not allow him to pet her for long. She settled down on the pillow next to his, her purring soothing him as sleep claimed him at last.

Chapter Eight

DATA WOKE, DISORIENTED. He did not know where he was, what time it was, or why he had been turned off.

When he sat up, unfamiliar feelings shot through his body. His sensors had gone wild! He could not access his diagnostics!

The feelings resolved into aches, and the stiffness of his body recalled what had happened to him. A rush of cool air hit his skin as he threw back the cover.

He was in his own quarters aboard the *Enterprise,* and he had not been turned off. For the first time in his life he had . . . slept.

It was not an illusion or a fantasy. He was human, with all the slings and arrows that flesh was heir to.

Something was wrong with that reference—but he didn't care. He felt himself smiling, then grinning, as he looked at his hands and feet, felt the bristle of beard when he rubbed his chin, stumbled into the bathroom and found a human face surrounded by rumpled hair staring back at him from the mirror.

It took him quite some time to prepare for the day. Shaving was more complicated than it looked, but despite Geordi's contention that it should be regarded as "a human art form," Data adjusted the shaver until it gave him a clean, comfortable, and completely automatic shave.

When he was finished with his preparations, he was the image of a proper Starfleet officer: face cleanly shaven, hair neatly in place and treated to stay that way, uniform unwrinkled, and boots shined. With practice, he hoped to get his morning routine down to a few minutes.

Only then, with a brief moment's panic, did he think to check the time with the computer. To his relief, he was not due on the bridge for almost seven hours; he would have time to help Dare and his gang as he had promised, and keep his appointment with the former Starfleet Security Officer on the holodeck.

Mystery had been in his quarters last night—unless that had been a dream. Odd . . . he did not recall anything else that might be a dream; hours had simply passed without his being aware of them. There was no sign of the cat now; perhaps she had learned to make automatic doors open for her.

Meanwhile, Data was hungry. He had forgotten to eat again before going to bed. Instead of using the food console, though, he decided to brave Ten-Forward.

The smell of coffee drifted through the lounge. As an android, Data had not drunk coffee or tea; they contained no nutrients, and his organic fluids had had no use for stimulants.

However, the aroma was very pleasant, so Data sat down at the bar and asked Guinan to pour him a cup. She looked at him with her enigmatic smile and slight slow shake of her head. "So you got what you wished for. That can be very dangerous, Data."

"I know," he replied. "I am trying to . . . ease into the human condition."

Both smile and head shake became broader. "It doesn't work that way, my friend. We're all thrust into the world, willing or not, kicking and screaming. From then on, we must make the best of it."

"I seem to have no choice but to do likewise," he said, and took a sip of his coffee. It was so bitter he could hardly swallow it. "Gah!" he said involuntarily, and stared at the steaming liquid. "How can something that smells so good taste so terrible? I had the impression that people found it pleasurable."

"Many do. It's an acquired taste, Data, but there is no need for you to acquire it today. If you want a hot drink, try some tea—and I suggest milk and sugar in it at first."

"I will try it. Have you any suggestions for breakfast?"

"What a challenge," Guinan said. "Both balanced and palatable to someone just experiencing true tastes for the first time." She gave him juice, a small portion of a warm grain porridge, and a delicious spiced meat on flaky pastry.

Data ate it all, and found the tea with which she followed it up far more palatable than the coffee. "Thank you," he said. "There are so many choices, and little of my previous experience seems to carry over."

"Yes," she agreed, "but you really have no more choices than before. They are merely different."

"Perhaps," he said. Even when he had attempted to

resign from Starfleet to avoid Bruce Maddox's experiment, Data had perceived only limited possibilities. Leaving Starfleet had appeared to negate far more than half his options.

Now . . . the possibilities were endless. He could continue his career, join Dare or other adventurers, or decide to live on a planet somewhere.

As with Pris last night, Data found himself intensely aware of Guinan as female. For the first time it dawned on him that he had an entirely new option: within Starfleet or without, he could form or join a family unit. *I am no longer merely mechanically functional. I am capable of fathering children!*

He blinked and deliberately dismissed that overwhelming thought. Less than one full day human, he was hardly ready to think of taking on *that* responsibility.

Data excused himself, and went to the shuttle bay. Only Sdan was there now. He looked up from the program he was working on with a wicked grin. "Data, that kid you assigned to us is *great*. Bright, disciplined as a young Vulcan, with imagination and intuition to boot. Look at the shortcut he came up with for figuring geodesics."

Data examined Wesley's work, and found it both sound and innovative. The boy had obviously figured out how the startube Data had given him worked, for he had applied its technology to the navigation program. "I shall congratulate him on his efforts. I think you can see now why we are challenging Wesley to channel his abilities in positive directions. Before Captain Picard put him on the bridge, his curiosity and talent frequently caused mischief, even when he did not intend it."

Sdan nodded. "I hope Starfleet doesn't stifle him. Only thing I see wrong with him is that he's too damned polite. Yes sir, no sir, if you please sir." He shuddered. "Makes me feel like his grandfather, or his instructor at the Academy. Maybe workin' with us'll get him to relax a little."

"I do not think so," said Data. "Wesley's life is geared toward Starfleet." He took up the programming when he reached the point to which the debugging was complete—only to find Sdan growing impatient with his slowness. While Sdan claimed to have an unlikely mix of Federation and even non-Federation races in his ancestry, his appearance and intelligence were Vulcan. As an android, Data had been able to compute faster than any organic species. As a human, he was easily outclassed by any of the Vulcanoid races.

"Data, it's obviously four pi to the twenty-third! What's the matter with you?" Sdan demanded.

Data looked up at him, and answered deadpan. "I am only human."

Instead of provoking the laugh he had intended, the words brought a stricken look to Sdan's face. "Hell, I'm *sorry!* Course you are, and I wouldn't treat Poet that way. I was just used to the speed you calculated at before. You're still faster'n keyboarding in the equations."

The end was in sight by the time Data had to leave for his appointment with Dare on the holodeck.

"I miss this technology," Dare admitted as he looked around the bare room. "As active as we are, we can get rusty practicing only with one another—and wealthy as we are we'll *never* afford a ship capable of supporting a holodeck."

"Starfleet has not closed the option for you to return if you wish it," Data reminded him.

"Oh, no," the mercenary replied. "I couldn't live with such regimentation any longer. I enjoy my independence too much." He grinned self-deprecatingly and added, "I also enjoy command. Few Starfleet security chiefs ever move up to captain."

"Few live long enough," Data said—and was immediately sorry. He had been thinking of Tasha Yar, of course, and forgotten for the moment that Dare was not only the man responsible for setting Tasha on that career path but also the man who had loved and planned to marry her.

But Dare only said, "Too true," veiling his eyes as he turned away. Then he took off his jacket, and began to do warmup exercises. They were familiar moves to Data, who had often seen Tasha do them. However, this was the first time he had had reason to try them himself.

Data found at first that he suffered twinges of pain left over from yesterday, but as he bent and stretched in imitation of Dare's moves they became less noticeable. He was clumsy, but Dare pointed out proper positions and after a time he began to understand what was meant by "getting a feel" for an activity.

"You can bend further," Dare told him as Data touched his fingertips to the floor.

"I am doing what you did," Data replied.

"Yes, but you are years younger than I am and have never had your back broken. No—don't bounce!" Dare warned as Data tried to force his human body to do what his android body would have done easily. "Never force—that's how you get injured," Dare explained. "Let your body's own weight stretch you."

It did seem that his muscles stretched, and soon he was able to put his palms flat on the floor. "Excellent!" Dare told him. "Up slowly, now—don't lose your balance."

Data straightened, feeling the slight disorientation of changing pressure in his head, but he was not dizzy. He found Dare studying him with a frown. "Did I do something wrong?"

"No—but you mustn't let yourself lose that flexibility, Data. Children are born with it, but almost every human loses it by age twenty. It's one advantage a smaller man has over opponents with greater strength and weight." He glanced upward. "Computer: padding on floor and walls, and a safety field." The padding appeared immediately; the safety field would activate only if either of them were thrown so hard as to suffer injury despite the pads. "All right, Data, let's start by finding out what you already know." And Dare lunged for Data's throat.

Automatically, Data brought both hands up inside the other man's forearms, and struck them aside. That did not stop the mercenary, however; he twisted a shoulder into Data's chest. Data went down with the impact, too stunned at how easily he had been bowled over to recover before Dare had bounced to his feet and planted one boot on Data's Adam's apple.

Dismayed, Data simply lay there, realizing for the first time how helpless he was against anyone who knew what he was doing.

Dare removed his foot, and offered a hand up. "Analyze," he instructed.

"I—I never learned that kind of combat. I had no need of it."

"Negatives won't help," Dare said. "Your first move

169

was right. What was wrong with your second move was that you didn't make it."

"I . . . beg your pardon?"

"Attacking an android the way I just did you, I would have sprained, perhaps broken my shoulder, while the most I might have accomplished was to stagger you. Right?"

"That is correct. Worf could probably have knocked me over, but even he might have injured himself."

"But now we're both flesh and blood, and pretty well matched in size. Come at me the same way," Dare instructed.

Data did so, expecting the first move, turning slightly when his hands were knocked apart just as Dare had done, and trying to ram the man—

But Dare simply turned aside and let Data be carried on several steps by his own momentum!

"That works *once*," Dare warned him. "Unless your opponent is drunk or very stupid, don't try it a second time. Come at me again."

This time Dare moved only slightly to one side, grasped Data's arm, and tossed him over his hip. The safety field caught him and provided a soft landing.

Data climbed to his feet, feeling exactly where Dare's hands had gripped him. "Let me try that."

The first time, he succeeded only in bringing the two of them to the mat in a tangle; Dare twisted and had him pinned. The mercenary let him up, saying, "Spread your feet to keep a solid base for your own balance."

On the second try, Data threw Dare, who got up, laughing. "You're a natural, Data. If you had to trade that finely honed machinery for flesh and blood, at least you got good resilient flesh and blood."

170

"Dr. Pulaski says I am in perfect health."

"I don't doubt it. But it will be up to you to stay that way. Let's see you do that a few more times, until it feels natural."

Twice more Data threw Dare, but on the third try Dare suddenly swerved and kicked his legs out from under him. Data found himself on the mat again— but Dare was down, too. Data bounced up and dived for him, only to get two feet in the chest and be tossed with such force that the safety field had to catch him before he hit the wall.

Nonetheless, Dare was saying, "Good instinct, Data. Always take advantage of a weak moment. Now let me show you the right way to do it."

The hour sped quickly. It seemed no matter what move Data learned, though, Dare always had a counter move. So would Worf, he was sure.

"Of course he will," Dare agreed. "That's his *job,* Data, but it isn't yours. It could be, but I know you science-minded types. You'll settle into a routine of minimum physical maintenance, stay reasonably healthy and fit, but you'll begrudge every minute of it."

"I do not begrudge this past hour," Data said. "Thank you, Dare. At least now, with practice, I have some hope of having Lieutenant Worf clear me. Perhaps after my duty shift—"

"No more today, Data," Dare told him. "You're going to feel that workout in a few hours. Hell, *I* may feel it. I don't often go a full hour like that anymore."

Data was hot and sweaty again. He hadn't anticipated that when he made the holodeck appointment; he barely had time to shower and change clothes again, appeasing his stomach with a simple chicken sandwich, apple, and milk. Even so, he was fascinated by how different the flavors were, and had to pull himself away from savoring the meal.

He had hardly left the turbolift, though, when Picard turned and said, "In my ready room, Mr. Data."

When they were in the captain's ready room with the door closed, Picard said, "Sit down, Data."

Data sat on the couch, his hands folded in his lap. The captain, however, remained standing, neither taking the armchair nor retreating behind his desk.

"You assigned Wesley Crusher to help your friends with their computer."

"Yes, sir. Wesley is not cleared for priority duty, and so does not come under your proscription."

Picard shook his head. "You did not break any regulations. I am concerned about the effect on the boy's progress."

"Practical application of his lessons can only enhance his education. As a matter of fact, he discovered a formula for computing geodesics that I intend to test myself. If it proves as useful as it appears, I will incorporate it into our own navigation program."

Picard folded his arms, then lifted one hand to rub his chin. Data recognized the gesture as indicating that the captain was debating as to whether to say something unpleasant.

A movement caught Data's eye. He looked down, to see his fingers twitching nervously. Deliberately, he forced them still.

The captain said, "Mr. Data, I have no doubts about your judgment concerning the boy's education. Under your tutelage he has made remarkable progress. What concerns me is his exposure to . . . certain personality types."

"I . . . beg your pardon, sir?"

Picard sighed. "I have no objection to Wesley's interaction with anyone who comes aboard the *Enterprise,* provided other crew members are present. However, he has come to the bridge today full of the most outrageous stories of what he appears to consider high adventure."

"Ah," said Data. "He was working with Sdan and Poet. They were quite impressed with Wesley, as well."

"That," said Picard, "is precisely what concerns me."

For a moment Data didn't understand. Then he realized, "You cannot fear Wesley might run off and become a mercenary?"

"Adin's people have seen his potential, they are flattering him, and they are filling his head with tales of intrigue and heroism. What do *you* think they have in mind?"

"Providing him with an enjoyable experience in exchange for the help he is giving them," Data replied. "Captain, I know these people. Even if Sdan or Poet thought it a good idea to tempt Wesley to join them, which I do not believe is the case, Darryl Adin would not hear of it."

Picard nodded. "Yes, I am sure you are right about that. I am more concerned about Wesley's feelings."

"We cannot protect him forever. He lives among people he respects and admires. If he even thinks of joining Dare's gang, they will quickly disabuse him of the idea. That may hurt him, but he has weathered

173

disappointments before. If we do not let him grow up, he will be severely handicapped when he enters Starfleet Academy."

Picard stared at him. "You've developed tremendous wisdom in one day as a human."

"I would have said the same thing as an android."

Picard nodded. "Of course you would. Perhaps I am being a bit . . . overprotective. Still," the captain said, turning to face the stars visible in the viewport beyond him, "if anything happens to Wesley, I will have to answer to Beverley Crusher."

"I would not envy you that task, Captain."

Picard turned and gave Data a puzzled frown. "Thank you, Mr. Data. Continue assigning Wesley's lessons as you have done thus far. You may return to your post. If you have time, run the navigation test programs; I want you requalified as rapidly as possible."

Requalified? Data had understood that his physical abilities and emotional health were under question, but not his ability to fulfill his day-to-day duties. He started to protest, but quickly changed his mind; after all, he *didn't* know what gaps in his active memory might have been left by his experience on Elysia. The fact that he had not yet found any did not mean there were none.

The requalification process was required of any officer who had been away from active duty on a starship for six months or more. Picard's applying it to someone coping with an entirely new physical structure was only common sense.

But how long would it take? And . . . what if the process should reveal deficiencies that could not be quickly remedied? If he had to return to the Academy for retraining, he could be assigned to another ship—but the *Enterprise* was where he had found a home, made true friends, and—now quite literally—come alive.

"Yes, sir," Data told the captain, and headed for his post, determined to requalify as rapidly as he could. If there was any way to prevent it, he had no intention of losing his home, *and* friends, aboard the *Enterprise*.

Chapter Nine

DATA WAS BACK ON DUTY at navigation. The regular rotation of crew members had brought Ensign Serena Gibson to the Ops position. As they were in routine flight, the standard rotation, designed to give all qualified personnel bridge experience, would continue until they came within range of the conflict. After that only experienced officers would man the bridge.

Gibson looked over at Data as he took over the helm from Wesley Crusher, who moved to the science post on the upper bridge. "If you have any questions," Data told her, "feel free to ask."

She dropped her eyes. "I'm sorry; I didn't mean to stare at you. What happened to you is all over the ship. I will save my questions until after duty shift." And she turned her full attention to the board in front of her.

Data frowned at his board. He had not meant to imply that she should ask personal questions on the bridge; in familiar surroundings he was, in fact, starting to forget for minutes at a time that anything out of the ordinary had happened to him.

Until he was forcefully reminded. He keyed his I.D. into the navigation console, and the helm log scrolled past in the blink of an eye. Hoping no one had noticed, he set it to human reading speed, and brought himself up to date.

They were on course for the Samdian Sector, just below maximum warp, all systems normal. The viewscreen showed only passing stars.

Data glanced over at Gibson. He did not know her well, could not recall ever having a conversation of any length with her. Did that mean they had never had one, or that his memory had human gaps in it? Surely he would not have forgotten such a lovely woman. Gibson was blond, and wore her hair softly loose on her shoulders. Starfleet uniforms left no one's figure to the imagination, and hers was lithe and graceful. She smelled of something cleanly sweet and—

"Am I doing something wrong, Mr. Data?" she asked when she noticed him studying her.

"Oh—no. Just keep on with what you're doing," he replied, turning back to his board in embarrassment. He would have to cultivate the human ability to shut out the overwhelming load of sensory information when he was on duty.

Determined not to be chased off the bridge when the *Enterprise* reached its destination, Data called up the helm testing program and began going through the exercises. It was programmed with random situations, designed to test the user in a variety of navigational situations. Of course the tests would instantly disappear from the board if sensors detected any reason for the helm console to be operative. Data did not have to worry about his frightening inability to divide his attention like an android; the ship was designed to compensate for human fallibility.

Data was becoming accustomed to the perceptible time lag in his performance. To his relief, when he called up his scores he found his reaction times well within Starfleet tolerances.

As he settled back in his chair, he became aware of someone behind him, and found Will Riker looking over his shoulder. "Good performance, Data," he said. "First try?"

"Yes, sir."

"Excellent, then. You're obviously qualified for helm duty. I will so note it in the ship's log."

"Thank you, sir. However, it is not navigation or Ops or science skills that concern me most," Data admitted, having gained confidence from the ease with which he had passed this first test.

"Worf?" Riker asked softly.

"I do not know if he will clear me for active duty."

"Want me to give you some practice before he tests you?" Riker asked.

"Thank you, Commander, but Darryl Adin is already doing that."

"From what I hear," said Riker, "he used to be damned good. Probably still is, since he's still alive. Get him to help you with target practice, too, Data. His record as Starfleet sharpshooting champion still stands."

For the first time Data experienced the feeling described in the human cliché, "his heart sank."

He had never given a thought to target practice, for as an android he had accessed the same telemetry that controlled the ship's phasers and photon torpedoes.

The only way he ever missed was if his target moved unexpectedly after he had fired.

Now all that was gone. It would be as if he had never had a phaser in his hand before.

Despite a suddenly dry mouth, Data managed to say, "Thank you, Commander. I will ask Dare to help me with that, too." But he could not help feeling that when the *Enterprise* came within range of the Samdian–Konor conflict, Data would find himself off the bridge, assigned to some assistant's position in science or engineering.

Toward the end of the duty shift, Captain Picard returned to the bridge and took the command chair to bring his log up to date. Then he said, "Mr. Data, the bridge log indicates that you have proved your competency at navigation. Trade assignments with Ensign Gibson next shift."

"Yes, sir."

From his position on the upper bridge, Worf said, "When will you be ready to qualify on physical conditioning, weapons, and unarmed combat?"

Data had to force his voice down into its natural register as he attempted to conceal his fears. "Those particular requirements are the ones most affected by my change in, uh, status. I respectfully request further time to practice before testing."

"Sensible," Worf replied, but his tone of voice made it an insult. "Inform me when you are prepared."

"I hope to be ready before we reach the Samdian Sector," Data told him.

"Data," Counselor Troi said gently, "I do not think you realize yet how much you are affected psychologically. You cannot be ready for away team duty so soon."

"But I—" Data broke off. He had never argued with his fellow officers before; if he started doing so now, they would surely think him emotionally unfit.

"I shall of course abide by your judgment, Counselor—but I feel compelled to add that—"

"Don't worry, Data," Troi interrupted, giving him an understanding smile. "We'll try to clear you for bridge duty as soon as possible. And don't try to control your emotions so harshly. After what has happened to you, it's normal for your feelings to be in warp drive. Suppressing them will only cause greater stress."

Damn her Betazoid empathy! She must have been eavesdropping on everything he had felt since he came on the bridge. Oh, no—that would include his lapse in attention to duty when he had been diverted by the sensory impressions from Ensign Gibson.

Data felt his face grow hot, and knew he was blushing again. Troi, however, said nothing more, just gave him her understanding smile.

Somehow, that only made him feel worse.

Their relief crew began appearing on the bridge just then, and Data was free to make a strategic retreat. Having sat still for several hours, he felt the aches Dare had promised from their workout this morning. *Those* aches would respond to the sonic shower; he did not know what would assuage the growing ache in his conscience.

But as Data entered the turbolift, Wesley Crusher hurried across the upper bridge to dart in beside him. "Data, can I change my lesson for tomorrow?"

"For what reason, Wesley?"

"Working on the gang's computers, I got an idea for improving our own navigation equations."

"I know. I plan to study your discovery."

"No—not the star charts," the boy protested. "That was yesterday. This is a new idea. Let me show you," he added as they walked along the corridor leading to both their quarters.

Wesley still occupied the senior officer suite he had shared with his mother, for the other officers now responsible for him wanted him to remain nearby.

Knowing Wesley's enthusiasm, Data realized that if he allowed the boy to start working at Data's computer he would have a guest for the next several hours. So he paused at the door to Wesley's quarters, saying, "Very well. Show me."

But although Wesley started the program on his computer he did not immediately sit down and start to work. "You hungry, Data?" he asked.

Data was startled when, before he could speak, his stomach answered with a distinct gurgle. Wesley laughed. "That sounds like a 'yes.' Any preferences?"

"I am open to suggestions."

The boy grinned. "Mom always let me have one dessert per day—but I'd rather have it as an afternoon snack when I can appreciate it than after a meal when I'm not hungry anymore."

Data assumed that the boy still followed his mother's regime, for he was obviously healthy, and growing like the proverbial weed. "That sounds like a good idea," he agreed.

Wesley stood before the food dispenser. "Let's see—do you like chocolate, Data?"

"I do not know."

"You're human now. You've *gotta* like chocolate.

What would be the best way to introduce you? I know . . . Computer, two hot fudge sundaes!"

When Data tasted the concoction Wesley handed him, he was astonished. Only the chocolate sauce was hot; it was ladled over frozen ice cream, creating an incredible blend of hot and cold, bitter and sweet, matched visually by the dark-brown chocolate against the almost-white ice cream. "A study in contrasts," Data observed in a pause between mouthfuls. "Wesley, I think you have just taught me something about human art."

Caught with his mouth full of ice cream, Wesley choked on his laughter, his eyes watering in the struggle to swallow. When he had succeeded, he laughed openly.

"Did I say something funny?" Data asked.

"Not really—except that you're the first adult to agree with me that chocolate ought to be considered an art form. I'm glad you like it, Data. Next time I'll introduce you to chocolate mousse."

It took nearly an hour for Data to study the equations Wesley was working on—something he could have done in minutes as an android. Leaning over the boy's shoulder, he felt the stiffness in his muscles again by the time he agreed that Wesley should continue that line of research. Then he headed for his own quarters, yearning even more for the relief of a sonic shower.

He had hardly reached his cabin, though, when Geordi was at the door. "Well?" his friend demanded with a grin. "How'd it go on the bridge? At least you didn't do anything requiring an emergency call to Engineering."

"I suppose it went well enough," Data said. "There

is just so *much,* Geordi—so much I never gave a thought to. Wesley Crusher may be a senior member of the bridge crew before I am again."

"Oh, come on now," Geordi said sympathetically. "It's not that hard to be human."

"Perhaps not if you were born to it," Data responded. "Geordi, how do you remember what you are doing, when you are constantly bombarded by sensory information? I can no longer store extraneous information for later recall—when I look for it, it is gone. Whenever something new engages my attention, I lose track of what I was doing before."

"Data, that just takes experience. In a few days you'll learn to sort out what's important and what isn't. If it's really significant, but you can't deal with it immediately, tell the computer to store it for later recall."

"Yes," Data agreed, "you are right. That is an excellent way to decide what is important: if it should be recorded, it is; if not, then I should ignore it. Thank you, Geordi." Then he added, "Do you have difficulty ignoring the . . . sensory impact of . . . women?"

Geordi laughed. "I should have known—you've lost your halo, Data. Welcome to the world of temptation. There's no reason to ignore the more delightful aspects of the opposite sex when you're not on duty. But you'll learn the time and place to indulge yourself. You're obviously a fast learner." Then he sobered. "May I make a suggestion that might smooth your path in that area?"

"Please do."

"I shouldn't have said indulge *yourself,* Data. Indulge the lady. Look, I'm hardly a great expert, but I know this much. Until you get a whole lot of experience, let her set the pace. Never assume; let her show you what *she* wants. I don't think women know they go around tempting men just by being female."

"Then my reactions are not abnormal," Data said with relief.

"Not at all. But don't act on them until the woman in question tells you she wants you to."

"I hardly have time to think about that at the moment," said Data. "That is why I find it disturbing that women are so . . . distracting. I shall consider it a normal human response, and ignore it until I have resolved my other concerns."

"And what concerns are those?" Geordi asked with a smile Data didn't quite know the meaning of.

"Requalifying for full duty status. The *Enterprise* is headed into a difficult situation, and her Second Officer is not fit either to go on an away team or to take command of the bridge."

"Well," Geordi said, "what have you accomplished so far?"

"Officially cleared on navigation. I am scheduled to test out on Ops tomorrow."

"A good start. What are you worried about, then? You'll be back to full duty status in a few days."

"Not if Lieutenant Worf and Counselor Troi have any say in the matter."

"Worf's not as tough as he pretends," Geordi reassured Data. "He'll growl a lot and talk about Klingon superiority, but if you show reasonable competency he'll pass you. Hell, I pass his checks, even though he takes great pleasure in wiping up the holodeck with me before he grudgingly clears me for continued duty. He doesn't expect of the regular crew what he demands of his security people."

That was true. Data realized with intense relief that he was already as good as Geordi at unarmed combat. That left weapons. Thank goodness ordinary crew members were not required to be expert with a variety of exotic weapons, as the security personnel were. If Data could conquer phasers, he would pass.

Which still left Counselor Troi.

"Data, don't push yourself so hard," Geordi said. "When you get checked out on everything else, you'll feel confident—and Troi will sense that. She'd be wrong to clear you for full duty before you've had time to adjust. Think about it: would you *want* the responsibility for leading an away team right now?"

"No," Data admitted. "Especially not after the fatal mistake I made last time."

"What do you mean?"

Data got up and walked to the mirror. "Look at me, Geordi. You can see it better than anyone else. My . . . self-indulgence destroyed the balance of the *Enterprise* senior crew. There is nothing I can provide as a human that you and Picard and Riker and Pulaski do not already have between you. As an android I had strength, speed, and instantaneous access to information. Now I provide nothing special at all."

"Nothing but your skills, your experience, and the indefinable things that make you *you*," Geordi said. "Data, you have no reason to feel guilty. Good God, man, do you think I would have given one second's thought to the value of my special vision to Starfleet if I'd been in your shoes? If I'd *earned* my fondest wish, the way you did? If you think anyone resents your taking your chance, forget it. Now come on—we're off duty. Let's go to Ten-Forward for a drink, and see who's around for some more cheerful conversation."

In the lounge, Data spotted Darryl Adin sitting alone at a table near the viewports, looking out at the stars. While Geordi ordered drinks, Data went over to him, saying, "Sdan will complete the computer repairs in a few hours, and you will be free to go."

Dare looked up at Data with a sardonic smile. "It doesn't matter any longer. A message from Brancherion reached us today: as we did not arrive in time, the people we were to train and organize were forced to face their enemies without us. And won. It turns out we were not needed after all."

"Have you another assignment?" Data asked.

"Oh, yes. There is always work for the Silver Paladin. Starfleet won't be very happy about this one, though." He pulled a small tricorder from his pocket and inserted a message clip. "Your ship's security delivered this to me, still scrambled to my code. But Captain Picard has the right to know."

It was a plea from the government of the Samdian Sector for the aid of the Silver Paladin in resisting the Konor. "They are seeking help from everyone who will listen. Will you go to their aid?"

"I hate lost causes," said Dare, "but I cannot resist a challenge. Problem is, I cannot determine which this is."

Just then Geordi joined them. He set a tall glass of light brown liquid in front of Data. "Arcturian cider. Guinan suggested you try it, Data. If you don't like it, there are plenty of other things to try."

"Thank you, Geordi. Dare—?"

"Oh, join us, Geordi. I'm not keeping this a secret. I'm sure Captain Picard will make a fair decision, after I've made mine."

"What decision?" Geordi asked.

"Whether to let us ride at the *Enterprise* maximum warp, and arrive when you do, or to drop us off as soon as our ships are repaired, leaving us to trail you into the Samdian Sector by several days." While Dare brought Geordi up to date, Data tasted the cider. It was tangy-sweet with a hint of some odd but pleasant flavor beneath the fruity essence.

He pulled his attention away from the drink when Dare asked, "What unclassified information can you two give me about this conflict?"

Data's automatic attempt to access still occurred when people asked him direct questions. There was nothing to access. "All I know is that the Konor are attacking the planet Dacket in the Samdian Sector, apparently without provocation."

"That information is available on the public news services," Dare replied dryly.

"I don't know any more than that, either," said Geordi.

Data had not lost his curiosity with his android body; he was seized with a compelling need to know. "Let us move to a computer terminal," he suggested.

Ten-Forward was intended for leisure pursuits; however, just across the corridor were smaller recreation lounges complete with terminals. They found an empty one, and Data called up information on the Samdian Sector.

It was a trade community of three planets colonized many centuries ago by a single humanoid race. To this day they had only subwarp space travel. They had a thriving culture and trade among their own planets, but did not seek or encourage interaction with the rest of the galaxy.

Before the Federation was even formed, the three

planets had joined forces to fight off an attempted Klingon takeover. After that, they had been pretty well left alone, as even when the rest of the galaxy developed faster than light travel they were technologically advanced enough to be difficult to conquer, and their planets offered nothing like gold or dilithium to tempt invaders. Cultures seeking conquest turned to easier pickings, and the Samdians continued to live in peaceful isolation.

There were a few pictures, a generation out of date. The few Samdian artifacts the Federation had were confiscated from Ferengi or Orion pirates, who were occasionally successful in attacking Samdian ships on the outskirts of the sector. Such raids were one-time affairs, however; repeated attempts were met by well-armed resistance. The three planets always supported one another.

Because of the Samdians' isolationism, which deprived them of the intercultural feedback that made the Federation so vigorous, surrounding cultures had outgrown them technologically. It might have been possible within the past century to conquer the Samdian Sector without major sacrifice of life and equipment—except that before anyone tried the Federation and the Klingons had made peace, and the Ferengi, Orions, and other aggressive cultures recognized that an attack on such a peaceful population was not worth the risk of having it interpreted as the first shot in a war of aggression.

Few cultures cared to test the combined strength of the Federation and the Klingon Empire. And so, possibly without knowing why, the Samdians continued to live in peace—until the appearance of the Konor.

According to the reports received from Dacket, approximately five Federation Standard Years ago the Konor began attacking the Samdian Sector ruthlessly, taking the planet Jokarn with brutal efficiency. Now they were moving on Dacket, with Gellesen obviously their next target.

The Konor did not take goods or raw materials. They took planets. Like the Klingons, they were all warriors, but unlike them they appeared to have no compunction about attacking unarmed opponents. They quickly and efficiently killed men, women, and children who opposed them, and enslaved the rest. Then they settled into the ready-made homes, took over whatever agriculture and industry there was, and acted as if the planet had always been theirs.

Dare shook his head. "This is far beyond my capacity to handle. Have the Federation ever met up with these Konor before?"

Data searched for references. "Nothing," he said.

"Data," said Geordi, "doesn't it seem odd that the Samdians haven't sent more information on their attackers?"

"Perhaps they do not know any more than this," Data reasoned.

"But where did the Konor come from?" asked Dare.

"Negative information," Data replied after another fruitless search. Then he frowned. "Computer—spherical scan of inhabited worlds within fifty light years of the Samdian Sector."

"Working."

"Give us a visual display."

Over the table before them, a holographic representation of that quadrant appeared, inhabited worlds indicated by dots of white light. Dare said, "Revolve it, Data."

He did, first on a vertical, then on a lateral axis. "This should not be possible," Data said, for there was no direction the Konor could have approached from in which they would not have passed dozens of inhabited worlds. "Computer, have any of the inhabited worlds on this display reported attacks by the Konor?"

"Negative."

"Then," said Dare, "they came specifically to attack the Samdians."

"A peaceful people who have not ventured outside their own Sector in centuries?" Data asked.

"Wait a moment," Geordi said. "You said *inhabited* worlds, Data. The Samdian planets are class-M. Computer, delete from the display all inhabited planets which are not class-M."

About a quarter of the lights winked out, but it was still clear that no matter what direction the Konor had come from they would have passed by numerous worlds as suitable to their needs as those in the Samdian Sector. "It is not logical," said Data. "Their actions suggest that they are seeking worlds to occupy, and yet they have ignored all these potential planets. Why?"

"Perhaps," said Geordi, "because they want exactly the cluster of similar worlds, near to one another, that the Samdians have."

"Or they're afraid to pick on their equals," Dare added. "Strategically, the Samdian Sector is in an excellent position. If the Samdians had had the sense to keep up technologically, and form alliances with their neighbors, they wouldn't be in this predicament.

What weapons do the Konor have? What kind of ships?"

"Negative information," the computer replied unhelpfully.

"Damned fools don't even know how to ask for help," Dare grumbled. "We need every piece of information they can give us to form a defense strategy."

"We?" questioned Geordi.

"We're all on the same side, I should think," said Dare. "I hope Captain Picard will let us continue to hitch a ride on the *Enterprise.* Although there probably won't be anything in it for us, come to think of it. This situation appears to be a clear case of Starfleet rendering aid to people under attack by an unprovoked aggressor."

"Sure looks that way," Geordi agreed. "Data, I think we should tell the captain what we've learned."

"May I join you?" asked Dare.

"Your input may prove beneficial," Data said. "Computer, where is Captain Picard?"

"Captain Picard is on the holodeck."

As a matter of fact, most of the senior officers were on the holodeck, which was configured as a tropical holiday resort. Picard was sitting with Kate Pulaski at one of several small tables on a sun deck overlooking a swimming pool. Will Riker was in the water, watching Serena Gibson do a rather shaky dive, then making suggestions to improve her form and encouraging her to try again.

Pulaski looked up as Data, Geordi, and Dare approached. "Oh, no," she said, "just when I persuade the captain to relax a little, here comes trouble."

"Not trouble," Geordi said. "Just information."

"Can't it wait?" asked the doctor. "In three days we will enter a situation that is certain to take everyone's concentration. Data, don't use the captain as a model in this. Use—" she glanced around, to see Riker laughing as Gibson splashed him, "—Commander Riker. He knows relaxing when he's off duty makes him more efficient when he's on."

"Doctor," said Picard, "how can I relax while wondering what information is so important as to cause two of my officers to track me down on the holodeck? Let's go inside, gentlemen."

The holodeck obediently gave them a well-equipped conference room, where Data showed the captain what they had learned about the Konor and the Samdians.

Picard studied the display, pursing his lips. "So the origins of the Konor are a mystery. We have no records of them or their ships. Curious."

"Intriguing," Data agreed.

Picard gave him one of his snorting smiles. "Nothing will change your love of a mystery, will it, Data?"

"I do not think so, sir. It is a trait we seem to share."

"Ye-es," drawled Picard. "Now, Mr. Adin—why are you here?"

Dare explained what had been in the two messages he had received. "Our ships are almost ready," he said. "They're the fastest private space vehicles available, but no match for a Galaxy-class starship. From what we know of the attack on the Samdians, I can't see how the Federation could refuse to render aid. Still, I must answer the call. If you put us off, we'll arrive several days after you, probably just in time to watch the last of the Konor shove off for wherever they came from. A waste of our time and power. If we may continue to ride with you, however—"

"Of course you may," Picard replied. "But don't assume that we are going to enter into a war."

"Oh, I haven't forgotten my lessons in Starfleet," Dare said. "To be forced to fight is to have lost the first battle. However, this war has begun without us. The only possible way you could stop it without entering in is if the Konor either retreat or agree to negotiate when the *Enterprise* shows up."

"We can hope for that," Picard agreed. "It appears we will be first on the scene, but the Klingon cruiser *Pagh* will arrive within eight days, and other ships are on the way. If the Konor are not true berserkers, as appears from their settling into domesticity once they have taken a planet, they may bow to superior force."

"If our force is superior," Data said.

Picard gave him a questioning look, and Data continued, "The Samdians have provided no visuals of Konor ships. Are they cloaked? Or are they so many and so powerful that the Samdians fear even the Federation might not be willing to send the ships and personnel necessary to overcome them?"

"Find out, Mr. Data. Search for clues to Konor origins. Get me something Troi and her psych team can work on, or something I can hand over to Thralen in Sociology. We need some idea of what the Konor care about besides killing. I'm tired of dealing with shadows."

"Yes, sir," Data said, and got up to leave.

He was at the door when Picard suddenly said, "Data!"

He turned. "Yes, sir?"

"Not now, dammit. I'm sorry—I forget you are not a machine anymore, and apparently you also forget it."

"I am frequently reminded, sir."

"Yes, well, you came off duty and jumped right into a computer search for the information you've just given me. Now I want you to relax for a few hours, get a night's sleep, and start fresh in the morning. Meanwhile why don't you join us here? Take a swim."

Oh, no—another Starfleet requirement. "I cannot swim, sir."

"Well, here's a perfect opportunity to learn. Geordi?"

"Come on, Data," his friend urged. "No time like the present."

They did not have to leave the holodeck to change into bathing trunks; they were conveniently available in the changing rooms beside the pool.

By this time Riker and Gibson were lying on lounges beside the pool, both apparently asleep. Geordi dived in cleanly, his VISOR as well insulated against moisture as Data's android workings had been.

Data hesitated at the edge, feeling oddly nervous. That did not make sense. He would have been perfectly safe in this pool as an android; had he fallen into the deep end, he could simply have walked the bottom to the shallows. Now he was light enough to float, so where was the problem?

"Come on in, Data!" Geordi urged, and Data sat down on the edge, letting his feet down into the water. It felt cold.

Steeling himself, he slid all the way in, and stood shivering in the chest-deep water.

Geordi swam over, and stood up beside him with a frown. "You're really scared, Data. Why?"

"I—I do not know. Human instinct?"

"No—fear of water is a learned response in humans. Babies learn to swim without a second thought. What happened to you the last time you were in this much water?"

"It was on Elysia. I was already severely damaged, and the water got through my insulation and shorted me out."

"Of course—no wonder you're scared! But think a moment. It can't short you out anymore, can it?" Geordi asked reasonably.

"No. Now all it can do is drown me."

Geordi laughed. "Not on the holodeck. The water would simply disappear if anyone started to drown. This is the safest place in the world to learn. First you put your face under and hold your breath, then you learn to float—and after that, the rest is easy."

Easy for Geordi, perhaps. Data felt hideously awkward as he doggedly imitated what Geordi demonstrated. He knew perfectly well that human bodies were less dense than water and would therefore float, yet when he lifted his feet from the safety of the bottom and stretched out in the water he fully expected to sink like a stone.

He didn't.

The feeling turned from astonishment to exhilaration as the water cradled his body. It was another of those unexpectedly delightful sensations, being suspended weightlessly, rocked gently by the movement of the water—

Until Geordi moved abruptly, and the water splashed into Data's face.

He collapsed, went under, and came up snorting and coughing. Geordi was laughing at him. Data splashed him in return, and his friend retreated into the deep end of the pool. "Point your hands ahead and kick with your feet," he instructed, floating on his back and moving effortlessly with the occasional flip of a hand or foot.

Having proved to himself that he was not going to drown, Data began trying to swim. Before long he was able to propel himself from one side of the pool to the other without putting his feet down. Once he learned the simple expedient of keeping his mouth shut and breathing out through his nose when his face was under, he stopped choking and made some progress.

Suddenly the water churned with activity. Data surfaced to see three new people in the pool: Poet, Aurora, and Pris Shenkley. Apparently Dare's gang had been invited to join the party. Dare was still up on the deck, talking amiably with Picard and Pulaski.

Pris swam over to Data. "Dare said you were learning to swim. It looks to me as if you don't need much teaching." She sounded disappointed.

"I still have a great deal to learn," he replied. "I must be able to swim six lengths of the pool to fulfill Starfleet requirements."

"You mean they're making you pass *all* your tests over again?" she asked.

"It is necessary. If they did not, I could be left unfit for duty in some undiscovered way. On an away team assignment, or even on the bridge, such a flaw could prove fatal, to me or to a fellow crew member."

"You're right, of course," she agreed. "You don't seem to be having much trouble adjusting."

"In many ways the physical adjustments are easier

than the mental ones," he told her. "The Elysians gave me a body in perfect health. Dare says I will probably not keep it in the peak of condition, and he is probably right. I'm not security; I will not want to devote more than a minimum time to exercise. There is so much to do, and humans are robbed of almost a third of their time by the requirement of sleep."

She laughed. "But sleep is one of life's pleasures."

"It is? I don't even remember it, only the moment of panic when I woke up this morning thinking someone had turned me off."

"You'll see," she said. "May I show you some strokes?"

Data suddenly remembered Geordi, but his friend had made a strategic retreat and was now sitting on one of the lounges at the edge of the pool, talking to Riker. So Data accepted Pris's offer. She taught him only one stroke, something called a crawl even though it was one of the most efficient swimming strokes humans could use. After a great deal of splashing and sinking, he finally got his arms, legs, and head working together, and he and Pris swam side by side for a time.

"I think I'm shriveled up enough," Pris announced.

For a moment Data didn't understand, then saw how his own skin had wrinkled up from the exposure to the water. It began to smooth out again the moment they got out of the pool.

The sonics in the changing rooms dried them instantly. Pris emerged in a soft blue dress the color of her eyes, her hair a halo of blond curls. Data's hair was also free of anything to tame it, for he had not brought any such thing with him. Neither had Riker, he noticed; apparently after swimming it was acceptable to be rather disheveled, for although the first officer had changed back into his uniform and was now up on the deck with the captain, his hair fell in a fringe over his forehead.

"Would you like to have dinner here?" Data suggested to Pris. Tempting food smells floated in the air, and after the exercise he was quite hungry. The deck above the pool had been transformed into an outdoor restaurant through the magic of the holodeck.

Data allowed Pris to suggest the menu, and discovered that he liked roast beef and baked potato, that his palate seemed neutral toward carrots, and he did not care at all for the taste of either mustard or horseradish. More "acquired tastes," it seemed. His salad, though, was the first thing that tasted as it always had—the raw greens had little flavor, while the texture felt the same to a human as to an android.

As they ate, Data found himself able to hold a conversation at the same time, as well as maintain a free-floating awareness of Pris as a beautiful and desirable woman. He remembered when they had first met on Treva, how intrigued Pris had been with him. He recalled accessing his flirtation files for a pleasant interlude that had led nowhere.

Tonight, he discovered, he was flirting without the aid of data banks, and enjoying it.

Until Tasha crossed his mind. If he had been human then, he would have responded to her in this strange new way. Or if Tasha were still alive—

She would be over there with Dare, he realized, taking the opportunity to be with the man she had loved since the day he rescued her from the hellhole of her home planet. In fact, by this time they would probably have gone off to be alone together.

"Data?" Pris questioned. "Where did you go?"

"I am sorry," he replied, his pleasant mood broken. "Please forgive me, Pris. I am still learning to be human, and sometimes I don't do a very good job of it."

She smiled. "I think you're charming. You just have to learn how to relax when you're off duty."

Accepting her rationale, he said, "I am tired, something I do not yet know how to cope with."

"Try getting some sleep," she suggested, apparently not at all perturbed. "There's always tomorrow, Data —several tomorrows for you and me to get to know one another better, you know. Captain Picard has agreed to let us ride along to Dacket."

"Yes, I know," he said. "Then you will excuse me?"

"Certainly," she replied. "I'll see you tomorrow."

"I will look forward to it," Data replied, honesty compelling him to admit to himself that he spoke the truth, even though some confused emotion suggested it was wrong to be attracted to Pris.

Logically, he did not know why it should seem wrong, but many aspects of human emotion had always been a mystery to him. Perhaps it would be best to avoid women for the time being, at least until he had completed his requalification.

He returned to his quarters, but although he was physically tired after the long and active day, he did not feel ready to sleep.

Something led him to the shelves behind his computer console, where he displayed those objects that had somehow acquired importance to him. He picked up the crystal hologram base and set it on his desk, hesitated, then turned it on. The image of Tasha stood before him.

Dark emotions churned within him, more intense

than any he had known as an android when Dare had reentered Tasha's life; his sorrow at her death; his guilt when he had revealed the secret Tasha had asked him to keep, in order to preserve his own life. Captain Picard had said Tasha would understand, and Data was sure he was right—yet he still felt as if he had betrayed her trust.

Someone triggered Data's door signal. Without thinking, he called, "Come."

The doors slid open. Someone walked across the room toward him, and halted abruptly.

Data looked up, to find Darryl Adin staring at the figure of Tasha, his expression a painful mixture of surprise and sorrow. Then his eyes narrowed. "What are you doing with Tasha's image, Data?"

"We were . . . friends," Data replied hesitantly, but his voice betrayed him.

Dare's gaze moved upward from the holographic figure to Data's face.

"Oh, my God," he said in a voice devoid of inflection. "You were in love with her."

Chapter Ten

DATA SAT FROZEN, unable to confirm or deny what Dare had said. He didn't *know* if he had loved Tasha, knew no more now what love was than he had known as an android.

He saw a flicker of raw anger deep in the mercenary's eyes, and prepared to be thrown across the room.

But it didn't happen. Instead, he watched as Dare's anger faded and was replaced by sadness.

"I'm sorry, Data," Dare said, his voice rough-edged. "Dammit, I knew you were capable of friendship, loyalty, sympathy—I should have realized it when you brought me Tasha's farewell: you understood what I was going through because you suffered the same loss."

"We were never—" Data began. But Dare did not deserve a lie. "You were the one Tasha loved," he said truthfully.

Dare came to Data's side of the desk, looking at the image of Tasha. He said nothing for a few moments, then reached out and turned off the display. Without looking at Data, he said, voice tightly controlled, "If Tasha were still alive, you and I would be rivals. Especially now."

"I told you—" Data tried to reassure him, but Dare interrupted him.

"It's ironic: because the woman we both loved is dead, instead of rivals we are closer friends. I should have realized it when you said you needed my companionship as much as I did yours when you brought me her farewell."

Data breathed a sigh of intense relief. "I am glad you see it that way."

"As you have always done," said Dare, giving Data his rare sincere smile. "I wonder—will you be able to remain so selfless as a human? You risked your life to clear me of treason and murder. No one would have known the difference if you had done nothing, and I would have been out of Tasha's life again, for good."

"Had I been human, I could not have done it," Data pointed out. "Only a positronic brain could interface with a starbase computer and access deleted and altered files." He got up, leading the way to the comfortable chairs at the back of the room, deliberately turning his thoughts away from what his transformation had cost Starfleet. "What did you want to see me about, Dare?"

"Captain Picard has invited me to act as advisor in the Samdian situation. He told me to work with you." The mercenary smiled again, this time in his usual sardonic way. "I take it that's a polite way of keeping me aboard the *Enterprise?*"

"I'm afraid so," Data replied. "I will be confined to

the ship for some time. But you are a free man, Dare. You can always take your ships and leave."

"You're right, of course. Actually, this puts me in an enviable position: *Enterprise* computers and scanners will provide the most accurate information, we'll arrive at Dacket in the shortest possible time, and if for some reason the Federation should refuse them aid, we'll be right there to offer ours."

"I don't think the Federation will refuse," Data said. "However, your experience may prove invaluable if we are forced to fight. Which reminds me, may I presume on our friendship for further lessons? Commander Riker tells me your accuracy with a phaser still stands as a Starfleet record."

"Does it? After all these years?" He was obviously pleased. "All right, Data, I'll help you with that, too. It would probably be a good idea to alternate days of practice at weapons and unarmed combat."

They made an appointment for the next morning, and Dare got up to leave. He paused, glancing toward the crystal holograph base still on Data's desk, then turned back. "Data," he said, "you know it is no betrayal of Tasha's memory to interact with other women, perhaps eventually find someone . . . special."

"As you have done?" It was out before Data realized what he was saying.

But Dare's mouth only quirked up in a one-sided smile. "Probably," he replied, and Data understood the veiled admission that he had little success following his own advice.

Dare continued, "Pris likes you, Data. She wouldn't expect commitment from a Starfleet officer, but you seem to enjoy one another's company."

"I enjoy hers," Data admitted.

"And you've met twice already within the past year. The galaxy is not so large as the planet-bound tend to think." Dare paused. "When you left the holodeck so abruptly, I thought you might have feared I would object—not that any of my people would allow me to influence their personal affairs. But when I found you . . ." He shrugged. "Enough. You and Pris are both adults. There is a great deal to be said for an . . . intimate friendship."

The next morning Data awoke disoriented again, but this time without panic. He knew that he had dreamed . . . and yet, peculiarly, he could not recall *what* he had dreamed. He thought of consulting Counselor Troi, but instead called up information on human dreaming from the ship's computers and was quickly reassured that his was a perfectly normal experience. That made him smile. He *would* tell Troi; it was evidence that his psychological state was settling into a human norm.

But he had work to do. He dressed, called up breakfast, and settled at the computer.

Three hours later he logged off in frustration, when the computer reminded him of his appointment with Dare on the phaser range.

There was nothing in Starfleet records that he could connect with the Konor. If the Samdians did not insist that they were attacking their planets, there would be no reason to believe they existed.

On the phaser range, Dare started Data with a fixed target. "Loose grip," he instructed, positioning Data's fingers around the weapon. "Your thumb points at the target. Most people push down with the thumb, which jerks the hand and spoils the aim. The secret is to hold the thumb steady and squeeze with the fingers. Try it."

Data concentrated, aimed—and missed the target by a meter. Then by half a meter in the opposite direction. "Hold it loosely," Dare kept telling him, and "squeeze—gently, gently!" but Data could not seem to follow the instructions. He eventually began hitting the target, but the *Ploink! Poot! Ping! Thud!* told him even before the computer confirmed it that his shots were all over it with no consistent pattern. Holding the bursts too long, in order to drag them onto target, he finally exhausted the charge.

"Damn," he said, transferring the phaser to his left hand and wiping his cramped and sweating right hand on his uniform. If he had gripped the weapon that hard with android strength, he would have crushed it.

Dare stood back, watching him, saying nothing. For some reason it seemed like heavy criticism to Data, and in frustrated anger he threw the phaser at Dare, demanding, "You're the expert. *Show* me!"

It was the small, light hand phaser; although it hit Dare dead center in the chest, it would not even cause a bruise. The mercenary caught it as it bounced off him, stared down at it for a moment, then at Data—and burst out laughing.

"It's not funny!" Data exploded. "My career in Starfleet is at stake."

"No—no," Dare gasped. "I'm laughing at my own stupidity, Data. I watched you eating last night and should have realized it then, but I didn't see it until you chucked that weapon at me. I put the phaser in your right hand when we started. I should have realized: you're left-handed!"

Data had been aware that humans favored one hand over the other, the majority of them the right, but as an android he had of course been ambidextrous. He looked down at his hands, recalled eating, shaving, brushing his hair, cleaning his teeth . . . Dare was correct. He instinctively used implements with his left hand. "Let me try again," he said, reaching for the phaser with his left hand this time.

As Data put the exhausted phaser back in its charger and took a fresh one, Dare said, "Wait a minute, Data. I want you to try something."

"What?"

"Pretend that fiasco didn't happen. It was my fault, not yours. Relax for a moment, take some deep breaths. Let the tension drain away."

Data tried to do as he'd been instructed, relaxing his muscles.

"Good," Dare said. "Now, forget that you're human."

"What do you mean?"

"Nothing has happened to change your shooting skill. You've always been dead-on with any weapon, the way you hit me dead-on when you threw without thinking just now. So don't think. Use the same instincts you've used all your life. Go!"

Data fired, not consciously aiming. *Ping! Ping! Ping! Ping! Ping! Ping!* Burst after burst hit dead center of the target.

He stopped shooting, stared, looked over at the computer results. They confirmed it.

He tried aiming as he had earlier, and although he

did better than he had with his right hand, he scattered shots over much of the target.

"Data—" Dare began.

"An experiment," he replied. "That is what happens when I try to aim. But if I let my automatics function—" He resumed firing—and again scored a perfect round.

Dare increased the distance, and said, "Do it again."

Ping! Ping! Ping! Ping! Ping! Ping!

Dare clapped him on the back. "I think you've got it!"

Data wondered, "How could that possibly carry over? I don't *have* automatics anymore."

"Of course you do: they're called reflexes. Don't question it," Dare warned him. "Just use it. Let's try moving targets."

As with the fixed target, Data proved as good as ever, as long as he simply forgot that anything was different from the last time he had used a phaser. Dare drew one also, and they practiced back-to-back security maneuvers, letting the computer keep score. Together, they drove it straight up to the limit of human reaction time, never missing a target they aimed at and only beginning to miss tracking some when the machine went into lightning barrage, sending targets at a rate even the fastest human reflexes could not match.

When they were forced to give up and end the program, Data called up their score—and found they had surpassed the *Enterprise* record.

Dare looked up from the screen with a wolfish grin. "Data, can you delete that record?"

"I *can*," Data replied, "but I *will* not. It is part of the ship's log."

"Of course," Dare said. "Well, then, we'll have to move quickly, before Lieutenant Worf routinely reviews phaser range scores."

"What are you planning, Dare?" Data asked suspiciously.

"Just a little wager. Computer: give me Security Chief Worf's phaser scores."

"You are not cleared for that information," the computer reminded him.

"Give it to *me*," Data said.

Dare studied the scores and gave a low whistle. "He's *good!* It will be a close contest. Hmm. You're never going to match a Klingon in unarmed combat skills—that's not an insult, as neither am I—so here's how we'll set it up—"

After one last session with Dare, Data informed Worf that he was ready to test for requalification on security skills. He had requalified at Ops on his last duty shift; security clearance would put him back on the senior bridge crew if Counselor Troi approved it. Data was feeling much more confident by now, and was certain she would fulfill her earlier promise.

Geordi was on the bridge, making some adjustments at his engineering station. The long journey at a steady warp seven allowed minute relativistic distortions to be detected.

When Data approached Worf with his proposal, Geordi looked up. "Are you sure you're ready, Data?"

"As ready as I'll ever be, probably," he replied. "Don't you think I can do it, Geordi?"

Geordi's VISOR made the exact meaning of his frown uncertain, but he said, "Sure, Data. You can do anything you set your mind to."

Worf looked down at Data from his imposing height. "After only three days' practice, you think you are ready to qualify at unarmed combat?"

"Both unarmed combat and phaser accuracy," Data replied confidently. "Darryl Adin has been helping me. He says I am capable of qualifying at the required Starfleet level. After all, I am not seeking a post in Security."

"So Mr. Adin thinks you're ready," Worf growled skeptically. "We shall see. 1600 hours on the holodeck."

As Data headed back toward Ops, Counselor Troi said, "I sense that you are completely confident, Data. Is it possible that you are *over*confident?"

"I do not think so, Counselor," Data replied. "Would you care to wager that I cannot do it?"

"I'll take that bet, Deanna," said Commander Riker. "I don't think Adin would encourage Data to attempt to qualify if he wasn't ready."

"Men!" Troi said, exasperated. "You have to make a game of everything. Data, why did you ever allow this man to teach you to play poker?"

"It was a challenge," Data replied. "But the current issue is not poker. Will you wager, Counselor?"

"I don't, usually," she replied. "However, just to temper your egos—"

There were very few, though, who bet against Data, as the wager was simply on his qualification. Everyone knew Worf's growl was worse than his bite when it came to non-Security personnel. Because he was judging, Worf did not bet. Everything was going exactly as Dare had told Data to expect.

The news spread, and by 1600 hours so many people had bets on the contest, and therefore wanted to see it, that the holodeck could not hold them all. As the odds were grossly in Data's favor, no one stood to win much; Data was sure curiosity about how he was handling being human was at the heart of their interest. Still, interactive ship's communications were hooked in, so that bets could be placed at each step in the qualification process.

Dare and his gang had wangled their way onto the holodeck. Riker, Pulaski, and Geordi were also there, as was the ship's counselor, even though she protested that she needed to gauge Data's emotions during the test, and had no interest in encouraging gambling. If the captain was watching the event, it was from the privacy of his quarters.

The mats and safety field were in place. Data felt a moment's trepidation as he faced Worf. But he didn't have to beat him, Data reminded himself; he only had to demonstrate the required skills. If he performed them properly, Worf would allow the takedowns.

Worf began with the simple standard attack basic to all such lessons. On Dare's advice, Data used the unorthodox maneuver of stepping aside. Worf wasn't expecting it—and to the Klingon's annoyance, his stumbling two steps beyond his smaller opponent drew a laugh.

Worf turned and lunged again—and for a moment Data feared he might be annoyed enough to skip to a degree of difficulty that Data couldn't cope with. But no, Worf would never betray his sense of honor. When

Data executed the proper turn and tossed the Klingon over his hip, Worf went down gracefully—to a round of applause. Data hoped their chief of security understood that it was more for his sportsmanship than for the minor skill Data had demonstrated.

The next skill Dare had had Data practice with the holodeck warrior projection, for the mercenary was not large enough himself to pick Data up as Worf could, and throw him. When an opponent had that kind of size and strength, it was best to let him toss one out of reach, then come back with speed and flexibility moves in an attempt to exhaust him.

So Data did not struggle when Worf grabbed him, but spent his effort on landing without injury, to bounce up and come at the Klingon from behind.

By this time, the spectators were making new bets. "Fifty that Data takes Worf down twice more!"

"I'll take that!"

"Twenty-five that Worf can pin Data."

"Naw—he's too fast. Look at 'im!"

But Data could not listen to the crowd. Dare had warned him, *Your only concern is to qualify. Do the very best you can, and don't let anything distract you.*

As a result, he performed the required moves adequately if not expertly, and as a good instructor Worf allowed himself to be bested when Data demonstrated the correct technique.

As the match continued, Data heard the bets on his ability increasing, and didn't understand why. Surely these people knew he was nearing the limits of his skills. To his amazement, he heard Pris wager, "One hundred that Data pins Worf!"

That, anyone ought to know, was impossible. A

man of Data's size might knock a larger skilled opponent off his feet—but never keep him there! In a genuine fight, he would try to exhaust or befuddle such a man, and then either escape, find a weapon, or simply survive until help arrived.

None of those options was available in a test situation, so it was not long before the tables turned. The next time Data attempted to use Worf's own weight against him, the Klingon grabbed Data's wrist and pulled him over, twisted, and kicked the smaller man into the safety field with such force that had he connected with the wall he would have been a mass of broken bones.

Even with the safety field, it knocked the breath from him, and before he could recover Worf had him again. Data struggled gamely, but all his moves were elementary; Worf countered easily, and in seconds he was pinned helplessly beneath the Klingon.

There were moans from those who had lost their foolish bets, but Data's attention was on Worf, who carefully removed himself without hurting Data, then offered him a hand up. "You qualify," he said, no hint of a grudge in his voice. "If you learned that well in three days, I'd like to see what you could do with advanced training."

Worf was not even breathing heavily. Data was panting, dripping sweat, his heart pounding. Still he managed a smile. "Thank you, Mr. Worf." He paused to gulp down more air before he could continue, "However, I do not wish to transfer to Security."

Worf glared. "I didn't say you were *that* good."

Their audience laughed, and people who had won sensible bets came up to congratulate Data. He was surprised to see Dare and his gang paying off quite a number of crew members. Dare, of all people, should have known his limitations.

Before moving on to the next test Worf and Data took time to rest and drink some water, then Dr. Pulaski ran her scanner over them. Worf, to no one's surprise, showed no effects at all. "You've got a few bruises and strains," the doctor told Data, "but nothing serious. So you won't stiffen up, go take a sonic shower before you move on to the phaser range."

When some of the audience protested the delay, Pulaski said, "You want Data to have his best chance, don't you? Give him ten minutes to get his breath back, then."

Data was glad of the break. The holodeck provided sonic showers on request, of course, as so many people took exercise there. The shower cleansed both Data and his clothing, and the massage effect relieved the aches Worf had caused him. By the time he reached the phaser range, his audience was waiting eagerly.

Before Worf could set up the target, Data turned to the Klingon as Dare had instructed, and asked, "Why don't we make this a contest, Mr. Worf?"

"Data!" Counselor Troi exclaimed in a tone of surprised warning.

"What did you read?" Pulaski demanded.

"Data believes he can outshoot Worf," Troi replied. "He is actually supremely confident."

"You don't think he can?" Dare asked.

"How could he? You have proved an excellent teacher, Mr. Adin. I'm sure you have made Data competent, or you would not allow him to test, but to bring him up to the level of a Starfleet Security Chief in three days? No, I do not think so."

"I'll wager that he can win over Worf," Dare challenged. "Will you take the bet, Counselor?"

"If she won't, I will," Worf said. "I am not judging this contest; the computer is."

In moments wagers were flying. Dare and his gang bet on Data, but most of the *Enterprise* crew bet on Worf. Except for Dr. Pulaski, who asked, "Data, aren't you going to wager?"

He hadn't thought of it. But he recalled, "Worf says one should always bet on a sure thing. Yes, one hundred that I will win."

"If you are that certain, then I will also bet on you," said Pulaski. "One hundred."

It was not a suspenseless contest; Worf was the *Enterprise* champion, and could not miss a fixed target. After six rounds at various distances, with both contestants making perfect scores, it began to get boring. They went on to moving targets. By this time people were marveling at Data's surprising ability, but there were no complaints, as it was an even match.

It took more than half an hour, with targets appearing at faster and faster speeds. Would they reach beyond the range of human reflex before there was finally a miss? What about Klingon reflexes?

At the thought, Data felt his hand spasm, and almost missed a shot. Desperately, he sought to retain the state of mind in which his hand automatically tracked the targets without his conscious volition.

Then the "sky" was filled with flying missiles, and there was no hope of hitting them all. Again Data lost himself, firing rapidly in as efficient a pattern as he could see. All around them "explosions" indicated missiles that had gotten past them, but he closed out the noise and flashes and kept firing . . . firing—

The sky went black.

Data dropped his shaking hand to his side, almost losing his grip on the phaser.

The audience remained hushed, waiting, until the computer's voice announced, "Lightning barrage scores: Lieutenant Commander Data, 37; Lieutenant Worf, 36."

A cheer went up from the assembled audience.

Worf turned to Data. "Congratulations," he said. "You pass." The Klingon then turned to Darryl Adin, saying, "Could you tell me, sir, how it is possible to so successfully transfer one's skills to one's students?"

"If I knew how to do that consistently," Dare replied, "I would know the secret of the universe. Data is something special."

"Indeed you are, you little hustler," Pulaski said softly, coming up next to Data.

"Hustler?" Only then did he realize the game Dare had played. He had understood that his mediocre performance in unarmed combat would encourage bets against him on the phaser range, but had not anticipated the gang's wagers on the impossible. Now he realized they had driven up the size of the later wagers.

"Don't play innocent with me," Pulaski was saying. "I can smell a hustle—but I'm not complaining, as I won a pretty penny on you." She shook her head. "If I hadn't just scanned you, I'd swear you'd turned back into an android. How'd you do it, Data?"

"That is exactly what I did, Doctor: Dare told me to

forget being human, and shoot as I had all my life. I don't know how it works without the telemetry, but it does."

"And how did you get Deanna to play along in this little game?"

"I didn't, and I don't think Dare could have. Her reaction to my confidence was . . . fortuitous."

"It could as easily have blown the game," Pulaski said. "Your friend Mr. Adin is a master con man, Data. Be careful how you let him use you."

"He came very near to losing," Data replied. "In the lightning barrage, aim is less important than the pattern of attack."

"Only when the contestants are as good as you and Worf," she told him.

"So the score could have gone either way. In the end, I won by . . . luck."

Other people came up to congratulate Data; even many of his crewmates who had lost money wished him well as they paid up. He sensed no hard feelings; the match had been truly close. Dare might have "hustled" to increase the size of the bets, but he must have known that either of such evenly matched opponents could have won. He and his gang could have lost just as much as they had won.

Now that the test was over, Data found he was both hungry and tired—and learning to distinguish between different kinds of tiredness. He did not need to sleep; he needed a meal and some time sitting down, preferably in pleasant company.

That was easily arranged: Pris Shenkley left the knot of people still paying off bets, and came over to Data. "Congratulations. You did beautifully, Data. Do you have plans for this evening?"

"No—would you care to introduce me to more new foods?"

"Certainly. Where shall we go?"

Just then Counselor Troi came over to them. "Data, you have passed all objective tests to requalify you for bridge duty, and I have observed no extraordinary emotional instability. Your confidence was justified. I think you should resume all your duties now, except away team assignments."

"Thank you, Counselor."

"So even more congratulations are in order. Will you come to Ten-Forward for a drink to celebrate?"

"Certainly."

As they walked through the corridors, Pris asked, "Why shouldn't you go on away teams if you've passed all the tests?"

"Bridge duty is relatively predictable; away team duty is not. In only these few days, how can I know how this body will react in new situations? Furthermore, should any crew member on the bridge fail in his duty, he can be quickly replaced. That is not true of an away team member. Pris, I have no complaints; look at the progress I've made already."

He did not add that, aside from the android strength and information retrieval abilities he had lost, his job on away teams included the scientific skills in which he had majored at the Academy. Those he had not yet been retested for, as he had been concentrating on what was . . . humanly . . . possible in the brief time he had: achieving active bridge status.

"You're right, of course," Pris agreed. "Let's go celebrate your achievement."

The party in Ten-Forward was fun. Data tasted

champagne, and found that it tickled his nose as it had his nasal sensors as an android, but was not particularly appealing in taste. There were a good many toasts, though, and after a while he began to feel slightly . . . intoxicated. It was a pleasant feeling, so he just let it happen.

After a time, the party began to break up. Pris asked, "Are you hungry, Data?"

Yes, he still was, now that he thought about it. "Let's go get something to eat," he agreed, climbing to rather unsteady feet.

Out in the corridor, he realized he didn't know where they were going. Pris seemed to. He let her lead him, enjoying the pleasantly muzzy sensation of his head seeming to float just slightly above his body.

He was vaguely surprised when they reached his quarters. "You want to eat here?"

"You have a food dispenser, haven't you?"

"Oh, yes. Only the best for Starfleet officers."

"Excellent," she said, and while Data watched, bemused, she started ordering, not food, but a lace cloth for his worktable, settings of crystal and china, a rose in a bud vase, and more champagne. The bottle arrived chilled but sealed; Data got the wrappings and wire off, and laughed as he popped the cork and the champagne fizzed up.

Capturing the bubbling fluid in glasses, he and Pris drank another toast before she turned back to the food dispenser. "Let's have some oysters," she said.

"And quetzi ramekins," Data added.

Pris turned to stare at him with a surprised smile. "Marallel fowl with sennabar sauce."

"Aldebaran wine," he suggested.

Pris giggled. "I think the champagne will be enough. I don't want to get drunk, Data, just . . . friendly. Let's have some freshly baked bread—I love the variety you can order here on the *Enterprise*. Our food synthesizers are very good, but nothing compared to these."

They ate, talked of inconsequentials, and laughed a good deal more than Data had thought possible over things that were not to his knowledge funny. But he felt good, successful, even triumphant with his restoration to active duty. Everything smelled and tasted wonderful, and Pris was so lively, so beautiful—

After they had eaten, they moved to the couch with one last glass of champagne. Pris sat close to Data, and it seemed the most natural thing in the world to put his arm around her. In response, she snuggled up against him. It felt good. He breathed in the clean sweet scent of her hair, and beneath it the lovely aroma of woman.

Pheromones, something from his android past analyzed.

Shut up, Data told the analytic response. *I'm human and I'm off duty. I have a right to enjoy myself.*

For a while they continued to talk and sip champagne. Then Pris sat up, set the glasses aside, and came back into Data's arms in a position from which it was very easy to touch her lips with his. So he did.

He remembered Geordi's advice: *let the woman show you what she wants.* That was nothing new; as an android he had never initiated such a situation.

Then he didn't need advice from anyone as Pris got up and led him from his workroom toward the bedroom.

* * *

The next morning Data was wakened by his door signal. He started out of an unsettling dream, but its content disappeared the moment he came fully awake, leaving him with only the sense that it had been unpleasant indeed.

"Wha—? Who's there?" he asked, fumbling for his robe.

"It's Wesley. We have a lesson, remember?"

Data remembered—but how could it be so late?

Covering himself, he went into the outer room, saying, "Come in, Wesley." As the boy entered, he continued, "I am sorry. I seem to have . . . overslept."

Wesley stared first at Data's disheveled appearance, then past him at the worktable still covered with the lace tablecloth and place settings for two. "You had a *date* last night!" he said as if surprised. Then he blushed. "Well, why shouldn't you? I'm sorry, Data—I just never thought of you as . . . well, I'm growing up, too. I understand what it's like to notice girls. Sometimes it's hard to concentrate in my classes, when certain girls sit next to me."

"I know exactly what you mean," Data said, clearing the evidence of last night's carousal into the recycler. Now he understood why Pris had insisted on leaving several hours ago. Embarrassed as he was, it would have been far worse if Pris were still here.

Data put Wesley to work at the computer, reviewing the Samdian–Konor situation. That took long enough for Data to set his quarters to rights and prepare for the day.

When he returned to the computer, Wesley looked up. "It's all one giant dead end."

"Any ideas for getting out of it?" Data asked.

"I don't know. It isn't like an equation in quantum

mechanics. That I could solve. This is . . . trying to prove a negative, which is impossible."

Data frowned. "Who is trying to prove a negative?"

"The Konor. They've covered their trail so completely, it's as if they don't exist. Data, have you tried the starscope you gave me on this problem?"

"It cannot do anything the ship's computers cannot."

"I know. I figured out how it accesses the star maps. I meant, have you had the computer check the charts from the Samdian System outward to the limits of explored space? I don't see any record of it here."

"It's not feasible. Such a task would tie up the computer for—" He drew an utter blank.

It would be an impossible amount of time, but Data could not say if it were days or months. His mind could no longer grapple with such mathematical complexities.

"Computer," said Wesley, taking Data's lapse as a teacher's pause for student response, "how long would it take to examine star maps from the Samdian Sector outward in all directions to the limits of explored space?"

"Parameters of examination?" the computer asked.

"Locate class-M planets which—" He looked up at Data. "What do we look for? Evidence of wars or conquests? Movements of fleets of ships?"

"A trace of class-M planets yielded nothing. Beyond that, we do not *know* what to look for," Data explained. "That is why the computer cannot do it for us. Even if we knew what to ask it to trace, the star charts vary from as recent as our last update from Starfleet to more than a century old. If the Konor made their move out of a quadrant that has not been

221

mapped since they did so, there would be no evidence in our records."

Wesley sighed. "You're right, Data. I would have wasted time on an impossible task."

"So we must find a different approach," Data said. "You often find new approaches that people with more experience don't consider, Wesley. That's why I wanted you to see these studies."

"But this isn't what I'm good at, Data. If you want me to build or repair something, or invent a device, that I can do. This is more in your line: solving a mystery."

"Wesley, do you think your Starfleet duty will consist only of things you are good at?"

"No, sir," Wesley replied, chastened, and turned back to the screen. "Maybe I should try an opposite approach."

"In what way?"

"Look at the Samdian System itself. Try to see what those three planets have that the Konor want. Then we could check the star maps for planets that have the same thing, and see if they have ever been approached by the Konor."

"Good thinking, Wesley," agreed Data, and together they went to work.

At the end of two hours, although Wesley had had a thorough workout in the practical applications of set theory, they had been able to isolate nothing about Jokarn, Dacket, or Gellesen that was not common to a thousand other class-M planets. Wesley had to leave for history class, and Data went to Ten-Forward for a combination of breakfast and lunch before reporting to the bridge.

It was now only hours before they would reach

Dacket, and Data was no closer to solving the mystery of the Konor than when he had begun. Last night's triumph had ebbed away; he might be able to pass the minimum requirements for a bridge officer, but he was third in command of this vessel, not an ensign on first assignment. More was expected of him than minimum abilities.

He should not have overslept; he would have to learn to discipline himself, to resist temptations like last evening's. Pris was a beautiful woman, but . . . something nagged at the back of his mind, something he could not bring to his consciousness to be examined. Memories of Tasha? Or something else?

He didn't know; but deep inside him was a sadness, a yearning for something beyond his reach. Something he desperately needed, and yet couldn't even name.

Chapter Eleven

DATA HAD ANOTHER APPOINTMENT before his duty shift: Dr. Pulaski was recording his physical adjustment to humanity. "You're doing fine," she told him. "Your muscle tone has improved, but I don't suppose we can expect much more now that you've passed your security qualification."

"Probably not, Doctor," he agreed, remembering what Dare had said.

"Well, that's refreshing honesty," she said. "Hmm—despite the exercise, you've gained almost a kilo of weight. What have you been eating, Data?"

"Orange juice, alphabet soup, kosa juice, Secarian meat rolls, verne porridge, an apple, a chicken sandwich, milk—" He paused. Was that the day he had first tasted roast beef? "I am afraid I can no longer recall everything precisely."

"It doesn't matter—you're certainly getting enough variety! But cut back on the portions, especially if you're not going to keep up your present level of exercise. It's far better to avoid becoming overweight than to have to diet back from it. And continue the swimming lessons; swimming exercises the whole body, and you still have to pass that test before you can be cleared for away team duty."

The mention of swimming, though, brought up the image of Pris, and along with it the odd feeling that Data had somehow treated her unfairly. He could not "put his finger on," as the human expression had it, the reason for his sense of ingratitude.

Dr. Pulaski did another brain scan, and showed him the comparison with the first. "Some change," she said, "but you still think like an android." She shrugged. "Perhaps those thought patterns will never change completely. That also doesn't matter, Data, so long as you are able to function."

It crossed his mind to say that he was indeed functioning fully, but he didn't. The thought was not amusing today.

As Data was getting ready to leave, the doors opened to admit two ensigns with an antigrav trolley piled high with equipment. "Here are your new diagnostic consoles, Doctor."

"Now?" Pulaski objected. "I gave Ship's Supplies the specs weeks ago. So now, when we're hurling headlong into potential danger, when in the next thirty-six hours I could have this place full of casualties, *now* you decide to tear my sickbay apart to install new equipment?"

"We're just following orders, Ma'am," said one of the ensigns.

"Well, you just follow *these* orders," the doctor said acerbically. "March all that stuff right back to Supplies, and tell Lieutenant Carson in the future to do her job on time."

As the two ensigns struggled with the unwieldy

trolley, Pulaski continued, "And you also tell Carson that if I have any problems before this Konor situation is resolved, that could have been prevented if you had installed this equipment while we were in transit, I'll hold her personally responsible!"

In their eagerness to escape the doctor's scathing tongue, the two ensigns were working at cross-purposes. The Vulcan at one end had kept his head and was attempting to reverse the controls to remove the trolley without turning it. The human at the other end was attempting to do just that, his fingers hastily punching the control buttons to make the trolley rotate.

"No, Tom," said the Vulcan, "we don't have to turn it. Just reverse the controls."

"Reverse the—" repeated the very nervous human —and began hitting all the switches in turn.

"No!" exclaimed Data, who could see what the man was doing. The Vulcan's vision was obscured by the pile of equipment. "Not the inertia and friction—"

But it was too late. The forcefields which increased friction and reduced inertia to keep the components in place shifted to do exactly the opposite. The trolley was still moving; the Vulcan could not stop the rotation Tom had started.

And Tom, by reflex, did exactly the wrong thing when Data yelled at him: he hit the Emergency Stop.

With friction reduced and inertia increased, the components tumbled off the trolley and into the ship's Earth-normal gravity. A sharp-edged metal box on the very top pitched off, right toward Dr. Pulaski.

Data darted forward, caught the falling equipment —and was propelled backward off his feet as efficiently as if Worf had slammed into him.

But there was no safety field to catch him here.

Data fell, the equipment slamming down on top of him. It was sheer luck that the flat side struck him, rather than a corner or an edge, which might literally have cut him in half.

As it was, he had the breath knocked out of him. Then he felt a wave of unbearable pressure, which swiftly changed to pain as his already bruised ribs protested with renewed anguish.

Then Tom and the Vulcan ensign were lifting the weight off him as Pulaski warned, "Data, don't move!" A second later, she was bending over him with a scanner, white-faced and thin-lipped.

He couldn't have moved if he had tried. In his brief human life he had never known such pain! He struggled to draw air into his lungs.

Pulaski studied her readings and said, "Thank God," in a tone of relief. "Nothing's broken, Data, but you have four slightly cracked ribs and a badly bruised diaphragm and spleen." She turned to the two ensigns from Supplies. The human was pale and quaking, the Vulcan standing with hands folded behind his back, face impassive, the posture of intense emotional control.

"You two—get that junk out of here." Then she raised her voice. "Selar! Get in here and help me get a patient onto a treatment couch!"

Data gritted his teeth, helpless to stop the tears that leaked from his eyes or his gasps of pain as they moved him, but once Dr. Pulaski turned on the treatment field, his pain disappeared and he became able to think again.

The doctor adjusted the controls and studied the readouts. Finally she announced, "Dumb luck,

Data. You're far less hurt than you deserve for that stunt."

Despite the pain-relieving field, Data still could not pull a full breath into his lungs. "Is that—the thanks I get—for saving your life?" he managed to ask.

Pulaski shook her head. "Thank you," she said. "But you didn't have to risk injury to do it. I'll go tell the captain you'll be late for your duty shift. You think about how you *should* have handled that emergency."

By the time she returned, Data had no alternative solution. "I didn't realize—I would be hurt," he agreed. "But I could not—let the equipment hit you."

"You *are* still thinking like an android," said Pulaski. "No, not your thinking, your reflexes. Data, you are human now. If you can't think of *yourself* in those terms, suppose you had not been there. Suppose Geordi had been in your place. What would he have done?"

When it was put in that way, Data saw the answer instantly. "I should not have attempted to catch the equipment. I should have moved *you* out of its way."

She nodded. "It would have taken a flying tackle, I suppose. As an android you would never dare use such a move on a human; your impact would have injured me as surely as being hit by that machinery. But if a human knocked me aside, the most I would have suffered would have been a few bumps and bruises. No more than you got from your bout with Worf."

"I understand," Data said.

"Yes," the doctor said with a nod, "I know you do. But understanding isn't the problem. Breaking the habits and reflexes of a lifetime—*that's* the problem." She shook her head. "I don't know, Data. Your adjustment to being human may be more difficult

228

than any of us imagined." She studied the readouts again. "On the other hand, you weren't hurt as badly as you might have been, and you're healing nicely. They say the gods protect fools and children. In some ways you're a child, Data, only a few days old. We can hope that you will grow to develop proper human reflexes."

But Data wasn't listening. His mind had suddenly flashed back to Elysia's caverns, and Thelia saying, "The gods temper the wind to the shorn seja."

He wondered how she was, feeling an oddly pleasurable pang at the thought. Perhaps when he had the time, he would return to Elysia, and seek her out . . .

No. She had undoubtedly forgotten him by now, and was swept up in solving the problems of her land. He would never know what had become of her, and whether she found being rewarded by Elysia's gods as mixed a blessing as he did.

Data was back on the bridge, injuries healed, when the *Enterprise* came in range of Dacket's communications.

"Chairman Tichelon of the Samdian Planetary Council hailing you, sir," Worf announced.

"On-screen," Picard instructed.

Tichelon was a middle-aged Samdian, a lavender-skinned humanoid with bluish hair and beard, whose brightly colored flowing garments were distinctly at odds with his mood.

"This is Captain Picard of the U.S.S. *Enterprise*. We have come in response to your signal."

"Thank Providence! You must help us. The Konor have taken all the southern continent, and are moving toward the capital, killing any who try to stop them."

"Our sensors will soon verify that," Picard answered. "We have tried to contact the Konor, but either they do not receive our signals or they ignore them."

"They ignore ours, as well," Tichelon said. *"We have tried to negotiate, but they kill our emissaries. Captain —they will not even accept surrender! In the city of Eskatus, the Konor so far outnumbered our people that they laid down their weapons—and the Konor slaughtered them. Only a few escaped to tell us what happened—and is still happening as we speak! You must use your starship's weapons to destroy these aggressors!"*

"Let me investigate," Picard replied. "When we have seen these Konor for ourselves, we will decide what aid to offer."

"They will kill you if you go among them!" Tichelon warned. *"We are peaceful people, Captain Picard, but the Konor are an abomination upon the face of the galaxy. There is nothing to do but destroy them!"*

Picard shook his head. "First, we must seek a peaceful resolution of the problem. Have you any pictures of the Konor, their ships, their weapons?"

"Why . . . no. To approach closely enough to obtain pictures is to be killed."

"Captain—" Troi interrupted softly.

Picard cut the voice transmission. "What do you sense, Counselor?"

"Tichelon is telling the truth about the destruction, and the refusal of the Konor to respond to negotiation or surrender. He is truly terrified of them. However, his anxiety level peaked when you asked for pictures. I think it is true that they kill anyone who attempts to record them, and yet . . . I do not think it is true that there are no visuals."

"He did say some people escaped," Riker pointed out. "They've seen the Konor. If no recordings, there must be descriptions, drawings."

"Which Tichelon does not want us to see?" Picard walked forward toward the viewscreen, as was his habit when dealing with people he did not trust. Data wondered if he thought closer inspection would reveal details unobservable from the command chair.

"Open frequency." Picard told Tichelon, "We will reach orbit in one point three hours. We will contact you when we have investigated these Konor for ourselves. Picard out."

The captain turned to Data, who was back in his customary place at Ops. "Mr. Data, prepare for a detailed scan of the area of the planet the Konor have conquered."

"Yes, sir," Data replied, and moved to the science station.

"Mr. Worf," the captain continued, "full sensor scan of space around Dacket. I want to know about any vessels in orbit—even if they're cloaked."

"Aye, Captain."

Data made his preparations while listening to the talk going on about him—and suddenly realized that he had regained the ability to do two things at once, if one of them was as routine as setting up a sensor scan of a planetary surface. He smiled to himself. Dr. Pulaski was wrong: he *would* develop human reflexes. If only he could do it without further lessons as painful as the one this morning.

Worf was soon growling at his equipment and his

assistants, for sensors could detect no ships in orbit around Dacket. Eventually he said, "If there's a cloaked ship in orbit, it's using technology we don't know. But I'm sure there is no ship, Captain. I've even done a gravity scan. The power required to maintain a cloaking device for so long would be an unacceptable drain on a ship's power. Either the Konor arrived in ships that they landed on the planet, or a mother ship left them there and departed."

"Sensor scans will show any ships on the planet," Data said, and began providing orbit coordinates to put them directly over the southern section of the continent which the Konor were taking.

In the far south, the terrain was typical of an inhabited class-M planet: cities and farms, crops in the fields, electrical power in operation, numerous humanoid life-form readings.

"But something . . . is missing," said Data, unable to determine what it was.

"Ships, for one thing," Riker observed. "The only deep-space vessels grounded there are Samdian sublight trading ships. If the attacks began at the southern end of the continent, the Konor ships should have landed there. Your theory of a mother ship may be correct, Mr. Worf."

But Data still felt something was missing. As the scan continued northward, the cities were not in such good condition; many buildings lay in rubble, although roads were clear. Here, too, the farmland was being cultivated.

As they neared the edge of the territory the Konor had taken, though, the fields were uncared for and the cities lay devastated. Heavy equipment was clearing the worst of the destruction. It was as had been reported: The Konor defeated the populace, and then took their homes and lands.

The level of technology was quite high—powered vehicles sped through the air and along well-designed highways. There was no evidence of radiation, not surprising if the Konor were seeking planets to colonize.

But there was still something missing! Data was becoming thoroughly annoyed at what he now recognized as a "mental block," until the scan crossed over into the territory the Konor had not yet reached, and the missing element suddenly leaped into prominence on his screen.

"Communications!" he exclaimed.

"What was that, Mr. Data?" asked the captain.

Data swiveled his chair around. "Captain, throughout the lands held by the Konor I can detect no use of long-distance communication. No radio on any frequency, no wires carrying electronic messages, nothing."

"You can't coordinate a planetwide assault without communications," Riker said.

"I know, sir, but at least we now know why the Konor do not respond to our attempts to communicate with them: whatever means they use is so incompatible with ours that our sensors do not detect it. It is therefore reasonable to assume that they never received the messages sent by either the Samdians or the Federation. It is even possible that they misunderstood attempts to surrender."

"That is true," Worf said. "Tichelon said his people laid down their weapons. There is a Klingon form of challenge in which the challenger lays a weapon down and backs away, daring the one he challenges to reach for it. If the Konor could not understand the Samdians' words, they could misinterpret the gesture as a similar challenge."

"Thank you, gentlemen," said Picard. "Data, optimize those scans so we can get a good look at the Konor. If we watch them, perhaps we can determine how they communicate. If we can talk with them, there may be hope of ending this conflict."

Once again the captain called for the skills of Thralen, the Theskian sociologist, taking Riker, Data, Geordi, and Worf into his ready room to study the enhanced scans of the cities the Konor held.

"There are many ways of communicating besides the words and gestures we are accustomed to," Thralen said. "I take it we have eliminated sound on all frequencies?"

"Detectors find no sound-transmission equipment operating," Data assured him. "Samdian telecommunications devices are still in place, but inoperative. If the Konor use a visual code, such as heliograph or semaphore, our energy scans would not necessarily detect them."

"Visual symbols are the second most common means of communication among intelligent species," Thralen continued. "If we can see these people at their day-to-day activities, we will quickly see any evidence of a visual language. You remember studying the Verwar, Mr. Data."

"The . . . Verwar?" Data had no memory of that name.

"The classic example of visual language: they communicate by color change. They do not have eyes as we have, but visual sensors in many areas of their bodies so that their range is as complete as our range of hearing." His antennae swiveled to demonstrate.

Data, however, was staring at the tabletop in shock. He had majored in exobiology at the Academy, Thralen said casually that the Verwar were a "classic example," and yet Data had no memory of ever having heard of them! How could he perform efficiently at navigation and Ops, and then discover such a formidable memory gap in his own specialty?

Data dragged his attention back to the display Geordi was working on. Large pixels vaguely sketched what might be a street scene in a city, but there were no details until Geordi carefully focused it. The pixels divided and subdivided until the image resolved into a clear picture, and began to move.

It was indeed a street in a neat, clean city. People were walking and riding in vehicles—people who must be the Konor. After all the secrecy, they were certainly getting an excellent view of them now: except for sandals to protect their feet from the heat of the pavement, the Konor wore nothing at all.

Data did not know what any of them had expected —some kind of brutal monsters, surely. Instead, they saw humanoids with serene faces: men, women, and children going about their business like the most peaceful people in the galaxy. There were no soldiers in evidence, no weapons, and no rushing or pushing among the people moving efficiently but politely across the screen.

The Konor looked superficially like the Samdians, except that their skins were golden-green, their hair lavender. They were also more slender and willowy, and none wore beards.

Not only were they unclothed, they were also unadorned. There was no jewelry, no makeup, not so much as a flower in anyone's hair. They had no need of such enhancements, for all had the attractive quality of good health.

"*These* are the brutal killers Tichelon is so terrified of?" Riker asked, astonished.

"We haven't seen them in contact with the Samdians," Picard reminded him. "Thralen, can you make out how these people communicate? I don't see any gestures."

"No," the sociologist replied, "and also no speech. They hardly look at one another. Scent is not probable; they do not sniff at one another, either. I've never encountered scent as the primary method of communication among humanoids, and these people are too well organized not to have long-distance communication. Scent will not communicate in crowds or over distances."

"Or through the vacuum of space," Geordi put in.

"I think we must hypothesize that they are telepathic," Thralen said.

"Telepathic!" Riker exclaimed. "Thralen, telepaths are rarely aggressive unless they're psychotic—to harm or kill someone forces a telepath to experience the other person's pain, fear, death."

"Then you tell me how they communicate," Thralen said.

"Perhaps they *are* psychotic," Geordi said. "Data, can you call up what's happening in Eskatus?"

"What was happening there approximately an hour ago," Data agreed, and switched the image to one of the last ones their scan had recorded.

236

The city of Eskatus lay smoking in the aftermath of battle. There were bombed-out buildings, overturned vehicles, and bodies both Samdian and Konor—but Samdian corpses far outnumbered Konor ones.

Some of the Konor wore shielding clothing, heavily padded suits with helmets hanging at their belts. They were heaving Samdian bodies onto trucks—and as the *Enterprise* officers watched, horrified, one of them discovered a Samdian alive, calmly slit her throat, and with the help of another Konor soldier slung the body on top of the others.

"Earlier reports said they took slaves," Picard said. "This looks as if they kill everybody."

"There are only adults among the dead," Thralen pointed out. "The people of Eskatus may have sent their children to cities farther north at the approach of the Konor. Among societies which practice slavery, though, children are often separated from adults. If we scan further, we may find that the Konor have the Samdian children in a secure area."

"We saw no Samdians in the earlier scene," Data recalled. "Neither adults nor children."

"We don't know how they treat their slaves, if indeed the reports of slavery are true," Thralen replied. "People may cling to the hope that missing friends and relatives are alive, by assuming those unaccounted for have been captured. We have only the Samdians' word for what the Konor are like—and those reports are hardly comprehensive."

"Hardly," Riker agreed grimly. "You'd think they'd have reported that they can't communicate with the Konor because the Konor don't have a spoken language!"

"But slavery is inconsistent with telepathy," Geordi pointed out. "Thralen, are you sure the Konor are telepaths?"

"No. It is simply the only means of communication I can hypothesize without going down among them."

"No one is going down there," Picard stated. "Not until we know a great deal more. What we see here confirms the reports by the Samdians: We could expect an away team to be killed before it could communicate—especially as we are not certain *how* these people communicate."

"Then let's beam up one of the Konor," Geordi suggested, "and try talking to him. Or whatever they do. In that situation he'd surely try to communicate with us, and the translator might be able to work out what his method is."

"Mmm," the captain mused, "that is a possibility. Do you think you could isolate an individual and bring him up safely?"

"Not at this distance. We can only enhance the images *after* we've recorded them. We could send someone down into a sparsely populated area to get a lock on someone, and beam them back together."

"Risky," Picard noted, "but it may become necessary. Go find Transporter Chief O'Brien and sort out the specifications, but don't do anything without my order. Number One, consult with Security about precautions should we decide to bring one of the Konor aboard. Data, Thralen, I want you to study everything on all the scans—search for clues to Konor motivations. If we do decide to bring one of them aboard, what will persuade him to cooperate?"

"Yes, sir," Data said as the meeting began to break

up and everyone rose to go to his assigned task. "We will set up in Briefing Room Three."

"Very good," the captain said, a hint of weariness in his tone. "If you'll take something from *my* years of experience," he added, "you have the most important task. We're going to have no success in dealing with the Konor until we can talk to them. I've asked Darryl Adin to act as advisor. He has direct experience with a wide variety of aggressive species, both in Starfleet and in the private sector. See what suggestions he might have."

Dare brought Aurora and Poet to the briefing. "Our communications and tactics specialists," he explained. "If you don't want them here for security reasons, though—"

"I think we can use everyone who wants to help," Data cut in. "Thralen?"

"I agree."

They began with the first scene, the serene Konor occupying the Samdian city just as if they had always lived there. "The serpent underneath the rose, eh?" Poet said. "You're sure these are the bloodthirsty Konor we've heard so much about?"

"Oh, yes," Data replied, and called up the scene in Eskatus.

"Cold bastards, aren't they?" Dare observed. "I take it with this evidence there won't be any problem with the Federation offering aid?"

"I don't think so," Data answered. "We are trying to avoid fighting. They're civilized. There should be *some* line of reasoning they'll listen to."

"Except they don't speak," Dare observed, "so they probably don't listen. How do they communicate?"

239

"Our best guess at the moment is telepathy," Thralen said.

"Telepathy!" Dare exclaimed. "Telepaths don't act like that. Unless—Data, I think Sdan should see this. There have been aggressive Vulcans, although I don't think there's anything *that* coldblooded in their history. But he knows how telepaths react, better than any of us."

The Vulcanoid member of Dare's gang studied the scenes and said, "It's possible—but they'd have to be mighty sick. 'Suffer the death of thine enemy' is an ancient Vulcan tradition, even though most Vulcans are only touch-telepaths. Even that made pre-Reform Vulcans very selective about killing—it had to be worth accepting the other's pain. But these Konor act as if they don't feel what they do to the Samdians. They'd have to be so jaded that pain wouldn't affect them. Madness." He shook his head. "I can't see how they can be so vicious to the Samdians and then so calm with one another."

As the computer enhanced the other scans, they got a larger picture of Konor activity, but not a clearer one. Just as they were about to give up, though, one dramatic scene increased the mystery.

It was again a street scene, on the edge of a city captured by the Konor but not yet rebuilt. Two adult Konor, a male and a female, led a group of a dozen or so small children into a plaza with bombed-out buildings on two sides. Like all the Konor they had seen so far, this group did not talk to one another, although the children looked about them, wide-eyed.

"Those kids look surprised," Poet observed. "I wonder why."

240

Some of the children began to cry. "There's definitely something wrong," Dare said.

The group stopped, the adults lined them up, and just stared at them, it seemed. Most of them stopped crying, but one little girl shifted from sniffling to wailing. An older girl turned and put her arms around the crying child—and her mouth moved. "That child is speaking!" Data exclaimed.

The crying child said something back.

"The children have a spoken language and the adults do not?" Dare questioned. "That makes no sense."

"Unless," Thralen said pensively, "those are not Konor children."

The scene continued. The two adults came to the children who were conversing, separated them, forced their struggling hands down to their sides, and put gentle fingers on their lips. Each one then stared into the eyes of the child he or she was calming—comforting?—and the little girls' tears abated.

All the children moved obediently back into line, and the procession continued.

"Bloody hell!" Sdan said in a vehement whisper. "That's the way Vulcan parents help their kids learn emotional control. Little doubt now that the Konor are telepaths."

"But those children *spoke,*" Thralen said. "Data—"

"Look!" Poet pointed excitedly, as the little girl who had cried so hard suddenly broke from the line of children and ran back across the plaza the way they had come.

They watched, mesmerized. The man led the other

children away, while the woman doubled back after the fleeing girl. The picture followed the child and her pursuer, taking them into an area unseen before, where perhaps thirty more children were held in cages.

"Bloody bastards!" Poet swore as he viewed the picture of terrified children caged like animals, some beating futilely on the bars, some crying, and some huddled hopelessly on the floor of their prison.

The little girl ran to a cage where a boy a bit older sat against the bars. When she came up to him, he thrust his hands through, and she grasped them, sobbing.

The boy spoke to her, then tried to push her away just as the woman caught up and grabbed the little girl away from him.

The child fought, kicking, scratching, biting—but not for long. After a moment she stopped, screaming as if she were herself in pain, while the woman who held her set her down, put her hands on the child's shoulders, and stared into her face with a smug expression. The girl subsided into hopeless weeping. The woman turned to the boy staring in anguish . . . and spoke to him.

"They *can* speak!" Aurora exclaimed. "But—how can they treat children that way? It's inhuman!"

"These cannot possibly be Konor children," Thralen said. "Data, I thought you had accessed all records on the Konor."

"Everything in the computer, which is practically nothing."

"What about the Samdians?" the Theskian asked.

"I got the same briefing as everyone else," he

242

replied, and suddenly swallowed hard as he realized that he had not followed through on it.

Data should have had the biological specifications of the Samdians ready at hand, but he didn't. As an android he had had all data on all species known to the Federation in his personal memory banks, adding to it as new life-forms were discovered; there was no need to access the information until there was an application for it.

As a human, though, he should have called it up from the ship's computer immediately. "I'm sorry," he said. "I have allowed this investigation to proceed on incomplete information."

The scene they had been watching ended with nothing more dramatic than the woman leading the grim-faced little girl away.

"Computer," Data addressed the ship's system, "biological briefing on the Samdians."

And there it was, the missing information that made sense of what was happening on Dacket: The Konor had not arrived from some unknown sector of the galaxy, but from right there in the Samdian Sector!

Samdians, it seemed, were all born with green-gold skin and lavender hair. That coloration continued until puberty, when under the influence of the atmospheric conditions and sun's emissions on Dacket, by the time they reached early adulthood their skin coloring deepened to lavender and their hair to blue. Conditions on Gellesen turned Samdian skin dark green and hair a reddish brown. Only on Jokarn, the planet the Konor were reported as having "taken," did skin and hair remain the same color as in childhood.

"I knew it couldn't be their own children they were treating that way," Aurora said. "It's Samdian—or rather Dacket children they're enslaving and separating. Those were probably brother and sister we saw."

"Standard slaving technique," Thralen agreed, "separating family members to prevent mutual emotional support."

"I . . . am sorry," Data repeated, wishing he could melt away from the heat of embarrassment pouring through him.

"It was my mistake, too, Data," Thralen said. "I studied all the information on Samdian culture and customs, but did not think to look for clues in the biological information."

"Because that was my job, and you assumed I had done it," Data said flatly. It was an incredibly stupid mistake—something an ensign straight out of the Academy would be severely disciplined for. Forcing himself to face up to his responsibility, and ignoring a cowardly impulse to run away and hide, he said, "If you will excuse me, I must report this piece of information to the captain."

"You don't have to go in person, Data," Sdan said. "Just call and tell 'im."

Dare said, "Let him go, Sdan. He's a Starfleet officer with a duty to perform. Data, we will— That is, Mr. Thralen, I suggest we inform the First Officer of this finding."

Captain Picard was in his ready room. "What's wrong, Data?" he asked in concern when his second officer entered. "Is everything all right?"

"No, sir," Data said grimly. "It is not." And he told the captain what he had so belatedly discovered.

"Has Commander Riker been informed of this finding?"

"Yes, sir."

"Very well, then. The error has been corrected, and we are now proceeding with all appropriate information at hand."

The words seemed tantamount to a dismissal. Data was tempted to grab the chance to run, but his first duty was to the *Enterprise* and Starfleet. "Sir, I must report myself unfit for active duty. Perhaps for any Starfleet duty at all."

"Why, Data? Dr. Pulaski reports your injuries healed, and you have passed all the tests for return to active bridge status. We all make mistakes from time to time—"

"I almost got myself killed, and then I nearly ruined our mission, both in one day," Data said wretchedly. "I—"

"Data," the captain said softly, "sit down." As Data did so, Picard got up and went to the food dispenser. "Coffee? Tea?"

As his mouth was very dry, Data said, "Tea, please." Then, as an afterthought, "Uh—with cream and sweetener."

"Milk, Data," Picard admonished. "Cream is for coffee. With tea you have milk." He turned to the dispenser and ordered, "Tea. Earl Grey, hot. One with lemon, one with milk and sugar."

Data accepted the tea, took a sip, and set the cup down. "Captain," he tried again, "I think I must be removed from duty. I cannot function as I did before."

"No, of course you can't," Picard said, "but that's

245

no reason to give up your career. Tell me precisely why you think you are not fit for duty."

"I no longer function efficiently."

"Understandable. You are going through a period of adjustment such as the rest of us cannot even imagine. But if I take you off the duty roster, how will you regain your efficiency?"

"I don't think I can, sir."

"Why not?"

"My strength is gone. So are my special sensors. But we have machinery to compensate for those. The most important thing I have lost is my total recall and direct access to information. I made a foolish mistake today—"

"Two, I believe, but you are referring to your error in not informing us upon first sight that the Konor are a branch of the Samdians."

"Yes, sir."

"And what did you do when you discovered your error?"

"I called up the missing information from the ship's computer."

"Data, as an android, when a piece of necessary information was not in your memory banks, what did you do?"

Data blinked. "I . . . called up the information from the ship's computer."

"And what did you learn from today's experience?"

"That I should not assume my own memory will provide the cross-references I need, but should always look up the applicable files."

Picard smiled. "Will you make that mistake again?"

"I hope not, sir. But what other mistakes will I

make? I have discovered important gaps in my memory."

Suddenly the captain was seriously concerned. "Oh? What kind of gaps?"

Data frowned. "I am beginning to cope with the way human memory fades and distorts with even a brief passage of time. Still, I have an . . . awareness that events occurred, so that if it were important to trace, for example, what I had eaten forty-eight hours ago, I know that the information on what I ordered from the dispenser exists, and I could ask the computer to locate it."

"But you have had an instance in which you did not know that certain information even existed?"

"Twice now," Data admitted. "Thralen gave an example of a species supposed to be a 'classic example' that I could not remember even having heard of. And then the Samdian biological specifications."

Picard frowned. "That *is* a potential problem. Yet your memory, both intellectual and kinetic, proved accurate enough to pass the helm and Ops tests at a first try. Those are very stringent tests, as you well know: a starship cannot have someone liable to error at either post during sensitive maneuvers. Have these two instances of memory lapse anything in common, Data?"

When he compared them he realized, "Yes—both are the kind of information that was simply dumped into my memory banks at the Academy, without my consciously examining it. I think . . . I seem to remember, or at least know that at some time I had contact with, those things that I have either personally experienced or accessed into my consciousness. Material stored in my memory banks that I've never had occasion to access . . . is lost."

"Is it, Data?" Picard asked softly.

"It's all in the ship's computer, of course, but—"

"But you have to remember to ask for it, just like any other organic crew member." The captain smiled. "It takes time to develop new habits, but you'll learn."

Data nodded. "I must not assume information does not exist without first asking the computer. Yes, I can do that. Still, my efficiency—"

"—is not expected to be up to your usual standard at present. I will assign you no more unsupervised duties for the time being."

"Yes, sir," Data said glumly. "I am sorry. My self-indulgence on Elysia cost Starfleet a valuable asset."

"Data," Picard said, "Starfleet was started by humans. Its membership is still more than half human. Most of the officers of this ship are human, including myself."

"All with unique qualifications for their positions. I threw away my uniqueness."

"But not your value. There is no reason you can't perform as well as any other officer in the fleet. From what I observe, your desire to perfect yourself has carried through your metamorphosis in full force. That means you will be *better* than most, if you don't allow yourself to accept 'I'm only human' as an excuse for shoddy work."

"No, sir," Data said, beginning to feel better. Of course the captain was right; if he took Picard and Riker as his models, he could become as valuable to Starfleet as he had ever been, if in a different way. "Thank you, Captain. I know what to do now. The

248

Prime Directive forbids us to take sides in what we now recognize to be a civil war among the Samdians, but we *have* been asked for help. I shall delve into their history, culture, philosophy, and biology to try to find some way we might legitimately persuade them to settle their differences in a more peaceful way."

"Work with Thralen," Picard directed. "Ordinarily I would tell you to take time out for relaxation first, but—"

"I've done too much relaxing the past few days," Data stated firmly. "My priority now must be to stop the Konor conquest of Dacket—before more people are killed."

Chapter Twelve

DATA AND THRALEN redoubled their efforts to decipher the mystery of the Konor, working at the computer complex in Data's quarters. They were poring over all the information on the Samdians when Data's intercom buzzed.

It was Pris Shenkley. *"Would you like to have dinner together, Data?"*

With a start, he realized he was hungry—he and Thralen had been working for hours without a break, but he couldn't stop now. "The captain gave me an assignment, Pris. I'll be busy all evening."

"I understand," she replied easily. *"Why don't you call me when you're free."*

"Uh—I don't know when that will be, Pris."

"Hey," she said, *"I'm a pro too, you know. Just remember when you have a break, I'd like to spend more time with you."*

"I'll remember," Data assured her. It was the truth: he certainly would remember. But not for the right reasons.

Data couldn't fathom why something he could only

identify as conscience prodded him each time he recalled the events of last night. Ethically, he had done nothing wrong: two consenting adults with no beliefs opposing intimacy, and no ties to anyone who might be hurt by their actions, had shared a most enjoyable experience. So why the nagging doubts?

Perhaps they had to do with his right to involve anyone in his life when his future was so uncertain. If he performed his duties during the present crisis with no further lapses, he would probably look forward with pleasure to seeing Pris again.

Meanwhile, he had more urgent things to occupy his mind. Data and Thralen took a break only long enough to order food from the dispenser, and took it back to the computer screens.

"We are overlooking something," Thralen said.

"I don't find that difficult to believe," Data replied, "but what is it? These records are extremely sketchy. The Samdians have been isolationist up to now."

"There must be another approach," Thralen said, his antennae extending and retracting in frustration. "We need to know *why* Jokarn suddenly began attacking Dacket."

"The call for help said the Konor had *taken* Jokarn," Data pointed out. "From what we saw earlier, they appear to be natives of Jokarn. Why would they say that they had taken their own planet?"

"The people of Dacket may have put it that way in an attempt to guarantee our coming to aid them," Thralen said. "But there is nothing here to indicate that the Samdians possess ESP. Yet what else could account for what we witnessed? The people of Jokarn must have recently developed telepathy. Yet . . . telepaths are normally nonaggressive."

"What if not all of them developed it?" Data asked. "The name 'Konor' does not appear in the historical information on the Samdians. Could the powers of a few have frightened the people of Jokarn? Galactic history certainly provides enough instances of people with new powers being persecuted. Could the Jokarn have hurt them so badly that they were driven to revenge on all Samdian non-telepaths?"

"Possibly," Thralen agreed. "Giving a group of people a new name is a way of distancing them, making them less than yourself so you can mistreat, even kill them."

"Let's find out," Data said. "Computer: language banks. Morphemic structure of the Samdian language."

"Working."

"What is the historical meaning of the word 'Konor'?"

The computer took several seconds to access the information before reporting, "It is an archaic word, believed to derive from the language of the ancestors of those who colonized the Samdian planets. In that language its base meaning is 'human.'"

"That can't be right," Data said.

"Provide context," Thralen prompted.

"People: sentient, sapient organic beings. Persons, as opposed to animals."

That was why Data had heard it as "human," the generic term for "people" as used casually by the more specifically human people he had spent most of his life among. Still, Data found himself frowning. "Why would the Samdians call the Konor that? It must be the Konor's own word for themselves."

Thralen nodded. "But just 'people' is strange. Computer: analyze by connotation. Does the word 'konor' have implied meaning, such as 'enlightened people,' 'chosen people,' or similar semantic layering?"

"Working."

There was an even longer delay as the computer utilized the universal translator's most detailed comparative analysis. Finally the reply came. "Denotative, not connotative. In the language from which the Samdian language derived, the meaning of the morpheme 'k-nr-' is 'soul.' Root derivation of 'konor' is 'those who possess souls.'"

"Gods," Thralen whispered, the blue of his face paling to a washed-out hue. He pushed himself up out of his chair, and began pacing behind the terminal. "If that is what we're up against, we haven't a chance."

Data turned to stare at him. "I don't understand."

"History, Data. The fiercest wars in all the history of the galaxy have been fought over religious differences. What ought to be the balm and consolation for the trials of life is made the instigator of fury and grief." Thralen stopped pacing, and rested his hands on the back of Data's chair.

"In my own family, those who denied that the Great Mother literally gave birth to the world, who understood that the story is a beautiful symbol of creation—we were cast out of our Ancient Den for daring to examine the facts of the universe as She presents them to us."

"I am sorry," Data said, recognizing that the Theskian sociologist was sharing something very painful. Recalling the sorrow he had felt when he had thought himself forced to leave the closest approximation to family he had ever known, Data could only guess at the agony of exile from true family that one had grown up in.

Thralen shook his head. "I believe in the Great Mother as strongly as those who seclude themselves on our home world and claim that the rest of the galaxy is Outer Darkness. We agree on the most basic tenets of our faith, Data, and yet those of us who have ventured beyond our home planet are considered heathen." His antennae retracted slightly. "Today, of course, the vast majority of Theskians, both on Theskia and on colony worlds, perceive the Great Mother as a manifestation of the generative force of the universe. But for some reason, She sent my spirit to be born into a family of the Old Faith." He sighed. "If I was meant to enlighten them, I failed. When my studies led me to Starfleet Academy, they cast me out."

The Theskian paused, as if waiting for a response, or perhaps contemplating what he considered a failure. Data was far out of his element here. Still, he had to say something.

"At one time, I had stored in my memory banks gigabytes of information on gods throughout the galaxy. I could quote it, but it never meant more to me than any other information. Then I met up with some 'gods,' and experienced what many would call a miracle. I do not understand any better now than I did before."

"Those were not gods as I believe in a God," Thralen replied. "One day we will understand the kinds of powers those Elysian 'gods' possess. But beyond us, beyond them, beyond anything the sentient mind can comprehend, there is a force that drives the universe. While we are alive, we can only understand it in some familiar form, such as the Great Mother. But when we leave this state of existence, we will experience that force directly. I will go to the arms of the Great Mother; Mr. Worf would say that he will enter the Black Fleet. We both mean the same thing."

"But you believe in an existence after death. You believe you have a soul."

"Oh, yes. There is no doubt of it."

"I do not know if I have one," Data said.

Thralen smiled. "*I* know you do," he replied, "and you did not get it on Elysia." Then he sobered. "But galactic history is full of atrocities committed by those who could not recognize that people unlike themselves have souls. If this particular group of Samdians, the Konor, refer to themselves as 'those who possess souls'—"

"Then," Data realized, "by implication the other Samdians do *not* possess souls, and may be rightfully treated as animals or . . . property. Oh, yes, Thralen," he added grimly, "I understand *that* reasoning."

Thralen's coloring had returned to normal, and his antennae unfurled. Data recognized that the invocation of his religious beliefs was something sustaining to the Theskian.

"We must go down to the planet," Data said, rising. "We need more information to verify our conclusions. What do the Konor call the other Samdians, for example? Are they really telepathic, or are we misinterpreting what the scans picked up?"

Thralen nodded. "And how can a telepath think other intelligent beings are not people when he can perceive their thoughts and feelings? You're right, Data—let's take this information to the captain."

Captain Picard contacted Chairman Tichelon, who provided the information that the Konor called the other Samdians "Ikonor"—which meant simply "not Konor," he explained.

"It is more than that, Captain," Thralen said. "It confirms our fears, for it means 'those without souls.'"

It was obvious from Tichelon's expression that he had not expected them to derive the root meanings. He immediately went on the offensive, protesting, *"The insults they cast at us are not the issue. Our people are being murdered, Captain. You have been here for almost a day, and done nothing!"*

"You could have speeded our investigation, and therefore potential action, by telling us the truth," Picard replied. "The Konor are your own people. We cannot become involved in your internal affairs."

"They are not our people! They might once have been, but they are the ones who deny us. Have you seen them? They do not respond to our pleas—they only kill!"

Picard took a controlling breath, and said, "We are going to attempt to communicate with the Konor. If we succeed, will you accept representatives of Starfleet as mediators? May we say you have agreed?"

"Yes—yes, of course! But they will not listen to you. Do you think we haven't tried? Approach them with a well-armed force, for they kill even those who offer surrender."

So Captain Picard called another strategy session in

the observation lounge, with everyone who had been involved in previous discussions taking part. It was decided that a small away team would transport down to the city where the Konor were well settled in, and things appeared peaceful.

"I should be included in the away team, Captain," Deanna Troi stated.

Picard pursed his lips. "I'm not sure that's a good idea, Counselor. This is potentially a very dangerous situation."

"Sir, we have no full telepath in our crew," Deanna insisted. "I may be our best chance to communicate."

She was right, of course—in fact, if the Konor's lack of response was due to accepting none but telepathic contact, she was their *only* chance. Her training in mental communication was the best both her home planet and Starfleet Academy had to offer. Still, Data understood why the captain hesitated to send this gentle woman, untrained in any but the most basic of Starfleet self-defense, into such a dangerous situation.

Data watched Will Riker watch the captain, the commander's "poker face" betrayed by a slight wince when Picard nodded.

"You'll need the best protection we can give you," the captain continued. "Mr. Worf, Number One." He looked around at the rest of the group assembled there.

Again Data felt inadequate; once, he would have been the automatic next choice.

"Captain," Thralen said, "I should be there." His antennae quivered nervously. "If I have misinterpreted what we saw, I may be able to correct any errors before they cause diplomatic chaos. And even if Data and I are right, on direct contact I will certainly see more."

"Agreed," Picard said. He shook his head. "I still don't like it, but we know they're not receiving our messages. Data, you and Chief O'Brien handle the transporter. I want all communications left open, and a tricorder channel providing a visual to both the bridge and the transporter room. At the first sign of a threat to the away team, they are to be beamed up instantly."

"Yes, sir," Data said, glad to have at least some part in the mission.

"All right," Picard said. "Are there any questions?"

"Only what else Chairman Tichelon might not have told us," Worf growled.

"I doubt there is anything left to tell," Troi put in. "The Samdians do not seem to understand the Konor any better than we do."

"What about the fact that they go naked?" Worf asked, grimacing slightly. "Should we beam down unclothed?" The idea obviously pained him, but as Security Chief he had to consider every possibility to keep the away team safe. "We cannot go unarmed, and we certainly will not be mistaken for Konor. But what if there is some taboo against clothing, as the Ferengi have against clothing women?"

"An excellent question," the captain noted. "Meff Tichelon may know the answer."

"We go naked before Providence when we pray," the Samdian explained when they contacted him. *"The Konor pervert our beliefs by displaying their nakedness in secular activities."*

"But did anyone ever attempt to approach the Konor nude?" Riker asked.

"Oh, yes," Tichelon replied with a grimace. "Yes, some broke our own taboos, and were murdered in the midst of their error. Aping the Konor's sacrilege will not save you from their madness. You will see: the Konor are raging beasts which must be destroyed before they kill us all."

So finally, ill-prepared as they might be, the away team gathered, fully clothed and armed, on the transporter platform.

Geordi had made detailed and enhanced scans, to locate the place within the city most likely to be the seat of government. Data and O'Brien each kept one eye on the transporter console, to make certain the team was tracked for immediate pickup, and the other on the drama playing out on the viewscreen.

With the direct communication link through combadges and tricorder, they could see and hear everything that happened. Riker, Troi, Thralen, and Worf materialized on the steps of the building the city's traffic pattern indicated was the center of local government.

They never got through the doors.

At first, people nearby just stopped, stared, but did not move or speak.

Then suddenly, from all sides, Konor men, women, and children converged on the away team.

Looks of astonishment crossed the faces of all four Starfleet personnel. Thralen's antennae retracted reflexively, and Worf put his hands to the sides of his head.

"Do you hear them?" Troi asked, smiling, her eyes huge and unfocused.

"Yes—inside my head!" Riker replied in tones of utter amazement. *"Deanna—no!"* he exclaimed suddenly as the counselor stepped ahead of the others, hands outstretched toward the Konor before her.

Data knew Troi must be projecting a message of peaceful greeting to the Konor, using Betazoid techniques. If what the Konor required was telepathic contact, surely her sincere attempt would at the very least get them a hearing.

But if they understood Troi's message, none of the Konor surrounding the away team gave any indication. They stalked closer, faces angry. *"I hear you,"* Troi gasped, the look on her face changing from joy to confusion to horror. *"Such terrible anger—but why? Why will you not listen to me?"*

At the same time, Riker gasped, grasping the sides of his head for a moment before he regained control. Pain was clear in his movements as he kept to Troi's side. Thralen staggered, his skin paling and his antennae retracting again as his mouth opened in a grimace of pain.

Even Worf winced—but the Klingon did not lose stride. He put his hand on his phaser, ready to draw at the first sign of attack.

The Konor converged on Troi, the serenity of their faces gone, although their looks seemed more disdainful than angry.

"We must beam them up!" Data exclaimed.

"They're moving, and there are Konor too close—" O'Brien began, fingers playing over the controls.

"Bring the Konor along, but *beam them up!*" Data ordered, activating his own controls as Picard's voice came over the ship's system, *"Get the away team out of there!"*

Even as they tried, the Konor attacked. The away team became four rapidly shifting foci.

Worf and Riker drew phasers, and two people trying to grab Troi fell, stunned.

That did not stop the Konor. The crowd converged, parcels suddenly turned into weapons, then stones and bricks passed in from the outskirts of the mob.

Data and O'Brien fought for a fix on moving bodies. "Get Troi out first if we can't get them all at once!" Data instructed. She was both the focus of the Konor attack and the least skilled of the four at self-defense. She was also lithe and quick, moving just fast enough to constantly change her coordinates.

Worf knocked aside a brick aimed at him, which threw him slightly to his right—just far enough off balance for the split second it took a Konor to thrust a metal rod past him, toward Troi.

It wasn't a weapon, but some kind of building material. That made it no less lethal.

Troi stumbled back, and the attacker missed spearing her. He shifted his grip and swung his improvised weapon up, ready to bring it down on the woman's head. With the power of his fury behind it, it would split her skull.

Riker, cut off by other Konor, shouted *"Deanna!"* and lunged desperately toward her.

Worf raised his weapon to stun the attacker, but another Konor struck his arm. The shot went high.

From the other side, though, Thralen did what should have been exactly the right thing: he flung himself at Troi in an attempt to knock her out of harm's way.

The crowd surged against them. Thralen slammed into Troi, but they did not go down.

The blow fell with full force on the Theskian's head, shearing off one of his antennae. He collapsed forward onto Troi, red blood spurting over his yellow hair and blue skin.

And in the second of horrified stillness that followed, the transporter finally found its fix and beamed the away team up.

Thralen's assailant came with them. The moment he congealed on the platform, he raised his blood-stained weapon again—Worf fired, and the Konor collapsed, stunned.

"We've got them aboard, Captain," O'Brien reported.

Data ordered, "Medic to transporter room!" and dashed from behind the console as Worf tapped his combadge and called for Security to come take the prisoner.

Riker and Troi bent over Thralen, but Riker's concern was divided. "Are you all right?" he asked the counselor. "Those thoughts and emotions they were sending were painful enough to me. With your sensitivity—"

"I am learning to deal with pain," she replied. "What they projected at us was not real, although it was extremely disorienting. No wonder they have found it so easy to win their battles."

"All the less reason for them to slaughter people," Riker added.

Data, meanwhile, picked up the fallen Theskian's tricorder, set it to medical scan, and checked out Thralen's vital signs.

His heart had stopped and he was not breathing.

Data quickly checked the head wound—concussion and severe nerve damage where the antenna had been ripped off, but the brain was undamaged. It was shock that had stopped his heart and respiration. At worst, if prosthetic help were not possible, Thralen would be deaf on one side. The thing to do right now was to save his life.

"Help me," Data said, straightening Thralen's body while he tried to remember how to do CPR on a Theskian.

Oh, damn, *damn, DAMN!* The knowledge had disappeared into one of the gaps in his memory!

"Counselor," he pleaded, knowing she had a good knowledge of physical medicine as well as her expertise in psychology. "Please help me revive him."

As he spoke he made sure Thralen's breathing passage was clear—at least that step was the same for all air-breathing beings.

Troi knelt beside him. "He's stopped breathing?" she asked. "Data, what is his—?"

The doors swooshed open to admit Dr. Pulaski, followed by two assistants with an antigrav gurney. "How badly is he hurt?" she interrupted, seeing from the tricorder and scanner lying separately on the platform that Data had already assessed the damage.

"We must resuscitate him," Data said. "I will breathe for him if you will try to restart his heart."

"Data—no!" Pulaski exclaimed, aghast.

"Doctor—it's less than five minutes," he protested. "We can save him!"

Troi put a hand on his shoulder, saying softly, "Data, we *can* revive him, but we *must* not."

He stared at her gentle face, anger welling up. "He saved your life! How can you let him die? Doctor," he turned to Pulaski, horrified to find her also standing back, refusing to render aid.

"Data, Thralen is Theskian," she said. "You know their beliefs. At the moment of death, they believe the soul leaves the body and cannot return. If we were to resuscitate Thralen, he would never forgive us . . . nor would he be likely to survive long. He would be an outcast from his people, for they would believe him to be a body without a soul."

Riker put in, "He would believe that himself, Data. Let him go now."

Data swallowed hard over a lump in his throat. He should have known that about Theskians; he had been programmed with information on what to do—or not to do—in an emergency concerning any race in the Federation.

He looked down at the body of his colleague. If he had been alone he would have done everything to revive him . . . and if Theskian internal physiology were similar enough to human, he might have succeeded.

Which to Thralen would have been worse than death.

Data sat on the edge of the transporter platform, feeling worse than useless, while the medical team took away the remains of what had been a friend, and the security team took away the Konor.

He couldn't think. His mind leaped from one image to another, incoherently.

Counselor Troi remained behind. She knelt beside him, putting a hand on his shoulder. "Data," she murmured, "it is all right to cry. Let out your sorrow. We have all lost a colleague, but you knew Thralen better than any of the rest of the bridge crew."

Only then did Data realize that unshed tears burned

264

in his throat and behind his eyes. When he stopped fighting them and let them fall, they brought physical but not emotional relief.

He looked up at Troi. "Thralen believed that he would go to the arms of the Great Mother. I . . . hope he was right."

"I hope so, too," she replied. "In any case, his belief was a great comfort to him in his life, Data. He never feared dying, and he died bravely."

"And not without purpose," Data agreed. "He gave his life to save another."

But as far as their mission went, Thralen's loss was pointless. They had had no success in communicating with the Konor.

"Mr. Data, Counselor Troi, report to sickbay," came Commander Riker's voice over the communications system.

Troi sighed. "I'm all right, but I suppose Kate won't be satisfied until she checks me out for herself."

But what does Dr. Pulaski want with me? Data wondered.

As it turned out, neither Troi nor Data was the patient: the doctor had insisted that Worf bring his prisoner to sickbay, where the Konor was just now recovering from the phaser stun.

Pulaski had placed him in a restraint field used to protect hallucinating patients who might otherwise harm themselves or others. The Konor could sit up, but not get beyond the forcefield that kept him on the examination couch. It was a one-way field, however; the doctors and nurses could reach through it to treat the patient.

Picard, Riker, and Worf were already there. The

captain turned as Troi and Data entered, saying, "Counselor, are you well enough to work?"

There was dirt on Troi's usually immaculate face and clothing, along with Thralen's blood, which stained her pale skin and deepened the wine color of her uniform. Her long hair was in disarray, but she was unhurt except for minor bruises and abrasions. "Yes, Captain, although I don't know what I can do."

"See if you can get through to this man, one-on-one."

"You've done it with me, Deanna," Riker reminded her, "and I'm not telepathic at all."

"Nor am I," Worf added, "but down on the planet I also heard these Konor inside my head. There is no doubt that they are telepathic."

"They are broadcast telepaths," Troi said. "They do not seem to be receptive, like Betazoids."

"Try," Riker urged her. "Here, in private, without a crowd to drown you out, you may get through to him."

By this time the Konor was pushing himself up groggily onto his elbows, looking around.

Dr. Pulaski moved toward him, saying, "You are in our medical unit. We are not going to hurt you. We just want to find out why you fight everyone who tries to contact you."

//Ikonor animals! I understand your primitive noises, but, thank Providence, the Konor have no need of such. We communicate soul to soul. You may be powerful enough to kill me, but you soulless beings will never defeat the Konor.//

Data was astonished. He had never before felt . . . heard . . . there was no word he knew for receiving

266

another's thoughts inside his head. The words were accompanied by the Konor's scorn at being forced to deal with a lower life-form.

But Dr. Pulaski was undaunted. "We'll leave the state of our souls to the theologians. Right now we are trying to communicate. I'm Dr. Pulaski. Will you tell us your name?"

//Konor have no need of names. We identify one another by the essence of our souls.//

Troi stepped forward. "He is sincere," she said. "But then, you could all feel that, couldn't you? Let me see what I can do." Data could see her concentrating, but he did not receive any thoughts she tried to transmit. At first.

Then, faintly, it seemed he heard her gentle voice inside his head, feeling with it her sweet emotional presence. //Is this the communication you need to recognize us as your equals?//

Data glanced at Riker, saw him smile proudly at Troi.

Captain Picard looked surprised, then pleased. Pulaski smiled as Data remembered she had done when the boy from the Genetic Research Station on Gagarin 4 had communicated with her telepathically. Worf almost allowed a smile, then caught himself and took up his most military stance.

There was no response from the Konor.

//Do you not hear me?// Troi asked. She was even paler than usual, and strain showed around her huge eyes. Her "voice" still seemed very faint to Data, but surely that was because he was not a telepath.

Still no response from the Konor.

After a third try, Troi turned away, trembling with

267

the effort. "Doctor, this man is adept at shielding his feelings—a common ability among telepathic races. However, it prevents me from telling whether he does not hear me, or whether he is simply refusing to respond."

"That's easy enough to test," Pulaski said, and set her instruments to measure the electrical impulses of the Konor's brain.

They quickly found the problem: When they spoke to the Konor, his response indicated that he heard and understood what the universal translator transmitted to him. When Troi broadcast to him mentally, although her crewmates received her thoughts there was no indication that the Konor heard them at all.

Pulaski frowned. "I don't understand this."

"We don't know how telepathy works," Troi said. "It doesn't operate on any frequencies we can measure; that's why it cannot be artificially reproduced."

"Perhaps this man's telepathy operates on a different frequency from yours?" Data suggested.

"I suppose you could use that analogy," Troi said with a tired smile. "It's not a physical thing, though, Data. I shouldn't have used the word 'frequency'— but whatever the reason, while the Konor can broadcast to Samdians, humans, Andorians, and Klingons, they cannot receive Betazoid thoughts."

She turned to the Konor, who lay impassively waiting for their next move. "Let me make certain we understand your beliefs. You believe that the ability to communicate without speaking is evidence that a person has a soul?"

//That is correct, but you speak of *belief*, while we *know*. We communicate soul to soul.//

"How can you claim we have no souls if we can understand you?"

//The soulless recognize our state. It is their own they refuse to accept.//

"And what do you think our 'state' is?" Troi demanded.

//You Ikonor are to the Konor as beasts of burden are to you. Providence created you to pave the way for our coming. You have built well, and we are pleased—but now you foolishly attempt to deprive us of what was built for our use. We are forced to destroy you, when you might have pleasant and productive lives in our service.//

"Never mind that," Commander Riker broke in. "What would prove to you that we are as much people as you are?"

//Any among you who can respond soul to soul are recognized as Konor. We have rescued many from among the Ikonor on Dacket.//

"That's what was happening with those children," Data realized. "They were separating out any telepaths among the Dacket children, and making slaves of the others."

Troi asked, "If we can find someone who can communicate with you, 'soul to soul' as you put it, would you accept that person as your equal and listen to what he or she has to tell you?"

//Certainly. Providence may have created Konor among other races than the Samdians. We would welcome contact with them.//

Troi turned to Pulaski. "Then there is a chance we may find an ambassador the Konor would respect. I suggest you try Dr. Selar's Vulcan abilities."

"She's not a very strong telepath," Pulaski said. "That's why she's a physician instead of having taken the training to become a Vulcan Healer."

"All Vulcans have enough telepathy and training to broadcast to other telepaths, even if they must touch to do so. We must try, Kate."

"Of course," Pulaski agreed.

However, although Dr. Selar also received the Konor's thoughts clearly, she, too, failed to reach him mentally. So did two other Vulcans from among the ship's families, whom Selar recommended as having stronger ESP than hers.

Data, meanwhile, called up from the computer the names of all crew and family members with high ESP ratings. One after another, they tried to contact the Konor; one after another, they failed in their attempts.

When they had tried thirty people of a variety of races, all with the highest ESP ratings, Captain Picard called a halt. "It's obvious we're not going to succeed at this. Prepare that man to be returned to the planet."

"Captain," Worf said, "is that wise? You heard what he said: his people think all the technological advancements made by non-Konor are theirs for the taking. Now he will report what he has seen here, and the Konor will want starships."

"They knew of the existence of starships before our arrival, but they hardly have the technology to take them from us, Mr. Worf," Picard said.

"Now," Worf growled. "What about a generation from now?"

Picard stared at nothing. "We can only hope," he said, "that by then we shall have found a way to convince them they are not masters of the universe by divine right."

Before beaming down the Konor in sickbay, Picard tried to do just that one last time.

The Konor stared defiantly. //This is nonsense. We have *proof* of who and what we are. Providence provides. Dacket is ours by right, as Jokarn is and Gellesen will be.//

Data spoke up. "You have no right to take other people's lands and property. Might makes right only until greater might comes along."

After the Konor was taken back to the transporter room and returned to Dacket, Captain Picard called a meeting in the observation lounge.

"We have now done everything that Starfleet allows," he explained. "The Samdians have obviously heard of the Prime Directive. They knew we couldn't fight the Konor for them once we knew it was a civil war; that's why they tried to keep us from discovering that it was their own people attacking them."

"Captain," Dr. Pulaski said, "we can't just desert the people of Dacket!"

Geordi added, "Surely the Prime Directive will allow us to stop the Konor before they kill or enslave all the other Samdians!"

"You know it will not, Lieutenant," Picard replied. "It does not permit us to aid some planets even in case of plague or natural disaster."

"That's only when such aid would interfere with their natural development," Pulaski said. "That's not the case here; the Samdians have star travel, even if it is sublight, and are perfectly aware of progress made elsewhere in the galaxy. We would help if they were suffering an epidemic or an earthquake. This situation is as bad. We have to help them, Captain!"

"I agree," Geordi said. "The development of this broadcast telepathy—couldn't we say that's a medical emergency?"

"You would have us break the Prime Directive?"

"This is a clear case in which it would be wrong to invoke it," Pulaski argued.

"Doctor," said Picard, "there have been rare instances in which Starfleet officers ignored the Non-Interference Directive and were ultimately exonerated. But those cases have never included interference in the politics of a planet. Perhaps Starfleet Command was wrong in not punishing those who gave aid in cases of epidemic or natural disaster, no matter what the mitigating circumstances. The consequences are that we sit here arguing over a clear-cut situation in which we are strictly forbidden to take sides: war between two opposing forces from the same culture, plain and simple."

"But it is not plain and simple," Darryl Adin spoke up. "This is not a dispute over laws or lands or resources. When both sides *choose* to fight, it's none of our business to get involved. Or when people allow themselves to be mistreated, because they are afraid to fight for their own rights, it's not our place to do for them what they will not do for themselves.

"But when a mighty force rises up and destroys a weaker populace, those who are killed and enslaved don't make a choice, any more than those who die in an epidemic choose to be attacked by disease. The Samdians *are* fighting; they are simply outnumbered by the Konor, and unable to match them in viciousness."

"Mr. Adin is right!" Pulaski agreed. "The Konor's prime weapon is this form of broadcast telepathy, intangible but deadly when they use it to disorient those they attack. They're more like an epidemic than an attacking army."

"Or locusts," Geordi added, "gobbling up what other people have worked hard and long to cultivate."

There were murmurs of assent all around the table. Picard looked from face to face, his features hardening. "Listen to yourselves!" he demanded. "My God, don't you realize that you are doing to the Konor exactly what they do to those they call Ikonor: refusing to see them as people? They *are* people. They are not bacteria or viruses, Doctor. They are not insects, Chief Engineer. They are people, and part of the natural population of the Samdian Sector."

"Natural?" Dare scoffed, his voice taking on the tight nasal quality it had had when Data had first met him, when he had been a disillusioned fugitive from Federation justice, convicted of a crime he had never committed. "Is it natural to turn on your own kind, Captain?"

Picard said sadly, "From galactic history it would appear that it is only too natural. I am sorry, my friends, but the Prime Directive forbids our interference in the internal conflict in the Samdian System."

"But it doesn't forbid mine," Dare said.

Data was startled, but realized at once he shouldn't have been. "But what can you do, Dare?" he asked. "Eight people, two ships, a few weapons?"

"And many years of experience," the mercenary replied. "I'd advise the Samdians left on Dacket to refugee to Gellesen. That should give them some breathing space while we train them. Sdan knows

273

mental techniques to avoid letting telepathic transmissions disorient people. We all know how to devise defense systems. We can prepare."

"When the attack comes, and it will," Data said, "it will be the population and resources of two planets, Jokarn and Dacket, against one, Gellesen. I thought you did not take on lost causes."

Dare gave him his old non-smile. "Who says this is a lost cause? And who says everybody will be as reluctant to help as Starfleet?"

Picard's mouth was a thin line. "There is no way we can stop you from involving yourselves in this dispute, Mr. Adin. If you plan to stay here, I suggest that you remove your ships from the shuttle bay before we leave orbit."

"Oh, we'll leave immediately," Dare said, his voice acerbic. "Thank you for your hospitality, Captain."

When Dare and his gang had gone, Riker said, "He's going to escalate the situation. Captain, you know Adin's reputation: he'll deal with anyone to accomplish his ends. The Klingons will honor the Prime Directive, but the Ferengi will have no qualms about selling him weapons. We're close to the Neutral Zone, too. This dispute among three minor planets could erupt into interstellar war."

"Number One," the Captain said grimly, "the moment we found ourselves helpless to resolve the situation peacefully, interstellar war became a distinct possibility. Any act on Mr. Adin's part will have little or no influence in the matter."

Chapter Thirteen

DATA COULD NOT SLEEP that night, could not stop thinking of Thralen, or any of the events of the last few days. He was not invited to the holodeck for Thralen's farewell to his colleagues, as he had really only gotten to know the Theskian sociologist during their work on the Samdians.

The personal loss of a colleague was aggravated by the general sense of failure hanging over the *Enterprise:* They had left Elysia without solving the problem of the power surges, causing Starfleet to warn anything smaller than a starship to make a costly detour around that system, and now they had failed to make peace among the Samdians.

It was far from the first time in Starfleet history that a starship was forced by the Prime Directive to refuse aid to oppressed people, but it was the first time Data and his fellow crew members had had to face such a situation. It felt like betrayal.

After his duty shift, Data found his quarters oppressive. He felt closed in, confined. All the other senior officers' quarters were on the outer hull, with viewports. Data's were as large and well-equipped as theirs, but on the opposite side of the corridor. Androids did not suffer claustrophobia.

But he wasn't an android anymore.

Wanting a sense of open space, he went to the nearest observation lounge—only to find Will Riker there before him. The first officer turned when the doors swooshed open.

"I'm sorry," Data said, starting to back away.

"No, it's all right—come on in, Data," Riker said. "You probably need as badly as I do to be reminded of what we're out here for." He looked back at the motionless stars. "Exploration. Expanding horizons." Data realized that the view from the first officer's quarters, on the other side of the ship, would include the planet they still orbited. Riker continued, speaking with little inflection, "New knowledge, new life, new civilizations. We have to balance that against the hard choices."

Data could hear that Riker had not yet restored that balance after the events on Dacket. Trying to find a point of contact, he offered, "Experiencing personally what had been only theoretical knowledge is sometimes . . . painful."

"God, yes," Riker replied, still staring out at the stars as if he could not face Data and say what he had to say. "Do you remember when we found the Portal of the T'Kon Empire, Data?"

"Yes. The first time we had direct contact with the Ferengi."

Riker nodded. "And they accused us of obstructing commerce, withholding technology and defenses from backward planets."

"We have to do that," said Data. "It would be unforgivable to put modern weapons into the hands of those who do not understand their potential. They would destroy themselves."

"Oh, yes," Riker agreed. "That application of the Prime Directive is easy to understand. But this is the other side of the coin, Data, that we know is there, but somehow never expect to turn up. The side that forces you to walk away, when you know the strong and violent are going to close in behind you and devour the weak."

Data could think of nothing to say to that. "Perhaps," he suggested after a pause, "Dare's plan will work."

Riker turned to look at him. "You don't really think so any more than I do. Adin will be lucky to get his own people away from here alive."

Data opened his mouth to argue, then closed it again. Adin was a survivor, but he had lost followers before. Data didn't want to think what this job might cost his friend.

So he just stood for a time, looking out at the panorama of space, trying as Riker was doing to remind himself of the reason they were all out here. After a time, with little improvement in his attitude, he left the first officer of the *Enterprise* still staring out at the unresponsive stars.

He ate dinner with Geordi that night—although neither had much appetite. For once the two friends could find little cheerful to talk about. To avoid more useless rehashing of the Samdian situation, Data told the engineer about the gaps in his memory. But there was no escaping the topic uppermost in everyone's mind.

"I learned today that there can be things worse than to let someone die," Data concluded. "I don't know, Geordi. Is there an analogy there to what we are having to do—or rather not do—about the Samdians?"

"We probably won't know in our lifetimes," Geordi replied, and turned to a subject on which he could offer advice. "You really didn't remember that Theskians aren't to be resuscitated? That's in the required Social Anthropology course at the Academy, Data."

"I didn't *take* that course," Data now remembered. "There were a number of courses in which the subject matter was just to be memorized, that I didn't have to take."

"But you must have tested out of it. I tested out of basic math and science, and went straight into the advanced courses."

"It was different for an android," Data explained. "I didn't come there with that knowledge, as you did with math and science. But when a course was nothing but facts and statistics, the Academy computer just downloaded them into my memory banks. There was no need for me to take a test afterward; the information was there for me to access any time I needed it. The courses I had to participate in, and which I found very difficult, were the ethics and other philosophy courses—the ones without clear-cut right and wrong answers."

"Yes. You still keep looking for neat solutions to messy problems. But don't feel bad, Data; so do people who've been human a lot longer than you have."

"What about the messy problem of not knowing where there are gaps in my memory?" Data asked. "Geordi, the next one could kill someone, or jeopardize the ship."

"Well, plug the gaps, man!" Geordi said in tones of annoyance. "You know what's missing: it's all on your Academy transcript. Study the texts for all the courses that you originally downloaded, and then take the tests. What's the matter—you too lazy to take a little of the medicine you dole out to Wesley?"

"No. I will do that. At least I can resolve those problems that *do* have neat solutions."

There was a moment's silence. Then Geordi said, "I think this time Starfleet is wrong. The Prime Directive is a neat solution sometimes, but the Samdian situation is a messy problem. Dammit, why can't the Konor just stay in their own territory and practice whatever beliefs they have among themselves?"

"Because they believe in manifest destiny," Data replied. "To the Konor it would be wrong not to take what they believe to be rightly theirs. You weren't in sickbay, Geordi. That Konor wasn't making excuses for selfish acts. He honestly believes that Providence is . . . providing. To him, we are an annoyance to be dealt with as efficiently as possible. That means if we, and everyone else who cannot project telepathically the way the Konor can, don't knuckle under and become their willing servants, they'll just kill us."

"Unless we kill them first," Geordi said.

"That," Data said flatly, "is genocide."

"So we warp away and let the Ferengi or the Romulans or the Orions do the dirty work."

"This is why I was so confused by the ethics classes

at the Academy," Data said. "Sometimes there is no right solution, neat or messy. The best we can hope for is not to be caught in such a situation. This time we didn't get the best we could hope for." He stood. "Good night, Geordi."

Data left for his quarters, intending to start restoring the Academy coursework that had disappeared along with his memory banks. Instead, when he passed the shelf of personal belongings at the entrance to his computer area, he picked up the crystal holograph base, set it on his desk, and conjured up Tasha Yar.

He had been far closer to Tasha than to Thralen, yet although her death had caused him sorrow, he had not known the aching grief he felt today. Tears slid down his face, unbidden. As an android he had had tear ducts, but they had functioned only to lubricate his eyes. How absurd he had been then to think he could comprehend human feelings!

The old grief washed over him, joining with the newer anguish of loss and failure. This was what it meant to be human: to feel pain, to know loss, to suffer failure, and eventually to die, perhaps as senselessly as Tasha had.

Why did I want this? Data asked himself.

Honest to a fault, he admitted that comprehension of the human condition, not the flesh with all its dangerous pleasures, was what had always beckoned, just beyond his reach.

Why? Why would anyone desire such pain? How did humans live with it?

"Tasha, Thralen," he whispered, "you are well out of it."

But Data was still here, with a life to live, with duties to fulfill, and without the companionship of those friends lost along the way.

Another memory surfaced with the clarity of a computer log, this time from the mission he and Tasha had been assigned to on the planet Treva. There Tasha and Dare had been reunited. Then, Data had controlled his response without much difficulty. Now, he wondered if he would have been able to or if, as Dare had said, they would be rivals if Tasha were still alive.

But she was not. He would never see her again, except in the hologram, frozen there forever young and strong and beautiful. As artificial as he had once been.

For the first time, Data wondered what his own fate would be. Was he a survivor? Would he grow old, outliving all his friends and colleagues, the fate he had accepted would be his as an android? Or would he die young, like Tasha and Thralen?

Which was worse, dying before one had fulfilled one's potential, or living not only to lose friends but to experience the kind of frustration that lay like a shroud over the *Enterprise* tonight as they waited, impotent, for orders to abandon their assignment on Dacket?

"I remember how frustrated you used to get when you could take no action, Tasha," Data said. "The Samdian situation is worse than anything we encountered while you were alive."

But those memories were dimming. Only the ones that decided to intrude on him surfaced from his human mind of their own accord. Tasha looked at him out of the hologram, but when he tried to remember her on board ship, or on a planet, the images were blurred.

Wanting her to seem more real, he touched the switch that put the hologram into motion. Unintentionally, he hit the sound setting as well, and Tasha's last words to him sounded in the small room: "You see things with the wonder of a child, and that makes you more human than any of us."

Horrified, Data hit the switch to turn off the hologram. "Oh, Tasha," he said wretchedly, "you have no idea how wrong you were. I'm glad you never knew."

Data put his head down on his arms, and wept.

Worn out emotionally, he fell into uneasy sleep.

His door signal woke him.

Data felt feverish and headachy, and regretted the automatic "Come in" almost before it had passed his lips.

His visitors were Darryl Adin and Pris Shenkley.

"We've come to say goodbye," Dare said. "Or—"

"Come with us, Data," Pris said.

"We may die trying," Dare continued, "but we are going to *do* something for the Samdians. We would welcome you along for the fight."

"What good would I do you now?" Data asked. "As an android I had unique strengths and skills. Now I'm just another human."

"Like the rest of us," Dare replied. "For one thing, you shoot as well as I do. You've got Starfleet training, which I admit is the best basis there is for a life like ours, once you strip away some of the naiveté that goes with it. There's probably not a computer in the galaxy that you and Sdan couldn't finagle between you." He attempted a smile. "I don't ask very many people to join up with us. We have to depend on one another in too many life-or-death situations."

"Thank you for your confidence, but I think not," Data said. "At least not now."

"If you change your mind," Dare said, "it's never difficult to locate me. Pris, I'll see you at the ships."

Pris watched the door close behind her, then turned to Data. "I'll miss you," she said.

"I—" Some new human sense warned him not to tell her honestly that he regretted their brief liaison and could not for the life of him tell why. And he certainly could not say that for the past twenty-four hours he had completely forgotten her existence.

Fortunately, she mistook his fumbling, saying, "Don't be embarrassed—I'm not holding you to any promises. Neither of us made any, did we?"

"No. It's best that way, when we don't know if we'll ever meet again."

"We will, Data—I'm sure of that. And I hope it will be under happier circumstances." She smiled, but it was a sad smile. "Think of us when your current tour of duty is over. You may be ready to leave Starfleet once you've proved you can still handle anything they throw at you."

Again he allowed her to misinterpret his motivations, let her kiss him softly on the cheek, and say good-bye.

He recognized his emotion, but not its source. There was no reason, no reason at all, that he should react with embarrassment to Pris. He *liked* her! He honestly found her attractive and appealing, and yet he had been unfair to her.

When that thought surfaced, he examined it more closely. What had he done that was unfair to Pris? She was not in love with him. She liked him, he liked her, and they had spent a most pleasurable time together. How was that unfair to her?

Too tired to think, and yet with the thoughts repeating in his head, Data decided he ought at least to try to sleep. By habit, he turned to put everything in his outer room back into place before turning out the lights—and saw the hologram base still on his desk.

For the first time he realized how much Pris was like Tasha. Both were slender, blond, intelligent, and assertive. Both had chosen a life of action and danger.

Is that it? Did I accept Pris because she reminds me of someone I cannot have? That would certainly be reason enough to feel I have been unfair to her.

Accepting that as a working hypothesis, Data decided that tonight he would not think further about his mistake, except to vow never to repeat it. He also refused to let his mind return to the Samdian situation. While the rest of the *Enterprise* crew might have to invent ways to take their minds off their inability to help the Samdians until permission came to abandon their mission, Data had necessary work to do, restoring the knowledge he had lost. He ordered the computer to set him a course of study to begin in the morning, and went to bed.

By Data's next duty shift, Starfleet had given the *Enterprise* a new assignment, and everyone breathed a sigh of relief as the reminder of their failure swung off the viewscreen.

In routine flight, Wesley Crusher returned to the helm. Midway through the shift, Captain Picard sent Data to the science station to study the records of seismic activity on Beta Tharsis Four, where a mining colony needed help in reinforcing their underground compound before it collapsed from shifting gravitational stresses.

Ensign Serena Gibson came to take Data's place at Ops. As before, he noticed how lovely, how *female,* she was—then caught himself. Another slender blonde. Was this an obsession?

The time it took to examine his reaction kept him lingering beside the Ops console long enough to notice Wesley look over at Gibson, blush, then return determinedly to close inspection of his own console—on which, as they were in routine flight, he had absolutely nothing to do.

Data went up to the science station, and soon became immersed in the problem of Beta Tharsis Four. He took his conclusions to Geordi, and by the time the *Enterprise* reached its destination they had designed a method of reinforcing the mining colony without forcing the inhabitants to evacuate.

From there, the *Enterprise* went to Starbase 92 for vaccine to deliver to Ghandi Seven. After that, they ferried a bevy of scientists to the science colony on Nisus.

No one missed the pattern: The *Enterprise* was being given obviously beneficial assignments as a reminder that Starfleet missions seldom ended in the kind of frustration they had known in the Samdian Sector. Slowly, tensions eased and people regained confidence.

Data completed his self-imposed refresher course, retested in his personal specialties, and was recommended by Captain Picard and First Officer Riker for restoration to full active duty.

But the medical personnel disagreed.

Dr. Pulaski was concerned that Data's blood pressure was elevated. "It's not above the human norm," she told him, "but it's consistently higher than it was when you came aboard from Elysia. So are your cholesterol levels. They're not dangerously high, Data —but if they continue to rise this way, in a few months I will be forced to take you off the duty roster."

"Surely they'll level off," he said diffidently. "You said I couldn't stay in the state of perfect health the Elysians gave me."

"Are you exercising?" she asked.

"Every one of Mr. Worf's required sessions."

"Then what are you eating?"

"Oh, I don't know. A variety," he replied. That was true as far as it went, but his appetite had never returned to the state of his first days as a human, when everything had been fresh and new. When his stomach reminded him that he needed to eat, his mind frequently rejected the idea of a balanced meal. Sometimes he craved spicy foods, and sometimes he placated his stomach with endless cups of tea instead of the nutrition it was signaling for. He sometimes woke in the middle of his sleep period with unpleasant sensations he had identified as indigestion. Ship's stores provided remedies, and Data deliberately ignored the warnings to report frequent need to the CMO. He simply swallowed a tablet or two and went back to restless sleep.

Often, usually after an afternoon's lesson, Wesley would introduce him to another new concoction featuring their acting ensign's favorite flavor and secret vice: chocolate. Data discovered a "sweet tooth," and sometimes cut back on other foods to allow himself those treats when his uniform started getting tight around the middle.

Nightmares plagued him, yet on some nights he had dreams that filled him with joy. Oddly, although he would waken with a sense of great pleasure, he could not remember the good dreams any more clearly than the bad ones.

To be human, Data had known in the abstract, was to have a subconscious mind. Whatever his was doing, it was skilled at hiding from his consciousness. It was a new and frightening experience not to be able to access information that he was perfectly aware *did* exist somewhere in his mind.

When Pulaski would not give him an unconditional medical clearance, Data forced himself to eat a computer-designed, perfectly balanced diet for ten days, and increase his exercise schedule before reporting back for another check. He dropped over two kilos of weight in that time, and his blood pressure was closer to what Pulaski considered desirable.

She reluctantly cleared him—but nothing he could do would persuade Counselor Troi to clear him once and for all on the psychological level. The problem was, he could not tell her why he was still depressed after the rest of the crew had recovered from having to turn their backs on the Samdians.

Wesley, noticing that he and Data had a certain moodiness in common, tried talking with him.

"Do you miss that woman from Darryl Adin's gang?" Wesley ventured.

"Pris? Yes, I suppose so," Data replied. But Pris was not the cause of his unidentifiable feelings. His problem was that he didn't know what *was*.

Wesley persisted. "Are you dating anyone else?"

"That is really none of your business, Wesley."

"Lots of the women on the crew would like to date you, you know."

"How would you know that?" Data asked.

"They keep asking *me* about you," the boy replied. "They think you're cute."

". . . Cute?"

"Yeah . . . Ensign Gibson asked me about you."

Oh, no—he was not going to risk disappointing another woman who looked like Tasha. "I don't think it's wise to become socially involved with someone whose bridge performance I will soon have a hand in evaluating," he improvised.

Wesley grinned. "Thanks, Data. I'll tell her that. She's on bridge rotation for another two weeks." He blushed and admitted, "Maybe if you're not available I can get her to take an interest in me."

Data smiled. "I'm hardly an expert on such things, but I've observed that a small difference in age creates great barriers until humans get at least into their twenties. Why don't you approach girls in your classes, Wesley?"

The boy shrugged. "Lots of them are pretty, but they're hard to talk to. They're not interested in the things I do." With painful honesty he admitted, "And some of the kids resent that I get to work on the bridge. I don't really fit in with them anymore. Data," he asked, "has a woman ever turned you down?"

"Certainly they—" He stopped, frowning. Why did he automatically start to say yes? Why did he *feel* as if he understood what Wesley was talking about? Since becoming human, he had never put himself in that situation; Pris had taken the risks in their liaison. As

288

an android, he had had no personal desires on the subject; it had always been the woman who initiated any relationship. His closest approximation to Wesley's disappointment was the time Tasha had told him "It never happened." That had bewildered him even without the added turmoil of human hormones.

Finally he said, "Wesley, you have to understand that I probably have less experience with women than you do, at least as a human. You'd better ask Commander Riker or Lieutenant La Forge for advice on dating."

Data did empathize with Wesley's feelings . . . and realized that his own chronic wistful anguish closely resembled the acting ensign's adolescent yearnings.

So he decided to take his own advice, and consult Will Riker.

The first officer was taking a break in Ten-Forward, drinking *café au lait* and watching the passing stars. Not knowing how to open the topic he wanted to discuss, Data also watched them for a moment. He remembered, "On Elysia, when I told Thelia I was from Starfleet, she asked if the stars truly moved swiftly there."

"It sure looks that way, doesn't it?" Riker replied, then turned to Data. "Sit down. Enjoy the view."

Data sat, saying, "It is something I have learned to enjoy."

At that Riker, who had momentarily returned to looking at the stars, suddenly turned squarely toward Data and fixed him with a hawklike gaze. After a few moments' study, he nodded sagely. "Woman trouble."

Data felt his eyes widen. "How did you know?"

"What other kind of trouble sets a man to staring at the stars?" When Data started to answer, Riker shook his head.

"You opened with something romantic a woman once said to you."

"Romantic?"

"In the broad sense of the word. If you'd been human at the time it would probably have led to a flirtation. So what's the problem now?"

"I'm not certain. Wesley asked me for advice about women, which made me realize how little I know about them. I have too many of my own feelings I don't understand."

"And don't want to discuss with Deanna because she's also a woman," Riker concluded.

"That is correct. I do not wish her to think me even more unstable. For . . . I sense that I want something, very badly—and yet I cannot say what it is I want! You are correct that my feelings are exacerbated by proximity to a woman."

Riker smiled. "Data, you're not unstable. You're reacting perfectly normally to having hormones for the first time in your life. Don't be afraid to tell Deanna—it's her job to know more about men than we know about ourselves."

Data wondered for a moment how much that had to do with Riker's not making a permanent commitment to the beautiful counselor. But Riker continued, "All you need is more experience, Data. More variety. Women are one of life's greatest pleasures, and certainly nothing to be afraid of."

"I'm not afraid."

"But your experience is limited."

"Extremely," Data admitted.

"I think right now your feelings about women are exaggerated by their uniqueness, my friend. Get to know some more women. Play the field for a while. It won't be long before your emotions reach an even keel.

It sounded like good advice.

So when he saw Ensign Lee Ann Su in Ten-Forward the next day, Data struck up a conversation, and they ended up having a pleasant evening together. She had none of the liabilities of Ensign Gibson. Instead, she was a short curvaceous brunette, more pretty than beautiful; she bore no resemblance at all to Tasha Yar, and her rotation on the bridge had ended several months ago.

Their evening went no further than dinner and public entertainment afterward; Data was still following Geordi's advice to let the woman set the pace, and it became apparent that Lee Ann was just a bit unsure of what a senior officer might expect of her. He made sure she felt no pressure on that account, and simply enjoyed her company through dinner and a concert performed by some of the crew who had formed a very fine string quartet. After that, Data and Lee Ann went their separate ways.

And the next morning Data woke again with that sense that he had done something wrong—that somehow he had betrayed someone! Whom did he think he had betrayed? Tasha? But she would *never* be jealous, even if she were still alive. No, his feelings could not be about Tasha.

Flashes of his dreams were starting to surface—he remembered one from last night in which he was with a woman. A brunette. Lee Ann, but not Lee Ann. A face he could not pull into the forefront of his memory, but someone he knew. Someone he . . . loved?

That was not possible. He didn't know any woman well enough to love her.

"I need that information *now,* if you please, Mr. Data."

To his horror, he didn't even know what information the captain had asked for. He glanced over at Wesley, who asked, "Has Starfleet ever had an armed confrontation with the Waykani before, Captain?" That was enough for Data to recall that on the periphery of his attention Picard had asked for specs on the Waykani space fleet.

Glad the captain could not see his burning face, Data rapidly punched up the statistics while Picard told Wesley, "We are not going to have a confrontation now, if we can avoid it, Ensign."

They didn't have to avoid it; the fleet of heavily armed vessels had no interest in the *Enterprise.* They passed by, incommunicado, but their course told where they were headed: the Samdian Sector.

"The war is on," Worf remarked.

"So it appears, Lieutenant," Picard replied, "but it is not *our* war. Mr. Data, I don't expect to have to repeat an order on my bridge."

"No, sir. It won't happen again."

It didn't the rest of that watch, but Wesley had to track Data down in Ten-Fore later, as he had forgotten they had a lesson scheduled. His computer would have reminded him, but he had not returned to his quarters.

"I owe you an apology for forgetting our appointment," Data told the boy, "and thanks for 'getting me off the hook' with the captain today. I didn't know what he had asked me for till you mentioned the Waykani."

"Data," Wesley said with genuine concern, "what's wrong? You didn't make mistakes like that when you first came back from Elysia."

"I don't know," Data admitted. "Possibly this is . . . a letdown, after the tension of learning to be human, coping with requalifying, and the stress everyone was under with the Samdian situation." He smiled. "I may be overconfident. I just have to face the fact that I can't think about two things at once anymore."

The lie flowed so smoothly that Data hardly realized he was twisting the truth. Wesley appeared to accept what he said. It was only later that he realized what he had done. As an android he had been perfectly capable of lying when a situation called for it; what had been hard was recognizing the situation, and then producing a convincing lie.

Why was so much about being human negative?

And his dreams continued, night after night, although he could never see the face of his dream woman. *Definitely hormones!* Data told himself. Yet he found himself looking forward to the dreams, which were now quite pleasant.

Then one day communications from Dare and his gang stopped. An ion storm? A hasty evacuation in which there was no time to send messages? Or the exigencies of war?

With that nagging worry foremost on his mind, he went for another interminable session with Counselor Troi. He seated himself in a chair opposite hers.

"Tell me what's troubling you, Data."

"I am concerned about my friends," he began.

"They'll be all right, Data. Darryl Adin has been in tight spots before." She smiled reassuringly. "So has Pris, I'm certain."

"It's not just Pris—" Data began, harsher than he intended. He shook his head. "I'm sorry, Deanna. It's also these dreams I've been having."

"Why don't you tell me about them," Troi suggested.

He shook his head. "They're not that important," he said, averting his eyes.

Troi leaned forward across the table separating them and covered his hand with hers.

"Oh, Data," she said, "don't be afraid of me. Or of what is troubling you. The only way to resolve it is to bring it out into the open."

He felt exposed, threatened. He wanted to run. Only Starfleet discipline held him, pinned beneath her gaze. "There's nothing to resolve," he protested weakly. "But . . . I will tell you of my dreams anyway."

"They bring you pleasure," she said after he'd finished. "Yet they also cause you pain. You yearn for something you cannot have. Fantasizing about it may be pleasurable, but it also prevents you from enjoying what you *can* have."

Data sat back in his chair, abruptly pulling his hand out from under hers. "I could have called *that* speech out of the computer files on elementary human psychology."

"It would not be there if it were not true," she pointed out. "It's all right to fight me, Data. That way we'll get at what you're fighting for."

"There isn't anything I'm fighting—"

As he spoke, she leaned forward slightly in her chair, her huge dark eyes unfocused as she probed his

294

feelings. Then, "Oh!" she gasped. Her eyes suddenly focused on his. "Data, what you are suffering is something I have sensed before, but only once. It *is* an obsession, but not a destructive one. You are in love."

"Counselor," he protested, "how could I be in love without knowing with whom?"

"I think you do know. Somewhere in the back of your mind, you know who this woman is."

Data frowned. Despite all he felt, "Could it be Pris, Counselor?"

"No, Data. If you had unrequited feelings for a woman on the ship, or for Pris, you would not hide that from me, or from yourself. What I sense from your dreams is something you can't admit because you don't want to face it and possibly lose it." She frowned. "An obsession."

Data frowned. "I can never see her face. But you are right: I know her, Deanna. We work together as if we had been colleagues for a long time, and at the end of the dream she always kisses me. So why can't I see who she is?"

Chapter Fourteen

"DATA," SAID COUNSELOR TROI, "will you permit me to hypnotize you?"

He nodded. His hostility had disappeared—now he wanted only to know the truth. "Yes, if that's possible."

"There's no reason it shouldn't be. We will work together, and you will remember everything we discover."

So Data lay down, and Troi spoke softly, intensely.

He didn't fall asleep. Rather, his dream came slowly to life. He started to tell about it, and then to live it, climbing, climbing ever upward, a woman at his side. It was the Quest he had undergone on Elysia, he recognized, but not accurate in detail. And he was human, not android. He and his companion overcame wild beasts. They scaled cliffs, swam rivers, encouraged each other through a burning desert.

Twilight fell.

Data and the woman prepared to rest, but still he could not see her. In the dream state, he didn't care.

"Data," she said. "Look at me, Data."

For some reason, he could not.

"Data, look at me."

Slowly, helplessly, he turned toward her.

"Thelia?"

He felt no surprise.

For a moment she was the dirt-smeared gamin of their struggle through Elysia's sacred mountain, smiling as she did each time she overcame an obstacle.

Then she was as he had last seen her, a breathtaking vision in gold and white. She held out her arms, and he went joyfully into them. They kissed—

And Data was wide awake, alone, on the couch in Counselor Troi's office. Troi stood beside him, her face calm but concerned. "Data," she said, "you should not have left Elysia."

"What?"

She smiled. "Can't you see it? You're in love with Thelia. Passionately in love with her. No other woman can overcome such a force."

He sat up slowly, rubbing the back of his neck.

"Then . . . that's why I feel guilty when I have a pleasant time with another woman."

"Yes," Deanna said. She sat down on the couch beside him. "I've rarely come across such intensity of emotion, Data."

He nodded. How could he not have known? It was so plain now, the feelings overwhelmed him. He wanted Thelia, and no one else. "Counselor—what can I do?"

"Isn't it obvious? You must get permission to return to Elysia. If my experience means anything, she is probably yearning for you in exactly the same way."

He nodded, still half-dazed. "I hope so, but . . . why couldn't I see it for myself? Why didn't I *know* it was Thelia?"

"For completely understandable reasons, Data. At first, you were overwhelmed simply by the sensations of being human," she reminded him. "More recently you have been consumed by your duties—but Data, if Thelia feels as you do, you will have little trouble persuading her to join you on the *Enterprise.*"

"Yes!" he said, feeling a grin spread across his face. "She will . . ." His voice trailed off, his grin faded, and his expression turned to one of surprise. "Deanna, she doesn't *know* we can be together! She was sent back to her land before my transformation took place. She must think she's in love with an android!"

When Data approached Captain Picard with his request, and Troi confirmed it, the captain considered the options. Data could spend several months in a shuttle or several weeks working his way from starbase to starship to reach Elysia in stages. "And then how long to get you back again? No—the study of Elysia is far from complete; I expect Starfleet will approve our having another look."

There was no way to hail Thelia from orbit so, using the ship's sensors, Data and Geordi worked out which habitat was hers. Atridia turned out to be by far the biggest of the habitats, more heavily populated than the ones the *Enterprise* crew had visited, with one large city, several smaller ones, and numerous towns and villages.

Data shook his head in frustration. "Geordi, how am I ever going to find her?"

His friend laughed. "She's a local heroine, remember? We'll put you down in the biggest city, and I'll bet the first person you ask can tell you where she is."

Data nodded. "You're right. I guess I'm just not thinking straight."

"Don't worry about it." Geordi clapped him on the shoulder. "Everyone's rooting for you, Data. Good luck."

He beamed down near the bustling city—and from the moment he materialized, Data was overwhelmed with happiness. Thelia was somewhere nearby, breathing the same air, being warmed by the same sunshine.

When he reached the town itself, he couldn't help but think that the entire place shared his mood, for all about him were healthy, well-dressed people in the midst of preparing for some sort of celebration.

Banners and flowers festooned the buildings, some just being hung up as Data watched. Loops of white and gold intertwined with loops of blue and maroon, while huge garlands of yellow, pink, and orange flowers turned the street into a rainbow.

At first no one took particular notice of him. His uniform was of different material, cut, and style from the clothes of the passers-by, but among the gaudy colors the greenish gold and black did not command immediate attention. And of course he now appeared as human as any of the natives.

He looked along the street in either direction. There was nothing to see but people and buildings one way, but in the opposite direction there rose above the city a turreted castle that he recognized: the one in the background when Elysia's gods had unsuccessfully tempted Thelia with the vision of her home. He set out in that direction, winding between people busily cleaning and decorating the city.

The place had obviously grown up without the advantage of a designer; the cobbled street twisted and turned, providing quaint and charming nooks and crannies. Data kept expecting to turn a corner and come face-to-face with Thelia.

Which he did.

Not Thelia herself, but a huge tapestry displayed in an open square, depicting Thelia dressed as she had been when he had first met her, and a man. Or rather, from the white cloth chosen to represent his face and hands, and the rather good representation of his Starfleet uniform, an android.

The portrait of Thelia was recognizable, although that of Data was not. The artist with a needle had obviously had a model for the female figure, while the male must have been done from Thelia's own description.

The two figures were depicted symbolically, proportionally far too large for the mountain they stood upon, the sacred mountain of Elysia's gods. Data had seen primitive artwork before; for the period before a culture grasped the concept of perspective, this was exceptionally good.

It also proved Geordi right: Thelia was a local heroine. There would be little difficulty finding out where she was.

Data turned, ready now to ask someone, but people were streaming toward one area of the square, where an elderly man climbed onto a platform to the accompaniment of musical instruments that sounded a cross between a guitar and a mandolin. The crowd cheered, then hushed, waiting expectantly.

In practiced, professional tones, the man began to tell a story. It was not just a simple recitation; it was poetry, chanted to strums of music. Data listened for a while, then decided it was time to move on when he heard his name mentioned.

"The one from afar, promised by the gods, turned out to be magical indeed. Not a flesh and blood being, but a man of metal and light, with greater strength than a team of oxen but the gentleness of a mother caring for her child."

At that, Data decided to stay for the rest of the performance, using his tricorder to record the poetry for later appreciation. In its bare essentials, the story was accurate: Thelia, permitted by the gods to undertake the Quest, successfully negotiated the swamp, met Data at the sacred island, and together they climbed through the mountain. In detail, though, the story was compressed, omitting the many long hours of weary climbing, and stressing Thelia's feats over Data's. That was only right and proper: she was their local champion.

The story ended with Thelia's return to Atridia, bearing the news that the gods had agreed to unite their land with that of Tosus. A cheer went up from the gathered crowd. The union of the two habitats must be what the celebration was all about.

It was time to find Thelia. Data turned away from the storyteller's platform—and found himself facing another tapestry. He had walked past this one when he entered the square, and it had been behind him all this time.

This tapestry featured Thelia and another man—definitely not Data. This man's portrait was as detailed as Thelia's, and had clearly been done from a live model. He was tall, with brown hair a few shades lighter than Data's, worn long in back in the Elysian style, and was dressed in a suit of blue and maroon, while Thelia in this version was all in gold but for a garland of white flowers on her dark hair. She and the man were depicted holding hands in the center of the tapestry, the castle in miniature beside Thelia, an equally imposing structure beside the man, the sacred mountain in the background, and a stylized sun pouring benevolent rays over the smiling couple.

He strode closer to the tapestry. It almost looked as if the two of them were . . .

Murmured voices sounded behind him. "It is true . . . he wears the attire of the land of Starfleet!"

Data turned to see who had spoken—and found himself being stared at by a small crowd of curious people.

"Welcome to Atridia, stranger." An elder man detached himself from the group and stepped toward Data. "I am Lodel."

Data nodded. "And I am—"

"You are from the land of Starfleet," another man interrupted. "You wear the same attire as Data!"

"I do," Data smiled, letting the second man feel the fabric of his uniform. Generations from now, if the Elysians succeeded in reuniting their entire planet, would they wonder what had ever happened to the land of Starfleet? Perhaps to them it would be like lost Atlantis on Earth—or perhaps by then both Thelia and her mysterious "one from afar" would be long since forgotten.

"Princess Thelia will be so pleased you have come!" a woman cried out, clapping her hands together. "You must tell us all whether her Quest companion got what he quested for, and how he has fared since."

"Have others braved the swamp to share our celebration?" another woman asked.

"What happened to Data, the one from afar?" someone else wanted to know.

"Enough questions," Lodel said, stepping in front of Data and turning to face the crowd. He held up his hands. "You must be tired, stranger. You have come a long way, and will want to rest before the wedding. I will take you to my own home, and—"

"Wedding?" Data asked, his heart sinking. *"Whose* wedding?"

"Why, Princess Thelia's. She marries Prince Sharn of Tosus tomorrow afternoon," he replied.

Data sat down heavily on a nearby bench.

Thelia's wedding? Tomorrow? His head was spinning. It couldn't be. He couldn't have come this far only to lose her.

"Are you all right, friend?" Lodel asked.

"Yes," Data said—though in truth he felt sick. "I'm just . . . surprised."

Lodel frowned. "You did not come for the wedding?"

"No," he shook his head. "We did not know about it. Little news travels across the swamp."

"Then you don't know about Sharn," a woman added. "He is a true prince—a worthy husband for Thelia." She snorted. "Though he did not succeed in his Quest, as our princess did."

"Now, Ulia," Lodel chided. "Sharn failed his Quest only because Thelia had already accomplished hers. The princess herself has said as much."

303

Data sat listening to the two argue, his head still reeling. He didn't care to know any of this. All he wanted to do was get out of here, get back to the ship, and forget all about Thelia, and Sharn, and Elysia itself.

"They were promised to each other as infants," Ulia continued, oblivious. "And now their marriage will unite both our lands."

Data clasped his hands in his lap to hide their shaking. It was as if he could hear the message from Elysia's gods: Thelia's duty is to her people. She must marry Prince Sharn to complete the union of the habitats.

Then why did you let me fall in love with her? he wondered hopelessly.

As if in answer, another woman spoke up. "Aye— when Thelia gives Sharn the Kiss of Bonding at their wedding, then he will love her forever."

Ulia laughed. "Thelia has no need of that ancient gift. Sharn fell in love with her the moment he laid eyes on her."

"That's as may be," the other woman answered, "but the Kiss will guarantee that he'll never stray."

Data's head snapped up. *The Kiss of Bonding?*

He recalled Thelia mentioning it in passing, and his own skeptical response. But now one of those log-clear memories flashed through his mind: At the end of the Quest, when he and Thelia met in the knowledge that both had succeeded, she had kissed him on the cheek, saying, "It is safe for me to accord you such a token of affection."

He had wondered what she had meant then, but . . . a kiss could do that? It was impossible. . . .

As impossible as making an android human?

304

"This . . . Kiss of Bonding," he asked. "Thelia had that power before her Quest?"

Lodel nodded. "From her many-times grandmother, Melinia, who Quested to end a war between feuding factions within the land of Atridia itself. All the women descended from that line have it."

Another gift from the gods of Elysia. Now he knew what Thelia had meant by "safe." Well, it might have been safe for her to kiss an android, but clearly her family gift had operated in full force on the man he had become. Elysia's gods repaying Data for his skepticism? Well, he had learned *that* lesson quite thoroughly!

"This kiss," Data asked, "is its effect permanent?"

"Oh, yes," he was told. "Melinia's husband pined away less than a year after she died, great strong warrior though he was."

"But," Data swallowed hard, but knew he had to ask the next question, "what if a woman with that gift were to use it with more than one man? Does it work only once, or is the spell lifted from one man if she kisses another?"

"Oh, she could hold many men under her spell," Ulia put in, "as one of Melinia's daughters did. An evil woman, that one—misused her gift and died when one of the men she made her slave attempted to poison the others so as to have her all to himself. In error, she drank of the poisoned wine herself, and good riddance!"

"But Thelia would never give her Kiss to any but Sharn," Lodel said.

"Of course not," Data said flatly.

So his condition was permanent. He could not have Thelia—her duty was to unite the two habitats—but neither could he escape her spell. Somehow, he would have to survive. The best thing was to get away as quickly as he could, and call for beamup.

But his planned departure was interrupted by the sudden arrival of two men wearing gold and white tabards.

"You are the visitor from the land of Starfleet?" one asked.

"Yes," Data replied.

"Princess Thelia wishes to see you," the messenger told him.

Data's heart stirred with hope. Thelia's wedding had not yet taken place. How well could she know the Prince of Tosus? She and Data had shared more in their brief time together than many close friends in years of acquaintance.

The union of the habitats—that was what Thelia had asked for. The gods had granted that. If there had been any mention of a marriage, Data would certainly remember. If Thelia deserted her bridegroom, it might provide generations of stories for the people of Atridia, but she had already done everything they had asked of her. And once she knew that Data was human, and could and did love her—

The gods must have arranged his return. Of course —that was why Thelia had kissed him in the first place, the only way she dared indicate to the gods her fear of entering into a loveless marriage. She did not owe her people her happiness. The Kiss of Bonding might make Sharn love her, but the story of Melinia's daughter made very clear that it would not create love in the one who bestowed it.

The gods had brought Data back here, in human form, just in time to deliver Thelia from a life of

306

dutiful obligation. In a daze of hope, he entered the reception room where Thelia waited.

She was more beautiful than he remembered.

And her eyes lit with joy when she saw him.

"It is true then!" she said, crossing the room swiftly, taking his hands in hers. "Though I had hoped—"

He looked into her eyes—and saw disappointment. He did *not* see recognition.

Thelia shook her head sadly. "Do not mistake me. I am pleased that someone from Starfleet could come to share my happiness, but—" she let go of his hands, and lowered her gaze—"I had prayed it would be Data himself."

"No," Data said, lowering his own eyes, for fear he could not keep Thelia from seeing what was in them now. "He could not come."

"Of course. I should have known," Thelia said. "You must tell me what has happened to Data. Does he ever speak of our Quest? Is he happy with the gift he received from the gods?"

Data sat beside her, his hands folded stiffly across his lap. "I cannot say if Data is happy with his gift," he began, "but I know he would want me to ask if you are happy with yours."

"I have been rewarded many times beyond what I desired," Thelia said. "Not only will our lands be united, but the gods have provided me with a husband beyond my dreams. Sharn's only regret is that he was denied the Quest—but what does that matter? He is everything I could ask—not only handsome and strong, but wise and gentle, intelligent, and—" she smiled, and for a moment, despite her elegant clothes and jewels, she was the Thelia he had known once again "—he makes me laugh."

"You knew Sharn before—?"

"Before my Quest? No. All the agreements for our marriage were arranged by go-betweens many years ago." She lowered her eyes. "To be truthful, I feared that it would be difficult to enter a marriage with someone I did not know, but," her eyes raised and met his again, "I know him now. So you can tell Data I am happy."

Data hid his agony. Thelia had no idea who he was, and now that he knew she loved another he wanted only to keep her from knowing. He yearned to flee, and yet, knowing this was the last time he would ever see her, he wanted to stay in her presence forever.

"Now you must tell me about him," Thelia said. "Did he receive the gift he desired from the gods?"

"Not . . . exactly," Data said.

Her face fell. "Ah, I was afraid he didn't know how to ask it, or wouldn't because he doubted the gods' powers. But surely they gave him something precious. And healed him? That is, repaired his injuries? His damage?"

"Of course," Data said, "the gods would not leave anyone in such condition. You need not be concerned about Data. He is . . . back in Starfleet where he belongs. And he remembers you . . . with great fondness."

He had to fight not to blurt out who he was, but what good would that do? Thelia didn't want him. She might care very much for the android she remembered, but only as a dear friend. And she showed no response whatsoever to Data as he was now. She was in love with another; he could not win her if he tried.

Nor did he want to cause her distress. He could not

308

stand to provoke her pity, or the guilt she might feel at causing him pain, however unintended.

He could not have said what answers he managed to her questions, but she had made time in a busy day for the unexpected visitor from Starfleet. Soon her duties called her back to her schedule, and Data was ushered out.

There was nothing left for him to do but go back to the ship and try to forget her. He would throw himself into his duties, and try to find some meaning in a life without joy.

Unsatisfied? It was a gross understatement of Data's condition—a condition he would not be suffering if he had not gotten precisely his fondest wish. He remembered telling Thelia the story Ira Graves had told him, about the tin man who had found his heart without being transformed into something he was never meant to be. "I understand that story now," Data said to himself. "Why did I ever want to be something other than myself?"

He returned to the spot he had beamed down to before and tapped his combadge. "One to beam up, Mr. O'Brien."

The transporter took him—but when he coalesced, he was not on the *Enterprise* transporter platform.

He was atop the sacred mountain, in the rainbow sanctuary of Elysia's gods.

"Data of Starfleet," the now-familiar voice said to him, *"our gift was never intended to bring such pain."*

"Then relieve it," he said. "I shall not ask you to make Thelia love me—she is fulfilling her destiny, and I could not give her any greater happiness than she already has."

"You speak wisely," the voice replied. *"What do you ask, then?"*

"Make me stop loving her. Let me make what I can of my life without that pain."

"That is not possible. The only way to remove the effects of Thelia's kiss would be to deprive her and her descendants of the gift our predecessors bestowed upon her ancestor."

"Your . . . predecessors?"

"Or perhaps our descendants. The languages you know have no words for our condition."

"What are you?" Data asked.

"Like you, creatures bound by the natural laws of the universe. Although we have no physical form, neither are we immortal nor infallible. We erred in not preventing Thelia from binding you. However, we cannot take a gift from another in order to alleviate your pain."

"Then take back *my* gift! Make me an android again—then surely Thelia's kiss will have no effect."

There was a long silence, but finally the voice said, *"That is also not possible. We gave you what you most desired."*

"Yes—but that was not what I was sent to Elysia for. I should have asked to know what *you* are, how you maintain the habitats on this hostile planet, how you can entirely change a person's form."

There was another pause. Then the voice spoke again. *"Would you exchange the gift we gave you, then?"*

"Gladly!"

"We can show you what we are. But the human mind cannot comprehend it."

"I see," said Data. "You're counting on the fallibility of human memory. I'll take that risk."

"No, Data of Starfleet, you do not see. There are a few rare points along the space-time continuum at which choices govern vital events in the structure of galactic history. We have shown you the result of one such choice."

Data frowned. "The last major change in galactic history was the Federation-Klingon Alliance. I had not even been activated then."

"No, Data. The last major change in galactic history, from your present perspective, was the failure of the Federation to bring peace to the Samdian Sector. The interstellar war you started will escalate until all the major cultures of your galaxy waste themselves in its destruction."

"Then we have to go back to Dacket and find a way to make peace!"

"It is not possible in the time-choice of your present experience. You should have taken a different path at the point at which you made the choice leading to Starfleet's failure."

"I made the choice?" Data exclaimed.

"When you involved yourself in Thelia's destiny," the voice of the Elysian "gods" replied. "When you placed your curiosity above your duty."

When I . . . sinned, Data realized. He had been human indeed, in the only sense he had ever truly intended . . . and he had never known it.

"Put me back there!" he asked desperately. "I can beam up before Thelia sees me, and I interfere with her destiny."

"You can do so," the voice replied. "We have no assurance that you will."

"Why—?" Data began.

"Our law is much like your Prime Directive. We

311

*cannot interfere with your free will, Data of Starfleet.
We cannot 'put a person back' at the point in time at
which he made a fatal choice and allow him foreknowl-
edge of his error."*

"Then . . . nothing can be changed," Data said in
despair. "My pain at losing Thelia is insignificant
against the destruction I have somehow brought
about. But how could my foolish error change galactic
history?"

*"You wished to know what it would be like if you
were human. That knowledge includes all the consequences, past and future, of your humanity. We will
show you."*

Without warning, knowledge flooded Data's per-
ceptions. His human mind was not equipped for such
an overload of information. There was no hope of
assimilating the billions of details; rather, overall
impressions came into his consciousness, and he
understood. . . .

That time was not a constant. That the knowledge
of these beings the Elysians called "gods" was not
confined, as that of humans was, to a stream of time
moving in a single direction. To them all of history
was a single event, where time, and space, and thought
were one.

He understood the Elysian habitats: the barrier
between the swamp and the habitable territories was
that of probability. They were protected by . . . an
expectation, a union of space and thought on the
molecular level. When he observed it, all was perfectly
clear—and yet he could not have reproduced the
effect in a thousand years.

A forcefield based on probability theory was within
Data's comprehension. His android mind might have

been capable of understanding the rest of what the Elysian gods showed him, but his human mind could only create analogies.

Within the event which was all of time to the Elysian gods were . . . "threads," as it were: events that met and intermingled, each life interweaving with others, a mutable pattern upon a fixed substructure.

The Elysian "gods" showed him his life, influencing numerous others. There was only the "what" to be seen. He could not understand "why" his transformation meant interstellar war.

The Konor extended their dominion from Dacket to Gellesen. He saw Darryl Adin and his gang training the Gellesenians in guerrilla warfare, hoping to make the price of taking the planet too high in Konor lives. He saw the Ferengi arrive, seeing a quick profit in selling to the Konor a fast-dissipating poison dropped from the sky, with no risk to the Konor. He saw the cities of Gellesen become necropolises, among the corpses those of his friends, of Dare, and of Pris.

He saw the Konor pretend to seek another deal with the Ferengi, take hostages, and commandeer their ship. Now they had warp capacity, shields, phasers, photon torpedoes.

He saw the Ferengi retaliate, taking some of their ships through the Neutral Zone in their haste. The Romulans challenged—and the Ferengi had no idea how to deal diplomatically with that obtuse and difficult race. The Romulans took their presence as an act of war.

When the Romulans retaliated against the Ferengi, the Orions came in on the Ferengi side. They attacked Federation outposts—claiming they were secret Romulan strongholds—in an area patrolled by

Klingon Birds of Prey. The Klingons, pleased to honorably dispense with peacekeeping, blasted the Orion ships out of space.

Ever since the Klingon-Federation Alliance, the Orions had been waiting for an excuse to attack the heart of Klingon Territory. They were met by Starfleet.

The Waykani increased their claims on disputed territory. War escalated, system by system. The Konor were forgotten, a minor annoyance in the face of galactic conflict.

At last, somehow, Data was able to form a coherent thought: *No more! Stop! Show me how to stop it!*

He was distanced from the fabric of history, although it remained within his perception.

"You asked," the voice of the Elysian "gods" reminded him, *"to know what we are."*

Again he found his mind filled with incomprehensible knowledge. These were not physical beings, but creatures of pure mind.

"Behold."

Data's attention once more focused on his own life's "thread" within the fabric. As he "watched," it dissolved, freeing other threads.

Data realized that the link was not an inevitable line of destiny, which for all their powers the Elysian gods could not change, but *his* life, subject to his choices, his will. With that thread removed, the whole area of interstellar conflict . . . unraveled.

The other "threads" lost their pattern of aggression and misunderstanding and war. They were pure potential, to be woven into the horrors Data had just observed . . . or into a new pattern dependent on the decision of one young android programmed with insatiable curiosity.

Data understood: From their perspective outside time, the Elysian gods could observe any time-choice at will. Their "gifts" were potential time-lines in which the Questor was strong, or wise, or beloved or . . . human. The choice was the Questor's, and he alone was responsible for what he made of his gift.

Data understood that he, not the gods, controlled his life-choices. But that was all he understood of what they showed him. What he needed was the information as to what he could do *now* to mitigate that hideous vision of the future.

"But I do have the knowledge you have provided me," he said, grasping at the hope. "Perhaps there is a clue from the human perspective that an android can utilize."

"No, Data of Starfleet, you will not retain that memory. All you experienced is, for you, no more than a dream—a dream forgotten, once you accept your true self."

"My—" Data lifted his hands. Pale synthoskin covered them. His diagnostics began a routine systems check, reporting all functions normal. He was restored, yet, "I do remember it all."

"It was an illusion, Data, a possibility, but not reality."

Automatically, Data accessed his knowledge of illusions—these "gods" had produced many that were beyond his ability to penetrate.

But . . . the entire experience he had just lived through? His love, his pain, all a dream? Then how could he feel them as forcefully now as he had in human form?

As always, Data's curiosity set his memory banks to searching for knowledge related to the topic at hand. They responded with a puzzle from one of his philosophy courses at Starfleet Academy: "Am I a man who dreamed he was a butterfly, or a butterfly who dreams he is a man?" His classmates had argued endlessly over the question, while Data had found it incomprehensible.

He understood it now.

"Am I a man," he asked the Elysian gods, "who dreams he is an android, or am I an android who dreamed he was a man?"

The gods chose not to reply.

Instead he was told, *"Your wish has been granted. You have experienced what your life would be like as a human. The dream is ended, Data of Starfleet. It never happened."*

Data smiled. Did these "gods" truly think that saying it never happened would erase his memory of the dread scenario he had experienced so vividly? He would put an access denial code on it, of course, but—

The Elysian transporter effect began to pulse around Data. As if suddenly released from denied access, his internal clock told him it was not fifty days into the future.

Why should he need to be informed that it was not fifty days from now? He knew when and where he was, in the transporter beam on the way to investigating Elysia's mysterious island.

It was as if he had been switched off and back on.

There was always a momentary disorientation as he adjusted his active memory to his internal clock.

When his diagnostics reported everything normal, Data dismissed the absured idea that his memory had adjusted backward, rather than forward. It must be an effect of Elysia's peculiar gravitational anomalies. It could not be imagination. After all, androids do not dream.

At the foot of Elysia's sacred mountain, four *Enterprise* away team members regrouped after circling the island, frustrated at finding nothing to report but a cave opening, invisible to the organic eyes of Riker and Worf and even to Data's instrumentation, detectable only by Geordi's VISOR.

"Wait," said Data as they moved into position for beamup. "There is a life-form reading—but it is faint. No . . ." he frowned at the faint flicker on the tricorder screen, and turned up the gain. "Commander, I cannot get an accurate directional reading, and on open range your readings interfere."

Riker nodded. "We'll get out of your way, then." He tapped his combadge. "Three to beam up, Mr. O'Brien. Mr. Data to follow at his command."

"Are you all right, sir?" O'Brien's voice was tight with tension.

"Of course. Why wouldn't we be?"

"The ship's Red Alert warnings suddenly went off, with no reason for activation—and then there was another of those power surges. It seems to be over now, but—"

"Is your instrumentation working?" Geordi demanded, tapping his own badge.

"Yes—everything reads normal."

"Then get us out of here!"

Data stepped away from the other three. They dissolved in the transporter beam, and he turned up the gain on his tricorder again. Nothing. He turned full circle, annoyed; he could not have been fooled by that flicker—

He was about to signal for beamup when he heard a sudden splashing noise.

Looking toward the swamp, he saw nothing until he used infrared vision to penetrate the fog. There was someone coming!

Fascinated, Data watched the boat with its lone occupant approach the shore. Suddenly she looked up. It was a woman, tired and bedraggled from her arduous journey.

Data was overcome with a sensation unique in his experience. It was as if he had been in this situation before, watching the boat approach—

Did he have a memory circuit malfunction? Was he affected by the power surge?

At the same moment, he realized that the woman was now close enough to glimpse him through the swamp fog.

She must not see him! This was a religious sanctuary to the Elysians; she must be here on one of their sacred Quests.

Data darted behind a rock.

He must have had *some* kind of malfunction to have stood staring at her through the fog, letting her get close enough that she might have seen him. According to the Prime Directive, he had no right to risk discovery. And by closing the channel he had trapped himself: the chitter of his combadge would carry to

the woman's ears, as would the sound of the transporter.

He could not risk having her come to see what the
noises were, just in time to see a person disappear into
thin air.

Still, his error gave him a chance to watch, to see
whether the Elysian "gods" would communicate with
this Questor. Data held perfectly still, waiting for her
to go on up to the mountain, before he called for
beamup.

The woman, though, was looking around the island.
She did not seem to be seeking the entry point to the
cave; rather, she peered along the shore in either
direction, as if expecting someone.

From the opposite direction, there came a splashing
and scraping. The woman started working her way
over the rocks toward the sound, a difficult process.
But soon she would be far enough away—

A man came around some rocks. Both he and the
woman stopped, looking at one another. The woman
was small, with dark hair and eyes. The man was tall,
with lighter brown hair. Like the woman, he was
somewhat the worse for his journey, but he smiled
when he saw her.

The woman spoke. "You are the one from afar the
gods promised as a companion on my journey. My
name is Thelia."

The man's smile widened. "And you are the one
promised me—by our parents, and now by the gods. I
am Sharn."

"Sharn!" she exclaimed. "I should have known it
would be you. Surely together we will succeed in our
Quest."

The man took her hand. "I saw a spring of water

back there. We'll need to fill our water bags before we try to find our way up the mountain."

But they would not have to climb it, Data saw: the cave opening Geordi had discovered was now clearly visible; the two Elysians would easily find it when they returned from the spring.

It was balm to Data's conscience, if not his curiosity, when the two disappeared from sight and hearing. He hit his combadge. "One to beam up."

Geordi had lingered in the transporter room, waiting for his friend. "Dammit, Data," he said, "how many times do you have to be reminded you're not indestructible! What if there'd been another power surge while we were beaming you?"

"I think," said Data, not knowing why he felt certain of something on such slight evidence, "you would have been warned, as you were of the last one."

"You think that Red Alert was deliberately triggered? By whom?"

"Elysia's 'gods.' I just saw them in action."

"What?"

"No, I did not see the gods themselves," he explained, "but I saw their response to people they had invited. When two Elysians came ashore for one of their Quests, that cave entrance you detected was suddenly visible."

"You're sure they didn't see you?"

"I am certain. But Geordi—the two events suggest a pattern. They did not want us on the island, so we could not see the cave. But apparently we are not unwelcome on Elysia, as they have started to warn us of those dangerous power surges."

"Intriguing, as you always say." Geordi was rubbing his hands. "You'd better go tell the captain your theory. I think I should let one of the doctors check some of these cuts."

"Let me see," Data responded automatically, and Geordi held out his hands. They were cut and bleeding from climbing over the sharp rock formations on the sacred island. "They should be cleaned and medicated against infection," he agreed.

"Which will hurt even more," Geordi complained. He shook his head. "I don't know why you'd ever want to be human, Data. We get hurt awfully easily— especially compared to you."

"I do not want to be physically human," Data replied. "It is just that I wonder if it will ever be possible for me to understand the human spirit . . . the human soul."

"Either way, Data," Geordi replied, "the only way you'll ever understand is to understand human pain —and my friend, that's something you should pray you *never* have to experience."

Chapter Fifteen

THE *ENTERPRISE* SPENT three more frustrating days trying to solve the puzzle of Elysia's dangerous power surges and their relationship, if any, to the elusive "gods." Then they were called on an emergency mission to the Samdian Sector, where the local populace were being attacked by beings known as Konor, and another ship was assigned to verify that the space lane past Elysia was safe to travel.

Within an hour of setting out, Data was deep into a fruitless search through every cross-reference he could think of for records of the Konor. And an hour after that, he was certain he had left no potential source unsearched. He found nothing: the Konor were new to this part of the galaxy, and until the *Enterprise* reached the Samdian Sector they would know no more about them.

As it was an otherwise routine flight, Data had time to spend with his friends, both among the crew and among their unexpected guests. He brought Darryl Adin to the regular poker game one evening, and Dare won, resoundingly.

After the game, they joined the rest of Dare's gang in Ten-Fore. Data sat down next to Pris Shenkley, with whom he had had some intriguing conversations when they first met on Treva. She seemed pleased to talk with him again. This time he was not preoccupied with a mission, as he had been then, so he focused his full attention on her and learned a great deal about improvising weapons systems from outmoded technology.

Eventually they found themselves the last people in the lounge. Guinan relieved the other hostess and put on coffee to brew for the next shift's early risers.

Pris looked around, saying, "You know so much about technology, Data. You could probably do my job better than I can."

"I do not think so," Data replied. "Perhaps the construction, but not the design. It is not possible to program inspiration, intuition, improvisation."

She gave him a softly wistful smile that he didn't quite understand. "No, I suppose not. But perhaps you can learn those things. Especially . . . intuition." With that she stood and stretched. "Good night, Data."

"It is actually morning, ship's time," he pointed out.

Pris chuckled. "Good morning, then, but I'm going to bed anyway. Perhaps we can work on your intuition at a time when I'm not so sleepy."

Data stared after her a moment, perplexed. Then he went over to the bar. He had drunk a glass of juice with Pris earlier, and had no need for further nutrients at the moment, but he often found Guinan's conversation enlightening. So he sat on a stool and said without preamble, "I think I missed something."

"Yes," Guinan replied, "you did."

"What?" he asked eagerly.

"Your friend wanted to know more about you."

Data frowned. "She did not ask me any questions."

Guinan's face took on that infuriating smooth complacency which meant she was about to say something it would take the hearer a considerable time to understand—or that he might never figure out. "There are certain things a woman does not come right out and ask a man," she told him.

"But what could she not ask *me?* And why?" Data asked.

"When you work out *what,*" Guinan assured him, "you'll know why."

Data then went to see how Sdan and Poet were coming with the repairs to their ships' computers. After that he had scheduled a science laboratory demonstration for the ship's schoolchildren, and then he was due on the bridge.

Two days later Data helped put the finishing touches on the guidance systems for the ships of the Silver Paladin—just as his friends received word that their presence on Brancherion was no longer needed.

"Damn the luck," Poet cursed. "We'd of made easy money if the matter was that simple to settle. Ah, well, win some, lose some."

One day Dare received a message from the Samdian System, in his private code. He made no secret of the contents, however: he, too, was being called upon to help the people of Dacket against the Konor.

As the *Enterprise* was far faster than Dare's ships, he and his gang requested that they be allowed to "hitchhike" the rest of the way. Captain Picard agreed —and as the *Enterprise* approached the Samdian

Sector, Data was plunged into the mystery of the Konor.

According to the planet Dacket's leader, Chairman Tichelon, the Konor had recently taken the planet Jokarn, and were now attacking his own world. The third planet that made up their economic community was Gellesen, which had sent Dacket weapons and troops, to no avail.

Geordi's scans showed Dacket in detail. Where the Konor had established themselves, all technology was operating except communications. No wonder messages from the *Enterprise* had been ignored: although the communications equipment built by the people of Dacket was still there, it had been shut down.

They focused in on a city the Konor had taken months before. People went about their business as if they had always belonged there, to all appearances peaceful and contented beings. What was odd was that no one spoke, no one gestured, yet it was clear that people understood and cooperated with one another. Thralen, the Theskian sociologist, hypothesized telepathy.

But where the Konor had recently conquered, as in the city of Eskatus, the scans recorded graphic scenes of slaughter. "Surely telepaths could not treat people so," Deanna Troi said in disbelief. "They would feel their pain, their deaths."

"Perhaps they do," Will Riker said grimly. "Perhaps they are psychotic."

Further scenes provided nothing to counter the hypothesis of telepathy as the Konor means of communication, and also confirmed the contention of the Samdians that they took slaves. But . . . the children they saw caged like animals did not look like Chairman Tichelon and the other people of Dacket. They were slender, willowy beings with green-gold skin and lavender hair, like the Konor.

Data accessed his memory banks for information on Samdian biology—and started in amazement. "Captain!" he interrupted the briefing. "We have missed something Chairman Tichelon obviously wanted us to overlook: The Konor are not an alien species recently arrived from some unexplored area of the galaxy. They are simply another group of Samdians!"

"Explain," Picard ordered.

And Data did.

"So," Picard said ominously, "Chairman Tichelon lied to us. The Konor didn't 'take' the planet Jokarn, but originated there."

"If our conclusions are correct," Data continued, "the Konor are a branch of Samdians who have recently developed telepathy. There is no indication in our records of high levels of ESP among the Samdians."

"Perhaps," said Picard, "the Samdians will be willing to tell us the truth now that we have penetrated their deception. This is not an attack by outside forces, but a civil war."

"And so we cannot offer assistance other than as mediators," Riker added. "And that only if both sides agree."

"I'll have another talk with Chairman Tichelon," said the captain. "Data, Thralen, study the rest of these records. Look for what motivates the Konor, other than conquest. If we are to act as mediators, we will need leverage. Obviously the other Samdians don't have that key, or they would have used it."

Data and Thralen ran the records several times, but found nothing.

Thralen said, "We must be overlooking something."

"What else is there?" Data asked. "Our records are extremely sketchy, as the Samdians have always been isolationist."

"There must be another approach," Thralen said, his antennae extending and retracting in frustration. "We need to know *why* Jokarn suddenly attacked Dacket. The people of Jokarn must have recently developed telepathy. Yet . . . telepaths are normally nonaggressive."

"What if not all of them developed it?" Data asked. "The name 'Konor' does not appear in the historical information on the Samdians. Could the powers of a few have frightened the people of Jokarn? Galactic history certainly provides enough instances of people with new powers being persecuted. Could the Jokarn have hurt them so badly that they were driven to revenge on all Samdian non-telepaths?"

"Possibly," Thralen agreed. "Giving a group of people a new name is a way of distancing them, making them less than yourself so you can mistreat, even kill them."

"Computer: language banks. Morphemic structure of the Samdian language."

"Working."

"What is the historical meaning of the word 'Konor'?"

After several prompts, the computer concluded it meant "People: sentient, sapient organic beings. Persons, as opposed to animals."

Data frowned. "Why would the Samdians call the

Konor that? It must be the Konor's own word for themselves."

Thralen was not satisfied either. He prodded the computer to even deeper analysis. Finally the reply came. "Root derivation of 'konor' is 'those who possess souls.'"

"Gods," Thralen whispered, the blue of his face paling to a washed-out hue. He pushed himself up out of his chair, and began pacing behind the terminal. "If that's what we're up against, we haven't a chance."

Data turned to stare at him. "I do not understand."

"History, Data. The fiercest wars in all the history of the galaxy have been fought over religious differences. What ought to be the balm and consolation for the trials of life is made the instigator of fury and grief." Thralen stopped pacing, and rested his hands on the back of Data's chair.

He then told Data of his own experiences with religious disputes, revealing more than Data had ever learned before of the ship's sociologist: his own family had rejected Thralen when he pursued a course of study opposed to their fundamentalist beliefs in the Great Mother.

Data felt inadequate, but Thralen did not seem to notice, accepting Data's comprehension the way Dare had that time Data had taken him Tasha's Farewell. Data was far out of his element here. Still, he had to say something.

"I have stored in my memory banks gigabytes of information on religions throughout the galaxy. I can quote it at length, but I do not understand it. I am sorry, Thralen. I have no way of knowing what gods are—which is why I had hoped actually to meet up with the gods of Elysia."

"If you had been able to do so, it would have proved they were not gods as I believe in God," Thralen replied. "Beyond anything the sentient mind can comprehend, there is a force that drives the universe, Data. Only when we leave this state of existence will we meet and comprehend it."

"We?" asked Data. *"You* believe in an existence after death. You believe you have a soul."

"Oh, yes. There is no doubt of it."

"I do not know if I have one."

Thralen smiled. *"I* know you do," he replied, "and not because of a Judge Advocate's ruling."

"Her ruling was that I have the right to try to find out if I have one," Data pointed out.

"Well then," Thralen said, "perhaps the Konor can tell you. If they call themselves 'those with souls,' that implies that they can recognize a soul when they see it." But Data heard the sarcasm in the anthropologist's voice; neither of them could credit people of such viciousness with any degree of sensitivity.

"It's time to go down to the planet," Thralen said decisively. "We must have direct information to verify our conclusions. Come on, Data—let's take our findings to the captain."

On the trail of clues to a mystery, Data was in his element. Captain Picard called Chairman Tichelon, who provided the information that the Konor called the other Samdians "Ikonor"—meaning simply "not Konor," he explained.

"It is more than that," Thralen said. "It confirms our fears, for it means 'those without souls.'"

It was obvious Tichelon had not expected them to

derive the root meanings of the terms. He protested, "The insults they cast at us are not the issue. Our people are being murdered, Captain. You have been here for almost a day, and done *nothing!*"

Picard took a controlling breath and said, "We are going to attempt to communicate with the Konor. If we succeed, will you accept representatives of Starfleet as mediators? May we say you have agreed?"

"Yes—yes, of course! But they will not listen to you. Do you think we haven't tried? They killed all of our people who tried to communicate, even those who offered surrender."

There was another strategy session in the observation lounge. It was decided to send an away team to meet the Konor. Deanna Troi insisted on being part of it.

Data watched Will Riker watch the captain, the First Officer's "poker face" betrayed by a slight wince when Picard agreed.

"You'll need the best protection we can give you," the captain continued. "Worf, Riker, Data."

"Captain," Thralen said, "I should be there." His antennae quivered nervously. "Even if Data and I are right, on direct contact we will certainly see more. Perhaps something that will persuade them to make peace."

"Agreed," Picard said. "I want all communications left open, and a tricorder channel providing a visual to both the bridge and the transporter room. At the first sign of a threat, the away team are to be beamed up at once."

"What about the fact that they go naked?" Worf asked, grimacing slightly. "Should we beam down unclothed?" The idea obviously pained him, but as

Security Chief he had to consider every possibility to keep the away team safe. "We cannot go unarmed, and we certainly will not be mistaken for Konor. But what if there is some taboo against clothing, as the Ferengi have against clothing women?"

But another conference with Tichelon assured them that the idea had already been tried, to no avail.

So the away team, fully clothed and armed, beamed down to Dacket.

They materialized on the steps of the building most likely to be the center of local government. A few people nearby stopped, stared at them, but did not move or speak.

//Strangers—who are you?//

Counselor Troi stepped forward, smiling.

From all sides, Konor men, women, and children converged on the away team.

//Are you soulless cattle, or Konor? Answer, strange ones, or die!//

The command was so loud Data reduced his audio gain. It didn't help. Thralen's antennae retracted reflexively, and Worf put his hands to the sides of his head.

"Do you hear them?" Troi asked, her smile now forced through pain, her eyes huge and unfocused.

"Yes!" Riker replied in tones of utter amazement. Then he shouted, "Deanna—no!" as the counselor moved ahead of the others, hands outstretched toward the Konor.

Data knew Troi must be projecting a message of peaceful greeting to the Konor, using Betazoid techniques. But the Konor only stared at her, their faces angry. "I hear you," Troi gasped, the look on her face changing from joy to confusion to horror as the din in

Data's head increased. "Such terrible anger—but why? Why will you not *listen* to me?"

Data had to focus his attention on vision alone to be able to keep pace with Troi as she strode into danger.

His companions could not so easily cope with the bursts of furious noise. Riker grasped the sides of his head, fighting for control. Pain was clear in his movements, but he forced his way to Troi's side. Thralen staggered, his skin paling and his antennae retracting again as his mouth opened in a grimace.

Even Worf winced—but did not lose stride, keeping his hand on his phaser as he moved forward.

The Konor converged on Troi, the serenity of their faces gone now, although their looks seemed more disdainful than angry.

//Ikonor! Strangers! Heathens! Barbarians! Soulless animals!//

"Beam us up!" Riker ordered.

"Stand still!" came O'Brien's voice. *"There are Konor too close—"*

"Bring them along, but *beam us up!"* Riker repeated.

Picard's voice confirmed, "Get the away team out of there!"

Even as the faint hum of the transporter began, the Konor attacked, flinging missiles. The away team had no choice but to run, taking them out of the transporter focus.

Worf and Riker drew phasers. Two people trying to grab Troi fell, stunned.

That did not stop the Konor. The crowd converged on them, faces contorted in anger. Parcels suddenly turned into weapons, and other, more deadly implements began to appear in the mob's hands.

"Get Deanna out!" Riker shouted as Konor shoved him away from her. The counselor was both the focus of the Konor attack and the least skilled of the five at self-defense.

Worf and Data managed to keep pace with Troi, protecting her on either side. Worf knocked aside a brick aimed at him, which threw him slightly to his right—just far enough off-balance for the split second it took a Konor to thrust a metal rod past him, toward Troi.

It wasn't a weapon, but some kind of building material. That made it no less lethal.

Data tried to intervene, but four hefty Konor working in concert shoved him aside.

Troi stumbled, and the spear missed.

The attacker shifted his grip and swung his improvised weapon up, ready to bring it down on the counselor's head. With the power of his fury behind it, it would split her skull.

"Deanna!" Riker shouted, lunging desperately toward her.

Worf raised his weapon to stun the attacker, but another Konor struck his arm. The shot went high.

Data threw off his attackers and ran to protect the counselor. From the opposite direction, Thralen flung himself at Troi to knock her out of harm's way.

The crowd surged against them. Thralen slammed into Troi, but they did not go down.

Troi's assailant attempted his swing again—

Data dived at him, not caring if he broke the man's ribs if he deflected his aim.

The weapon missed Troi, but struck Thralen a glancing blow to the head, connecting with one of his antennae. The Theskian collapsed forward onto Troi, red blood spurting over his yellow hair and blue skin.

Gasping in pain and clutching his middle, the Konor fell on top of them. Worf's phaser hummed, and he strode over stunned Konor to the scene, as Riker, face white, converged from the other direction.

And in the moment of stillness when the away team all stopped, the transporter found its fix and beamed them up.

Thralen's assailant came with them. The moment he congealed on the platform, he tried to raise his bloodstained weapon again—but Worf fired, and the Konor collapsed, stunned.

"We've got them aboard, Captain," O'Brien reported.

Data slapped his combadge. "Doctor Pulaski to the transporter room—emergency!" He pulled his tricorder from its holster, and knelt down by Thralen's side.

At the same time, Commander Riker was bending over Counselor Troi, who had fallen as soon as the transporter beam released them. "Deanna!" he cried out.

Blood caked on her fair skin, and stained her uniform a deeper wine color.

"I'm all right," she said. "But Thralen . . ."

Worf moved the unconscious Theskian off her while Data continued to scan his vital signs. Thralen was fading fast. Data slapped his combadge again.

"Dr. Pulaski," he ordered, "you will require Theskian life support—stat! Please hurry, for if we lose him—"

Data left the last words unspoken: they all knew

what it would mean if the faltering heartbeat stopped entirely. A Theskian was not to be resuscitated. His people believed the soul left the body at that moment, and could not return even if the body were revived.

"Do not die, Thralen," Data whispered. "We are back on the ship. You are safe. Hang on!"

Again he felt that odd disorientation, the feeling he had had on Elysia's sacred isle that somehow this event had happened before.

The doors slid open to admit Dr. Pulaski and two assistants, with an antigrav medibed.

"He is still alive!" Data reported.

"Good," Pulaski said in her brisk way. "Let's keep him that way." They hurried Thralen to sickbay, while other medics carted off the unconscious Konor. Data, Troi, Worf, and Riker followed.

The Konor quickly recovered from the phaser stun. Despite his broken ribs, on which healing rays were already at work, Pulaski had placed him in a restraint field.

Picard was already there, asking anxiously about Thralen.

"He will recover completely," the CMO said, much to Data's relief. "The scalp wound was superficial, and there is no concussion or brain damage, but a bruise to a Theskian's antenna is extremely painful. That's what put him into shock, but he's stable now. He's sleeping, but he'll be up and around tomorrow."

The captain turned as the rest of the away team entered. He took in Troi's disheveled appearance and asked, "Counselor, are you well enough to work?"

"Yes, Captain, although I don't know what I can do."

335

"See if you can get through to this man, one-on-one."

"You've done it with me, Deanna," Riker reminded her, "and I'm not telepathic at all."

"Nor am I," Worf added, "but on the planet I also heard these Konor inside my head."

"They are broadcast telepaths," said Troi. "They do not seem to be receptive, like Betazoids."

"Try," Riker urged her. "Here, in private, without a crowd to drown you out, you may be able to reach him."

By this time the Konor was groggily looking around.

Dr. Pulaski moved toward him, saying, "You are in our medical unit. We're not going to hurt you—"

//Ikonor animals! I understand your primitive noises, but, thank Providence, the Konor communicate soul to soul. You may be powerful enough to kill me, but you are soulless beings who will never defeat us.//

But Dr. Pulaski was undaunted. "We'll leave the state of our souls to the theologians. Right now we are trying to communicate. I'm Dr. Pulaski. Will you tell us your name?"

//Konor have no need of names. We identify one another by the essence of our souls.//

Troi stepped forward. "Let me see what I can do." Data could see her concentrating, but he couldn't receive any thoughts she might be transmitting.

He glanced at Riker, saw him smile proudly at Troi.

Captain Picard looked surprised, then pleased. Pulaski smiled. Worf almost allowed a smile, then caught himself and took up his most military stance.

Obviously Counselor Troi had managed to communicate with all of them.

But there was no response from the Konor.

After a long attempt, Troi turned away, pale and trembling from her efforts. Dr. Pulaski's tests of the Konor's responses showed that he understood what was spoken aloud, but did not receive the Counselor's efforts to reach him, any more than Data did.

So Troi tried a different approach, speaking aloud. "How can you claim we have no souls if we can understand you?"

//The soulless recognize our state. It is their own they refuse to accept.//

Commander Riker asked, "What would prove to you that we are as much people as you are?"

//Any among you who can respond soul to soul are recognized as Konor. We have rescued many from among the Ikonor.//

"That is what was happening with those children we saw in the scans," Data realized. "They were separating out any telepaths among the Dacket children, and making slaves of the others."

Troi asked, "If we can find someone who can communicate with you, 'soul to soul' as you put it, would you deal with that person as an equal?"

//Certainly. Providence may have created Konor among other races than the Samdians. We would welcome contact with them.//

So they began trying everyone aboard the *Enterprise* with a high ESP rating, but none could reach the Konor.

The Konor stared defiantly. //This is nonsense. No one is both Konor and Ikonor. We *have* proof of who and what we are. Providence provides. Dacket is ours by right, as Jokarn was and Gellesen will be.//

At that, Captain Picard called a halt. "We're wasting our time. Prepare that man to be returned to his home planet."

"Captain," said Data, as what he had stored up over the past several hours as raw data suddenly took on a significant pattern. "Please do not send him back yet."

"Why not?" Picard asked. "We're not going to persuade him that he and his kind are not masters of the universe by divine right. Our only hope, and it is a slim one, is to scour the galaxy for telepaths who somehow might succeed where the ones aboard this ship have failed. In the meantime—"

"That will not work," Data said. "What the Konor have developed is not telepathy."

Everyone in the crowded sickbay stared at him. Pulaski frowned. "Data, we all heard everything this man said to us, although he did not speak aloud. He is a broadcast telepath."

"That is how I know, Doctor," Data said. "I should have realized it the moment we beamed down to Dacket. I could not perceive Counselor Troi's attempts today, for an android can receive only emanations that have a physical component detectable to his sensors. The Konor's means of communication cannot be telepathy—because *I* hear everything they project just as clearly as the rest of you."

Chapter Sixteen

CAPTAIN PICARD and Commander Riker adjourned with Data to the nearest briefing room. Data called in Chief Engineer La Forge to help with his plan. "What the Konor must do is transmit their thoughts on a frequency common to both your sense organs and my sensors," he explained. "If we can trace that frequency, Geordi and I can build a transmitter—and we shall all be able to communicate with the Konor."

"As will the Samdians," Riker said with a pleased grin. "Data, I don't know what we'd do without you! We'd never have guessed what the Konor have isn't ordinary telepathy."

Picard's mouth thinned in a moment's pain at the thought. "We might have been forced to abandon them to their fate—and the tender mercies of the sharks drawn here by the bloodbath. Thank God you are what you are, Mr. Data. You and Mr. La Forge get to work on that transmitter as fast as you can. Until we can reach the Konor's minds, they will continue their destruction."

Finding the frequency, however, was easier said than done.

"I don't understand," Geordi complained. "Why can't your diagnostics tell you what frequency you are receiving the Konor's transmissions on?"

"Geordi," Data explained for the third time, "my diagnostics say there *is* no transmission. They detect nothing, yet I hear the Konor as clearly as you do."

"Then maybe it's telepathy after all," said his friend. "Medical tests can't detect telepathy, either."

Nor could either Geordi's or Dr. Pulaski's most delicate instruments tell what it was that Data—or the rest of the crew for that matter—received from the Konor.

So close to a solution, Data felt his failure very strongly. He spent hours listening to the Konor as he focused on one set of interior sensors after another, determined to discover how he could hear something that had no detectable physical manifestation.

Meanwhile, the Konor on the planet below continued their conquest, killing or enslaving all but those few who were able to return the mental communication. The ones who, as they saw it, had souls.

"Perhaps the Konor are right," Data said. He and Geordi had come to Ten-Forward to "drown their sorrows," as the engineer had put it. "Perhaps they do speak with the voice of the soul."

"Then we just have to answer the same way," Geordi said firmly.

"*I* am not the one to answer, then," Data said. "If souls exist—"

"Data." It was Thralen, just released back to active duty after his injury. The Theskian took the stool next to his. "Don't let the Konor distract you with their misinterpretation of their telepathic powers. They've got it exactly backward, can't you see?"

"No, I cannot," Data admitted.

"Can the ship's computer detect the Konor's telepathic transmissions?" Thralen asked.

"No, of course not," Geordi said.

"We do not know that, Geordi," Data pointed out. "We have not tested that possibility."

Geordi shook his head. "The computer would tell us about the transmissions—unless," he snapped his fingers, "unless it interpreted them as conversations not addressed to it!"

Data nodded. "Excuse us, Thralen—but we have work to do." He climbed down off his stool.

"And I'm coming with you," the Theskian insisted, following them out the door.

The Konor, healed of his minor injuries, had been moved to the brig. Worf had left standing permission for Data to interview him at any time, so there was nothing to hamper their experiment. In half an hour they had verified that the ship's computer indeed could not receive the Konor's transmissions.

//What is the point of all this?// he asked them. //Do you think to manufacture mechanical souls?//

The sarcastic question made Thralen smile, but Data was distracted by another of those odd moments of *déjà vu*. There was definitely something odd about his memory circuits, ever since Elysia.

They returned to Ten-Fore, and found an animated discussion in progress. Worf and Riker were teamed up against Dare and his gang.

The news was not good. Starfleet reported Ferengi and Waykani ships on course to the Samdian Sector.

"If we don't give the Samdians help," Dare was saying, "they'll accept it from those who will do so."

"It's an internal conflict," Riker added. "The moment we found that out, our hands were tied."

"Ours are not," Dare said.

"What can you do?" Worf asked. "Two small ships, eight people? If you had time, you might be able to equip the Samdians with weaponry, train them to fight. But there is no time. The Ferengi will be here within four days."

"The Samdians have space flight, even if it is subwarp," Dare replied. "In four days the children of the remaining free people of Dacket could be refugeed to Gellesen. So could a good portion of the adults, perhaps all of them."

"So you would have them run," Worf said. "How long before the Konor attack Gellesen?"

"Not quickly, once they realize what they are likely to get for their trouble." For the first time since they had rescued the Silver Paladin at Elysia, Data saw in his friend's eyes the old hard look born of years of disillusionment. The shuttered face, the hard set of the mouth, bespoke a man who knew life to be solitary, poor, nasty, brutish, and short, but who refused to bow before that knowledge.

"Oh?" the Klingon demanded. "You would leave traps behind, then."

"Certainly," Dare replied. "Nuclear weapons are easy to build. The Konor want ready-built cities, cleared and cultivated agricultural land, industry and technology in place for them to take over without effort. Stop giving it to them! Destroy the cities with weapons that will leave them and the land around them contaminated for generations to come. Contam-

342

inate the fields so nothing will grow. Teach the Konor that if they try again to kill their fellows and steal what they have built, their efforts will win them only scorched and blasted territory, and many of their own dead in the process."

Data was an android. He was not supposed to have physiological reactions to emotion, yet although his hands were clasped before him on the table, he saw his fingers twitch spasmodically at Dare's words. "And would you have the Samdians use the same strategy on Gellesen?" he asked.

"No," Dare replied. "The Konor must be left thinking they would, to give us time to make plans and train people. Dacket is as good as lost—if it must be let go, make the Konor pay a high price for it. But on Gellesen the Samdians must take a stand or lose everything. We will teach them guerrilla tactics. If the Konor should succeed in taking any part of Gellesen, they must never be allowed to feel secure, never know when an attack will come, a bomb go off."

"That's terrorism!" Geordi exclaimed.

"Against self-righteous murderers who would kill the Samdians and take their children into slavery? What would you have them do, Mr. La Forge? Surrender? You saw what that got them on Dacket: mass slaughter."

Geordi got up. "There has to be another answer. We *can't* leave murder, slavery, and terrorism as the only options. Data—"

"I know, Geordi. We must continue trying to duplicate the frequency on which the Konor transmit. But there is no reason to expect me to be able to do it any better than you can."

"No," objected Thralen. "You are the only one with

a chance, Data. There are too many differences between one of us and the ship's computer for us ever to
find the right one. Look for the difference between *you*
and the computer."

"Thralen's right," Geordi said as they walked to
Data's quarters. "Let's try to reason it out. If the
computer can't detect the transmissions, chances are
you're not doing it with inorganic components."

"But most of my organic structure is no more than
nutritive fluids," Data said, sitting in the armchair
at an angle to Geordi, who had chosen the couch.
"It is not a sensing device any more than your blood
is. The answer has to lie in the organic/inorganic
interface in the anterior cortex of my positronic
brain."

Geordi sighed. "It figures. The mystery that died
with Dr. Soong."

"Or disappeared with him," Data corrected.
"There is no actual record of his death."

"Either way, we don't have him here to ask. But
Data, we do at least know, physically, where that
interface is located."

"It is the one thing I cannot allow even you to
touch, Geordi. I am sorry. If it were damaged, I could
lose . . . everything."

"No, Data, I'm not suggesting that *I* do anything.
You don't have to touch that area to isolate its
sensations."

"I cannot isolate them," Data replied.

"What? Why not?"

"It is my . . . my mind, Geordi. Not my brain,
which has a number of separate memory and program
storage areas. This is one way in which we *are* alike. I
share memory storage and computation capacity with

computers. With humans I share the ability to think. Can you isolate which area of your brain you think with?"

"No, but you've just described exactly what we're looking for. Never mind that you can't physically locate it. You can still use it."

"Yes."

"You're the Sherlock Holmes fan: after everything else is eliminated, what is left that is possible, no matter how improbable?"

"I detect the signals with something my brain has in common with yours, but that the ship's computer is lacking," Data responded. "It does not receive the usual sorts of telepathy. Surely telepathy such as Vulcans and Betazoids project goes directly to the mind." He frowned. "I have just contradicted myself. If I were receiving the Konor transmission directly to my mind, then I would perceive other forms of broadcast telepathy the same way. So what the Konor have is not telepathy."

"Then it's a physical emanation," Geordi said. "Detection is no problem; we can all do that. But how do we *duplicate* it?"

"By discovering the receptor and reversing it," Data said. "Eliminate direct mind reception, eliminate sensory reception, and . . . the receptor must be the interface."

"And the difference between you and us lowly humans, Data, is that you have conscious control of all parts of your body."

"Theoretically. I have no consciousness of that interface."

"Well, theoretically, then. Just try to switch over from 'receive' to 'send.'"

"You are suggesting that I try to stop operating with an . . . open mind?"

Geordi grinned. "Jokes under stress, eh? You *are* getting human, Data." He sobered. "You're constructed so you can't harm yourself, aren't you?"

"That could be the reason I am not aware of the interface. But then, the effect could be a necessary consequence of sentience. All right—I shall try."

Data sat back in his chair, so that he could focus all his awareness, even that small portion usually reserved for keeping his body balanced. Although he could call up information from sensors all around it, he had no sense that the interface was there. He remembered the first time Bruce Maddox had examined him, how he had tried to explain this very lack of awareness, and thus his inability to tell the man how the linkage worked.

He had been far less articulate in dealing with humans in those days, before his experiences at Starfleet Academy and later working with such a variety of fellow crew members in space. Looking back on it now, he could almost see why Maddox had decided he was not a sentient being.

After repeating several times that he had no sensory apparatus capable of isolating the interface, he had finally attempted an analogy. "Humans have a blind spot in either eye," he pointed out, "where the optic nerve is attached to the retina."

"Yes, that is so," Maddox agreed.

"Yet you are not aware of it. When you look out of only one eye, you perceive a complete field of view. There is no blank space, as it were, where the blind spot is."

"That's true," Maddox acknowledged.

346

"So it is with my lack of sensors to the interface: I have no perception that they are missing."

He wondered now if the mystery thus left as to his operation was what had tempted Maddox into the further study of positronics. Then he put the thought aside, recognizing it as a form of procrastination.

Geordi was right: he did fear tampering with a part of himself he did not fully understand. But there were lives at stake. The Konor would never listen to anyone who could not communicate by the method they thought to be soul to soul.

Data understood the structure of the filament links to his anterior cortex, but not the theory behind their function. Theoretically, they could *not* function as they did, because of the electron resistance . . . and yet they did function. Would that the interaction between his organic and inorganic components were as simple as that between matter and antimatter!

He and Geordi had intended, before encountering total frustration, to build a transmitter that could be hooked into the universal translator. Then any emissaries the Federation sent could communicate with the Konor. But there was no way to modify an organic brain to send as well as receive on a particular frequency.

Could a positronic brain be so modified?

//Either kill me or let me go!//

It was the Konor, in the brig, his thoughts so emphatic that they carried throughout the ship. Data realized that he addressed Worf, who was making a routine inspection.

Data tried to analyze how he had received the transmission, but he could not trace synapses, chemical changes, anything. What receptors had he used, where there apparently were none?

//Send me back to my home. If you are going to kill us, let me die with my own people.//

No, thought Data, *we do not want to kill you.* But if he could not find the solution, someone would have to kill the Konor or else imprison an entire society, to stop them from slaughtering innocent people. *How do I reach you?* he wondered.

If there had been circuits, he could have reversed them. If the transmission had been a beam or wave, he could have duplicated it. But it just came at him.

//Let me go!//

Wait.

The Konor's thoughts had not intruded on him before, nor had anyone else mentioned it. Data had gone close to him to test his reception. The transmission was usually limited to a small area around the Konor, but now the man was mentally "shouting," as it were.

He "listened" for the Konor to communicate again. He had stopped "shouting." Data strained to "hear" . . . //You will learn, eventually.// And then something that faded away as the man became resigned once more.

But in straining to "hear," Data sensed the activity of one of his semantic interpreters. It was not within the filament links, but fed information to them. If it fed information one direction—

He sat up. "I believe I have found it."

Geordi smiled, and followed as Data went to his computer and called up his own schematics. "Here— this is the receptor that transfers what the Konor sends to my positronic brain. Geordi, it does not matter how my mind works at all. If we modify this receptor to send as well as receive, as long as I can formulate thoughts I can send them to the Konor."

But the receptor was not a circuit, like the ones in most of Data's body. It was a tiny plasma electrode, its charge delicately balanced by electromagnetic activity.

Geordi whistled. "Data, we can't mess around with that. If we unbalance it, we might never be able to put it right again. I don't even have tools to deal with that kind of connection."

"I will risk it," Data said. "I trust you, Geordi."

"Absolutely not," his friend said. "Only the man who built you knows how that thing works. And don't tell me it's okay because *you* know—with that part out you wouldn't be able to *tell* me how to fix you!"

"Geordi—think of all the lives at stake. We have to try."

"No," Geordi said emphatically. "You might as well ask me to perform brain surgery on the captain. But . . ." he added, rubbing his chin as he studied the screen, "we just might be able to construct something else to connect to that plasma electrode, and use *that* to transmit."

"Yes!" Data exclaimed, seeing at once how they might accomplish their goal without disturbing the delicate components associated with his positronic brain. Like that brain itself, these were devices no one had yet succeeded in duplicating. They fed not only into his brain, but into his language banks as well—circuitry well understood since the invention of the universal translator in the previous century.

In moments they had the worktable spread with the tools and spare parts Data kept on hand, and Geordi started in on a tentative design. There was no way to miniaturize it to fit against Data's positronic brain, but Geordi had no intention of coming anywhere near that delicate area with what he described as "these clumsy tools."

Instead, they opened Data's chest, where there was room to insert the new circuit, and ran a connection to his language synthesizer.

The first several designs they tried didn't work at all. But after much trial and error, they got a measurable flow according to the instrumentation.

Geordi said, "Now it's got to work. There's no reason it shouldn't, Data. Besides, I'm flat out of ideas. If that thing was gonna work, it should've done so five adjustments ago."

Data sat at the worktable, his chest open and the circuit board lying before him. All the connections had been tested a dozen times; if the thing would only work, they could tuck everything neatly into his chest cavity, and he could go to the brig and try it out on the Konor.

//Geordi, can you hear me this time?//

Data waited. There was no response. *Damn!*

Geordi started. "Data? I thought I heard something, but it was too faint to be sure. Wishful thinking?"

Data remembered the Konor "shouting." He tried using more emphasis. //Geordi?//

The engineer tilted his head as if he were listening for something faint and distant. "I thought . . . Data, can you increase the gain?"

Treating the new circuit as if it were one of his speech amplifiers, Data increased the power to it, and tried again. //Geor—//

Burning shock ran through every circuit in his body.

Geordi screamed and tore off his VISOR.

It cut off the moment shock stopped Data's attempt to transmit.

Geordi was gasping, sweat popping out on his skin as he groped blindly for his friend. "Data, what—?"

The door bleeped, and they heard Riker's voice. "Data! Are you all right? What's going on in there?"

"Come," Data responded automatically, and the door slid open to reveal Commander Riker, very much out of uniform in a short robe and bare feet, his hair uncombed. He had obviously been wakened from a sound sleep.

Wesley Crusher, in a similar state, arrived in moments from his quarters a little farther down the corridor, almost colliding with Counselor Troi, whose rooms were about the same distance in the other direction. The captain, in black pajamas, arrived just in time for explanations.

By this time Data had analyzed the event. "It was not pain, Geordi," he explained. "It was electronic feedback. I am sorry. I did not know that was going to happen."

Realizing that what he had felt was not his VISOR overloading, Geordi put it back on.

Wesley came over to the table and studied the device they'd constructed. "Wow!" he said. "You've built a thought transmitter into Data!"

It was not, unfortunately, that simple.

If they could have built a plasma electrode like Data's own receptor, it would have taken almost no power to operate. The circuit Geordi had built, however, required at least fifty times as much power as a speech amplifier—and when Data tried to send at a level people could perceive, it created a power feedback that Data experienced as agonizing pain.

He made no objection to calling it that; it went far beyond "unpleasant," as he normally described the sensations he received as malfunction warnings.

There was actually nothing wrong with the transmission circuit; it simply required too much power to do a job associated with components of the greatest sensitivity. Unless they could duplicate or invent a device something like the plasma electrodes surrounding Data's organic/inorganic interface, Data could not transmit words without at the same time transmitting excruciating pain.

Which made his communicating with the Konor hopeless, and all the more frustrating because they had come so close.

"You did the best you could," Captain Picard told Geordi and Data when they reported their failure the next day. He sat down behind his desk, tugging the front of his uniform down. The gesture, a habit from the days when Starfleet uniforms were two-piece outfits, indicated the captain's frustration. "I'll report to Starfleet, and you keep working. You may yet invent something to do the job."

"Not before the Ferengi get here," Geordi said grimly, "and the rest of the galaxy after them."

"Darryl Adin and his gang are already here," Data added. "They have stayed aboard at my request, Captain, while we tried to find a solution. But if Starfleet removes the *Enterprise,* they will try to help the Samdians."

"And I can't blame them," Picard said. "Geordi—"

352

"I'm sorry, Captain," said the chief engineer. "Even Data doesn't understand the construction of his plasma electrodes. Their design is completely alien."

"They may *be* of a design alien to any we know," Data added. "Considering Dr. Soong's reputation, and the fact that there are times in his life that are unaccounted for, it is possible that he did not invent those components, but obtained them elsewhere. I know now that they are essential to my existence; without them, every communication between my mind and my body would be as painful as trying to use the mental transmission circuit."

"If I could only figure a way to get around that pain," Geordi said sadly.

"Get . . . around it?" Data asked.

"Prevent it," Geordi interpreted. "But nothing I know channels less power than—"

"No, Geordi," Data said, "get *around* the pain. Captain, I must experiment. You may wish to be out of range."

Picard looked up from staring at the tabletop. "You think you know a way to transmit without pain?"

"If I can block it, and just let the thought through. We do not know what thought is, for you, me, or the Konor. But I know what the pain is: excess power overloading delicate sensors."

"I don't understand," Geordi said. "You need that power to transmit strongly enough for anyone to receive you."

"Yes, but—" Data concentrated, allowing the power flow to increase to a painful level while diverting equal energy from his other systems. It met the power searing his nerves as he projected, //Captain Picard, Geordi—can you hear me?//

"Data!" the captain exclaimed.

"How did you do that?" Geordi demanded.

Data spoke aloud, as it was too painful to continue the mental transmission. "I was right; thought exists in some form we cannot measure. I diverted power from my other systems in resonance with that going through the transmitter circuit. Harmonic damping, Geordi. The pain is damped out; the thought is not."

"Then it didn't hurt you?" Geordi asked.

"That is . . . I believe the expression is the 'fly in the ointment.' The damping must be done *after* the power is used to boost the 'loudness' of the thought to a perceptible level. I cannot escape experiencing the pain, but I can prevent it from obscuring the message."

"Oh, Data," the captain murmured.

"I'm so sorry," Geordi said, with sorrow in his voice. "When I said you had to experience pain to understand what it means to be human, I never meant anything like this!"

"I shall be all right," Data said.

"Will you?" asked his friend. "Do you know what I saw happen, Data? Whether it's from the pain or from damping the power, you lost your halo, my friend. For that moment you looked to me just like any other human."

"Perhaps," Data said, "that is a . . . good omen. I shall go and communicate with our Konor guest in the brig. If that is successful, then I shall go down to the planet."

"Data," Captain Picard said, "we've been concentrating on creating a transmitter—but not on what we would say once we were able to communicate. Commander Riker is skilled in diplomacy—"

"Captain," Data said, "the Konor will listen only to the person who can communicate with them mentally. As I cannot confer the ability on anyone else, I will have to beam down alone. And I know what I shall say. Is it not obvious?"

Chapter Seventeen

DATA FOUND IT pitifully easy to fool the Konor in the *Enterprise* brig into accepting him. When he transmitted his first words without speaking, the man leaped up and embraced him wordlessly.

Through the lingering haze of pain caused by his transmission, Data forced a smile.

//My brother.//

The Konor answered with a smile of his own. //We knew Providence might have created Konor among other beings, but you are the first we have discovered.//

Then, to Data's relief, he began speaking aloud—for of course the security guards outside the cell could "hear" every word of mental conversation. "My brother, can you help me escape from the Ikonor you dwell among?"

"I can," Data nodded. "I am third in command of this ship. As I outrank everyone except the captain and the first officer, no one will question my orders."

The man did not question Data's willingness to leave the ship, assuming that he was in the midst of the same wonderful discovery each Konor knew when he became capable of speaking mind to mind—or as they saw it, soul to soul. "I wondered why you came back to study me so often—you must have felt our kinship under Providence. You must tell me of your people. Do they dwell far away?"

"Very far," Data told him, remembering a lesson taught him by Tasha Yar when she was *Enterprise* security chief, preparing those officers who would most often form away teams.

"When you must lie," she had said, "keep it simple. Don't make up involved stories. Often part of the truth—that which pleases your listener—will satisfy him, and you won't actually have to lie at all."

Data had depended heavily on that advice ever since, and now found it working once again with the Konor.

None of the people they passed along the way questioned them, though only the guards at the door and Chief O'Brien knew the plan. The transporter chief played his role well, questioning Data's intent to beam down with the prisoner, but backing off when told it was "Captain's orders."

They materialized in the same square where the away team had been attacked, but this time Data's companion led the way up the steps to the building which housed the Konor Council of Elders. Data easily proved his ability to communicate, although he kept his statements brief. It was getting no easier to concentrate through the excruciating pain which he must not allow to be broadcast with his words.

Luckily, the Council members were as easy to convince as the first Konor had been.

//We are not alone!// exclaimed their leader, who

was hardly an "elder" in the usual sense. In fact, none of the Council appeared to be much beyond middle age.

Before someone they regarded as an equal, the Konor spoke—or rather mentally projected—freely. They wanted to know all about Data, his people, what planet he came from. He gave them as few facts as possible, "letting slip" that he had a brother whose whereabouts were unknown so as to allow them to assume he came from what they would consider a normal family. For the most part he countered their questions with questions of his own, and learned that the discovery of a Konor of a race far different from theirs only confirmed their beliefs.

Unsurprisingly, the Konor "revelations" were rooted in beliefs shared by all the Samdians. They knew little of other cultures, because of their isolationist political and economic policies, but they were aware that the galaxy held many beings physically different from themselves yet with intelligence equal to their own.

When the Konor developed their unique mental broadcasting, they were naturally drawn to those they could communicate with. Thralen had surmised correctly: As the numbers of Konor grew, the ordinary Samdians began first to be uneasy about them, then to fear them. Prejudice spread.

Tolerance dropped to nil, however, when the Konor declared new interpretations of certain passages in Samdian teachings: intelligence and self-awareness were not enough. The ordinary Samdians were wrong in believing they had souls; the true Konor had come into existence among them only now, displaying absolute proof of their ensoulment to Konor and Ikonor alike.

It was difficult, they agreed, to realize that people one loved were mere soulless beings—but that was the test Providence placed upon them. Data's presence was proof that they were rightly interpreting what Providence required of them. He must display his ability publicly, and be welcomed into their company before the multitudes.

As that was exactly what Data wanted, he was perfectly willing to comply. Unfortunately, it would take several hours to spread the word, so that as many Konor as possible could gather to witness the ceremony. Forced to respond "soul to soul" to a barrage of questions and comments, he found the constant bursts of pain becoming intolerable. He might be able to contain his reactions, as a human could not, but despite the assurance of his diagnostics that his systems were thus far undamaged, he felt as if his circuits were burning out, one by one.

The agonizing sensations slowed Data's conscious thinking. It was not until he was invited to a feast in celebration of his arrival that he found a way to obtain a few hours of relief: //No—I must rather fast and meditate. Is there a place I can be alone?//

It was the right thing to say. Respect flowed from his hosts, and Data was shown to a small room, presumably a chapel, although he was not familiar with the symbols on its walls and what appeared to be an altar.

Although he correctly assumed there would be none, he checked for listening devices before tapping his combadge to give the *Enterprise* a brief progress report. "It will be a very public ceremony," he explained. "I will keep this channel open so you can hear, and you can scan the coordinates visually."

"Good work, Data," Captain Picard said. "However, we are pressed for time. Waykani and Ferengi vessels will be here within ten hours."

"The ceremony is in four," Data said. "If my plan works, I will try to persuade the Konor to negotiate with the other Samdians, and accept Starfleet personnel as mediators."

"Yes," Picard agreed. "That, and the presence of the *Enterprise,* should be enough to deter any action by the Waykani or Ferengi. It's all on your shoulders, Data. Good luck."

"Thank you, sir," Data replied, and cut communication.

All on his shoulders. He did not want to calculate the probabilities; with the Waykani and the Ferengi ready to rival one another in offering their services, out here so close to the Romulan Neutral Zone, interplanetary war was virtually unavoidable.

But worry was a waste of time and energy, so Data spent his time rehearsing his plan, attempting to create a flowchart of possible scenarios. He knew there could be omissions: sentient organic beings were simply not predictable. No matter how he rehearsed possibilities, when it came time for action, he would have to . . . improvise.

Finally Data was led out onto the steps of the Council Building, facing a crowd of thousands. They stood in the square, and massed at windows in surrounding buildings. Throughout the lands of the Konor, the Elders assured him, other Konor were waiting for those gathered here to send the proceedings soul to soul.

The Chief Elder introduced Data, who told them simply, //I bring you greetings.//

Overwhelming welcome and joy poured over him. He understood why the Konor found it easy to recruit those they wanted to their side—if it were not for the pain of communicating in return, it would be remarkably easy to allow these people to take him into their company. But he reminded himself of two facts: when faced with people who would not accept abject slavery, these kind and gentle people turned into ruthless killers; and their welcome was so joyful because they did not yet understand what he was.

The Chief Elder was continuing, //We welcome the first Konor we have discovered not born among our own people. The grace of Providence is here demonstrated, for he dwells among Ikonor, as we do, and knew not of his state until a Brother of our souls discovered him toiling in the service of the soulless.//

As the Konor they had captured had asserted, no names were used. Data was already catching the nuances in tone; the reference to the Konor who had been returned to them carried with it something of both the man's mental "voice" and the determination of his character. It was odd, though, to "hear" in references to Data himself not only a shadow of his speaking voice but a sense of . . . innocence?

That could not mean they knew what he was, could it? Was Dr. Pulaski right that he gave away his mechanical nature with every word or act?

But no, if the Konor knew what Data was, surely *artificial* would come through in the way they thought of him. They were not at a technological level to conceive of an android of his sophistication; they simply accepted his pale skin and different body movement as characteristic of the race he came from.

So long as they did not guess what he was before he was ready to show them, Data's plan had a chance. It *had* to work. With time pressing, there was no chance for an alternate plan if he failed.

The Chief Elder invited Data to step forward, //—and remove the barriers between yourself and your brothers and sisters. As Providence sees all, we disguise nothing. Hide not your body from Providence, nor from those who perceive your soul.//

Data had no innate body modesty, but had learned in his twenty-seven years among humans a variety of meanings to being clothed or unclothed. Here nudity was the norm, so he removed his boots, then peeled off the rest of his Starfleet-issue clothing, carefully laying it so that his combadge, with its open channel, was unimpeded in its function.

There was curiosity, but no prurient interest in his anatomy from the watching crowd. He had deliberately not resealed the synthoskin of his chest after he and Geordi installed the thought transmitter, but as his skin was all of one color the lines would not show from a distance, and up close appeared to be either thin scars or natural markings. No one paid them any attention. The Konor were obviously more interested in what they thought was his soul than in his body.

If only they were not so terribly wrong in the interpretation of their mental communication!

The crowd again sent warm thoughts to Data. //Welcome, Brother of our souls!//

But then the Council of Elders continued, //We are Konor, created by Providence to have dominion over the land, the water, the plants, the animals, and the Ikonor. We would gladly care for the Ikonor and treat them well if only they would accept that they are soulless beings provided as our servants.//

//Providence guide them to truth!// responded the gathered crowd.

The Chief Elder turned to Data. //Brother of our souls, you have brought us a great opportunity. You hold much influence with the Ikonor who inhabit the great ship you came in. Do they accept their role? Are they the servants of the Konor of your race?//

Here it comes, Data thought, and turned to face the gathered multitude.

//No, my colleagues aboard the *Enterprise* are not my servants, nor am I theirs,// Data responded, and pushed on before they could ask him to take over the ship for them, as he knew without any mind-reading would be their ultimate demand. //The people on the *Enterprise* are my friends.//

//But we are your brothers and sisters,// the crowd replied, giving Data the perfect opening.

//Are you?// The rapid-fire transmissions hardly let one wave of pain ebb before another began, but he forced himself to go on. //Am I Konor?//

//You speak to us, soul to soul.//

//But I am not one of you.//

//Providence provides. Wherever we go, we will meet our brothers, like you.//

//But the way Providence provides—it is the work of Ikonor that is provided for your use?// As the catechism continued, Data's sensors warned him that the transmitter was overloading. There was not only pain, but the danger of real damage.

//*Our* use, brother. You are one of us,// the Konor answered his last question.

//Even though I am different?//

//You are different only in body. In soul you are one of us.//

//But that which is made by Ikonor, that is property,// Data persisted through the static of pain, striving to turn the litany in the direction he needed before his transmitter shorted out entirely.

//Ours, to do with as we wish, as are the Ikonor.//

//Then,// Data said, sliding fingers into the unsealed seam down his chest and pulling it open, //what am I?//

There was sudden mental silence, then surprise, and the transmission from those close by to those farther back in the crowd of Data exhibiting not a gruesome view of heart, lungs, alimentary tract, but diodes, circuits, memory boards, sensory mesh, and conduits for his organic fluids.

Amidst all that, the telepathic transmitter sprouted the connectors that Data's sensors warned him were overheating. He had to cut his dramatic demonstration short, or risk damage that could disable him.

The moment's respite from pain was delicious relief, but Data had no choice but to go on. //Am I Konor?// he demanded again.

//Yes!//

//But I am not a man. I am a machine. I was not born, like you. I was built. You claim what is built by Ikonor is property.// Searing heat threatening to short him out at any moment, so he played his trump. //I was built by those you call Ikonor.//

Confusion and shock went through the crowd, but

364

they were accustomed to demand proof of the mind, not the body. //We touch your soul. You are Konor.//

What did it take to convince them?

Data did not project that thought, but even though he had stopped transmitting, his pain did not subside. The overloaded transmitter was generating excess heat now even when not in use.

//Is that the only proof of the soul?//

//Yes.//

//Can a soul be manufactured?//

Inarticulate confusion: they could not comprehend such a question.

Data grasped the transmitter and pulled it from his body, careful not to pull the connections loose as he removed it from the vicinity of the delicate components it had threatened. It burned his hand, but he ignored the warnings of the delicate sensors in his fingers.

//This,// he said, //is a thought transmitter. A friend and I *built* it, and installed it in me. *This* is what gives me the power to communicate with you. Is it a soul?//

Horror ran through the crowd, followed by anger. //You mock us!//

//I show you truth. You have the ability to transmit in a way any sentient being can receive. Perhaps reception is proof of sentience, but the ability to transmit proves nothing more than a mutation particular to your species.//

The mental atmosphere was rife with denial—but no one could dispute the proof before their eyes.

Then the realization began: if a mechanical object could transmit soul to soul . . . then it could not be the soul they touched in one another.

Anger surged toward fury. Data considered calling for beamup.

But then they might claim his demonstration was a trick. He had to stay, let them test him.

The Elders closed on him. //What you claim is not possible, one of them said. You cannot be a machine!//

//But I am,// Data replied. The surge of power to the transmitter melted a patch of synthoskin in his hand, and sensors just beneath sent a screeching protest through both Data's own diagnostics and the transmitter they touched.

The entire crowd gasped at the burst of agony.

//You are in pain!// exclaimed the Chief Elder. //A machine cannot feel pain.//

//Then shut it out, as you shut out the pain of your fellows as you kill them!// Data told them.

//But we *feel* your pain,// protested one of them, staring in bewilderment at Data's exposed mechanisms. //How can you be a machine, and have a soul?//

//How can you be a man, and believe your fellow men do not?// Data countered.

If the Konor had held their belief for generations, it might have been impossible to shake it, even with Data as living—or mechanical—proof before them. But few people in the crowd were children of Konor parents; most of them had discovered the transmission ability in themselves, or had it discovered by other Konor.

Doubt spread—and flashes of memory. Being separated from brothers or sisters who could not communicate mentally. Killing people like themselves, in the firm belief that because they could not transmit their fear and pain they were soulless beings no better than animals.

Doubt. It was the best Data could hope for. //What if you were wrong?// he demanded, again damping out the pain it cost him so as not to obscure his words. //You cannot *know* who has a soul. I do not know if I have one, but I can tell you this much: a soul is not something that can be manufactured. This—// he held up the transmitter as high as the trailing connectors would permit—//is not a soul. Yet it is what allows me to communicate with you.//

He looked into a sea of faces reflecting the turmoil he could feel in their minds, and pressed on. //I do not say you have no souls. All I know is that the soul is not what your test detects. If you will accept that those you call Ikonor are as probable as yourselves to be ensouled, and deal with them as equal in the eyes of Providence, the Samdians of Dɔcket are willing to negotiate with you. Will you stop your path of destruction and talk with them about making peace?//

The advantage to dealing with a society of mental communicators was that the scene before the Council Building was transmitted instantaneously throughout the Konor population; their disillusionment came all at once, with no dispute as to what they had actually seen.

But the agreement still took time, and while the debate raged Data removed the telepathic transmitter connections with great relief, closed up his chest, and put his clothes back on. The palm of his right hand was badly burned, the transmitter circuit fused to it in that final burst of energy; if he had left it inside his chest it would have damaged components far more difficult to replace and adjust than a few diodes, some sensor mesh, and synthoskin.

Emotions surged around him: guilt and grief, anger and denial, and finally resignation and acceptance. He knew the Konor answer before it was officially brought to him, although it astonished him anyway: yes, they would agree to make peace with and reparation to the Samdians of Dacket, and to accept a Starfleet mediator to help them make the treaty—but only if that Starfleet mediator were Data.

"I have removed the transmitter," he told them, displaying the charred and lifeless object. "I can no longer communicate in your way."

"We can speak," said the Chief Elder aloud, "and will do so in the negotiations. Providence sent you to teach us a harsh lesson, and we felt the pain it cost you to teach it. Please—help us to make amends as best we can."

"If my Captain agrees, I am willing," Data said, "although we have people on board ship who specialize in diplomacy."

"Ah, but the Konor are right," Picard said when Data contacted him. "You are the best negotiator under these circumstances."

So it was agreed, and Data returned to the *Enterprise* to contact Chairman Tichelon and set up a time and place for the negotiations. The Dacket chairman was flabbergasted that Starfleet had succeeded in persuading the Konor to negotiate, but when it penetrated that there was actually a chance to end the slaughter the man was close to tears.

Counselor Troi acted as interpreter for the scene on the planet, which was too far away for most of the crew to follow the mental transmissions. And Geordi, who had been hovering at his side ever since he'd beamed up, took hold of Data's arm.

"Sickbay for you now, Data."

"I am all right," Data assured him.

"We'll let Dr. Pulaski decide that," he said firmly. "Let's also see if the transmitter can be salvaged."

It could not, Dr. Pulaski discovered as she and Geordi carefully disengaged the charred and fused component from Data's hand. It took less than an hour to restore the parts that had been damaged, then replace and seal up the synthoskin, which formed itself into Data's own finger- and palmprints.

"Fascinating how it does that," Geordi said. "You couldn't change your fingerprints and start a life of crime."

"Why would I want to?" Data asked, flexing his hand. "If I wished to make a great deal of money easily, I would become a 'card sharp.'"

Pulaski laughed. "Don't let any Klingons in the game, then," she warned.

"Hey—" Geordi said suddenly, "that reminds me —you just lost a bet, Doctor!"

"I did?"

Data could tell Pulaski was genuinely puzzled. He had no more idea than she did what Geordi meant until the engineer continued, "Remember the wager that at the next opportunity Data would attempt to pass for human? He certainly succeeded with the Konor!"

Pulaski nodded, then smiled. "That is one bet I am only too happy to lose." The smile became a grin as she told Data, "What irony! Only an android could resolve the Samdian situation, and only by demonstrating forcefully that you are *not* human, after they were firmly convinced otherwise."

Data smiled in return. For once, he completely understood the humor.

As he started to slide off the examining table, though, Pulaski said, "Not so fast. Let's have a look inside you."

"There is no damage," Data assured her. "I have removed the extra connectors, so all I need do is seal up the skin."

But Geordi, too, insisted on seeing for himself, so Data had to lie back and let them probe.

As he lay there, Data pondered, "I still know only what I am not. Will I ever know what I *am?*"

"Why not be satisfied to be yourself, Data?" Pulaski asked. "You are unique."

"But do I have a soul?"

"I don't know. It's probably best that none of us know for certain."

"Yeah," said Geordi. "The Konor are a perfect example of what people do when they think they have all the answers."

"But if there is a God, a Providence, driving the universe," Data pursued, "why would it want us to live with such uncertainty?"

"To keep us humble," Pulaski asserted. "Data, do you know a saying that goes, 'If a man will begin with certainties, he shall end in doubts'?"

Data automatically accessed the rest: "'But if he will be content to begin with doubts, he shall end in certainties.' Francis Bacon, of Ancient Earth. Are you telling me to be content with doubts?"

"Look at the pattern," said Geordi. "Those who are

370

For a complete list of Star Trek publications, please
send a large stamped SAE to Titan Books Mail
Order, 42–44 Dolben Street, London, SE1 0UP.
Please quote reference NGG1 on both envelopes.

positive they know everything suppress and destroy those who disagree. But those who know they *don't* know explore and build and seek after wisdom. Stay a seeker, Data."

"I do not think I have any other choice," Data said resignedly.

"Shoo!" Pulaski said suddenly. "Cat hairs will not improve Data's internal workings!"

It was Mystery, who, determined to investigate, hopped up on the table and peered into Data's open chest cavity. A blinking diode caught her eye, and she raised a paw to pat at it.

"Hey—not so fast!" Geordi said, picking her up. "Here, Data—hang on to this creature till we get you squared away."

Data placed the cat on the couch between his neck and shoulder, holding her lightly while he petted her. She didn't struggle, but settled down against him, and—

"Listen!" Data said, leaning his ear against the cat's soft fur.

"What is it?" Pulaski asked, turning to face him as Geordi ran the instrument along the opening to seal his synthoskin.

"It is Mystery," he said in wonder. "She is purring."